For Hawthorn,
who hops now among eternal dandelions.

THE WILD FOLK

"You must go north, to the very end of the land,
where our sisters the Grizzly-witches dwell.
They are tenders of the elk herds, of the prairie
meadows, and of the northern star. In the middle
of their herd is the Elk of Milk and Gold herself.
She is very, very well guarded. Her hoofs are gold.
Her eyes are violet. Her fur is cream. You must
find her, and you must give her this feather,
and you must tell her what you've seen,
and ask her what must be done."

THE WILD FOLK

SYLVIA V. LINSTEADT

USBORNE

THE ISLAND OF FARALLONE

Mount Ash

Juniper Mountains

Sagebrush

Egret Valley

Madrone

Barn of the
Grizzly-witches

Tamal Point

Cattle
grid

Tamal Bay

OLIMA

Crab
Apple

Black
Oak

Lupine

Olima Borderlands

Quail

Vision Mountains

Alder

The Baba
Itha's Firwood

The Holy
Fool's Inn

1

THE GREENTWINS

Two newborn hares dreamed against their mother's belly in a nest of grass. The spring moon was bright as milk above them. The mother hare dozed lightly, one ear cocked for danger, rousing now and then to groom her small, sleeping children with a rough tongue. Near dawn, she heard a blue jay loudly declare news of a coyote sneaking across the meadow. Sitting up to sniff, she caught the unmistakable scent of him on the breeze – the damp, rank coat; the sourness of his breath; a hint of blood. She strained to hear which direction the coyote was coming from and made out the faint hush of his paws through the grass to her left. Her great ears, fully alert now, trembled.

Her little ones slept on: two curls of pale gold, four soft white ears. But she could hear the coyote's panting breath.

Fear shot through her body in a hot streak. She leaped sideways from the nest with all the force in her. The coyote, startled, stepped back a few paces. The mother hare zigzagged in mad, desperate arcs across the meadow, doing all she could to distract him from her sleeping babies. The coyote tore after her. It was early spring, the grass short and green. The hare had little cover, and though she ran fast, darting on strong legs, she stumbled once at the mouth of a badger hole. One stumble was all it took. The coyote was upon her.

The meadow fell silent.

A while later the coyote moved on, leaving only three splashes of the mother hare's blood behind in the dawn light.

The twin hares woke as the sun was breaking over the ridge. They turned sleepily to drink from their mother, but found a great cold spot where she had been. The sky over them and the ground under them felt suddenly very large and very empty. The brother twin began to shake. His sister made a small noise of comfort, her best imitation of their mother, and burrowed closer to him. Mother would be back. She always came back. Whenever she went off to graze, she told them never to move. *No matter what,* she said, *remain silent and still.* So they waited, and fell asleep again.

When the little leverets woke next, a warm hand was

scooping them up from their nest of grass. At first, the sister thought to bite the hairless thing that grabbed them, but the hand smelled of grass seeds and milk. From above, a voice hummed in familiar tones – wind through firs, mother's breathing. The tones sounded like the hare-words for *Be still, little hearts. Be at ease.* And so the twin leverets, drifting into dreams again, let themselves be carried away from the meadow of their birth, across a rushing spring creek, to a green-painted wagon in a patch of alder trees. Two glass windows tinted a reddish-rose gave the wagon the appearance of a creature with eyes. Smoke coiled from a silver chimney pipe. Four elk, unhitched from their harnesses, grazed on hedgenettle in the shade.

The leverets woke a third time feeling famished, and found themselves in a nest of grasses and hare fur in an old rusted tin by a wood-stove fire. A man and a woman sat side by side in front of the hearth. They looked almost identical, the male and female versions of the same broad-cheeked face, the same short-cropped fringe of fir-green hair, the same dark skin and pale, round eyes. They were called Angelica and Gabriel, and long ago they had been named the Witchtwin Doctors of the Land by the Wild Folk. But among the Country people, to whom they were little more than a legend, they were known simply as the Greentwins. Just now, they were feeding sticks into the flames with the hand they shared between them.

Being only infant hares, and therefore never actually having seen a human before, the leverets found this conjoined hand no more alarming than the green wagon itself or the fire held in the iron box; the ancient jars of herbs macerating in dark wine on low shelves; the piles of skins and rush-woven sleeping mats in a corner; the speckled old enamel pots and pans by the wood stove; the great basket of acorns by the door. All of this was an entirely new landscape of shapes and smells and colours. The leverets sat up, their little pale ears quivering, blinking their golden eyes and sniffing the air carefully, as they had seen their mother do.

Immediately the shared hand was near them again, this time offering a scrap of cloth that dripped with milk. They drank greedily.

"Welcome to the house of the Greentwins, small leverets," a voice murmured in words that they could understand. "Do not be afraid. We have been waiting for you."

All through the spring, summer and autumn, the Greentwins raised the two leverets like their own children, letting them sleep by the fire or out in the shelter of the bearberry bushes as they chose. They spoke to them in the languages of both humans and hares, and gave them human names. The sister they called Myrtle, after the silver-green bush that grew on ridgetops, and the brother Mallow, after the sweet weed that grew all along old roadsides.

Those months were gentle, full of succulent chickweed breakfasts in wet meadows and long evenings by the fire. There, Gabriel and Angelica told the leverets many human stories. They told the ancient creation myths of Farallone, about the Spider-woman who spun the dust from fallen stars down to earth, about the Elk who mixed that stargold with dark and milk and made all the animals, plants, waters and stones; about the many thousands of years of peace among human, plant, animal and sky; about the coming of the Star-Priests and the making of the City of New Albion, and their hunger for the energy they had figured out how to extract from pieces of stargold mined from rivers and hills and streams; about the time of the Collapse, when the City overreached itself and everything fell apart, when disease swept Farallone and the Star-Priests of the City built a giant wall to protect themselves; about the birth of the Wild Folk to heal the ravages done to Farallone by the hungry City, and the laws that presently kept the life of the island in a tenuous balance. They did not tell the leverets what they feared – that the Breaking was not over. That by building walls of fear and hurt between City, Country, and the territories of the Wild Folk, Farallone had become only more fractured, more wounded, and therefore more endangered than ever before.

Hares normally do not need stories to understand the world, for they live in the thick of each moment, ripe as new grass. But the Greentwins had chosen these hares for a purpose; for nobody is as good as a hare at getting over, under, round or through a wall. But for this they needed to understand the world in a human way. Stories helped them to see things in a human way, because it was through stories that humans understood their own world.

One evening in winter, a herd of thunderclouds came to sit above the ocean on the eastern horizon. The Greentwins and the leverets were camped on the Country's eastern-most ridge, the one that looked down over the Great Salvian Desert to the walled City of New Albion. Even two hundred years after the Breaking, the valley remained a desert. Only sagebrush grew there. No one ever crossed it. Even the hardy deer avoided it, and most of the lizards. The thunderclouds cast a black shadow over the distant silhouette of the City, where it sprawled across the far eastern peninsula. The long metal wall that surrounded it, sealing it off from the Country, gleamed ominously under the gathering darkness. Its rim of fluorescent lanterns flickered, illuminating one of the Star-Breakers. There were six in total along the City's Wall, great, round metal towers crowned with eight points. Each contained a reactor that could break the molecules of a flake of stargold into pure power, the power that the City had run on for many centuries before the Collapse. Now, the last beam of the setting sun split amber along the crowned top of one of the towers, its rays wheeling like the threads of a web.

Gabriel and Angelica looked at one another over the basket of acorns they were shelling under the sunset. They glanced at Myrtle and Mallow, who were grazing on fresh miner's lettuce at the edge of the wood, chattering to one another between mouthfuls. The two leverets were leggy, exuberant adolescents now, with strong muscled haunches and enormous ears with inner skin so thin that the setting sun shone through it, illuminating many small veins.

After a long silence, Angelica pursed her lips into an O. With quiet hoots she called down two barn owls from the winter sky. They landed, claws clattering, on the roof of the wagon.

It was time.

2

THE FIDDLEBACK

In the far corner of the room, there among the dust and dark of the catacombs' deepest chamber, Tin's invention gleamed. It was the middle of the night on the first day of February, and a storm thrashed the Fifth Cloister of Grace and Progress where it brooded just inside the City's wall. But Tin was underground, far from the storm and wholly absorbed in his secret invention. He called it his Fiddleback, and had kept it hidden under old rugs and a bit of canvas for the last three months, sneaking away nightly to add to it bit by bit. Tonight it was all but finished. He had only to connect the final wires of its circuitry, and polish it to a shine for good measure with a bit of oil from his lantern. But now, poised to pull off the rugs and close its looping wires, Tin felt a strange apprehension. Light from his lantern danced across the spindled legs where they peeked out under the carpets. Something about the Fiddleback felt different, almost alive. Like it might shake off the rugs all on its own. *It must just be the way the lantern is gleaming on it*, Tin thought to himself, and yanked off the coverings. But the impression was only stronger than before. The vehicle was luminous and strangely unfamiliar, as if he hadn't made it himself but had only found it in the catacombs like some impossible treasure from the time Before.

Don't be silly, he told himself, taking the loose wires very gingerly in his hands and setting to work. *You wanted it to look like a spider, didn't you? Well, maybe you just did a good job!*

It did look remarkably like a spider, a very large one, large enough to hold at least two twelve-year-old boys in its round body. Its shining, spindled legs folded up just like an arachnid's, with a small bronze wheel at each tip. They were attached to a round cab made of carefully quilted scraps of leather, wool and old tarpaulin, with an open-air viewing window and a door fashioned from an old polished piece of stained glass. On top he'd tried to make the shape of a violin out of thin sheets of copper, like real fiddleback spiders have on their heads. There were two seats inside, a small metal steering handle and eight dials that controlled the direction and speed of each of the eight wheels. Another lever stopped them all simultaneously. Beneath the outer layers of fabric, wires connecting the inner controls to the legs looped and netted every which way. There was a little engine hooked up to an old battery under the seat compartment, wishful additions given the fact that he had no source of energy to run them with. Next to the engine he'd attached a big bobbin from an old electric spinning wheel he'd found in a heap. He'd wound some thread around it and tied a grappling hook to the thread for fun. It was useless, of course, save that he could wind and unwind it from within, but it resembled the thread-making abilities of a real spider, and it made him smile.

Tin closed the circuit, hooking the final two wires into the rusted battery. He half anticipated some magical spark, but nothing happened. The Fiddleback was made, after all, entirely of scraps and wires that didn't really match. Mostly it was a dream-beast, made of his own imaginings. He'd put the wiring in for a sense of completion, a gesture towards the veins of a real body. All those odd pieces together could never actually work, but he liked the idea of the wires all the same. With a rag, Tin went over each of the Fiddleback's parts, rubbing the oil gingerly, as if his creation really was alive.

As part of their schooling, the orphan boys of the Fifth Cloister of Grace and Progress were taught the precise ways to use all the tools in the Metals Studio so that they could disassemble machinery from Before. None of them ran any more, given the shortage of energy, but their parts were endlessly recycled into new human-pedalled contraptions, or melted down for metal to supply the Alchemics Workshop and to provide the City people with nails and tacks and buckets and cans. Until the Fiddleback, Tin had only made very small contraptions from the scraps he found lying around the Metals Studio at the end of each day – a minute box that rang a bell when it opened; a tiny model of the sun with wings that could be moved up and down with wires. All in secret, for his own pleasure. The much larger Fiddleback had required thefts from the catacombs themselves.

"I never thought about what I'd do with you once you were actually finished," Tin said to his creation, oiling the wheels one by one. "If only I could get my hands on some of the Brothers' stargold. Then you could run!" He paused, watching the way the lantern light danced on the newly oiled parts. The shadows cast by the Fiddleback's legs seemed to dance too. Tin's chest felt light with the magic of that sight. "There's hardly any stargold left you know," he went on conversationally. "That's why they have us slaving all day in the Alchemics Workshop, to see if we can make any more. But even if I could get hold of some I wouldn't know what to do with it. The Brothers keep their secrets very secret. You have to have a Star-Breaker in order to extract power from stargold, and you'd be killed before you ever got inside one on your own, or learned how they work. Nobody knows how they break the stargold open up there in the Star-Breakers. I wish I did. Once the whole City was run on it, they say. The power made in the Star-Breakers fuelled everything. Once you could press a button and wash the dishes, wash the clothes, run a bath, send a message to someone on the other side of the City. The whole City was perfect, everything was connected, nobody wanted for anything. That's what they say…" Tin trailed off. Down here alone in the Cloister's old catacombs, full of dead machines that the City no longer had the energy to run, the words felt hollow. They echoed strangely. The room was very dark, the stone walls oppressive with shadows.

Suddenly nervous, Tin picked up his lantern, opened the Fiddleback's door, and climbed inside. The light from the oil lamp illuminated the stained glass from within, glancing blues and reds and greens off the careful stitch-work of old scraps, the silvery steering wheel, and the many small levers. Looking around, he sighed. Now that the Fiddleback was finished Tin felt oddly empty. It had been the thing he looked forward to each night, the thing that got him through the drudgery and danger of each morning's work in the Alchemics Workshop and each afternoon's grinding shift in the Metals Studio. He had filled it with his own most hidden dreams. Of adventure, of escape, of the lives of animals and stars. He smiled, remembering the little fiddleback spider he had encountered three months earlier in Hall Brother Christoff's closet, the first real animal he had ever seen and the inspiration for the creation of his own secret Fiddleback.

The only animals allowed inside the walls of the City were the cattle raised in sterile warehouses on sterile grain that supplied protein for the citizens. No one except their keepers ever saw them, and it was said their lifespans were very short, just long enough to become milk and meat. Still, Tin had always been obsessed with animals, with the strangeness and beauty of their bodies, which he had only seen in the few, censored books he and the other orphan boys were allowed to read as part of their narrow education. Mostly the books showed images of dangerous animals, animals the Star-Priest Brotherhood had eradicated after the Collapse. Even insects were forbidden within the City. It was, after all, the mosquitoes and flies that had been partially responsible for the devastating spread of the Plagues in the time Before. That's what the Wall's enormous, deadly lanterns were for – a defence against any and all insect-borne diseases. Any mosquito or moth or fly that passed by the City was drawn irresistibly to those lights, and promptly immolated with a quick spark and the smell of burning insect flesh.

How that little fiddleback spider had found her way into Brother Christoff's closet was still a mystery. It had been Tin's most recent stint of many in the Brother's closet, punishment for keeping the other boys up until sunrise telling stories. This time, Tin figured, someone had ratted, and that's why Brother Christoff had his ear pressed to the door at precisely the secret story-gathering time: when the clock struck eleven-eleven. Maybe it was Thomas, who acted tough and had strong muscles because he was always doing push-ups, but who only the month before had wet his bed from a nightmare.

"Do you know, Martin Hyde, just how many rules you are breaking at this very instant?" hissed the Brother, a young man with a balding patch in the middle of his head, who had pulled on his blue habit hastily over checked pyjamas. He stormed into the centre of the dormitory and all the boys scattered except for Tin and his best friend Sebastian, who glared at the Brother with fierce eyes.

"One for staying up past curfew, one for burning candles past curfew, one for telling a story, another couple for goading all the other boys to stay up with me. Baiting and abetting or whatever. So, I guess, five or so?" Tin had said with mock diligence, counting off on his fingers. His curly hair glinted in the candlelight and he faked a sweet smile.

"I swear by the City, you are hardly worth feeding for the trouble you cause. I would make it six rules broken and six hours in the closet without food or water, the biggest of course being blasphemy, to speak of the animals of the Country in that eager manner, when they of course are very diseased, and very dangerous to us." Brother Christoff shook his head at Tin's wide-eyed innocence. Sebastian snickered. At that, the Brother had grabbed Tin forcefully by the arm and dragged him out of the dormitory, giving him six belt lashes in the hallway and then slamming him into a narrow, dank closet alongside the mop bucket.

Groaning with pain, Tin had leaned back against the stone wall, his backside and thighs stinging too much to sit down, and lit the candle-stub smuggled inside the toe of his sock. He always kept one there when he held a story night – it had happened before, the closet-punishment, and he'd found it was more bearable with a little light.

As the flame had come to life, the candle illuminated a spider occupying a crooked web in the corner of the closet. It had long brown legs and a thick thorax with a strange pattern. Its body cast a wildly elongated shadow. At first Tin had gone very still. Could it truly be a *real* spider? With a little gasp of delight he'd leaned closer to examine the spider's markings. There was a funny shape on her coppery head, like a violin. He'd always liked the sound of the violin, lilting above the dusty drone of the organ during Sunday's brief hymns, before Father Ralstein's sermons about Grace and Progress. He'd remembered then, with a start of panic, the name *fiddleback*. This was in one of his books. It was a very deadly kind of spider. He'd leaned as far away from it as he could, and taken several deep breaths.

The fiddleback seemed to be regarding him from her web. If anything, she had retreated slightly onto a far edge of silk, tucking her legs in close. She hadn't looked especially interested in biting him. Nor had she looked particularly diseased, though Tin had heard over and over again the maxim *Do not trust in your senses for they will lead you astray; trust only in the Perfection of Brotherhood, and of the Golden Way.* She'd scuttled closer again. She was definitely watching him. He thought he could see her tiny eyes. Despite everything, despite his own panic, they looked gentle.

Even if I catch a flu, Tin had thought wildly, *I don't care! This is a real spider. And she is looking at me!*

After a little while, the fiddleback had turned away and set to repairing several broken pieces of silk on her web. Lifting his candle-stub nearer still, careful not to singe any threads, Tin had watched how she wove the silk of her body in and out. Where did it come from? How was it made? He gaped.

Nothing he had ever seen or been taught came close

to explaining the beauty of the fibres she wove, the grace of her quick eight legs, the perfect gleaming sphere of her body and its violin tattoo, her very otherness, alive but entirely different from him. Where had she come from? How had she got in? Was she from the Country? What had she seen? What was it like out there? His head had spun. She was a tiny mystery, perfectly encapsulating a much larger one. What if he made a model of her, one big enough for him to climb into, a vehicle of sorts? Maybe then he would understand more about what made her what she was, and the mystery that she contained.

For the rest of his stay in the closet, Tin had dreamed up plans in his mind. He'd sketched her every detail there in his imagination, every gleam and curve and line, her faceted eyes and the bends on her eight legs. He'd imagined that his brain was a pencil, and had sketched in the dark, unafraid of the deadly fiddleback in the corner. She had become his friend.

Now, sitting inside his creation three months later, he saw that he was no closer to understanding anything – not the mystery of fiddleback spiders, not the nature of spider silk nor the secrets of animals. And certainly not a thing about the much maligned Country outside the City's Wall. The mundane realities of his life settled around him where he sat. He was an orphan, owned by the Brothers at the Fifth Cloister of Grace and Progress since he was born. No matter what he did, what he invented or discovered, even if he did the thing they all tried for each day and figured out how to transmute scrap metals into stargold for the Brothers, would he ever be free? Would he ever be his own, and not theirs?

Every day, all day, the orphan boys and girls of the City's five cloisters were told they mattered less than the last of the stargold that powered the City. That their bodies were worthless and dispensable. Why else would the Brothers make children work with poisons to make new gold? Why else would they let them die trying? Only last week a vial full of liquid mercury had exploded, killing two boys in the shift just before Tin's. Father Ralstein had given a brief speech that praised the boys' sacrifice for the greater good of the City's progress and perfection. There was no funeral. Things like this happened so often that Tin had only felt a kind of cold dread during the speech. What kept him from giving in entirely to the listless hopelessness that so afflicted many of the other boys was making up stories and telling them, and inventing little contraptions with his hands. Otherwise he'd want to fight the Brothers, even the stone walls themselves. Otherwise, life in the Cloister would have been entirely unbearable.

A sudden movement all around him brought Tin back to himself. The lantern light seemed to be dancing across the dark room. There was a sound of well-oiled wheels, spinning. He almost yelped with shock. *The Fiddleback was moving.* It was rolling along on its eight wheels, its eight legs flexing gently as it went. What was more, it was glowing.

Tin instinctively grabbed hold of the steering wheel to keep from running into the wall. The metal wheel flushed gold under his hands. Every metal scrap inside the seat compartment flashed the same, the very colour of stargold. Now he really did yelp. Then he leaped right out through the Fiddleback's door and tumbled onto the stone floor, almost shattering the glass of his lantern. Abruptly the Fiddleback stilled and darkened, the glow snuffed.

Tin sat up, dazed and gasping. He started to tremble. What had just happened? Was it alchemy? Was it real stargold, or just the colour? He crept back and placed a shaking forefinger on the Fiddleback's side. Nothing happened. Taking a deep breath that was more joyous than fearful, he clambered back in again and sat down. This time he focused very hard, watching every scrap and wire and bit of metal around him in case the impossible transmutation happened again. This time he noticed a strange feeling stealing through his body. It was like a warm light in all of his bones. It settled right in the centre of him, a golden star. Then, just as before, the Fiddleback began to move. The engine below purred very gently. The wheels spun on their supple legs. Tin grasped the steering wheel and watched as it and the rest of the Fiddleback turned the colour of gold once again.

For the next hour, Tin zipped and zoomed around the dark stone chamber, testing out all the speeds and abrupt turns that the Fiddleback was capable of, getting used to steering eight legs at once, amazed at how fluid and lifelike his creation was, and how well it worked. For a little while the why and the how and the what of its miraculous animation didn't matter. All he knew was that he had never felt so happy in his life. He would think about it later, tomorrow in the Alchemics Workshop while grinding at the mercury they had been using over the past six months in the Brothers' latest set of experiments.

A noise outside brought him abruptly to a halt. The Fiddleback stopped without a sound. It cast a subtle, shimmering light on all the walls. Tin listened hard. It had sounded like a cough, quickly stifled, the sudden movement of boots outside the stone door. He hardly breathed. But the catacombs were silent now, so silent his ears rang. Maybe he had imagined it. Maybe it had come from the Fiddleback, something to do with the brakes or a wheel. He sat still for a long time, straining for any further sounds. All he could hear was his own breath. The last thing he wanted was for his Fiddleback to be discovered by the Brothers. This thought struck him, sickly. Whatever made his Fiddleback run, it had something to do with stargold; the stargold that the Brothers coveted. Tin didn't understand what had happened to make his invention run, but he knew that if it fell into the Brothers' hands, its beauty and mystery would be taken from him for ever.

But surely the sound was nothing; he was always so careful to make sure no one saw him when he snuck down to the catacombs. Still, just to be safe, he reluctantly climbed out of the Fiddleback and tucked it back into its corner, laying the rugs and bit of tarp back over it. The golden glow took longer to fade this time. For a moment Tin thought that it was emanating from his hands as well. But it was very late, and he was quivering with fatigue and excitement. He needed to tell Sebastian! Someone needed to share in this miracle, this mystery, and Seb was his best friend. He'd kept his Fiddleback a secret until now, but he needed to talk to someone about what had happened.

"Till tomorrow night then," he whispered to the Fiddleback, half-expecting it to reply. But it only sat silently under its rugs.

The way back was circuitous, winding through the kitchen cellars, below the Library and Alchemics Workshop and Metals Studio, zigzagging through the least-used and dustiest passages. He crept quietly behind old barrels of wine that the Brothers kept for themselves.

He skirted sacks of beans and tubs of the flavourless oats they ate daily. The oats came from the Albion Agricultural Facility, where all the fertilizers and pesticides were fabricated to grow just enough food and rapeseed lantern oil annually for the residents of the City.

Tin neared the trapdoor hatch he usually used to sneak in and out of the underground, taking from his pocket the clever lock-pick he and Seb had fashioned. It was the closest trapdoor to his dormitory wing, and opened at the edge of a worn-out red carpet in one of the side rooms that flanked the big Assembly Hall where Father Ralstein gave his weekly sermons. Several huge candelabras lined a large central table, but the room, as far as Tin could tell, was rarely used.

As he climbed the top stair and reached to unlock the trapdoor, he heard the voices of two men above him. The legs of a chair squeaked as somebody shifted his weight. But it was well past midnight. Why were any of the Brothers still awake? He had passed through the room dozens of times at this hour, and it had always been empty. Then he heard one of them speak his own name, and his whole body went cold. He froze, crouching there beneath the floor.

"Martin Hyde, he's called? Well, maybe this *is* worth calling me here for, straight out of bed at the witching hour." The speaker broke off into a rumble of low, delighted laughter. Another man, younger, said something whining in reply. Tin couldn't tell from their voices alone who the two men were, but he caught a high strain in the younger voice, and thought of Brother Warren, the slim, quiet fellow always transcribing texts in the Library. For a moment Tin's ears couldn't focus on their words above the sound of his heart – should he turn all the way round, try another exit point somewhere near the Cloister? But then he'd be locked outside, with no way in until mid-morning exercises. Should he just wait, curled on the stair, until they were gone? And why were they talking about him anyway?

Tin listened more closely to the cadence of the older man's voice, and realized why he hadn't recognized it at first. It was Father Ralstein himself. The boys never spoke to or interacted with the Head of the Cloister, only heard his weekly sermons on the subjects of Grace and Progress, always delivered in deep and booming tones. Now, he spoke in a conversational voice, and Tin only recognized him because of the crackling resonance of his laugh. It was a frightening sound. He listened harder.

"So you say this *thing* he has made, this contraption – it's shaped like a spider? And he's found a way to turn it into gold?" Father Ralstein's voice purred, horribly.

At this, Tin sank down to his knees in a sweat, his mouth dry. How did they know about his Fiddleback?

Had that noise been someone at the door after all? How long had they been watching him? And how had he not noticed? His Fiddleback! It was his secret, the only thing that was really *his* in the whole world. The idea of the Brothers getting their hands on it, taking its miraculous gold for themselves, made him want to break apart with anger, into a hundred little pieces.

"Yes, Father, yes!" intoned Brother Warren, his voice rising. "It seems impossible, I know, but I saw it before my very eyes. The thing turns to pure gold when the boy is in it, and runs. It moves just like a spider, with eight legs. It's ingenious."

"Your excitement is understandable, Brother," said Father Ralstein, his voice very deep now, so deep it was hard for Tin to hear. It trembled with anticipation. "This is indeed a revelation. But how do you know it's real gold – stargold – the gold we have been trying for a hundred years to create? Think of how many times a boy has managed some starry resemblance in the Alchemics Workshop, something with a golden sheen that only lasts a week or so, and melts to nothing in the Star-Breaker. Let's not get ahead of ourselves."

"Yes, Father. But it runs, you know, the engine runs! It has to run on something, and not just any old something. The boy must have made some very important discovery, some secret about the inherent properties of stargold.

We always knew he was uncommonly clever. I've had my eye on him." The Brother's tone wheedled and flashed.

Horror flooded Tin's chest now. He wanted to throw up. He hadn't made his Fiddleback as some tool for the Brothers, but as a wild act of imagination. Now they would take it from him and pick it apart until all the wonder was gone from it, like they did with everything. His whole life he had been told that his efforts to make gold were for the common good, the good of the City, to return it to its former state of glory. But he'd never felt as free or as glad in all his years as he had tonight. He wouldn't give the magic of it away! He couldn't.

"You know, Brother Warren, how dangerously low our reserves of stargold are of late?" Father Ralstein said after a pause, his tone grave. "They won't last us the year at current consumption rates. Probably not even through spring, unless we severely curtail Citywide use. It's the very last of the stargold in all the City. Stripped from every last façade and woman's jewellery case."

"Yes, Father, yes! That's why—"

But Father Ralstein ignored the Brother's wheedling. "I remember the tales my great-grandfather told when I was just a boy, of his own great-grandfather's boyhood Before the Collapse. How the City shone as one great golden star, brighter than the sun and more perfect. Now look what a shanty town it's become. What degradation we live amidst.

The slovenly poor running our Generators, turning the waterwheels day and night just to keep the lanterns lit. It's pathetic!"

"Yes, a disgrace indeed!" Brother Warren echoed. "But perhaps it's now at an end, Father?"

"Oh my dear Brother Warren, how little you know!" But Father Ralstein's voice brimmed with triumph, not defeat. It thundered through the room, and Tin found it hard to swallow; his mouth was too dry with fear. "I am going to tell you a secret, Brother," the man continued. "A Secret Ordain passed down from Cloister Father to Cloister Father since the time of the Collapse, we who carry what is left of the Star-Priests' knowledge. It was written by Solomon Pierce, last of the great Priests, last of the men who could read the patterns of the stars. He died of the Plagues, but not before he left two decrees. The first was that, on the two-hundredth anniversary of his death, the River Lutea would again run clean, and that on that day we should send a contingent of Brothers to test it for contamination and disease.

"The second, his Secret Ordain, sounded like little more than the deathbed ravings of a delirious man. It was written down nevertheless, though no one has been able to make sense of it since. Until I have, this evening." Father Ralstein paused with a self-indulgent smile. "*When the Spider makes Gold the Land will behold the return of the Old.*

Solomon Pierce, there always was a soft place in his head, they said. He predicted the Collapse, you know. So it seems he predicted our Rebirth, too. It was the Spider bit that nobody understood. Gradually we came to ignore it, thinking perhaps the scribe at his deathbed had misheard. Some thought it had to do with the legendary arachnid slain by the first of the Star Priests when they arrived here five hundred years ago, that monster big as a horse they found in the deep cavern at the City's heart where now we drill for groundwater. But still it didn't make much sense. Now at last it seems, Brother Warren, that the decrees have converged. In a fortnight it will be the two-hundredth anniversary of Solomon Pierce's death. A small contingent of the City's private guard has been informed, and is preparing for a covert mission to test the River Lutea and the Country itself for habitability. Of course it's a top-secret mission. We can't have ordinary City people finding out, and getting ideas about freedom, about leaving the City... And tonight you have brought me the Spider. You have answered the riddle. This Spider, it is a sign! A mascot for our Rebirth! The City shall rise! We are the Old, the old rulers, returning at last to cleanse the Country of savagery and turn it once more into the productive paradise it is destined to be. Without our intervention, this place has become but a wild and poisoned wasteland, without order, without meaning. It must be perfected once more!" Father Ralstein's voice rose to a feverish cry. But he quelled it abruptly. "Bring me the boy. Bring me the Spider," he demanded, and the words shook with greed.

At this, Tin turned in a panic to run back down the stairs as far and fast as he could possibly manage. But he was having trouble breathing, and his heart was thumping so hard in his chest that he stood too fast, dizzily, and whacked his head on the trapdoor. Horrified, head spinning, he ran.

"Well," said Father Ralstein, eyeing the trapdoor and rising to his feet. "I believe we have an eavesdropper." It was a growl.

"Tin, no doubt," replied Brother Warren smoothly. "This is his regular exit route."

At the same moment, both men leaped at the trapdoor and pulled it open. But there was nobody there. Brother Warren cursed.

"Headstrong brat," he hissed. "He'll make things difficult for us, that Tin. He won't give away his invention easily, I know him."

"All treasures can be bought," purred Father Ralstein, descending the stairs in a bound. "And all boys can be broken."

34

Tin was already out in the cloistered courtyard where the boys did their daily exercises. He'd sprinted there faster than he had ever run before. Now he gasped and gulped in rain and air. He couldn't tell, in the rush of adrenaline, if the heat on his face mixing with the raindrops was anger or tears. His mind spun and he couldn't quieten it. Why did he feel only dread and terror at the thought of these men using his Fiddleback to somehow rebuild the City's former glory? Wasn't it only for the Good of All that gold and perfection be restored, as he was so often taught? Then why was his strongest urge to run down to the cellars and destroy his Fiddleback with a hammer right then? Shouldn't he just stand there in the rain and wait for them to find him, lead them peaceably to his creation, and let them use him for whatever glorious fate they seemed to have in mind?

The rain fell harder and thunder slammed the sky, followed by lightning, very close. In the flash Tin saw something extremely odd: a pale bird passing low overhead. What was more, the bird was holding a leggy creature with long ears in its talons. Tin gaped at the sky. Was it a rabbit? A hare? He remembered the names vaguely from his books. And was that an owl that carried it? This night was surely one of wonders! What on earth was going on? First the Fiddleback, then the terrifying revelation of Father Ralstein, and now this! Rain fell against his teeth as he gaped and stared at the circling bird and the kicking animal in its claws.

Suddenly the owl let go of its captive, angling it right towards the boy's arms. Tin was so startled that he leaped sideways. A young hare thudded against his shoulder and with two yelps of shock they both tumbled to the ground.

3

THE BASKET
OF FATE

"You'd best be out with it, Comfrey," said Maxine to her daughter as she washed their clay bowls clean of porridge in a deep basin of rainwater. "You're never so quiet and still, except when you want something very badly." She turned to regard her daughter, wiping strong, dark hands on her trousers. The girl sat very still on a round yellow pillow at the big polished redwood stump where they ate all their meals. She looked fit to bursting with whatever it was she wanted to say. Her tawny hands were clasped and white-knuckled, her black braids already coming loose. A very fierce, almost secretive look glinted in her pale eyes, which were fixed on her mother's trousers, and not her face, studying their patchwork of salvaged fabrics. Comfrey had always thought her mother's trousers looked like a map of a thousand colours and places. They held bits of other worlds, from Before the Collapse – a scrap of faded green with tiny curling leaf shapes; a square of pink roses; another of indigo plaid. What had the world been like when people could make such intricate and colourful fabrics?

"I'd like to do the Offering-bundle tomorrow," Comfrey said all in a rush, unclasping her hands as she spoke and turning her long fingers to worry at her loosening braids.

It was such an unastonishing request that Maxine almost laughed. "Of course, my love, we do it together every year."

"No, I mean I want to do it alone. By myself," the girl interjected, getting to her feet. "I'm old enough, I'm twelve and tall for my age! Elspeth is doing her family's bundle this year. I know she's fourteen already but really I'm much cleverer than she is, and braver too." The words were tumbling out. "Remember how she shrieked only last summer when she saw a bobcat on the path near the square, because she thought it was a lion?"

This was getting a little close to the secret Comfrey had clasped inside her heart for the last two moons. But she couldn't help saying the word, just for the thrill of it. *Bobcat*. Since that December day two months ago when for the first time in her life she had actually *seen* one of the Wild Folk – a Bobcat-girl who had watched her from the hills just beyond the road – she'd been sculpting little bobcat figurines from creek clay for this very purpose. To be given as Offerings to the Wild Folk on the day of the Festival of Candles, in the hope that the Bobcat-girl might see them and remember her.

At the eight major seasonal holidays of their year, the Country Folk of the three villages called Alder, Quail and Lupine left Offering-bundles for the Wild Folk on behalf of all of Farallone. This was because their villages sat nearest the boundary between the Country and Olima, the land of the Wild Folk. At the summer solstice people from all eleven of the Country's villages gathered for three days of feasting and dancing in Alder after the Offerings had been left, so that each village could leave their own prayers and take home a bit of water from the stream that flowed across the boundary from Olima into the Country, to bless their children and their crops.

In exchange, a certain safety net was maintained. Serious illness was rarely a concern. Bees and goats and vegetable plots flourished. If some family forgot to leave out their bundle, or if they gave their second-best bushel of apples, or lumpy candles, a child came down with a case of pneumonia, or worse. A leak appeared almost simultaneously in the roof. Socks grew holes that refused to be darned. Salmon stopped spawning upstream and spawned only up the creeks through the thick fir trees where Wild Folk lived. It was a serious affair, this leaving of Offerings, and one carried out exclusively by women. As to the matter of interacting with the Wild Folk, well, it just wasn't done.

The Boundary was a fault line eighty kilometres long, where the two tectonic plates that made up the island of Farallone came together. To the human eye it looked like a long flat valley between two ridges and the very narrow Tamal Bay to the north, thin and straight as a blue ribbon. To the Wild Folk, it was a sacred delineation. According to the stories Comfrey had been told, crossing over that boundary into Olima meant you walked into the Realm of Creation, where the Wild Folk made their homes and guarded the heart of the island of Farallone. What exactly this meant she wasn't quite sure. All Comfrey knew was that everything was not entirely as it seemed in the land of Olima, and magic was real. Among the Country people, crossing that boundary was likened to a death sentence. It simply *wasn't done*. Stray across the fault line for what felt like a night, and if you were so lucky as to make your way back by morning, you might find your body an old woman's, and all your loved ones dead. Or you might find yourself no longer human at all, but a little green frog.

Comfrey had only ever heard second-hand stories

about people seeing Wild Folk, told by the old grandmothers, tales their own grandmothers had told them, and much embellished. They sat in the village's centre amidst the weekly market stalls of wool and carrots and goat's milk, honey, elderberry wine and cut firewood, spinning wool and gossiping and telling tales to little ones. Hardly anyone Comfrey knew had actually seen one of the Wild Folk first-hand, besides the cobbler's ancient grandfather. She'd pressed him before for stories of the Egret-woman he had seen on the marsh when he was a young man, but he would only get a faraway look, and speak of his dead wife.

It was considered very dangerous to see one of the Wild Folk. You might be kidnapped, or go mad. You might destroy the delicate Balance if you did something wrong, and bring on the Plagues again, or another earthquake like the earthquake that had coincided with the beginning of the Collapse. And doing something wrong was very easy, because no one really understood the ways or laws of the Wild Folk at all.

That day, two months ago, Comfrey hadn't just *seen* one of the Wild Folk. She had spoken to one. And the experience, much to her surprise, had left her neither frightened nor insane. On the contrary, it had left her strangely elated. It had happened a few weeks after her twelfth birthday. She was following her mother and aunt and three of her older cousins up the road from the beach. They'd all spent the morning there gathering flotsam. Comfrey had found three whole green glass bottles, completely unchipped, and was very proud of herself. She held them up to the sun to admire the green, hanging behind her cousins, who were all talking about their breasts growing and the boy named Jonah in the village called Pelican, the one nearest the ocean. Bored by their chatter, Comfrey dragged her feet and stared up at the steep scrubby hills on the far side of the road, beyond the wide patch of marsh. Wild Folk territory didn't begin until the other, unseen side of the ridge, but still it thrilled Comfrey just to imagine what might lie beyond it.

Her eyes suddenly focused on a girl's face. It was peering at her from behind a thick patch of coyotebrush and orange poppies. The girl moved into the open. Comfrey saw with a shock in her chest and a tingle in her hands that the girl had the pointed, dark-tipped ears of a bobcat, the hint of stripes down her face, a scrap of green rag for a dress. Her legs were furred and ended in paws. As sun rippled with wind across the hill, the place where the bobcat ended and the girl began seemed to shift. The girl wore a crown made of black spotted towhee feathers and a necklace of bones.

For a second, the Bobcat-girl and Comfrey made eye contact. She had never seen anyone with such mischievous, spritely, lively eyes. They glittered with light.

"Hello, Comfrey," the Bobcat-girl said. Somehow, even across road and marsh and hill, Comfrey could hear exactly what she said. She gulped and whispered "hello" back in a raspy voice. She quivered with the forbidden thrill of the moment, and the delicious sense of friendship she felt. Nothing bad happened. The Bobcat-girl didn't bound down the hill at her with sharp claws. The earth didn't shake. She just smiled. Her teeth glinted. Then she turned and darted back up into the brush. Comfrey saw a striped, bobbed tail sticking out of a slit in the back of her green scrappy dress. It moved as if in an invitation to follow. The Bobcat-girl looked back once more, not the way a cat eyes a bird but the way a girl looks invitingly to a new friend, because she has something marvellous and secret to share.

Just then Comfrey's mother called for her to hurry up and quit dragging her feet. When she looked back a final time, the Bobcat-girl was gone. And though Comfrey had gone looking almost every day since, all through early winter as the mushrooms grew in the woods and the rains began in earnest, she glimpsed no more of the mysterious Wild Folk girl who had somehow, impossibly, known her name.

She'd always been an inquisitive, independent child, peeking under rocks for salamanders and asking far too many impertinent questions about the Wild Folk when they had guests for dinner, but since that day in December when she first saw the Bobcat-girl, Comfrey had become a tinderbundle of curiosity, and with a short temper to boot. Maxine's answers about the Wild Folk were never enough, nor those of the old women who sat spinning sheep's wool in the sun in the centre of the village, nor even those of the old men who smoked wooden pipes over their fishing nets down by the nettle-lined stream. She didn't dare tell anyone her secret in case someone told her she'd been cursed, or had cursed them all. But she was always darting off before the morning weaving or the afternoon mushroom gathering to peer across the edge of the road into the marsh, towards the hills where, beyond sight, the land of the Wild Folk began.

"Well," said Maxine after a short pause in which she tried to weigh all the said and unsaid words in her daughter's eyes. Soft winter light found the kitchen window and moved sidelong in, illuminating Comfrey's feet in their rabbit-skin slippers, and her skinny girlish ankles. After all, it was a small enough thing, and only just beyond the edge of the village. She'd been helping Maxine lay the Offerings at every holiday since she was a girl of four, and knew all the words by heart. Generally girls did not begin to lay them on their own until after their first bleeding, but that was an old rule and not much mentioned. Besides, it seemed to matter very much to Comfrey, though Maxine couldn't quite understand why.

"Father would have let me go," blurted Comfrey, taking her mother's hesitation for a refusal. She regretted the words almost instantly for the way they made Maxine's face fall, but she couldn't help it. Her father was the only person she knew who had gone beyond the boundaries of their world – from the quiet village called Alder to the City's Wall, driven there by the premonition of a disaster he hoped to prevent. Comfrey had been four. Maybe Maxine knew what it was he had seen, but she never spoke of it. One morning, her father was simply gone. As far as Comfrey had been taught, nobody from the Country was ever let inside the City, and nobody from the City ever came out into the Country. Her father's going was unheard of. *He wants to bring down the Wall!* some said. Others called it foolhardy. Still others called it heroic. Maxine, depending on her mood, called it both.

That was eight years ago, and Thorne had never returned. The people of Alder had assumed him dead after a year without word, and held a funeral. For Comfrey's sake, Maxine went along with the village's proclamation. But somewhere in both of them, a little spark of hope remained. Maxine and Comfrey never spoke of that spark, and yet they both tended it in their own quiet ways. Their Thorne was too clever and too brave to die. Maybe it was a rash thought, for no man or woman can vanquish death. But Comfrey thought she would know it, if he were really gone. In her heart, she would know.

Now, Maxine struggled with an unexpected seam of tears. "I was about to say yes, child," she managed at last, trying not to sound harsh, busying herself with a jar of elderberry tincture that needed straining. She was the village herbalist for Alder and several of the children had colds. "Of course I trust you to take the Offerings. Of course you are old enough, my love. Your father – you're right. He would agree. He would be so proud of the brave young woman you've become."

Comfrey ran to her mother and threw her arms round her waist. There, she burst into tears – of guilt for keeping a secret from her, of sorrow at the thought of her father, and of giddy excitement that felt close to some premonition of change.

The next morning, the first day of February and the Festival of Candles, Comfrey stepped proudly out of their little cob house in her sturdiest walking shoes and her favourite blue walking cape, which she only wore on special occasions. The red cloth bundle of Offerings was tucked carefully into a willow basket which Comfrey made sure not to tip or jostle as she walked, as if it were a cake lit with candles. In the other hand she carried a pail of kitchen scraps for the eleven grey geese that lived in a neat pen beside the earthen walls of the house.

After feeding them and leaving the pail at the gate, Comfrey wound through the vegetable garden she and her mother carefully tended, now mostly brown stalks of summer thistles among rows of kale and winter potatoes, and stopped at the beehives at the garden's edge. There were thirteen hives in all, wooden boxes painted in reds and yellows and blues and greens. As she did every day, Comfrey stopped at that circle of hives, ringed with leggy rosemary bushes, and told them her news.

"Maybe you're dreaming more now since it's cold," she started, fidgeting the edge of the red cloth bundle in her hands. "I'm off to do the Offerings all by myself. Mother has let me! I've got to make sure I do it perfectly and then the Wild Folk will be pleased and it will be a good end to winter. We won't get hungry and we won't get sick either." She paused. Should she keep her secret even from the bees? "And...I'm hoping that the Bobcat-girl might see my gifts for her. That maybe she will come out again and—" Comfrey lowered her voice. "Well, I don't know. Only I'd like to speak with her again." Then she blushed, feeling selfish; after all, the laying of the Offerings was for the well-being of the village, and her home, not just her own curiosity. A cold wind came from the west, through the opening in the low hills that led to the willow valley and the Borderland. Comfrey breathed deep into the wind, which had the smell of the ocean and wet alders and mud and green grass and rain in it. She shivered a little, bowed her head to the drowsy bees, and set off down the footpath at the edge of the village, away from the other houses. It wound past fresh patches of nettles and crossed the creek at a shallow point, then passed between the hills, across a sodden meadow and into the valley.

The Offering places lined the hillside beyond the willow marsh, just on the near side of Wild Folk territory. Even though this borderland was technically still Country, nobody liked to get any nearer to Olima than they needed to, and the western ridge provided a natural boundary. Each of the families of Alder had their own altar-spot along this hillside, and there was some competition for the loveliest display. Comfrey and her mother had an altar on the flat, smooth top of a serpentine rock outcrop. Comfrey climbed the thin deer trail that led to their spot, slipping here and there in the muddy grass, until she was level with the rock. It was a steep short climb, and it made her calves ache. She set the bundle down and unrolled the red Offering cloth. It was striking against the pale green of the serpentine.

She took out the Offerings one by one with trembling fingers. A blue jay called, startling her. No one else was up with their Offerings, nor would they be for a few hours yet. Comfrey had wanted to get there early so she could take her time, and look around in case she glimpsed again the Bobcat-girl's green dress or her furred face. She set the nine beeswax candles in their nine clay holders on the red cloth, arranging them in a circle. They were painted dark blue with yellow dots like stars. In the centre she set the polished skull of a barn owl she and her mother had found in the alderwood while softening nettle stalks in the creek, upside down so that it created a bowl. Into the bowl she placed a fresh-baked acorn-flour cake, and beside it she poured elderberry mead into a wooden goblet made of dark red bearberry bark. Nine pieces of kale, freshly harvested from the winter garden, she arranged like the spokes on a wheel, radiating out from the owl skull at the centre, and around them she laid a beaded strand of red madrone berries.

All that was left were her clay bobcat figurines. She picked each one up to admire before setting them down on the red cloth. She'd spent a day on each, shaping and smoothing and reshaping, using a sharpened feather to carve eyes and noses, claws, spots.

"Like guardians," Comfrey said out loud, shifting the clay bobcats so that they sat on opposite sides of the circle, between the madrone berries and the outer round of candles. Then she struck a flint to light the candles, put her palms down by the two clay cats, and said the proper words. "Bless the sun through the night, bless the dark through to light, bless the green, bless the rain, bless the land come to life at the turning of the light. May the roots in the ground, may the birds flying south, be held in the comfort and shelter of dark. Thank you new seeds, thank you rain, thank you salmon, thank you stars. Thank you alder, nettle, deer and green. May we walk all in beauty. Blessed Be and Scree."

The last part, "Blessed Be and Scree", Comfrey and her mother had made up and added in when Comfrey was around seven at the summer solstice, and a red-shouldered hawk had wheeled above them so close they could see the snake in her talons. The bird had called out once, a sound like "scree".

"She's saying a blessing too!" Comfrey had exclaimed, and Maxine had laughed, and so it stuck.

Today, just as Comfrey finished saying the words and was beginning to wonder whether she should whisper any additional ones about the Bobcat-girl, she heard laughter. Deep, ragged, howling laughter. Coyotes, she thought at first. Then she heard the cadence of women's voices. Comfrey blushed and looked around. Were the other women starting to arrive already with their Offerings?

Were they laughing at her, thinking her too young to leave them by herself? She stood, ready with some sharp retort. Then she realized that the laughter was coming from up the willow valley where it widened and the ridge lowered, and where humans never ventured. The footpath did not go any further north, south or west. It ended here, beyond Alder. If you wanted to get to one of the other boundary villages, you went back inland and took the well-worn paths east of the fault line, safely on the other side of the low hills that lay between them and the marshland. The Olima Borderlands were a kind of no man's land. All willow thicket, tule marsh, meadow and sudden mists. Villagers only ever ventured into them for the leaving of Offerings, and then very quickly, using the same well-tested footpath.

But there it was again, that strange and ragged laughter! And it was most certainly coming from up the marsh. Could the laughter be the Bobcat-girl and her mother and aunts and grandmothers, feasting around their own holiday fire? Comfrey wondered. What harm would it do if she went just a little further to peek and see? Wasn't this what she had hoped for?

Comfrey bowed quickly to the Offerings and the altar and leaped from the rock. As she slid down the hill her boots got covered in mud, and when she tried to tiptoe up the path they squelched. The sky was growing dark with rain clouds, and the sun passed in and out of them, making patchy shadows on the ground. Comfrey made her way through a sodden, newly greening meadow. The laughter got louder. She smelled woodsmoke. Somebody belted out a soulful tune amidst a murmur of talk, and then more laughter. It sounded like it was coming from just beyond the willow thicket she could see on the other side of the meadow, which backed into the deeper hills of Olima.

Breathless with excitement, forgetting how far she had strayed into the borderlands, Comfrey clambered between the bare yellow branches and looked. On a flat bit of the grassy hillside, surrounded by low-growing sagebrush and lupines, she saw a group of three women sitting in front of two wooden carts. One cart was ox-blood red, the other yellow. While the carts were stationary, the wheels doubled as spinning wheels, their bobbins full of golden thread. Big deer, eight of them, were grazing nearby with leather harnesses unhitched but still attached to their necks. The carts had rounded canvas tops and metal chimney pipes. The women sat in the grass cross-legged, making baskets from straight, split willow sticks. They hooted with laughter and chatted and poked at a fire they'd made in a pit of stones.

Wild Folk.

The only thing that made Comfrey certain they were Wild Folk at all, and not odd human people from another village, was that their hair was done up in elaborate four-plait braids woven into cone shapes like beehive baskets. In fact, their hair wasn't hair at all, but fine fibrous plant stalks, growing right from their scalps. When one of them turned slightly, Comfrey saw that her hair-basket was hollow inside, and sheltered a chickadee.

The women grinned and joked like Comfrey's cousins, but she could see that their lined eyes and hands were ancient. Their lips were youthful though, as were their easy, fluid movements. Watching them, Comfrey felt full of more yearning than she had ever felt in her young life. More even than she'd felt at the sight of the Bobcat-girl. She wanted her hands to be so sure, so fast and strong, making baskets of such beauty. She'd never heard anyone laugh the way they laughed. She leaned forward more and her foot slipped. It broke a branch with a snap and her shoe slapped the mud.

One woman looked up. Her eyes were darker than her beautiful skin, which was the colour of bearberry bark. Her fennel-yellow dress stood out bright in contrast. Her quick hands kept steadily at their weaving.

"Hello, you naughty village-girl," she said in a rich voice, the kind of voice with woodsmoke in it. "Would you like to come join our fire? Would you like to learn to weave the basket of your fate? Isn't it your own destiny you are after, girl?" She winked a dark eye and flashed Comfrey a smile that made the girl's stomach flip upside down. She had been seen!

With a gasp she turned, slipping in the mud, batting aside the willows, and ran all the way home. As she ran, her heart leaped with a mixture of panic and a deep, wild excitement.

4.

MALLOW

"What was that?" came a scolding voice from beside Tin's left elbow. "You have hands, don't you?" It was the little rain-drenched hare, hissing as he disentangled himself and his long ears from under Tin's wrist. "I was the one falling from the sky! That demoness of an owl even did her best to drop me near your hands. What a blasphemy to all Haredom, to be carried by an owl!" The rain had let up a little, and the leveret shook himself as if to get rid of a bad smell, then leaned forward to sniff Tin's outstretched palms. The boy gaped. "Much talked of, the hands of your kind. Very clever, very dangerous, it is said. Well, at the moment they seem rather overrated to me."

Tin sat up slowly and looked down at his hands. They smarted from the fall, and he opened and closed them as he peered closely at the hare, who was looking right back at him with expressive, dark-brown eyes.

For a moment Tin thought he'd hit his head when he fell. The hare's voice must be some hallucination made of the rain splattering the cobblestones and his own spinning thoughts.

The leveret sniffed again at his palms. "It smells as though you are in some sort of trouble. Good timing, I should say. Off with a bang. Hope I'm not a roast over someone's fire by dawn. Well, let's see what we can do to get you out of whatever predicament is causing your palms to sweat. The Greentwins were clear that I am to help you." The hare sat up tall even as the rain coated his fur. His proud black tail quivered. "You can call me Mallow, by the way."

Tin kept staring. The wild loops of the boy's hair, normally an unruly golden mass, were flattened to his head. His work clothes clung to his skin, revealing the outline of his young chest and shoulders, which years of hunger had made bony and lean.

"What, you don't talk, either? A strange human indeed you've landed me with, old Greentwins. We always suspected life was unpleasant inside the City Wall, but this is more dire than I—"

"No, no, I talk. I'm sorry," Tin blurted out, leaning forward into a crouch with a burst of energy that scared

Mallow backwards. A sweet simple wonder had stolen over him while staring at that perfect wild hare. "I'm Tin. You're from…outside the Wall? I thought all the animals were dead! I thought it was a dangerous place, full of sickness and—"

"All dead?" the leveret exclaimed, flashing his ears with mirth. "All dead! Oh no, far from it my friend. Outside, well, it's far lovelier than in here, that's for certain. Not a bit of green to be seen in this terrible place, and I'm ravenous!"

They both started at the sound of heavy, running footsteps in the tunnels below the courtyard.

"I'm in quite a lot of trouble, as it turns out," said Tin, still wide-eyed. "I don't have any idea how I'm going to get out of this one." He ran his hands through his wet mop of curls, and even though his heart surged with panic at the sound of those footsteps, something in him had gone light and clear. It was as if the leveret had come in answer to a prayer he'd never known he had said. The creature was another piece of a mystery he hadn't realized he was bent on unravelling.

"Come on then!" said Mallow, already bounding away. "Nobody's better at a brilliant escape than a hare."

"It's not an escape!" called Tin. "It's a rescue!"

"Whatever you say!" retorted the hare.

Dripping wet, Tin and Mallow dashed down the

staircase that led under the library at the far end of the courtyard, Tin leading the way towards the catacombs. They left wet footprints in the tunnels as they ran. Tin paused to light the little rapeseed oil lantern he carried in his knapsack with a stolen scrap of flint. It cast a flickering muted glow, enough to navigate the tunnels. In gasping whispers, he tried to explain the wheeled Fiddleback, and how he knew it was crazy to be running right towards his pursuers, but he couldn't let them get it, his beautiful machine, his miracle. Suddenly Mallow skidded to a halt. Further down the dark corridor, down one more crumbling flight of stairs, was the secret room that hid Tin's eight-wheeled invention. Mallow cocked his ears forward.

"They're already inside, talking," he said.

"How can you tell?" Tin couldn't hear anything.

"Big ears, silly. They're meant for such things."

Tin felt his heart torque with despair, and his stomach too. They were already there. It was too late. He was trapped. Worse than that, Tin thought, they would take away his Fiddleback.

"You can't give up so easily!" said Mallow, reading Tin with his veined ears and white whiskers. "We've hardly begun!"

"It's not like we can just waltz in," Tin said, distracted. "Trust me. You don't want to get caught by these guys."

"No, no. We have to be craftier than that. Like foxes or ravens," said the hare, smug. "We hares learn everything we can from listening to the Ones Who Would Eat Us. Anyway, you yell, like you've fallen down and broken your leg. Tempt them towards us."

Tin snorted, thinking this was the stupidest idea he'd ever heard, but all the while in the back of his mind he thrilled at the mention of ravens and of foxes.

"Then we'll duck right here," Mallow continued, ignoring the boy. "Into this clever dip in the walls, this little cleft of bedrock."

Tin lifted the lantern and the light shone on a cramped crevice in the wall. "How did you know that was there?"

"Air currents. Smells different."

"So long as they don't look behind them," Tin muttered.

"Yes," said Mallow. "I'll show you how to freeze just like a hare. A tried and true technique. Go so still and vacant in your eyes, barely even breathing, vacant in your head too, so utterly uninteresting, that even if they *do* look over their shoulders, they will be too uninterested to process your presence."

Tin eyed the hare. His ears only reached the boy's knees, yet he was standing there, nose moving, full of perfect confidence.

"Then what?"

The hare flicked his ears back. "No idea."

Tin smiled at the leveret's cocky bravado, recognizing himself in it. Then he screamed, as if with great pain.

"Good," whispered Mallow after the echoes quietened. "They heard you. They're coming."

He directed Tin into the depression in the wall first. It was only a slight dip, a layer of stone that doubled back to make a cleft. Tin's left shoulder was still clearly visible, and his foot. The leveret tucked himself between Tin's calves. The boy blew out the lantern, and total darkness fell.

"Okay, now start emptying your head. Think of it like a pool of water just draining until there's nothing. And when I say so, don't move a muscle. Hold your breath."

For what felt like for ever but amounted to only a scant minute, Tin tried to quieten his mind. He pictured his thoughts like streams of water flowing down from his head and out of his feet, but an image of his friend Sebastian kept slipping in as everything else emptied. Sebastian, posted as a sentinel while Tin murmured stories into the dim candlelight. Sebastian, creeping through these same hardpack tunnels just a step behind, always a little bit more nervous, and a good fifteen centimetres shorter, but quick and clever and good with maps, stealing extra oats from a barrel in the cellars with a snicker.

"Hey, shh," Mallow whispered to Tin, breaking into his thoughts.

"I wasn't talking!" said Tin, startled.

"No, but your mind was. I could hear the sound of all that busy-ness like cracking twigs underfoot. Empty, quick, they aren't far!" The leveret nipped Tin's ankle for good measure. Tin let out his breath, but he couldn't stop thinking about Sebastian.

Escape, he thought. *What does the hare mean by "escape"?* Could they really escape the Cloister? Could they really escape the City itself? But then Seb came back into his mind. *I can't leave Seb behind*, he thought. *He's my only friend.*

Mallow glared, just a dark flicker of eyes. Footsteps clip-clopped round the corner.

Tin went totally still. A faint glow of lantern light skittered across the walls.

"Where could the little brat have got to?" came Brother Warren's voice just a little bit ahead of his feet, a high edge in it, nervous and under pressure. "That scream was so close by."

"He's a hardy lad," Father Ralstein replied, "maybe he tripped but kept on running, right back up to his dormitory, thinking we'd never be the wiser. Not wanting to get in trouble for eavesdropping."

Brother Warren paused in his stride suddenly, just alongside the crevice where Tin and Mallow had pressed themselves, frozen and vacant-eyed. Brother Warren stiffened and began to turn his head and the lantern in his hand. Tin's mouth went dry, but he remembered Mallow's soft voice, his perfect stillness, and filled his head with clouds, with sky, vast and empty.

"Strange," said Brother Warren after a long moment, sniffing. He began to walk again. Father Ralstein looked sharply to both sides where the younger man had stopped, scanning in a general way.

"I'm sorry, Father. I felt something, somebody near, like a shadow. Thought I smelled a whiff of burned rapeseed oil." He looked over his shoulder. Tin saw the man's eyes fall right on the edge of Mallow's golden haunch, but process nothing.

"Ghosts, Brother?" chuckled Father Ralstein. "Boy must've run this way back to the dorms." There was an edge of irritation in his voice, a cold metallic tone. "Why treat him like a thief in the night?" he continued. "If we want him on our side, if we want him to tell us the secret of his golden machine, which hardly looked golden to me though you have assured me that it was when you saw it, why not pull him from the Alchemics Workshop tomorrow morning, talk to him in the meeting room with a cup of chicory-root coffee, man to man, a treat. Flatter his ego a bit?"

Brother Warren was silent. "I sense he is wily," he said, after a moment. "I sense he will fight us. We should capture him and take his machine now."

"Nonsense, Brother," murmured the Father, their voices getting fainter. "Nothing we can't break. Nothing we can't bribe. And I know about the egos of young men. I understand these things. We don't want to make a scene, chasing him through the dormitories, making the other boys take up his side against us. We don't want them to think we are thieves, Brother. We want the boy to bring us his invention of his own free will. It will go much easier, thus. We must coax him, butter him up. Come now, Brother, it was a good attempt, but I'll take over from here."

Tin and Mallow stayed still, breathing shallowly for a good few minutes after the voices and footsteps echoing through the tunnels had faded away. Then Tin looked down at Mallow and grinned.

"That was close!"

"It's always close," said the hare, shaking out his long ears and grooming at his chest with nervous relief. "You get used to it. You learn to go so quiet even your heart isn't thundering. You rein it in."

Tin shook his shoulders, which had gone stiff, and began to walk in the same direction his pursuers had gone.

"Hang on just a minute!" cried Mallow, settling back onto his haunches. "I'm not hopping another step until you tell me what in the world is going on. And what this Fiddleback *is*. You were talking so fast the first time round all I understood was that you'd made a – a *thing* out of old bits that looks like a spider but isn't really a spider, and has something called an engine which is like a heart, and that when you sit inside it the whole thing turns to gold and comes to life? This sounds like utter madness! But I'm new to City things. Do enlighten me."

Tin smiled a little at the leveret's earnest expression, his big liquid eyes and quivering ears, and tried to explain – about the Fiddleback, about the Alchemics Workshop, about the Brothers and their gold and their Star-Breakers. As he spoke, the leveret's eyes grew wider and wider, until at last he interrupted.

"This is very bad, very bad indeed," Mallow said. "The Greentwins were more right than they even knew to send me to you. Do you know the true nature of stargold? Did they ever teach you that, or the stories of the Wild Folk?"

"The what?"

"Oh, dear…" The leveret sighed. "Well, we can talk about it all later. For now, escape is the name of the game! This Fiddleback of yours, we have to get it out of here. It's very dangerous in the wrong hands."

"Dangerous?" Tin was starting to feel afraid, and in very much over his head. Mallow had already started to bound back down the hall towards the Fiddleback. "Wait!" called Tin. "First we have to get Sebastian. He's coming with us. Wherever it is we're going."

"In the name of all Haredom, the boy knows nothing of quick escapes!" the leveret muttered to himself, hopping back again. "Who is Sebastian?"

"He's my best friend. I can't leave without him. We always said we'd get out together. I have to go back for him or I'm not worth anything." Tin frowned down at Mallow, lamp cautiously lit again. "I don't want to get in the habit of abandoning people. That's what I am, isn't it, an abandoned person? Well, I'm not going to do that to Seb." He'd gone down into a crouch, and was looking Mallow in the eye.

The hare understood in that fierce blue glare something of the strength Brother Warren had spoken of. You couldn't change this boy's mind about a thing once it was set. And in those blue eyes, Mallow saw his twin sister Myrtle, and a blue sky. He felt an old memory rise up, from when they were only just born, and their mother had left them in a bed of soft grasses with the big dawn sky above them. A coyote had taken her, the Greentwins had told them later. He remembered the warmth of his sister next to him that day, the only familiar being in the whole big green and blue world. His little strong heart thudded, thinking of Myrtle, the terror in her eyes as the barn owl lifted her off into the dusk in dreadful talons, winging her towards her fate, her duty, as Mallow had been taken towards his. Had it only been a few hours ago? It felt like a lifetime. But this was what the Greentwins wanted. *The boy and the girl are your charges*, they had said. *We can see from the Shape of Things that Farallone is in great danger again. That this time, the island herself might die, and that the Elk will not be strong enough to save her Creation as she did at the time of the Collapse. It matters very much that you find these children. All together you, and they, have something to do with wholeness, with the overcoming of Walls and Boundaries and the things that have kept us living in fear of one another – City Folk and Country Folk and Wild Folk – for the last two hundred years. So you must trust us, and go. We cannot see the small details, only the greater patterns: that there is great danger to the whole. Help these children. Follow where they go and help them on their paths. Hopefully this will be enough, before it is too late.*

But Myrtle had been taken to a village in the Country. How would he ever find her again, and not lose Tin in the process? The leveret lowered his eyes.

"Okay, Tin, no abandoning. I get it," Mallow said solemnly. "Your turn to come up with the plan, then." He sniffed the air, brightening. "Wouldn't want any rumours spreading that just because hares run fast, they're cowards."

Tin grinned again, and his eyes softened.

"A plan? You never told me *your* plan. Well, *my* plan is to wake Sebastian up, sneak back down here to the

66

Fiddleback, jump in, and then, you know…vanish?" He laughed, shaking his head.

"That's hardly a plan!" said Mallow. "That sounds more like No Plan to me."

A chill passed all down Tin's spine as he regarded the leveret. He still didn't quite believe that Mallow was real, much less this talk of escape. His head reeled a little. "Look," he said, swallowing hard and trying to act calm. "I bet Seb will have a better idea. He has the maps we've made. The other week we found this tunnel that went way deeper than the others, on the other side of the Cloister and down and down until it kind of got hard to breathe, but I bet that's the one, the way out."

"Burying us alive or vanishing into thin air, that's all you've got?" Mallow said with a small snort. "Brilliant. The Greentwins have sent me into a deathtrap! Well, let's at least not waste any more time running headlong to our doom! Hop to!" And with that, the leveret bounded off down the passageway, silent and quick.

"And hope they're not already waiting at the door," said Tin to himself as he followed after Mallow.

The boy and the hare reached the surface without incident, Mallow expertly guiding Tin through passageways he'd never explored before. Tin had to admit to himself that he would have become completely lost in those dark and twisting catacombs without the leveret ahead, following the smells in the air.

They emerged, to Tin's surprise, at the bottom of the west bell tower, through a very small wooden door behind a threadbare tapestry woven with fruits Tin had never eaten – pomegranates, apricots, grapes, a handful of almonds in their shells. A narrow staircase made of iron spiralled upwards towards the bronze bell, which was old, cracked and still rung daily at dawn and noon and dusk, but in strange minor tones. Tin had never been in either of the two bell towers, because there was nothing inside except that winding staircase, dizzying and steep. Holding up his little lantern – which by now was almost out of oil – Tin tiptoed across the room and towards the other door, the one that led out towards the dormitories. A heavy key sat in the lock. Mallow kept close to his ankles.

"Wait," said the hare, and turned his ears to the door. Tin's hand paused mid-air, just above the key. "Okay, quiet, turn it slowly. I can't wait to get out of this place. Creepy, hulking cavern. Whoever got the idea to live in such an awful warren of stone and shadow and cold?" Mallow continued, mostly to himself. "It's hideous."

The lock clicked low, and Tin swung the door open, trying to keep it from creaking. They were in the Main Assembly Hall now, on the side near his dormitory.

"Good," he sighed, ignoring Mallow's mutterings, and slid along the shadows of the outer wall. He was in familiar territory again – he and Sebastian had shimmied countless times along this big dark wall, whispering plans.

Outside the rosette window all spattered in raindrops, the storm had broken for a moment. A scrap of crescent moon shone through the clouds, making a long soft beam across the middle of the floor. Mallow stopped and stared up at the rosette glittering with raindrops and coloured glass and moonlight, having never seen such a thing before.

"Psst, come on," whispered Tin, holding the door open to the West Dormitory wing. He took his tattered shoes off – old canvas and rubber sneakers worn to a nondescript grey – and padded silent as the hare three flights up the stone stairs. The halls were that particular sort of quiet that only reaches its fullness at around three in the morning. The grey shadows themselves felt muffled.

Tin picked at the keyhole with his lock-pick. It scratched, clicked, and gave way. They were in. Tin closed the door softly. The familiar smells of crisped sheets washed religiously on Sundays, sweat, and the musty dampness of the walls, hit Tin as he entered the room. For better or worse, the smells comforted him; this crowded chamber was the closest place to a home he had ever known.

The dormitory consisted of a series of slim metal cots lined up in rows of eight across, with an aisle down the middle from door to bathroom. There were four rows in all. Each bed had a small wooden crate at the end for clothes, and another wooden crate on its side as a bedside table where a candle and a cup of water might be perched.

Tin spotted his own bed, quilt rumpled and mounded round his pillow, and Sebastian's directly behind it in the farthest row near the windows. His friend's thick black hair shifted softly over his eyes as he rustled in his sleep. Tin slipped silently over to his own bed, Mallow, just as quiet, at his ankles. The leveret stared and sniffed, trying not to tremble at the sight of so many human beings all in one room.

"Seb." Tin shook his friend gently. "Seb, wake up. This is it, Seb, wake up!" Mallow put his paws up on the bed and sniffed Seb's head, then sprang back as the boy jolted upright with a gasp, eyes bleary until they focused on Tin.

"What is it? What's going on?" Seb rubbed his dark eyelashes.

"This is it, Seb! We're escaping, this second!" Tin leaned close, tired and scared and excited all at once. He suddenly felt the weight of it as he said it out loud, leaning against the hard mattress pad in this hard stone room with the rain starting up again on the roof. Mallow hopped onto the bed and Seb gaped.

"What is *that*, Tin?" he whispered hoarsely. "What are you talking about?" He looked between the hare and his friend twice, rapidly.

"I'm a black-tailed hare," said Mallow. "Not a 'that'. My name is Mallow, and really there's no time to explain. Tin insisted we come back for you. Otherwise we'd be out and away through the hare-forsaken streets of this gloomy City and heading straight for the secret door in the Wall."

"The secret door in the Wall?" both boys whispered in unison. Tin's thoughts hadn't reached much beyond the walls of the Cloister, and Sebastian was trying hard just to assimilate so many miracles all at once.

The hare looked at them in astonishment. "What? Don't you *want* to leave the City?"

"But…isn't it dangerous on the other side of the Wall? And aren't the people in the Country very sick with poisons and disease? Wouldn't we…die?" stammered Seb, thinking of all the things they'd been told.

Mallow let out a little hare-snort. "Sick? Dangerous! Compared to this place? Oh, my poor humans, what have they been telling you here? The Country is the most beautiful place in the world. The hills in spring are full of delicious flowers – have you ever seen a flower? I suppose you haven't… Oh my stars, what sorry creatures you are! There hasn't been any serious sickness in a hundred and fifty years, and the streams are clean as rain!" Mallow trailed off at the memory of wild clover; at the memory of his sister; of home.

The boys looked at each other with their hearts in their throats. Tin, pretending he had known this all along, grinned at Seb.

"See? It's for real," he said to his friend. "Now c'mon, I can't explain here. We're going to the tunnels, fast."

With a trusting, big-eyed look, Seb quietly climbed out of bed, pulled on his grey trousers and a sweater with holes in both elbows, then tucked his own tattered shoes under his arm. Out of the dormitory windows, the distant City Wall threw white electrical currents in the rain.

"We're not coming back," Tin said, his face illuminated by the storm's light, trying to sound certain both for Seb's sake and his own. "So take any special stuff, but hurry. They're coming for me at dawn and they're going to take my Fiddleback."

"Your *what*?" Seb stopped midway through stuffing a knapsack with socks, his toothbrush, a little necklace made out of bright copper pennies given to him wrapped up in a blue bandana from the kitchen-girl named Sophie. He eyed Tin, wondering if his friend had finally snapped.

"Shh, never mind. I'll tell you on the way."

Mallow nipped at Seb's calves to hurry him along, and the boy could think of nothing to do but trust his friend, and follow.

They managed to make it to the door without causing more than a few boys to stir in their sleep. This was an old routine for Tin and Seb, and they were used to whispering and walking with almost no sound, cued in to each other's hand movements and almost able to lip-read. But the excitement of the evening was starting to wear on Tin. He'd been awake for almost twenty-four hours. After the adrenaline of the chase, of meeting Mallow, and of the Fiddleback itself, Tin's hands shook with fatigue as he went to open the self-locking door with his little pick. He dropped it, a clattering of metal on the cold stone floor. Seb winced. Mallow stopped, still and quivering, as somebody stirred, springs creaking, and sat upright in his bed.

"You again, Tin?" came a voice. Thomas, a hulking shape in the semi-dark, his hair sticking up like feathers.

"I swear to God, Thomas, you shut your mouth or I'll fill your bed with hot mercury," hissed Tin after a moment's tense silence.

"Oh, will you?" snarled Thomas, waking the boys around him.

"Out, out," whispered Mallow urgently, leaping to Tin's arms and nearly winding the boy.

"What on earth is *that*?" said Thomas. "Oh, man, have I got the dirt on you, Tin, an *animal*?"

"An animal?" another voice said softly. More covers

rustled and springs creaked as half the dormitory woke and craned to see.

"Hurry up!" urged Mallow, pressings his paws to Tin's chest. Tin looked at Mallow and Seb with desperate, bright eyes, then jiggled the door open. The boys ran in their socks, shoes thumping against their knapsacks where they were tied by their laces. Mallow leaped out of Tin's arms and bounded ahead. They made it all the way down to the trapdoor under the red velvet carpet in the meeting room where earlier in the night Father Ralstein and Brother Warren had sat in wait. Now the room was empty and the boys dashed in the dark down the earth-packed stairs. The door slammed above them.

They ran all the way to the kitchen cellars before stopping for breath.

"The Hall Brothers will be awake by now, and Thomas will've told," said Seb, panting. "You'd better have a darn good plan, Tin. What are you thinking? I mean, I know we've talked about this a lot but we're already in a mess and we've barely left the dorms!"

"Finally, a wise child!" sighed Mallow. "I've been trying to say this to him but the boy is headstrong and reckless and thinks No Plan and a lot of dashing about is the way to go."

The boy smiled crookedly at the hare. Seb was shorter than Tin, but broader, with wiry dark arms and thick eyebrows, which he raised now as he smiled.

"Yeah, that's Tin for you. But he can probably talk his way out of a hole in the ground, so maybe we'll be okay, as it looks like we're going to need just that. To be talked out of a hole in the ground." He looked up ruefully at the tunnelled walls around them. "Tin, you better start telling me now what in the world you're up to. First, the Fiddleback."

"We don't have *time*," said Tin, pulling Seb by the arm. "Now they'll be after us, and they'll confiscate the Fiddleback before we have a chance to save it! Come on, I'll explain once we are in."

"In? In *what?*" cried Seb, but Tin and Mallow were off at a sprint again.

5

MYRTLE

The rains began not long after Comfrey returned home from the Offering altar, and did not let up all night. They were lashing and wild. Thunder boomed. All the candles lit on all the altars along the borderlands hissed out. Comfrey didn't tell her mother about the Basket-witches. She faked some measure of normality, then escaped to her room. She pulled aside the piece of felt at her bedroom window that kept the wet out, and let the rain pelt in sideways and spatter her face as she stared out into the storm.

Her thoughts were back in the clearing, remembering the dark eyes and deep yellow skirts of the woman who had spoken to her. Why had she smiled that way, so warm and fierce at once? And the baskets the women had been weaving – Comfrey had never seen anything so delicate, so finely wrought, so beautiful.

"The basket of my own fate. The shaping of my own destiny," she whispered to herself, sticking her hands out of the window to feel the downpour. What did that mean? Did it have anything to do with the Bobcat-girl who had known her name? Her eyes took in the blur of rain without focusing. Was your destiny really something you could shape, like a basket?

Suddenly a white shape came winging straight for her window sill. She snatched her hands back in shock but didn't have time even to cry out before a wet barn owl veered so close its wing touched her hair. It set a squealing and squirming leveret on the sill and flew off, shaking its wings in disgust.

"This better be worth it, so help me all Hare-gods!" Eyes white with terror, the young hare leaped onto Comfrey's floor, creating a shower of raindrops from her fur. A fine mist smelling of damp wool and grass covered Comfrey's face. She wiped her eyes and stared at the hare, who began delicately to groom at the white patch of fur on her nose.

Comfrey couldn't keep back her excitement. Was this yet a *third* encounter? "I'm sorry to be rude, but – are you a Wild Folk?"

The hare laid her ears back and looked up.

"Oh for goodness' sake, me? What on earth makes you say so? Did I grow an odd human limb from that hideous owl-flight?" She looked down again at herself in horror.

"No, no, it's only…you're talking, and you're a hare. And that's not meant to happen. Only Wild Folk look like animals but talk too, like people, and normally they look like people also, but they rarely come here and we never go there so I wasn't sure," Comfrey said, breathless, the words stumbling out. "Did those Basket-witches send you?" She found her head was spinning, and sat down hard on her bedroll. "Am – am I in trouble?" The leveret hopped over and joined her.

"Basket-witches? Trouble? It seems I've come just in time," she said cheerfully, wriggling her whiskers. "I'm Myrtle. And actually I'm just a bit hungry, after all that owl business. Might I have a snack? Hard to talk in your human way on an empty stomach." She pawed about for a moment at the wool covers, then settled comfortably onto her haunches, eyeing Comfrey expectantly.

The girl dashed into the kitchen on quiet, slippered feet, hardly breathing in her excitement. She tucked a small acorn cake from the ceramic crock by the window into a nettle-fibre napkin, and a garden carrot for good measure, then tiptoed back, snack-bundle in hand. But she misjudged the corner of her own door frame and stubbed her toe with a thud and an outward hiss of breath.

Her mother shifted in the room next door.

"Frey?" Maxine called, her voice mossy with sleep.

Comfrey froze. Her heart thumped. She breathed out.

"Just getting water, Mama. Sorry to wake you," she whispered loudly at her mother's door. Maxine made a small noise in reply and turned over. Comfrey waited until her breathing went regular. Then she slipped back into her room, closing the door very slowly, and laid the bundle out before the leveret. Myrtle tucked in at once.

"Much better," said the hare after a silence broken only by voracious nibbling. She ate the whole acorn cake and part of the carrot before turning back to Comfrey, who was sitting straight up in bed, watching her closely. "Brilliant, whatever you've done with the acorns," continued the leveret between bites, white whiskers moving. "Much better than they usually taste, yes indeed."

Comfrey smiled politely, impatient. "Myrtle," she said after the hare swallowed her last bite. The candle's shadow flicked and ducked against the wall in a sudden wind. "What did you mean when you said you'd come just in time? Just in time for what? You can't just say that kind of thing and then leave it hanging."

The leveret looked up at the girl. She sat cross-legged on her bedroll, the two nettle-fibre pillows propped up against the earthen wall. In the candlelight her two dark braids, wind-blown but still intact from her clambering through the willows earlier that day, shone black as thunderheads. She was skinny and tall, like she had recently grown but hadn't quite caught up with the sudden gangly length of her arms and her bony knees, which stuck up now through the sturdy old linen of her nightdress. Sniffing nearer at Comfrey's hand, Myrtle paused.

The girl smelled oddly wild, despite the neat little earthen house, the fenced vegetable plot and beehives and goats. It was a certain sharp musk beneath the smell of peppermint soap and wild lavender. The hare looked up again. Comfrey's eyes were light against her dark skin, a greenish colour in the candle-glow, eager but utterly without guile. Myrtle was expert at sensing any kind of trickery or dishonesty. Any self-respecting hare learned those things not long after they were born.

"Look," she said, settling back onto her haunches beside Comfrey. "To be honest with you, it's something of a mystery to me too. I wasn't brought up like a normal black-tailed hare, with a hare mother, in the scrub and meadows, learning to leap and forage on my own. I was raised by your kind. Well," the leveret paused. "Somewhere between your kind and mine. The Greentwins. Me and my twin brother Mallow both."

"The Greentwins? They really exist?" said Comfrey, catching her breath. A smile of astonished curiosity spread over her face.

"Why of course!" said Myrtle.

"And you lived with them? What was it like? Do they really have green hair and—" Comfrey caught herself. "I'm sorry, I'm just so curious you see, because nobody here knows much of anything about the Wild Folk, or if they do it's pretty much a forbidden topic."

"Is it indeed? How strange humans are," the leveret mused. "I did live with them. For all the nine months of my life before now I've lived in their green cart pulled by elk, and they and my twin Mallow were my only family. The Greentwins sent us on various little missions – fetch this certain bunch of bearberry leaves growing out of this particular serpentine-stone outcrop, or fetch those mimulus flowers, the most orange ones from the hottest bit of hillside, or investigate the broken heart of the winding patch of road where several hundred raccoons were murdered many years ago, when there were automobiles."

"Roads can have broken hearts?" Comfrey whispered, her eyes wide.

"Why of course. And ghosts. Anyhow, the Greentwins are doctors, as you'd call them," Myrtle continued, "but they are doctors for whole hills or meadows or families of bobcats or old roads or haunted barns from long ago. Anything that was wounded by what happened during the Collapse, or has been since. And my brother and I are

– or I guess *were* until now – their swift little helpers. They taught us to talk to them in human tongues. They taught us the roads and paths through all the hills and valleys and mountains and deserts of the Country. And then, this very night, they asked us to be brave, and to allow two owls to carry us high up in the night sky. They explained to us that this was the biggest task yet. Angelica, the sister twin, she told me that the owl was going to carry me to a girl named Comfrey in a clay and straw house in a village called Alder, and I was not to panic or squirm, but to follow this girl. I was to be her guide, because it was a matter of life and death, not just for them or me but the whole island of Farallone itself. The same thing happened to my twin brother, Mallow, only he was sent to the City…"

"The City?" said Comfrey, hoarse, her heart beating hard. "And you were sent to me, here? The Greentwins know my name too, just like the Bobcat-girl?"

"Bobcat-girl?" said Myrtle. "You've spoken to a Bobcat-girl?" She groomed at her chest-fur, thinking. "Something is truly at work here…"

"I hardly said a word!" exclaimed Comfrey, feeling almost feverish with excitement now. "It was the Bobcat-girl who spoke to me! And then, today, I accidentally spied on some Basket-witches and they asked me if I wanted to learn to weave the basket of my own fate!"

"Did they indeed?" said Myrtle, her nose quivering.

"You *are* a curious human girl, just like you smell. Like I said, it seems I came just in time! You can't just go about meddling in Wild Folk ways all by yourself like this. Though what we're actually meant to do about any of it I can hardly say."

"Any of what?" said Comfrey, leaning very near.

"That's the trouble," replied the leveret. "The Greentwins didn't say! They are mysterious like that, you see. All I know is that I'm meant to follow you, and help you, and somehow this will help Farallone itself."

"All of Farallone?" Comfrey whispered. "But I've never been further than the town of Crab Apple in my whole life! And that was only once, for the Blossom Festival...I could see the Juniper Mountains from there, with snow on them! I've heard about Egret Valley, where the grapes come from, and once the cobbler went to Tule at the river delta for his sister's wedding. But I don't know anything about all of Farallone, Myrtle. Is it really in danger again? Will there be another Collapse? Everything seems so peaceful, so...normal. How could it be in danger?" She shuddered, thinking of the stories she had heard of that time. Sickness, even a regular flu, caused panic among the villagers, remembering stories their grandmothers had passed down from their own grandmothers about the Plagues and poisoned waters, and how many people had died.

"I don't know," said Myrtle, blinking her golden eyes.

"The Greentwins believe it is. That the way we've sealed ourselves off from each other – City from Country and Country from Wild Folk, so that nobody trusts anyone else or goes between the three – will be our undoing. But how two leverets and two human children can bring all those pieces together, I have no idea!"

Comfrey was silent for a time, worrying at a bit of her quilt between her fingers and watching the candle's shadows on the wall. Her thoughts were on her father and whatever it was that had sent him to the City eight years earlier. Visions, dreams? What did he know? What had he seen? Was she to follow in his footsteps? Her chest swelled a little, despite her fear.

"Listen, Myrtle," she said, trying to sound capable, trying to sound like somebody the Greentwins would set their hopes on. "The Basket-witches seem to know something about my fate. And if my fate has something to do with Farallone's fate, then maybe it's a good place to start?" The words came out a bit thin, as she could hardly believe them herself. She was only an ordinary Country girl! *And yet,* another voice in her countered, *and yet... Your eyes have been turned towards the world of the Wild Folk your whole life long. Maybe you are not so ordinary after all.*

Myrtle regarded her with admiring golden eyes. "But Comfrey, you don't know Wild Folk. Ask them a question and they answer you with another. Nothing is as simple as it seems, over the boundary line in Olima. Still, it's as good a plan as any. It's a start." And with that, the little hare yawned, showing long, blunt front teeth and a small pink tongue, and settled down, chin to chest, ears flat along her back. Within moments, she was fast asleep.

Quivering a little at the strange wonders this day had brought to her doorstep, and with a coil of pure excitement in her chest, Comfrey blew out the candle, pulled the wool blankets up to her nose, and tried to get some sleep. Somewhere below her awe and excitement, there was a feeling of strange certainty. At last, near dawn, she slept.

The next thing she knew her mother was shaking her awake, the sun broad and warm through the windows.

"Comfrey, love, are you sick?" Maxine was saying, concerned. Groggy, Comfrey opened her eyes with some effort. Her lids were heavy, sleep-dusted. She rubbed them and sat up suddenly, putting her hand on the empty place where Myrtle had been.

"Bad dreams, slept terribly," Comfrey muttered, trying to hide her concern about the hare.

"I let you sleep, lovely, because I thought maybe you'd come down with a cold. But you'd better get up now and feed the geese, and then help me make milk cakes for tonight." Maxine patted Comfrey's leg under the covers, scanned her daughter's face once with dark, searching, motherly eyes, and headed back to the kitchen. She bent to pick up a stray carrot top with a confused frown as she left.

"There's hot water by the wood stove to wash!" she called from the narrow hall, bare feet padding in that assured way Comfrey always liked to hear at night or in the morning.

When the door closed Comfrey sprang up. The morning light was warm and beaming all over the hardpack floor.

"Myrtle? Where are you?" Comfrey whispered. For a moment she heard no response and her heart dropped. Had she dreamed it all? She felt a shock of despair.

Myrtle sprang up to the window sill from a patch of calendula and peppermint that grew outside. Several sticky orange petals clung to her tawny fur, and the scent of mint came in with her.

"I'm not so easily scared off," said the hare, licking mud from her lean paws. "Just went out for breakfast. Lovely carrot patch, excellent kale."

"Myrtle, that's our *food*! And what if someone had seen you? It's dangerous. People kill rabbits and deer if they come over the line, into our villages. It's believed they're offering themselves as food, and that the Wild Folk have sanctioned it."

"I am *not* a rabbit! I am a hare," Myrtle huffed. "Very different. Much quicker. And I'm not worried about people catching me, only hawks or bobcats. Silent as silent can be, those ones, and claws sharper than any knife." Myrtle hopped down to the floor without a sound.

"Right," Comfrey stammered, a little startled at the hare's defensiveness. "Listen, I forgot that today's a holiday," the girl said. "It's a feast day in the village centre, for the Festival of Candles, the return of milk and sap and green. We all cook things and bring them to the fire and there's dancing and music while the sun goes down. I'm trying to work out when there might be a moment to sneak off, without my mother noticing." Comfrey went to a firwood trunk in the corner of the room and started to pull on a pair of wool stockings. The mention of her mother had given Comfrey sudden pause, and she fastened her stockings slowly, remembering how Maxine's face had fallen yesterday at the mention of her father. Was she crazy, to go rushing off after Wild Folk? How did she know she wouldn't upset the whole order of everything? What if her mother got a bad flu, or all the geese were eaten by a bobcat?

"Myrtle," she said in a voice much less confident than it had been the night before. The hare looked up from her grooming – the calendula leaf was very sticky, and hard to dislodge – and studied the girl's face. "Will I bring misfortune on my family if I go running after the Basket-

witches? Isn't it forbidden? I'm not afraid, not for myself."
Her voice dipped, betraying the lie. "But my mother –
she's already lost my father. I couldn't bear it if I did
something wrong that hurt her."

And yet Comfrey's eyes were far away, caught in the
memory of the Bobcat-girl peering from her thicket; the
smooth shaping of clay dirt into bobcats; the yellow willow
branches, watching those women and their hands as old as
rain. Myrtle regarded her a moment longer. The clouds
moved thin and white in the winter morning sky. A thrush
darted past the window, then a robin.

"I don't know what will happen," the leveret said at last.
"But I do know that the Greentwins would not have sent
us like they did unless it was very necessary. Still, it seems
best to stay on the safe side. Since I'm not a human, why
don't you send me across the border, a sort of go-between.
I'll investigate these Basket-witches, if they're still camped
nearby, feel things out, and report back to you. Then,
well—"

"Yes!" Comfrey's face was shining again. "*You're* not a
Country person, after all. That would be different, not a
breach. I'll come with you just as far as the Offering spot,
and if it seems safe I'll follow you, and we'll see what we can
find out. I'll just help my mother with a few things, and
then we can slip off for a little while. So long as we're back
by dinner. "

Comfrey washed quickly in the basin by the wood stove. Maxine watched her daughter from the corner of her eye, and noted a cheerful secretiveness in Comfrey's half-smile. She shook her head over the pumpkin as she sliced and peeled, wondering at the moods of twelve-year-old girls. Comfrey put on a brown wool dress and sweater. Then she fed and watered the geese, milked the three goats into a wooden bucket, cut several handfuls of sage for the cakes, all faster than usual. Her hands ached from milking at that pace, and the goats regarded her from their narrow milking platform near the beehives with odd, slant-eyed knowing.

"Going to check on the Offerings, Mama, just a peek!" she blurted out as she trotted back through the house, flushed from the cold mid-morning air and her bustling efficiency with the chores.

"Frey, I need help with all these cakes. I can't make twelve all on my own!" Maxine looked up from the kitchen counter, wrist-deep in milky sweet dough, her full mouth pursed. Comfrey knew that look, and didn't like it.

"Just half an hour, please? I only want to make sure they took everything!" Comfrey, not used to hiding anything at all from her mother, gave a quick big grin, her cold-flushed cheeks masking her blush.

Maxine rolled her eyes and waved her off. "Be quick about it."

In her bedroom, Comfrey put the blue cape on again, this time hiding Myrtle in its folds under her left arm. The hare complained and protruded slightly, but Comfrey kept her to the outside. Maxine didn't look up as her daughter left the house, deer-leather boots padding soft and excited on the floor.

"You're going to have to stay under here until we leave the village," whispered Comfrey as they passed the beehives.

"That's ridiculous!" said Myrtle, and twisted, then kicked free. "I can hide myself, thank you."

Comfrey sighed, looking down at the lanky stubborn hare, all fur and muscle. "Suit yourself."

The girl paused in front of the hives, inclined her head, murmuring about checking the Offerings. Then she introduced Myrtle to the bees. The hare bowed her head and ears respectfully, then added, "I come from the Greentwins."

Comfrey looked around instinctively, hoping no one was passing by to see a talking hare. Then she turned and walked quickly down the muddy dirt path, the hare bounding in the tall wet grass behind a patch of wild blackberry, nothing but a blur of gold. When they reached the road that crossed the marsh towards the Offering hills, they saw that a couple of silvery buckeye tree limbs had snapped and lay straight across it, downed in the storm.

The air smelled stirred up with fresh dirt and fire-smoke and resinous leaves. Ribbons of water carved the pathway, streaked with alder and laurel leaves. Comfrey ran ahead, eager to peek at her Offering bundle before leading Myrtle to the place she'd seen the Basket-witches.

"It's gone! Everything, even the cloth and candles!" the girl cried. "They don't normally take the whole altar!" She climbed up the slope to get a better look. All that was left of her Offering bundle was a single red thread snagged on a nearby thistle and a golden rivulet of wax that had hardened onto the smooth stone. Myrtle bounded up the hill in a stride and sniffed everywhere around the edges of the serpentine outcrop.

"I don't think I smell any Bobcat-folk," said Myrtle, nosing about the grass. "And bobcat is a smell I know well!" She raised herself up to her hind legs and sniffed the air, then lowered to the earth again. "I smell willow, and deer, and well-oiled wheels. But I can't be sure; it's a tangled-up smell. There's a mystery about it."

"Do you think it was the Basket-witches, Myrtle?"

"I'll go up over the hill a little way and have a look," said the little hare. "I'll be back in a flash!" She bounded off, pausing between each leap to smell the air and grass.

Comfrey swallowed hard, feeling a nervous quiver in her chest. What was she doing out here anyway, flirting with this forbidden boundary? Her thoughts spun. She twisted her hands and tried to take a deep breath but it was hard to get enough air.

A high-pitched squeal shook her from her thoughts. She saw a flash of red up beyond the slender trunks of the bay trees, well into the land of Olima.

"Comfrey!" came Myrtle's voice, pinched and frantic. "Help!"

There was no time to worry about forbidden boundaries now. She looked back only once, across the marsh towards the safety of the Country. Then Comfrey took a deep breath, muttered a prayer of protection to the Offering spot, and ran off up the hill, legs burning at the steepness of the slope, stopping once at the outcrop of bay trees to catch her breath. "Myrtle, where are you?" she called, gasping. The hill rounded off to its peak five metres higher up, and Myrtle's high little voice seemed to be coming from just beyond. Comfrey saw another flashing of red. This time it looked orange-tinged, like fire.

A large bird came veering up over the crest of the hill, flying lopsided, with Myrtle kicking her strong back legs into the creature's stomach. At first glance Comfrey thought it was a massive red-tailed hawk. Then, as it tacked right on a wind, showing its tail feathers and wings fully, Comfrey gasped aloud – the red, fanned tail was glowing orange as an ember and flickering with flames, as were the tops and edges of the wings.

"Stop!" yelled Comfrey, then realized how silly that sounded. Fiery birds didn't just stop at the command of a girl! With a leap she was running uphill again, straight for the flame-feathered hawk, who had pinned Myrtle on the ground under his claws and was about to slice at her white neck with a sharp beak. Some bounding panic gave Comfrey's legs extra strength. She thundered up the hill and yelled again, hitching up her brown dress with one hand and waving frantically with the other.

The bird jumped back apace at this sudden, yelling, dashing creature, two black braids whipping. Released for a split second, Myrtle flung herself right into Comfrey's arms. The hawk hissed, beak wide, showing his hot red tongue, and took to the air. Comfrey held the trembling hare close as she watched the flaming hawk wheel over them on deep orange wings, then swoop low down the far side of the hill. Sparks flitted in his wake. The bird alighted on the top of a leaning cart. A loom-ladder folded up one side of the cart and a woman with big cone-shaped hair, wearing a yellow dress that was bright against redwood-dark skin, stirred a pot over a fire beside it. Delight lit in Comfrey's stomach. She looked down at Myrtle, whose face was buried under the folds of her blue cape. The leveret's narrow chest rose and fell in great shudders of panic.

"Shh, it's okay, you're safe now," said Comfrey instinctively, stroking the leveret's delicate long ears, surprising herself with the assuredness in her voice. She looked down to examine the hare's back, where the hawk's big talons had grasped.

The woman looked up from her fire and pot of soup at the sound of the hawk landing. She set the soup ladle down with a clatter. Comfrey jolted back a few paces. Only now did she realize fully what she and Myrtle had done. They had left the Country altogether. This was the far side of the ridge-top. They were in the land of Olima. Panic jolted through her, quick as flame, and she turned to run.

"Not so fast, darling," the woman said. It wasn't a yell, but her voice somehow carried over the distance from downhill, strong and clear as an echo in a cave, with that rasp of smoke in it.

"We didn't mean to come this far. Well, that is, in a certain sense we did, but—" Comfrey stuttered, stumbling backwards. After all, the flaming hawk had tried to kill Myrtle. What might these women try to do with her? How naïve she had been to think they might become her friends! "But really, it's no matter, we should be getting home now."

The woman was walking uphill towards them now, the hawk on her shoulder, flaming, but somehow not singeing her coiled hair.

"Home? You can't go back Home now, child. You have crossed into the land of Olima. Look behind you," she said,

94

mellifluous, matter-of-fact, pointing. The hawk ruffled his feathers, and sparks flew.

Myrtle poked her head out of the cape, sniffed the air, whimpered, and ducked inside again. Comfrey turned. Down the hill towards the Country, a gathering of tall, golden-furred Coyote-men lined the marsh and the willow valley that marked the fault line and the boundary between worlds. They had long, fierce human faces that shifted frighteningly between laughter and menace, and wore the lean, close-fitting garb of warriors, ragged and black. Bone knives of various sizes bristled at their belts.

Their teeth were bared. One began to howl.

6.

SPIDER SILK

Sebastian gaped at the sight of the Fiddleback as Tin pulled back the ragged rugs, and Mallow bounded all around its shining legs, sniffing.

"How could you have kept this a secret? It's incredible!" Seb exclaimed. He ran his hands over the round leather seat, the little gold wheels, the colourful window.

"Just wait," Tin said, opening the door and starting to clamber in.

"Holy grasslands!" came Mallow's voice from near the engine. "You'd better come and look!"

Both boys crouched down at once and Tin held up his lantern. The light made long shadows of the gleaming legs.

"What is it, Mallow? What—?" But then Tin saw what Mallow saw and he almost dropped the lantern. Woven under and over the metal spokes that comprised the Fiddleback's underbelly was a thick web made entirely of golden thread. The bobbin, which only a few hours earlier had been wound with a little bit of cotton thread, was now thick with a spool of golden silk. The grappling hook hung from it, securely bound. Huddled up against the bobbin was a large fiddleback spider who seemed to have set up her house there. Attached to her back was an egg sac nearly as big as she was, woven of the same fine golden threads. Tin sat back on his heels, flushed and too astonished even to smile. Mallow leaned closer to the spider. She perched expectantly, watching them all.

"Most extraordinary, Mr No Plan," murmured the leveret. "It seems you've won the loyalty of a venomous mother spider. And not just any spider, but a spider who can spin silk into gold. A most ancient undertaking…"

Despite the awe in his voice, Mallow looked solemn. He sniffed at the spider and her egg bundle, his whiskers almost touching her.

"But – how is that possible?" Seb burst out. "We've been trying to turn scraps into stargold for the Brothers our whole lives! And all along spiders have been able to do it?"

"But they can't!" interjected Tin. "I saw a fiddleback in Brother Christoff's closet, maybe this one, and her web wasn't gold—"

"Hush!" snapped Mallow. "We're talking."

Tin and Seb looked at each other.

"What, in your minds, like telepathy?" said Tin.

"No, and yes. Too complicated to explain. And spiders are especially difficult to understand, I can hardly make sense of any of it." Mallow flicked his ears, exasperated, and turned away from the bobbin and the fiddleback, towards the boys. "Listen, as far as I can make out, the spider is hitching a ride with you. She's hoping that in exchange for this very fine spool of unbreakable gold silk, you will ferry her and her little children safely out of the City Walls. Those abominable lamps and their electric currents prevent her going on her own." Mallow explained all of this in quick tones, with surprise and new-found respect for Tin in his voice.

"At your service, Madam," Tin said after a stunned silence. He bowed low and flourished an imaginary hat. Seb laughed.

"This is no joke, young sirs," chided the hare. "This is a very serious task, a high honour if truth be told. Spiders are very secretive and very, very old. As old as the beginning of the world. Let's not completely botch it, please."

"I know," said Tin. "Bowing is what one does before a queen or a lady, right? Well, this is the Queen Fiddleback." He smiled at Seb, his voice light, but inside he felt a flood of elation.

The sound of boots on packed earth thundered suddenly in the tunnels; it came from somewhere near the kitchen cellars.

"In, in!" exclaimed Mallow, raising himself up on his hind legs. The boys scrambled inside, almost crushing the hare, who squirmed indignantly until he was perched, stiff, on Tin's lap.

"Okay, here goes nothing," muttered Tin. But for a moment the Fiddleback didn't move. His stomach dropped. What if it didn't work this time, with all of them inside it? He pushed his pale curls out of his eyes, set his hands on the silver wheel, and deftly managed several slim knobs at once with his fingers. Suddenly the Fiddleback surged to life, its every surface bright with gold. In fact it surged to life much more powerfully than it had before, lurching from its corner and wheeling rapidly towards the low, arched doorway, and upsetting quite a bit of dust in the process.

Seb almost shouted with surprise. "What on *earth*…!" he gasped over the sound of the wheels. The little lantern dangling over the front flickered, casting a dizzying light.

"Quite extraordinary," Mallow gasped from Tin's lap, trying to keep his balance.

The footsteps got louder behind them.

"They're in it!" came Brother Warren's voice. "Somebody give orders to cover all the trapdoors, fast!"

Footsteps retreated at a sprint.

"They'll have all the doors blocked," Seb groaned. "There's no way out! Where will we go?"

"Straight for the walls! It's now or never with that silk!" said Mallow urgently.

"What if the silk can't hold us?" said Seb over the jostling and veering of the Fiddleback, its eight legs flexing and retracting as Tin whipped it round corners.

"It will," said Tin firmly, looking ahead into all that dark.

"The courtyard, that's the nearest shot!" said Seb, closing his eyes briefly to visualize the maps he had made of the Cloister's underground. They were in his knapsack now, but the space inside the Fiddleback was too cramped to wrestle them out. He pointed left where the tunnels forked.

Tin nodded, turned, skidding slightly on the light gold wheels. A scuffle came from behind them, closer than they realized, as Brother Warren rounded the same corner on swift feet.

"Get out of that thing now, Martin Hyde! Give it over, and we can pretend none of this happened!" he yelled, gulping air between breaths. His brown habit was hiked up over his knees. Seb looked back, giving a mock wave. Tin snickered.

The tunnel narrowed dramatically as it neared the

surface and became a lean flight of stairs leading to a grate. The boys and the leveret threw themselves out of the Fiddleback. They used the top of the Fiddleback to press upward and lift the grate, then folded the legs in and shoved the whole thing through, careful not to harm the little spider and her egg sac tucked against the bobbin. She huddled, stoic and brave, in her web, the golden bundle cradled there amidst the threads. Behind them, Brother Warren was mounting the stairs, slowing from a run to a walk, pale with exhaustion. The boys slammed the grate down just as Brother Warren reached his hand up to hoist himself through, crushing several fingers. They righted the Fiddleback and scrambled back in as Brother Warren bellowed, cursing with pain.

By now the moon had set, and the sky, though cloudy, was dry again. Rainwater pooled among the cobblestones, and for a moment Tin remembered the sight of Mallow dropping from those owl talons only a few hours earlier. In those hours the world had grown so much larger around him that they may as well have been months or even years.

"Faster, faster!" cried Seb, pointing frantically at the southern door that opened onto the courtyard from the library, where four Brothers in tall rainboots came running, hiking up their habits. Tin giggled, despite the seriousness of the situation, at the sight of all their pale hairy knees pumping away under those stately robes. Behind them Brother Warren groaned in pain as he pushed open the grate.

"This is no time for laughter!" said Mallow, nipping at Tin's hands. "Honestly, is this your idea of fun?"

Smiling ruefully at the leveret, Tin reached his hand carefully through the hole in the bottom of the seat above the bobbin, wary of the spider, to grab the grappling hook. The silk was very sticky and taut as it unspooled in his hands, covering them in gold dust. The wheels skittered and bounced against the cobbles, but the Fiddleback whisked ahead, towards the far side of the courtyard. The long row of classrooms flanking the courtyard were backed by a high stone wall, smooth with age, and Tin pointed the Fiddleback straight towards it.

"Turn, turn, quickly!" exclaimed Mallow in his ear, seeing a tall, lanky Brother closing in on their right.

Tin braked and swerved, moving the supple Fiddleback like a darting animal, then swerved again and made straight for the wall behind the classrooms.

"I've never tried this, but it's all in place. I'm gonna throw the hook up, far as I can, and hope it holds to something. Then I'll wind this lever here, and we'll hoist up. But we'll all be upside down, spider style, so hold on to something!"

A gunshot rang out then, not aimed at them but up towards the sky.

"They're using the guns on us!" gasped Seb. "I thought bullets could only be used against criminals!"

Tin saw Father Ralstein standing just inside the door frame of the classrooms, right where they were heading, holding a smoking pistol.

"I'll shoot the legs off that thing, Martin Hyde, if you don't hand it over right now!" His voice boomed and cracked out into the dark courtyard, impossibly loud.

"I don't believe you! I know what you want!" yelled Tin, veering right at the last minute, swallowing his fear at the sound of that voice and the gun, startling Father Ralstein back just long enough. Tin leaned forward and threw the hook out of the front of the Fiddleback's carriage and up as far as he could, onto the steep roof of the classroom building. It hitched against the peak, and the silk stuck faster than any glue to the stone shingles. Tin looked wide-eyed at Mallow, who was in a stiff panic at this prolonged chase.

"Up, up!" yelled Seb, catching sight of Father Ralstein levelling the gun. With a gulp, Tin began to wheel them up. The Fiddleback skidded and flipped abruptly. Tin grabbed hold of Mallow just before the hare fell to the ceiling.

Outside they could see six or seven Brothers just reaching the place they'd left a second before, staring up with awe at the golden Fiddleback, which was upside down and shimmying skywards on a line of impossibly strong golden silk. Father Ralstein lowered his gun in pure shock.

The Fiddleback reached the first roof with a clatter. Tin leaped out, unhitched the hook from the slate tiles, and threw it again, aiming for the main Cloister wall above the classroom roof. But the wall was higher than he had anticipated, and the silk slackened as the hook fell back down again onto the roof where they perched. Tin's stomach fell with it. The air was cold and damp, the sky still dark. The sharply pointed crown of one of the Star-Breakers loomed to their left. A thin line of steam seeped from it into the sky. Tin looked at Seb.

"It's too far," he said, trying to keep the panic out of his voice.

Mallow let out a high-pitched sigh. He laid his ears back along his body.

"Okay, look, maybe we can take it bit by bit, hitch the hook halfway up the wall in a cleft in the stone, climb..." reasoned Seb.

Tin pulled furiously at a curl by his temple, thinking.

Mallow sighed again, more audibly, muttering something about "No Plan."

Down below, the Brothers had grown oddly quiet as they stared up at the spindly silhouette of the Fiddleback where it sat poised, spider-legged, on top of the classroom wing. Father Ralstein had ordered the Brothers to hold their fire. The last thing he wanted was to accidentally kill

Tin with a stray bullet, or damage his creation. The boy really had made stargold. Not just the golden Fiddleback, but the golden thread as well. They needed the boy and his Fiddleback unharmed. With a sharp gesture he called the Brothers to him. Then all together they filed back into the Cloister.

"Where are they going?" said Seb. "Are they giving up?"

Tin peered over the side of the roof, down into the dark courtyard. He felt a chill.

"It must be a trick," he said, straightening up again, his feet clinging to the sloped roof.

Mallow sat up suddenly, ears perked, as if he had caught the sound of danger on the wind. The boys looked around, but heard nothing. A pale line of blue was beginning to rim the eastern sky, beyond the ever-present blaze of the lanterns along the Wall.

Suddenly, a barn owl swooped towards them, her flight silent as the cold, damp dawn, making straight for the Fiddleback. Mallow leaped behind Tin's knees as the bird landed. Quivering, he peeked round at the owl. But the leveret understood as he watched the white heart of her face, the glitter of her black eyes, that she wasn't there for him. She hadn't eaten him the first time, he reasoned, so why would she now? Something larger was clearly at stake – owls cooperating with hares, spiders with boys. Mallow sighed for a third time.

"Give her the silk," he said to Tin, his voice trembling but certain.

"Why am I not surprised by this?" Tin said quietly. "Yesterday, I would never have believed it…"

He kept one protective hand on the hare's head as he scooped up the fallen hook and long rope of silk with the other, then held it out for the owl. She veered down fast, her crescent talons outstretched. Tin, watching the silent beauty of her wings, her speckled breast, her big dark eyes, didn't shy away. She plucked the golden silk from his hands, flew it up to the top of the wall, hitched it there in a cleft between stones, and perched at the edge, her caramel-brown wings folded.

Whooping with excitement, Tin and Seb clambered back into the Fiddleback, and Mallow followed. Then Tin began to reel them skywards. In a moment, they crested the top of the Cloister wall and balanced there, the wall barely wider than the Fiddleback's eight legs. Through the open front window Mallow and the owl regarded each other, Mallow secure on Tin's lap. Tin lifted up a hand to offer thanks. The owl blinked her solemn black eyes once, then took to the air in total quiet. Mallow went limp with relief on Tin's lap, and the boy put his hand on the leveret's ears, stroking them. Normally proud, Mallow let Tin keep his warm hand there. It reminded him of his sister, or sitting with the Greentwins by the fire when the fog came in.

"Tin, look," said Seb. He pointed a hand out towards the City, his palm sweaty from the chase. "We're about to go out there, into the real City."

"Not a place I want to stay a second longer than I have to," hissed Mallow, sniffing at the air beyond the Cloister walls.

Tin smiled, feeling almost dizzy with wonder at the sight of it. The City rose and fell below them and into the distance: hills covered in cement streets; old ornate houses and big apartment complexes, dense and steep and worn at the edges; the ocean, dark blue-black at this hour, far away to the east.

"We're really doing it," breathed Tin. He tried not to look at the Wall and its blazing lights. Even his metal and cloth Fiddleback would not survive a journey past those deadly electric lamps, let alone the real spider who hid in its bobbin. He reeled the silk in tight, then carefully manoeuvred the Fiddleback down the outside of the Cloister. It flipped, and they were upside down again. He let the silk out slowly, bit by bit, and they descended.

"Never thought I'd be hanging upside down from the outer wall of the Cloister," said Seb, his eyes bright. "Well, except maybe as some sort of punishment."

Tin laughed. "I can't believe the silk holds, and sticks!" he said, hands focused and precise on the bobbin lever. They lowered down some thirty metres, more or less exactly the length of the spider silk, as if the little fiddleback now perched in the bobbin had scuttled up the whole wall, measuring with her immaculate legs.

"Well, that was lucky," snorted Mallow. "Lucky you didn't kill me by accident."

Below them, they heard the sound of voices and the clatter of boots. The Brothers, accompanied by Father Ralstein, burst through the side doors with an unwieldy net. Three Officers of the Peace mounted on sleek bicycles zoomed round the corner onto the big street named Fifty-Second.

"Push, left!" yelled Tin as he let out the last of the line. The Fiddleback fell fast and flipped as the boys threw their weight against the leather walls of the seat cab. The hook and golden line fell with it. Tin let the legs out just as they landed, buoying the impact, and frantically began to reel the silk in as the Fiddleback zoomed on, wheels spinning like suns on long silver legs. One of the Officers skidded away from them with surprise and spun out of control. A pistol clattered against the asphalt.

"I'm going to be sick," came Mallow's voice from behind Tin's shoulder, where he had tucked himself amidst all the spinning, glowing chaos.

"Where are we going?" yelled Seb as they sped down Fifty-Second Street, open and smooth in the hour before dawn.

"No idea!" Tin hollered back, and both boys laughed at the absurdity of their plight. "Didn't you say there was a door in the Wall, Mallow?"

The leveret groaned. "Yes, but I haven't the faintest idea where it is! My brain's scrambled by all this bounding around and dangling upside down, and I've never been in a City before! It's utterly disorienting!"

"Now look who's Mr No Plan!" Tin teased.

"So long, suckers!" Seb called out over his shoulder. Two Officers sped close behind them, and a shot rang out just shy of one of the Fiddleback's legs.

"Don't damage it, you morons!" screamed Father Ralstein from somewhere behind them. "Just scare them!"

Tin cursed, guiding the Fiddleback in a quick right turn down a small side street. Several of the legs skidded off the ground, and Seb began to look a little green.

"They know the City so much better than we do, Tin, we can't hide," Seb said, swallowing the sick feeling in his stomach. "How much more conspicuous can we get?" He gestured at the round, golden walls of the Fiddleback and at Mallow, who sniffed haughtily at his hand.

Tin bit his lip. *You're the storyteller*, he thought to himself. *You've dreamed up a hundred escapes. What does a person do? Where does a person hide?* They'd lost the Officers for a moment, and the Fiddleback bumped slightly as it skidded over a protruding manhole cover. Tin pulled the brake hard, causing the vehicle to spin.

"Holy Mother of Haredom!" wheezed Mallow as Tin's weight pressed suddenly against him. "What are you doing?"

"I've read about this kind of thing," muttered Tin, leaping out. Seb followed when he saw his friend grunting to lift the manhole cover.

"Isn't that where sewage goes, or something?" Seb asked, grimacing.

"It beats where we came from," said Tin, trying to joke. He pulled several levers and the Fiddleback's legs tucked into a golden ball. "We'll have to squeeze it in."

They grunted and shoved the Fiddleback in through the manhole, its shape compressing into a long oval.

Mallow sat nervously on the cold cement street, sniffing at the black tar. "Where's the ground?" he said. "Where's the dirt? Is this City just one big human house?" His hare senses were disoriented, without any real soil nearby.

Tin clambered down into the manhole, finding a ledge to crouch on. "Mallow, come on," he called from inside the shaft, his voice echoing.

The hare leaped down onto the boy's shoulders. Seb followed, squeezing onto the ledge as well. Tin dragged the manhole cover back over them, getting his hands out of the way just in time. Three Officers sped overhead, pressing the metal grate securely back in place.

The darkness that closed in with them was thick and complete. The boys shivered. Seb's mouth felt dry, and Tin found that his breathing was shallow. The air smelled sour and rank, far worse than the mildewed showers the boys used after exercises in the courtyard. Tin lowered a foot cautiously and found a metal ladder extending into the darkness.

"Brilliant," said Mallow. "I'm afraid I'm not going to be much help, guiding us anywhere in this hare-forsaken underground. Can't hear or smell a useful thing, without earth around me or under my feet." He was doing his best to sound indignant rather than afraid.

"Nothing to do but climb down further, then find a place to rest. We can plan what to do next from there," said Tin, trying to stay calm.

"Indeed, as I expected. Carry on, Mr No Plan," said Mallow.

"I'd say it's gone pretty well so far, Mr Hare," objected Tin.

"Come on, you two," chided Seb, smiling a little. "This is no time to argue."

They began to climb down the ladder. Tin kept hold of the silk, and half shoved, half lowered the squashed Fiddleback as they went. Mallow balanced on Tin's shoulders. The rungs were slippery and had to be found by foot and faith alone. The scrape of the Fiddleback's metal against the narrow walls, and the clanking of their boots, echoed.

Little beads of sweat formed on Tin's forehead when he began to wonder how far the shaft extended, and what would happen if he fell.

"I hear running water," said Mallow, breaking the tense silence. "Below us," he added, with mock cheerfulness.

Tin's stomach knotted at the thought of dark moving water somewhere far below them, possibly thick with sewage, and in the same instant his foot slipped. As he reached up for a rung to steady himself, he grabbed Seb's leg instead, causing Seb to lose his footing and come crashing down on top of him. Tin lost his grip completely then, and fell onto the Fiddleback which was wedged below them. Mallow leaped out of the way, off his shoulders, and landed on the compressed top of the Fiddleback just as Seb landed too. The weight of the two boys loosed the vehicle from where it had been stuck, and they all tumbled five metres further down into the darkness of the shaft, clutching at each other and at the Fiddleback, which hit the water first, breaking their fall but breaking all eight of its legs too.

For a split second before splashing down, Tin wondered desperately about that little spider tucked below, and whether she had scuttled out of the way of the water in time. Seb fainted in panic in mid-air. Tin, on impact with the water, hit his head on the side of a pipe and lost consciousness. The spider silk was still wrapped round his hand. Mallow, better built to land from a height, crouched on top of the bobbing Fiddleback and stared down in horror at the two boys drifting, unconscious, in the fast-moving water.

7

THE FIRE HAWK

"You mean I can never go home?"

Comfrey stood at the top of the hill, trying to keep her voice steady. Myrtle was clutched in her arms. The Coyote-men were still ranged and snarling behind her, and the camp of the Basket-witches was just down the slope in front of her. She was perched at the edge of the Wild Folk territory, and the reality of what she had done made her want to cry. She hadn't meant to abandon her mother for ever in this way, only to ask the Wild Folk a few questions! The Basket-witch in the fennel-yellow dress beckoned her nearer, one hand on her hip. On the woman's shoulder the fiery hawk opened his beak and hissed, his tongue an orange flame.

"Don't show you're afraid, don't show weakness,"

whispered Myrtle. "Creatures like that Fire Hawk can smell fear."

"Fire Hawk? It has a name?" Comfrey whispered back, her eyes wide on the shining bird.

"Of course he does, silly! We are in Olima now!" retorted the leveret, shivering.

Comfrey took a deep breath. Hadn't she just been boasting the other day of her own courage? She sniffled, blinked several times to clear the tears from her eyes, and began to walk downhill, placing her feet carefully one after the other along a narrow deer trail to the base of the slope, away from the Coyote-men and towards the camp of the Basket-witches.

"I won't throw you in my soup and eat you, girl, cheer up," said the woman in the yellow dress as Comfrey drew nearer. She stirred at the pot of nettles, dandelion greens and the bones of deer. "And never is a very strong word," she added. "But what would have been the point in coming here, only to turn around and run home again? No one is ever allowed out of the land of the Wild Folk so easily. The Coyote-folk guard the borders well." She grinned as if this was perfectly amusing. On the woman's shoulder, the Fire Hawk opened his beak and a single flame curled from his mouth. Somehow, the flames of his feathers did not singe the Basket-witch at all. Myrtle quaked and squirmed deeper into Comfrey's cloak.

"Then..." stammered Comfrey, dizzied by the Hawk's bright feathers. "I'm not the first one to come here, to break the rules?" She was standing close to the fire now, and the pot of bubbling dark green soup. The woman set down the ladle with the force of her laughter, and the chickadee in her hair flapped its wings, cheeping, which sent the Fire Hawk flapping off into the sky.

"Oh my dear Comfrey, oh my dear Myrtle! Yes, you, little leveret, you can come out now." Myrtle popped her nose out of Comfrey's cloak. "You may be the first girl and hare combination to come here together. Yes, that is unusual, it's true. But how, child, do you think the tales about the Wild Folk got formed? How can you know where an edge between places really is unless somebody steps over and never returns, or returns in fifty years as an old grey man, with another piece of the map?"

"You – you know my name too?" Comfrey exclaimed. Myrtle eased herself slowly to the ground and stayed close to the girl's ankles, sniffing the ground and the air, where the Fire Hawk circled lazily.

"Just like the Bobcat-girl, and the Greentwins! How do all of you know who I am? See, that's why we came – that is, we were trying to find you..."

"Soup?" the woman said. She grinned at Comfrey's startled expression. This was not the reply the girl was expecting. It was not a reply at all. The Basket-witch held out a basket woven all of bracken-fern root fibres, big as a tea mug, and watertight. It was full of steaming green broth. The Hawk swooped lower and landed on the edge of one of the wagons. He lifted his head and the edges of his wings with a ripple of ember orange, a gust of heat. "Not for you, love," said the woman to the bird. "We are not making hare soup today. These are our guests. Now sit down, Comfrey," she said, turning back to the girl and the leveret. "Eat first, questions later." The woman placed the bowl in Comfrey's hands and gestured for her to sit on the ground and drink. Myrtle tucked herself away behind Comfrey's ankles.

Comfrey was about to make some impatient reply, but a warning nip from Myrtle stilled her, and she sat obediently. The taste of the soup filled her up like nothing she had ever eaten: dark-mineralled greens, salt and cream and the tang of the blood of deer bones. The woman laughed at the look of delight on Comfrey's face, and sat down with her own soup, reaching a hand to pat Myrtle's head amiably. Myrtle ducked round the other side of Comfrey in alarm.

"As for your name," the woman said after she'd slurped almost the entire bowl. "Well, that's the simple part. Wild Folk can see right into ordinary folk, didn't you know? And your name's right there on the surface, easy to pick out as a smell or a colour."

Comfrey looked up from her soup, startled. She found the woman's dark face solemn. Up close it was covered in a hundred fine lines.

"You can call me Salix," the woman continued, "and my sisters Sedge and Rush."

"Oh," stammered Comfrey, watching the two women Salix had just named emerge from the far side of the wagon. They carried tall bundles of tule stalks, of sedge roots, of young willow sticks.

"Can you tell me what you meant yesterday about the basket of my own fate?" the girl ventured, eyeing the other Basket-witches shyly.

Salix looked at her with a little smile. Then she ladled soup into two more basket bowls and handed them to her hungry sisters, her yellow dress hushing along the grass. The other Basket-witches had just laid their bundles down and were now seating themselves with contented sighs in the meadow.

"Careful what you ask for," said the one called Rush. "You never know what you might learn." Her fibrous hair was pale like oatgrass. She was creamy-skinned, the colour of the milk of mammals and certain flowers, and round hipped, and wore a braided skirt of pale cattail stalks. Comfrey had never seen anyone so white before. Her eyes were paler blue than the winter sky. In her tangled hair perched the yellow flashing body of a goldfinch.

"Well, what about the fate of Farallone?" Comfrey persisted. "The Greentwins say a danger is coming. The risk of another Collapse, worse even than before. That Farallone might die!"

"Nonsense, child," said the one called Sedge. She was slim as sedge grass, her hair the same green as the soup in its coiled cone-basket headdress, her skin the colour of acorns. She wore all green and her bare feet were covered in silver toe rings. Her voice was sharp and without humour. In her reedy hair a marsh wren rattled her call. "Don't you know your histories, and all the Elk sacrificed to keep Farallone safe? Those meddlesome Greentwins. One can't trust the sort who choose to go among your kind. You humans proved your foolishness and your inability to take care of Farallone long ago. You should be ashamed of yourself and of your people. If there was anything amiss we would be the first to know, not you, and not the Greentwins either, who do not respect the boundaries laid by the Elk at the time of the Collapse."

Comfrey turned to Myrtle, wide-eyed with both hurt and awe. So the Elk of ancient legends was *real*?

"Told you they were hard to talk to," the hare said, tentatively wriggling free of Comfrey now that the Fire Hawk had settled a good distance away. "They *are* Basket-witches, after all. As a general rule, Wild Folk aren't greatly fond of humans. They have good reason."

"But *I'm* not bad! And neither is my mother, or the old ladies who tell stories in the village, or the cobbler who has been to Tule. And I thought you said the Greentwins were doctors! I know it was very terrible, what happened between the City and the Country, but the people I know are good people…" She trailed off, eyeing Sedge, who eyed her back coldly, arching a disdainful brow.

A great cackling laughter rose up from the two other Basket-witches. Salix had her hands and eyes busy splitting willow switches, but her face folded with mirth, and the chickadee in her hair flapped and chirruped.

"Sedge is a bit hard going," said Salix, chuckling. "You are an innocent-enough young thing. Perhaps it isn't fair to blame you for the entire history of your kind. After all, before the coming of the Star-Priests, those men of Albion now called the Brothers, the ancient people of Farallone were quite respectable on the whole. But still, we Wild Folk have good reason not to trust humankind."

Just then, the Fire Hawk swooped low, his talons extended. The wind from his wings moved Comfrey's braids, singeing them.

"Great Hare-mother above!" exclaimed Myrtle, flinging herself back into Comfrey's arms and hiding in her cloak once more.

"You seem to have caught his attention," said Rush, watching the Fire Hawk with interest. She smoothed absently at her braided tule skirt, then turned to her sisters. "Perhaps we might see something useful in the girl's weaving. The Fire Hawk has been listless of late. These two have excited him."

"I'll say," muttered Myrtle. "It's called *being a hare*."

"Who is the Fire Hawk, anyway?" said Comfrey, gazing after the luminous bird. Myrtle nipped her from inside the cape.

"Impertinence!" the leveret hissed. "For goodness' sake, Comfrey, be careful, asking the wrong question of the Wild Folk never ends well, and nobody even knows what the wrong question is! All the more reason to take care."

Salix smiled, her broad face crinkling, and handed Comfrey a bundle of fresh willow. Biting her bottom lip to keep back more words, and breathing deeply, Comfrey took the bundle and sat down among the Basket-witches by their fire.

"The world is very much bigger than you can fathom, Comfrey," said Salix. "You do not know how one question, one particular path taken or decision made, can affect the whole. How that one little hermit thrush now singing in the firs speaks of the life of the whole forest, and the bobcat hunting voles at the meadow's edge."

Comfrey opened her mouth to retort that this was no answer, and to ask another question, but then remembered herself and shut it again.

"Now, help us split these willows, there's a good lass," said Rush, touching Comfrey's hand with a pale finger. "Then you may weave your own basket, and we will read it for you at dawn."

That night Comfrey and Myrtle lay under a sky clear of rain, cold with frost, and full of ice-pale stars. Comfrey's bed was a mat made of tule fibres, with a blanket of river otter skins and goose feathers.

"Myrtle?" Comfrey whispered to the hare, who was tucked warm under the covers. "Have I got us into a mess?" It had been a long day, and her basket had come out lopsided, with many holes. She realized how impatient she normally was with her weaving at home, and how rarely anyone entrusted her with the making of burden-baskets there, for this very reason. All of her subtle proddings had elicited little more information from the Basket-witches for the remainder of the day. They'd spoken of the birds calling in the forest, of how nicely the grasses and reeds were growing after the rain. Their words wove in and out and around like the fibres of a basket, making Comfrey dizzy and more confused than ever.

Myrtle remained silent for a moment, licking carefully at the place on her shoulder where the Fire Hawk had singed her.

"Well," said the leveret at last, peeping her ears and her nose out from under the blankets. "They *are* letting you weave a basket. Surely there will be something useful in it, once you're done and they can read it. But that Fire Hawk is taking a toll on my nerves. He had his eye on me all day!" Myrtle shuddered, and ducked back under the skins at the thought.

Comfrey lay awake for a long time watching the constellation called the Hunter move down the southern sky as the moon waxed across the dark heavens. She thought of her mother making milk cakes alone, her strong arms stirring at the dough, her smell of lavender and salt when she tucked Comfrey in and kissed her. Tears came hot down her cheeks, and she felt an overwhelming longing to be home with her mother, among people who loved her and valued her. Sedge's harsh words still cut at her: *You should be ashamed of yourself and of your people.* There had been so much hatred in her voice. All the stories that had seemed so clear and solid in her life felt unsteady now. Wasn't it the City people who were bad, not the Country people?

She realized she only had a simple story of the Collapse in her mind, the kind that's easy to memorize and repeat: the earthquakes, darkness, plagues from the water carried by insects, a handful of Brothers hoarding the last of the stargold greedily to power their City, building their Wall high and killing anyone who tried to get in. Outside, in the Country, the Wild Folk appearing in the hills and abandoned towns, as if they'd always been there, healing the water and earth and air. But where exactly did the Elk and the Fire Hawk fit in? So much had been lost during the Collapse, so many ancient mythologies from the First People destroyed, that afterwards the Country Folk had been left only with scraps, and new stories had emerged. She wasn't sure how much time passed between the coming of the Wild Folk and the emergence of the four human survivors who became the salvation of all who were left outside the walls: Old Man John, his sister Bethany, and Bethany's daughters Hatta and Rose, all farmers who knew about growing food. They knew about the shape of a landscape and where the water ran and how to make compost and what to grow next to what, and in what rotation, and how to make a house out of clay and straw.

Once they had established a clear code of conduct between humans and the natural world, a code that protected the land, water and animals from any further exploitation, and included not only the leaving of Offerings but a series of other rules that ensured that humans never took more than they needed, the Wild Folk retreated from the Country to the land of Olima, and were scarcely seen ever again. No one was certain why. That terrible time, the time of the Collapse, was shrouded in much mystery. Old Man John, Blessed Bethany, Hatta and Rose spread their knowledge. The villages formed out of those who had survived. Those names were household nouns to Comfrey – sanctified, heroic figures from the past who seemed only part human. In muttered prayers over dinner their names were often thrown into the thank yous to the lettuce and chicken and beets. "Old Man John" was a high compliment to any exceptional act of wisdom or competence, as was "Blessed Bethany". Sometimes Maxine called Comfrey "my little Hatta-Rose" when she had been especially helpful and thorough harvesting garlic in the garden, or turning the raspberry beds for new canes in March.

That was the extent of Comfrey's understanding of the Collapse, and it didn't have much to do with Before. She knew that Before, the greed of the Star-Priests had turned Farallone into a wasteland. That in their City of New Albion they had found a way to turn stargold, which they mined out of the earth, into fuel. That this was against the laws of nature and of wholeness, that the use of such fuel had covered much of Farallone with cement roads and aqueducts, enormous fields of corn, and that poison from mining and from the Star-Breakers got into the water and the air. That the earthquakes and Plagues had come as punishment for the overreaching humans, to put them in their place and protect the land of Farallone from total destruction. Since then, the Country people had been careful to do each thing right. She thought of herself and the other Country Folk as virtuous, as Good, while the people in the City were Bad. She didn't want to be Bad. She didn't want to be seen as thoughtless and selfish by the Basket-witches, by the Bobcat-girl, by Myrtle.

Her tears dried in salty lines across her cheeks as she lay under the cold stars, thinking hard.

"I'll prove them wrong," she whispered to herself. "I won't be what they expect. I won't be like the humans Before..."

She woke to what seemed a gentle dawn. A light smouldered along the horizon. Stirring a little under the heavy skins to sit up, she saw that there were still a few stars overhead, and that the horizon was dark. And yet there was a light breaking beyond the hill. It seemed to stretch its wings, sending sparks like droplets. Then Comfrey realized it was the Fire Hawk, rising from his own slumber, wheeling high to talk with the stars. She breathed a sigh of pure wonder. It was like watching one of the stars themselves, dancing. She fumbled her wool cloak over her shoulders and ran barefoot out into the meadow to get a little closer.

"What are you doing?" groaned Myrtle, clambering out

from under the covers, her ears crooked with sleep. But Comfrey was already away down the hill, following after the Fire Hawk as if in a dream. "Oh, drat, she's off!" cursed the leveret, but despite the fear pounding in her little heart, she bounded through the dewy grass, calling her name. "Comfrey! Come back!"

But Comfrey was wholly entranced by the bright wings of the Fire Hawk, and how, against the sky, the sparks he left behind seemed to form patterns – blossoms, spirals, webs. Now dawn really was beginning to lift the edges of the hills with light and, a long, glowing feather fell from the Fire Hawk's wing and drifted down to the ground. It hissed when it touched the dewy meadow grass. Comfrey gasped with delight and darted towards it.

"Don't even *think* of picking that up!" squealed the hare. The Fire Hawk, hearing Myrtle, wheeled towards the sound of her voice with hungry eyes. The little hare stopped still inside a thicket of green wild iris leaves, so as not to be in plain view of the Hawk, and fought between her desire to remain safely hidden, and her desire to stop the silly girl from doing something rash.

Comfrey ignored the leveret. She was in a trance, her eyes fixed on the bright glow of the feather. She stepped nearer. It was as long as her forearm, rippling its colours just as a hot ember does – gold, orange, red, silver – or perhaps a star. The sight of it made her feel faint, and suddenly she wanted it to be hers so fiercely she thought she would do anything to hold it and to keep it.

"What are you *thinking*? Stop it, Comfrey, really, just listen to me!" the leveret cried from her hiding place. The Fire Hawk, hearing Myrtle's small voice again, wheeled nearer. Comfrey only half heard. She was imagining what the feather would feel like in her hands. It was surely a thing of great magic and power, for the Fire Hawk seemed made partly of the stars himself. And it was so beautiful. Surely it wouldn't hurt, just to hold it for a moment? Without another thought, Comfrey's hand closed around the quill. It felt hot, but didn't burn. The beauty of each smouldering fibre and the sweet scent of pine resin and smoke made her chest ache.

She brought the feather closer to her face, marvelling at its intricate light. But the light was rippling and changing. No longer did it look like the fibres of a feather but a landscape on fire. The feather had become a molten mirror, and in it flashed a series of visions. First, Comfrey saw the land of Olima as if from the eye of a bird, high overhead, the shape of its coastline like a coyote's profile, the borderlands a green valley flanked by two ocean inlets north and south, and two ridges east and west. All across it were hundreds and hundreds of bright lights, like stars. The vision changed, and close up Comfrey saw that all those lights were the hearts of Wild Folk. Their veins were full of a golden light. And they were being chained together, one by one, by men in strange grey robes, men with ashen eyes and strong hands and many, many guns. In the vision Comfrey saw a Mountain Lion-woman with broad hips and tawny fur lash out at one of the men with the knife-like claws at her fingertips. A shot was fired, and the Mountain Lion-woman hit the ground. Around her seeped a pool of pure gold. Then the men in the vision went into a frenzy. Gunfire rang everywhere. All of Farallone caught fire. The feather's surface clouded with smoke.

Comfrey screamed. The feather went as hot as fire in her hands, but she couldn't let it go.

"Oh Holy Mother of Hares!" cursed Myrtle, bounding out from her hiding place at breakneck speed towards Comfrey. "Now you've *really* done it! Daft human girl. I thought you knew better!"

Comfrey looked over her shoulder at the leaping leveret as if waking from a dream. A bolt of orange flashed down from the brightening sky, leaving a streak of gold in its wake.

"Not again," whimpered the hare, frozen with panic. Comfrey, gathering her wits just in time, ran towards the Fire Hawk with a cry, trying to beat him away, but the bird landed on Myrtle and clamped obsidian-sharp talons round her neck. He didn't make off with the leveret as he had done the first time, but only stood there in the grass, smouldering. Myrtle's long, pink-veined ears trembled in the hawk's grasp.

"Let her go!" Comfrey pleaded, holding out the feather. "I'm so sorry. Here, take it back. I know it's yours. I should never have touched it, I should have known better! Oh, Myrtle, what have I done?"

The Fire Hawk whistled and hissed, fixing Comfrey with a smouldering eye as Myrtle went limp in his talons.

"Please!" Comfrey was screaming now. "Punish me instead!"

"What on earth is all the commotion?" came a voice from up at the camp.

Rush, who had slept closest to Comfrey, filling the night with the scent of lemon balm, rose from her bed mat, reweaving a few stray coils of her milky hair as she did so. "Oh my stars above," she breathed, seeing Comfrey down in the meadow with the luminous feather in her hands and Myrtle in the clutches of the Fire Hawk. "Never did I think it would happen thus."

The marsh wren in Sedge's green hair gave a rattling call. Her expression was strained and full of horror.

"Look." She pointed at the ground by the firepit, where Comfrey's basket was nothing more than a neat circle of ash. The other baskets, in varying stages of completion, were all whole and gleaming with dew, save the girl's.

But both Salix and Rush were already running down the hill towards Comfrey.

"Lay the feather down, child, and the Hawk will let the leveret go!" Salix cried, lifting her yellow skirts as she ran. "It is only a warning – he doesn't mean any harm. He has a short temper, that's all!"

Comfrey, her face red and wet with tears, fell to her knees before the Fire Hawk, dropping the feather in the grass. The bird hissed again and loosed his claws. Myrtle, with a frantic lunge, leaped inside Comfrey's cloak.

"I'm so sorry," she sobbed, curling her body over the leveret's and bowing her head before the Hawk. "Oh Myrtle, I'm so sorry. And what I saw in the feather…oh it was terrible! It was so terrible…"

She felt a warm, strong arm around her shoulders, and was engulfed by the smell of trees.

"You did what any human would have done," soothed Salix. Turning to the Fire Hawk, she chided, "No need for such dramatic displays, my love. You know she couldn't help herself and that you only expected as much." The bird blinked one smouldering eye and took to the air, showering them with sparks. "This is a very serious affair," she continued, turning back to Comfrey.

"I know I should have left gifts and asked the Fire Hawk's permission to touch his feather! I'm sorry, I'm only behaving like all the other greedy humans of my kind…"

A small sob caught in Comfrey's throat, and she was afraid to look up into Salix's face.

"Well…" the Basket-witch said, and there was a sadness in her voice. "That's not what I meant, though it is true, a Fire Hawk should be thanked for his feather with gifts and songs. That's why he lost his temper. But what I meant, my dear, is that this is a serious affair because our Fire Hawk has never dropped a feather before. He was entrusted to our care by the Elk of Milk and Gold at the time of the Collapse. She made him out of the molten fires of the fault line to be her messenger at that time; she left him with us, saying that if ever one of his feathers should fall, the one who found it must come all the way north to tell her, for Farallone would be in danger again. A feather dropped from the wing of the Fire Hawk means that the Fire Hawk is dying, and the Fire Hawk is but a microcosm of the soul of Farallone itself. If you bring me the fallen feather of the Fire Hawk, the Elk commanded long ago, it will be time to read the words of making and unmaking that I carry."

"It must be a mistake," said Sedge, her voice a sharp knife through Salix's gentle one. "Surely *she* cannot be sent across Olima to the Elk herself. Not a human girl! Surely that's not what the Elk wanted when she entrusted her sacred Fire Hawk to us. If we send the girl alone, she'll never make it. Or worse, she will betray us."

"I'd never—" Comfrey began.

"Now, now," soothed Rush, settling a pale hand on her sister and Comfrey both. "You saw how the Hawk burned Comfrey's basket as well. Surely *that* was no mistake." She took the embered feather gingerly from the grass and bundled it into a scrap of white deerskin from her skirts, guiding them all back to the fire.

She pointed to Comfrey's basket, now a silver ring of ashes, and kneeled to examine the patterns there.

"Isn't the message clear enough?" seethed Sedge, refusing to kneel. "He *destroyed* her basket. There is no pattern, only a warning. She is dangerous. She is a human. We must get rid of her, for the good of all."

Comfrey went very cold at these words. "Get…rid of me? Do you mean, send me home?" But inside her cape, Myrtle was trembling at the predatory edge in Sedge's voice, and Comfrey knew in her heart that the Basket-witch meant something far worse than that.

"Sedge," said Salix, her face stern. "Your wariness is of course well-founded. But this girl is only a girl, and if we were to do as you say, we'd be no better than them. Besides, it is not the time for sacrifices, and they are only ever fawns."

"It's all one unbroken thread leading to the Elk," murmured Rush, still crouched over the ashes, tracing their patterns with a gentle finger. Her creamy cheeks were flushed.

"The Elk?" managed Comfrey, who was finding it

difficult to breathe. "You mean, *the* Elk?" After what she had seen in the feather, and after the threat in Sedge's words, she wanted nothing more than to turn round and run right back home over the boundary, Coyote-men or no. Sedge was right. How could she, a human girl, possibly cross the land of the Wild Folk alone? How could she seek out the Creatrix herself? And what on earth would she do if she did find her?

"Cheer up, Comfrey, you've got me to help you!" Myrtle tried to quip, but her tone fell a bit flat and her trembling ears betrayed her fear.

"Yes. The Elk of Milk and Gold," said Salix, crouching beside Rush to examine the wheel of ash. She was silent for a long time. At last, as if reciting a very old hymn, she said, "In the Beginning there was only darkness, stargold, and the milk that comes from mothers and from moons. In the Beginning there was the Spider and the Elk, who made the island called Farallone and all who live upon it. The Old Spider Mother Neeth spun down the dust of stars to the earth, and bade the Elk shape it into the lifeblood of Farallone. The spark that animates everything. The gold that men have mined from mountains and from rivers. They are the same. The Elk's third stomach is a book of endless pages, and on those pages are written all the words of making and unmaking. It is called the Psalterium, and it too is made of stargold. It is only to be opened at the time of greatest need. Only if the very life of Farallone is at stake. No one knows what will happen if that book is opened, but it seems it must be opened now. For the Fire Hawk was not born to lie."

"We have heard nothing of danger coming from the City, nothing at all from the birds or the willowbuds or the roots, nothing in any of our baskets," said Sedge, raising a thin hand to her reedy hair to quieten the rattle-cries of the marsh wren there. "And you want to send this human girl we've never met across our sacred land, to defile it with her every step? What if *she*, this wretched human, is the true danger, and the Elk too old a Creatrix to notice?"

Despite the light-headed feeling these ancient stories of creation gave her, Comfrey suddenly found that she had been insulted quite enough for one day. She took hold of her long black braids defiantly and said, "I am no threat and I am no danger, and all my life I've done nothing but try to be good, and loving, and kind to all creatures! You may be right that I'm not equipped to travel this land by myself, seeing how your kind hates mine so, but I would never willingly or knowingly defile *anything*. This is the most beautiful place I've ever seen. And all of you – and the Fire Hawk too... And anyway nobody even bothered to ask me what I *saw* in that feather. Maybe you'd like to know why it made me scream. Well, I'll tell you. It was the most awful thing, lines and lines of *you*, of beautiful Wild

Folk chained by men in grey and being led away. All of your bodies glowed golden inside your veins, and then there were guns being fired and there was blood all over the ground, except it wasn't blood, it was gold, like liquid stargold, and the men, the terrible men in grey were leaping upon it all like starving dogs. They seemed to be *eating* it, or gathering it up, and…and…" But the memory overcame her, the horror and the terror of what she had seen. She sank to her knees, weeping. Myrtle wriggled from her cape and crouched beside her protectively, her ears flat, her amber eyes fierce, with a look in them that said, *Come near my friend and I will box you silly!*

Even Sedge was silent now. Rush and Salix had taken hold of one another's arms. The birds in their hair had vanished deep into their nests.

"She must go," said Rush at last. There were tears in her eyes. "The pattern is too clear, sisters. Already the Greentwins entrusted this noble little hare to her. She will not be alone. But the feather fell at her feet and hers alone. The feather flashed its vision for her and her alone. The Fire Hawk burned her basket and hers alone. It is she who must go to the Elk, and not one of us. I don't understand why. I know we always assumed it would be one of us, if the time ever came. But then, the ways of the Creatrix are mysterious."

"But she has seen what was never meant to be seen.

She has seen the stargold in our blood. She has seen what the Elk meant always to hide… That all living things carry a bit of the stars in their blood," Sedge said, but now her voice had no malice in it, only an ancient sorrow, and fear.

"It is precisely for this that we must trust her," said Salix, and she laid a gentle, dark hand on Myrtle's brow. The hare didn't flinch, but only blinked and moved her broad nose.

"Well, out with it then," the leveret demanded. "What are we meant to actually *do*? It's all beginning to sound a bit doom and gloom round here!"

Salix snorted, and even Comfrey couldn't help but smile.

"You must go north," said Rush, her voice ringing. "To the very end of the land, the very tip, the point called Tamal, where our sisters the Grizzly-witches dwell. They are tenders of the elk herds, of the prairie meadows, and of the northern star. In the middle of their herd is the Elk of Milk and Gold herself, but she will not necessarily be easy to find. She is very, very well guarded. Easy to spot, though. Her hoofs are gold. Her eyes are violet. Her fur is cream. You must find her, and you must give her this feather, and you must tell her what you've seen, and ask her what must be done."

"It won't be easy, child," said Salix, cupping Comfrey's cheek with a sturdy hand. Her eyes were sad, and old. "The Grizzly-witches have sworn to hate humankind for all time, for what your people once did to theirs. They will kill you if they can, not caring that you come as a friend. They are powerful and strong, but short-sighted. And the Elk might turn you directly to a pile of embers before you ever have a chance to speak to her. It depends on her mood. She is, after all, a Creatrix, and all Creatrixes wield destruction just as easily as birth, like the earth. And she carries much sorrow. Nevertheless it seems it is you who must go, and quickly."

"But – why not the Fire Hawk himself? He's magnificent and strong and ferocious. Shouldn't he just go and tell her? I'm only a girl! If so much is at stake, surely it's better someone magical goes to fetch this Elk!" Comfrey blushed. "I mean no disrespect, only—"

"It is precisely because you are a human girl that you must go," said Rush in a quiet voice. The yellow goldfinch in her hair sang a sweet, sad note. "Don't underestimate the power of a human hand, reaching out in friendship and in peace. I think that it is precisely because these ills are human-made, that their healing must therefore be human-made too."

8.

THE MYCELIUM

When Tin woke up, a full twelve hours later, head throbbing, he found himself in a warm bed covered with wool blankets and one faded but sturdy red quilt. The bed was in a lantern-lit chamber made of salvaged wood and the old metal parts of a forgotten vehicle. He could hear the lap of water beyond the walls. For a moment he wondered if he'd died and woken up in a new life, a sort of all-at-once reincarnation. He turned his head and through blurry eyes saw a tall, lean, dark-haired man sitting close to his bed. The man was holding a warm cloth covered with a paste of crushed leaves, which he had been applying on and off to the boy's bruised temple.

"Hello, Tin," said the man, smiling. Tin lurched his head up and was relieved to see Seb in the bed next to him, still asleep. Across the small room, Mallow was crouched near the wood stove beside an older man and a woman with a mound of grey hair. The hare sensed Tin's eyes and glanced over at him with a look of affection and relief. Tin felt a warm slip of happiness in his stomach, and turned back to the dark-haired man at his bedside. Mallow bounded over to the bed and leaped up.

"Where are we?" said Tin. His voice came out cracked and thin with sleep. "And...who are you?"

The man chuckled. "I'm called Thornton," he said. "And as for here – well, that's top secret. But as you were unconscious from the moment you hit the water until now, and since, according to your extraordinary friend Mallow, it seems you were running from the Brothers, I will tell you at least a little bit. You're underground, in the old waterways of the City. Water's nasty in these aqueducts – don't drink it – but it makes for a great mode of transportation. You're in the company of some of the Mycelium." Thornton gestured his hand around the warmly lit room. The older man and woman by the wood stove looked up and smiled. Tin noticed that their skin, like Thornton's, was so pale from the lack of sunlight underground that it was nearly translucent. "There are close to fifty of us in total, spread throughout the underground."

"The Mycelium," said Tin, savouring the word on his

tongue like a riddle. "What does that mean? Are you a secret society? What do you do down here?"

"Easy there, lad," said Thornton, chuckling. "Seems the head injury hasn't slowed your wits at all! And as your rescuers, it is *we* who should be questioning *you*." A certain intensity infused his features, like a kindled flame, and he looked at Tin keenly. His eyes were a very pale, piercing green.

Tin went red in the face, embarrassed and uneasy all at once. Could these people be trusted? But he had liked Thornton immediately, even before he was awake, just from the feeling of his hand, fatherly and capable, pressing the compress to his forehead. He liked that the man's black hair was scraggly and peppered with silver, and that it glinted here and there with a thin tight braid. He liked Thornton's voice – deep and commanding, but also calm and soft. He liked that Thornton looked lithe as an animal, able to slip through anything, any tunnel or grate. He looked every bit the part of an outlaw. He looked nothing like one of the Brothers. He looked like somebody Tin might tell a story about.

"Mycelium are little fungal root filaments, and when they fruit they make mushrooms," Thornton said into the silence, softening. "But meanwhile, underground, the mycelium are really the ones doing all the work – finding water and minerals and decomposing animals." He grinned at Tin, and Tin smiled back at the suddenly exuberant expression on Thornton's face, though he hardly understood what the man was talking about. Thornton continued. "They connect all the roots of all the plants, bringing them water and nutrients in exchange for sugars. They're like an underground secret trade network, or communication network. They know how every piece fits. There, your biology lesson for the morning." He stood, stretching.

"And…you live down here in the City's underground passageways and tunnels, all the time?" Tin stammered, trying to pretend this whole mycelium concept made perfect sense to him, even though he had never seen more than a stray dandelion sprouting in the Cloister's courtyard. "Do the Brothers know you are down here? How do you get around without anyone seeing you? Are you secret traders?" The words gushed out. Mallow tried to shush him with a leg-thump, but the boy ignored him.

"You certainly know how to ask the right questions. But that's all top-secret information, kiddo." Thornton winked. "Maybe I can answer some of it later. Right now, we've got to get this show on the road. We're heading south today, to an old buried creek." Thornton turned now to the old man and woman by the wood stove. "I hear there are bear bones in the strata there, very old ones with a ghost and a story," he said, addressing the woman in particular. Tin looked over with excitement at Seb, and saw that his friend was awake, and leaning nearer to listen.

"Seb!" he exclaimed. "We got found by underground pirates who are named after mushrooms and trade in bear bones!"

Thornton laughed. "Sort of," he said. "Hungry, boys?"

Tin and Seb caught eyes again, both gleaming. On top of the wood stove an iron pot of soup bubbled. Thornton ladled some into two beaten-up tin bowls and brought it over. Mallow sniffed at them in disgust, and leaped off the bed to go and examine the room for any other titbits he might eat.

"Stolen meat and dandelion roots," said Thornton. "Don't ask how we got either. Trade secrets."

The bitter roots felt nourishing right to the boys' bones, the soup buttery and well seasoned with flavourful herbs. Tin drank his so fast he got overheated and broke a sweat. He was thinking about mycelium networks underground, and what sorts of information these people might be gathering, and what mycelia looked like, as he drank his soup. Did they look like spiderwebs, but underground? Then all at once he remembered how they had got here, and choked.

"My Fiddleback!" He turned desperately to Mallow.

"Ah, yes! We have it, it's safe, not to worry, just some broken legs. Easy to fix," said the older man who had been

143

sitting by the fire. He came and stood between the two beds. "I'm Anders, and this is my wife, Beatrix." The woman joined him, smiling, her great pile of grey hair moving like a cat. She was stouter and taller than her husband, who was short and lithe. Beatrix looked to Tin like she could lift the whole wood stove over her head in one motion, without effort, but her green eyes were softer than any eyes he'd ever seen. They held what he could only imagine was a motherly look of concern.

"Did you make the soup?" asked Tin, not knowing what to say to a woman the age of a grandmother, having never encountered one before, and remembering some vague association between grandmothers and soup, from hearsay perhaps.

She laughed. "Oh, heavens no. Can't cook to save my life. It's all him." She gestured towards her husband.

Tin, surprised, looked back at Anders with new respect. "Where is my Fiddleback? I need to see it, I need to make sure..." He stopped himself, wondering how much to tell these Mycelium. He tried to get up, then realized his legs were bruised too, and ached terribly.

"It's there," Thornton said, pointing to a far corner beyond the wood stove. The intense, kindled-flame look was on his face again, and his eyes followed Tin.

"It's a genius piece of machinery," said Thornton carefully, narrowing his eyes.

144

"That's high praise, coming from him," said Anders. "He's the one who rigged most of our little canal boats so that they run on a combination of wood-fired steam and our own pedalling. Wood is exclusively old dead roots we find underground and dry." He smiled at Tin, then glanced a little uneasily back at Thornton. "Perhaps you lads can join them eventually. It will be a great help to our cause. We always need more young hands."

Tin's fingers tightened against Mallow's back. The hare stiffened too, looking quick and sharp at the two men. "You don't understand," the boy said. "We can't stay in the City at all."

"What?" said Seb, his slim face, coppery in the oil light, falling. "I didn't think we really meant it, Tin. Not that part, not *really.*"

Anders let out a snort of laughter. "You didn't expect we'd let you go so easily, did you? Not now you know about us."

"Especially since *we* still know so little of *you*," said Thornton, his tone and his face suddenly very hard. "You boys have some explaining to do." He wheeled the Fiddleback into the centre of the room with a swift, angry movement, despite Tin's protestations. "Something very strange is afoot. A change in the pattern of things. This Fiddleback of yours. You boys trying to leave the City. The talking hare. I am a seer of strangeness, of patterns,

145

and of change. And Tin, I must tell you, you've created something very powerful, and therefore very dangerous. So I must ask you to begin at the beginning, and tell me *exactly what is going on*. There will be no more talk of coming or going, until we understand each other better." His eyes flashed, and Tin felt queasy. This was not a man you wanted to make your enemy.

"But I don't have any idea what is going on!" he retorted. A bright anger was rising in him. How did he know that Thornton and his crew weren't just as greedy as the Brothers? How did he know they didn't just want the Fiddleback for their own ends? "Mallow has a better idea than I do," he continued, trying to calm his voice. "Mallow was sent by the – the Greentwins. From the Country." He paused, watching Thornton's face to gauge his reaction, to see if he could read anything there that would help him know whether or not the man could be trusted. To see if he might frighten him with talk of the Country. What he saw on Thornton's face took him entirely by surprise. It was a look of pure shock, followed by a sorrow, which filled the man's eyes to the brim. An expression of longing, love and loss settled there, the likes of which Tin had never known.

"The fiddleback spider who made the golden silk," he stammered, trying to figure out what to say. "I promised to get her out of the City, to freedom. I won't go back on my promise. Not after what she did for us."

Thornton seemed to be only half listening now. There was a faraway look in his eyes, as if he'd been spooked. He sat back on his heels.

"I didn't think anybody ever left the City," interjected Seb. "Can we really trust a hare's word that it isn't dangerous? Filled with people who are still infected with the disease of Before? Plus gangs and lots of violence?"

"Excuse me, young lad," cried Mallow, thumping his back feet on the ground. "My word is impeccable, how dare you!"

The sorrow on Thornton's face dissipated as he broke into a loud laugh. His teeth were crooked and sharp. Mallow jumped back several paces, alarmed by the sudden outburst, and the display of so many teeth.

"What's so funny?" said Seb, a little frightened.

"Will it kill you of shock to learn that I, my boys, am a Country lad?" Thornton said. Tin felt a tingle run from his feet to his spine. Mallow sat straight up.

"I thought there was something familiar about you," the leveret said, bounding off the bed to sniff at Thornton's trouser-cuffs and bare feet, which were filthy and covered in black hair.

"I should have expected that was the sort of nonsense they taught in the Fifth Cloister of Grace and Progress, diseases and gangs and all," said Thornton.

"How can you be from the Country, but live here?" stammered Seb.

147

Tin sat silent, feeling a lightness rise through his body at the thought of Thornton, and the Country, the little spider and his Fiddleback, somehow all wrapped up together. Despite the darkness of the tunnels, the closeness of the canal boat, he felt himself expanding in every direction. The City's Wall no longer felt like the end of the world, but only the beginning.

"An eye for an eye," replied Thornton. "You first, my lads. Tin, tell me of your Fiddleback; tell me how it is you came to make such a thing. Then I will tell you more of who I am, and what I know."

The hanging lanterns shifted as the canal boat took a sharp turn, flashing long shadows across Thornton's face. Beatrix called out an apology from the front, and Anders brought a battered kettle from the wood stove and poured a pot of tea, pushing cups towards the boys with a wink.

"Well," said Tin, taking a deep breath. The air smelled of rapeseed oil and woodsmoke and the steeping dark tea. And something else too, a fresh and marshy scent. It made him feel suddenly and inexplicably glad. And so he told the man everything, from the very beginning, from the fiddleback spider he saw in the closet three months past to the moment his own Fiddleback had glowed gold and begun to run, and all the way to the end, when they had fallen down the manhole into the underground.

"When the Spider makes Gold the Land will Behold the

return of the Old," repeated Thornton when Tin had fallen silent, his face suffused with wonder. "We are doubly blessed today, my dear boys!"

Tin and Seb looked at each other, and Mallow thumped a foot on the ground in alarm.

"Unwittingly the Brothers have given us a great gift," Thornton continued. "For even among evil men there are good ones lurking, or at least wise ones. This Solomon Pierce they spoke of…he read the stars truly, only did not properly understand their meaning. I know because I too once heard of this oracle, but only in part. You have completed it for me. All I ever knew was the first part. *Wait for the Spider of Gold*, it was said to me. *The return of the Old* – I take it your Brothers think this means themselves?" Thornton swallowed down the milky dark tea in one swift gulp and began to laugh.

"They aren't *my* Brothers!" Tin objected, eyeing Thornton uneasily. Why was the man laughing like that? Was he mad? "But yes, that's what they said. Something about perfecting all the land again, raising it up from savagery. Only I can't imagine they could perfect anything. Everything I've ever seen the Brothers touch turns to poison, or to sorrow. We orphans are hardly better than their slaves. I don't know what it used to be like out there in the times Before, but I bet they would have treated us orphans just the same, only used us for something different. Put us down in the mines maybe, digging for stargold. I know that, for the good of the City, I should give them my Fiddleback, but I can't. I know we need more stargold to make the City great once more. But I don't want them to have it, not after seeing a real spider, and meeting Mallow and – and you! There's a mystery in the world that has more to do with wonder than with their kind of progress. That's what I made my Fiddleback for, I think…"

"… and that is why your Fiddleback is so miraculous," cut in Thornton. "That is why your Fiddleback runs the way it runs. The Brothers will never understand that. Come, let me show you something."

He turned to the Fiddleback and opened its door. Tin began to protest, but Mallow thumped him in the stomach with his back legs to quieten him.

"Mallow," said Thornton. The hare started up in surprise. "Come here and hop in."

"Me?" said the hare.

"Him?" said Tin, trying to contain his irritation. What was Thornton trying to prove?

Mallow leaped in and settled down in the driver's seat, moving his whiskers and nose all about. The Fiddleback flashed to life in a single surge of gold. Then it began to move, though it was hobbled by its broken legs. Mallow thumped the seat in alarm and bounded right back out again. The Fiddleback stilled.

"Confounded human contraption," he snapped. "Taking a creature by surprise like that! It's indecent."

Thornton laughed. Tin stared.

"What does it mean?" the boy whispered. "What makes it turn on like that, without me in it? You know, don't you, Thornton?"

"It runs on stargold," replied Thornton.

"Well, yes," said Tin. "That's what I thought too. But how? There is no stargold left!" replied Tin. "At least, not that I could ever get my hands on to use. Although the little fiddleback made some, didn't she…?" He trailed off.

"Oh, there is," said Thornton. "There is indeed. Right inside your veins. Everybody has a little, a very little trace. But you, my lad, seem to have more than a little. The leveret, well. He is of the Country, touched by the Greentwins and by Wild Folk. His blood is practically all stargold, like theirs."

"What?" said Tin and Seb in unison, lifting up their wrists and hands and holding them to the light. Mallow blinked once, but did not reply. He was remembering a story told to him by the Greentwins. He had not understood it very well as a babe, not having any knowledge of humans or of the City or of gold.

"Let me tell you a story," Thornton said, smiling sidelong at Mallow. The leveret flicked his ears in surprise. Had the man read his mind?

"A story!" cried Seb. "But you said you would tell us about the Country, and about what you know."

"That is exactly what I am doing. Sometimes it is better understood in a story," Thornton said, crouching to a seat beside the Fiddleback and pouring himself another cup of tea. "Listen. It is a long story but it is a very important one and one you have never heard before. Stories matter, my lads. They tell us how to see the world. It's taken me eight years to piece together this story, for it was lost at the time of the Collapse, and Before, during the many centuries of the rule of the Star-Priests. Here it is. In the Beginning there was only darkness, stargold, and the milk that comes from mothers and from the moon." The man closed his eyes, his voice taking on a strange, rooted tone that made Tin shiver. Already he knew this story was going to be special.

"In the Beginning there was darkness, and Old Spider Mother Neeth who spun the dust of stars into matter, into an Elk as vast as mountains and a Bobcat fierce as bones. The Elk made the island called Farallone out of the Spider's weavings, and out of the milk and blood of her own body. It was an island of steep hills that turned golden under the heat of summer and sang with cicadas; of valleys that gleamed with streams and summer berries; coastlines green and many-flowered and often wreathed in fog; and many coves where the cold, wild ocean foamed and

152

crashed against the rocks. It was a gentle land, though rich and wild with animals and plants. There were leaves on the trees all year round, and there was food in every season too – be it nut, berry, seed, mushroom, fish or fowl – for the climate of Farallone was mild and agreeable. Life flourished in the world the Elk had made.

"In all of Farallone's rivers and streams, the stargold of its Beginning lingered, glinting in the silt. The stargold the City Brothers are still so hungry for. Unseen, deep underground below the mountains and valleys, the stargold coursed, and that golden matter of the cosmos gave the island its life. The most ancient people of Farallone – whom the Elk had made with the help of the Bobcat out of mud and a little stargold and the water from the sea – believed that their land was the most holy in all the world, though they had never seen anywhere else in the world because they had no need to leave. Whether or not they were right didn't matter, for Farallone was theirs, and they were Farallone's, and they had all they needed.

"Things went on like this for a very, very long time. The people of Farallone lived peacefully in small villages, mostly along the edges of the three great marshes and in the four great valleys between the low mountains that crossed the island. Families followed the food as it blossomed and ripened and fruited – acorns and salmon in autumn, migrating waterfowl in winter, deer and greens in spring, berries from the forest and seeds from grasslands in summer. Having made things to her satisfaction, the Elk went to live at the furthest northern tip of Farallone among a herd of normal elk, keeping an eye on their Creations for Old Spider Mother Neeth. She looked just like an ordinary elk, except her hoofs were pure stargold, her eyes the violet of galaxies, and she never died from one generation to the next.

"Now and then a human caught sight of her, and she became known as the Elk of Milk and Gold. She might have made all beings live for ever too, just like she did, if it hadn't been for the First Bobcat, who thought that this would make for an awfully boring, unchanging world. Change, said the Bobcat, was the nature of the cosmos. Even stars die, or how else would we have the stargold that gives Farallone its life? How else will they savour what has been given to them, without change, and loss, and then renewal? This was pretty wise on the whole, the Elk decided. So she let the Bobcat make an opening in the ground where the souls of the dead would go, all beings returning back to earth and to the seams of stargold deep inside. The First Bobcat went deep into the underworld with them, to watch over the dead. And so the balance was kept for hundreds of generations."

The clank and hiss of roots being added to the fire, and the purring sound of several propellers vibrating the floor, interrupted Thornton's mellifluous storytelling. Tin felt like he had been shaken rudely from a dream, and looked around for the source of the sound. It was Beatrix, starting up the engine to quietly steer the little underground boat downstream. She shot an apologetic look over her shoulder from the small chamber where she sat at the wheel.

"Word just came through the network that there are unusual numbers of Brothers gathering in the streets on the City's western side," she said in a quick, low voice to Thornton. "I'm taking us deeper east and south." She shot a meaningful look at Tin, then back at Thornton. "Don't mean to interrupt, captain," she added, grinning. "You never tell us the old tales; you'd make a fine bard."

Thornton snorted. "This I'm telling out of necessity. Don't get your hopes up for a repeat performance. Take us south, yes. Towards the old pelican graveyard, I think."

Seb and Tin looked at each other, round-eyed.

"Now where was I?" Thornton said, turning back to the boys.

"The hole to the underworld!" Seb said eagerly.

"Ah, yes," Thornton smiled. "I'm afraid it gets worse. But you already knew that." He let out a long breath, uncorked a bottle of something dark, took a swig, and continued. "And so it went peacefully on Farallone, the balance kept, until one day an enormous ship landed on the easternmost point of the island from somewhere very far away. Many men in gleaming metal armour came pouring out onto the beach. They had come sailing round the whole world in search of gold, for they knew how to break stargold into its most essential parts and extract the power and energy of the stars from it. They found what they were seeking in abundance on Farallone, and a gentle climate to boot, not to mention the great herds of elk, the flocks of geese, the streams full of salmon. It was more plentiful than any land they had ever seen before. They wanted it all, and so they took it all and set about devouring it. And there was nothing that any of the ancient people of Farallone could do to stop them, having no concept of conquest, war or greed. Murder and jealousy sometimes, of course, but always they had kept the original balance among themselves.

"The new people named the easternmost point New Albion. Before that, it was a sacred place where no one lived because Old Mother Neeth had her cave there. But the invaders found her in her cave, called her a monster, and killed her. Then they built a vast City there, covering up the sand dunes and the deep caves with cobbled streets and towers and bridges and observatories as white as bone, made from the island's limestone cliffs. They turned the inner valleys to farmland and founded many prosperous towns. The outer coast, with its long point and bay and ridges and prairie grasslands, they filled with cattle so that there was hardly room for any other creature, and the hills were grazed to the root. The streams and the great river that flowed down from the Juniper Mountains they mined for stargold. In their City they had built terrible machines called Star-Breakers, which had the power to break the pieces of gold open and release the energy they carried. Thus they fuelled their City. Those who knew the secrets of the Star-Breakers called themselves Star-Priests, and later, the Brotherhood. Greedily they blasted the stargold out of the banks with violent hoses. They gathered it in pans, in buckets, in carts. They enslaved the ancient people of Farallone to do much of the work for them, rounding them up from their seasonal homes and forcing them to live in a series of boarding houses, where the wives of the Star-Priests taught them to work hard, to speak the language of Albion, to worship the white towers and the sky. They were punished for telling these old stories, punished until the names of Elk and First Bobcat and Old Spider Mother were all but lost. Most of them grew sick and died – of new diseases brought by the people of Albion, or of grief. Those who survived did so by hiding what they knew and what they had been, until they themselves forgot.

"Farallone was a feast of stargold, and so the Star-Breakers ran day and night, providing the City of New

Albion with seemingly inexhaustible fuel. The Star-Priests, drunk on their power, created an elaborate system of hydraulics to water their carefully engineered crops, and when the rivers started to run dry they built a desalination plant along the ocean and pumped water through the City via a series of aqueducts and canals, out to the agricultural valleys, and via canal all the way to the dairies nearly sixty kilometres away. They called Farallone the Land of Milk and Honey, but the animals, plants, and ordinary people who were not rich with stargold knew the truth. That Farallone was being sucked dry. That it was turning into a wasteland. Century after century for five hundred years it went on, until Farallone was, in truth, a wasteland, and had been sucked dry of her water, her wild animals, her fragrant plants, and nearly all of her stargold, save the gold that lay very, very deep underground. The connections between living beings had been broken. The forests were empty of songbirds and old mother trees. The island itself was dying.

"For those five hundred years the Elk of Milk and Gold hid and mourned. Even the First Bobcat, who presided over the dead, was afraid. It took all of their energy just to stay alive and out of sight, both Bobcat and Elk. They feared that they would meet the same fate as Old Mother Neeth. They hid in the island's deepest tunnels, caves and forests. No one remembered their names after a while.

No one believed in them, and so their power was much smaller than it had been, broken down further and further as the Brothers broke apart every piece of star.

"But still, in the end, they had enough strength between them to do what needed to be done. To keep Farallone from dying, the Elk came out of hiding. She stamped down her golden hoof right on the fault line that runs through the island and a terrible earthquake rended Farallone. The earthquake turned half the City to rubble, though it was not strong enough to destroy its Star-Breakers. The Bobcat opened the portal to the underworld and unleashed a terrible, deadly disease known later as the Plague."

"The Plagues…" Tin whispered. "They started because of a – Bobcat? And this Elk?" He was having a little trouble breathing, and his tone was incredulous. Despite everything Mallow had tried to explain to him about the Country, and Wild Folk, Thornton's story was almost too much for him to take in all at once.

"They started because of *your* kind!" Mallow said, a little bit miffed that Tin wasn't more obviously impressed. "The First Bobcat and the Elk of Milk and Gold had to step in, or the whole island would have been destroyed."

"So you know these stories too?" said Seb, looking at the leveret with surprise.

"Of course! The Greentwins taught me well," Mallow replied, sniffing casually at his paws.

"So they did," said Thornton, his voice soft with affection. "So it is, my boys. I know it is a lot to hear, a lot to understand all at once, but it is important that you do. There is more left to say. Have a sip of Anders's dandelion root cordial, it will revive you so you can listen all the way to the end."

As Tin and Seb, with wrinkled noses, took small swallows of the sweet, earthy stuff, Thornton picked up the thread of his telling and continued.

"When the earth had stopped moving, the Star-Priests of the City of New Albion did everything they could to save their own, quarantining themselves in their towers and their Cloister in the City's inner sanctum. They built a Wall around what remained of their City by smelting dark metals into a terrible impenetrable fortress. It had only one door, a secret one, so no one could come in and no one could get out, save those who kept the key. Only the most favoured were allowed in as the world outside sickened and flooded and burned. The best workers, yes, and also the families of power. They called themselves the Brothers, and pretended to be saviours.

"After a year they sent a scout out to investigate the habitability of the island outside the Wall. He came back very ill, and died two days later. Five years later, more cautious, they sent a second scout. He came back sick as well, and with stories that turned even the Brothers' blood cold. Before he died he described how the poisons that had seeped into the water and the air had created human and animal mutations. How else could he explain the horrible creatures he had seen out there, part human and part animal? It was a toxic waste, it was a danger to civilization and progress and humanity. Heaven forbid any such contaminants reached City water or City air. Some left the City in ships, seeking aid, but none ever returned.

"Meanwhile, in the Country, something extraordinary had happened. Not poison, but true and organic transmutation. The Elk of Milk and Gold, a very old and weary Creatrix by then, had used what remained of her generative powers to protect the last of Farallone's heart, the last of its gold. She took that stargold from the ground where men had discovered they could mine it, and turned it into beings, demigods, so that the animals, plants, stones and rivers might be protected from human greed. For every sort of plant and animal and stone, and every stream, lake and river, she created a clan of protectors. She named them the Wild Folk. Their blood was made of gold, and they shared the features of both wild being and human, for they were mediators, and had to speak and move in human ways, so that humans would listen to them and learn from them and revere them. What was more, their bodies now sheltered the last of Farallone's life-giving stargold, hidden right in sight.

"All the land west of the recently active fault line, on the peninsula called Olima, became theirs and theirs alone. East of the fault line, in the many valleys, hills and marshlands called the Country, the survivors of the Collapse learned from the Wild Folk and from each other how to live in balance, in reverence, in peace and in abundance. For many years the Wild Folk looked after all the land of Farallone outside the City's Wall, coaxing seeds back to life, healing deep scars in stone, tending to forests and waters and the last of every animal. But heal Farallone did. Under the hands of the Wild Folk the land began to flourish again. Then, one day, they left all of the land east of the fault line to the Country people, vanishing into the wilds of the west, across the fault line to Olima so that they might live near the Elk, in that land without time, where no humans dared walk.

"What nobody knew was that when the Elk of Milk and Gold made the Wild Folk, some of that final stargold seeped into the bodies of ordinary humans, ordinary plants and ordinary animals. It was impossible to tell who had some just by looking at them. Only if you could see through flesh right to the blood, and beyond it to the very essence, there you would be able to see a shimmer of gold, and to feel the life-giving power that emanated there. It did not make such a person better in any essential way than another, for all of Creation was made with love. Only it made them able to see more clearly than others, to look sometimes beyond the veil of ordinary reality, to understand the patterns of Farallone itself. Such people often became healers or menders, or were sought out for their miraculous green thumbs, their ability to prophesy small truths about the future, or their uncanny way with animals.

"You, Tin, have stargold in your blood. I do not know how it got there, but I too have it in mine. I've known it since I was a boy, and saw things in my dreams that other children did not. It was this that brought me here to the City as a grown man many years ago. Because of the visions I suffered. Visions of the City invading the Country, tearing up the earth and all the villages to get at the gold again. Only my visions were unclear. It was hard to know what was truth and what was only nightmare. I'd experienced this since I was a lad no older than you – some visions came true, others did not. It tormented me. All I saw clearly was that there was some part for me to play. That the lines drawn across the land of Farallone would be its undoing – the lines made between Wild Folk, Country and City. I came to the City Wall as a foolish young man with the dream of offering myself as a kind of peaceful ambassador. Luckily for me, I was intercepted by the very ones who sent you, Mallow. The Greentwins found me on my way across the Great Salvian Desert, and warned me of the danger I would pose for the Country if I showed myself to the Brothers and thus revealed the health and wholeness of Farallone beyond the Salvian Desert and the Salvian Mountains to the west, which hide the Country's bounty. They showed me a secret tunnel through an old well and a buried stream bed that burrowed under the Wall, and so I came to the City, and found others there who dreamed of something more, of a life beyond Walls, a life of freedom. They were common people who worked in the watermills or swept the streets, mothers with children to feed and dreams in their hearts, grandfathers who hid the seeds of common weeds in their pockets. Together, we became the Mycelium."

Thornton stopped speaking. The fire had died down. Anders's face gleamed with tears. Thornton's face was dark for a moment, folded in on itself, inaccessible. Seb sat open-mouthed, looking as if he'd lost the hinges holding up his jaw. Mallow thought of Myrtle, and the Greentwins, and the muddy lanes hung with bay branches, the scrub-covered hills of his beloved Country, lush with twigs and leaves to eat, and keened with longing. Tin sat absolutely motionless. His whole body hummed. He was sure that if he moved, or tried to say a word, it would all vanish – Thornton, the Fiddleback, the story of Farallone and the Elk of Milk and Gold, the stargold in his blood. *Stargold, in my blood?* He looked at his wrists, at the blue veins, trying to see a hint of gold there.

Thornton took a deep breath. He wasn't quite finished. "I do not know quite how you did it, my boy," he said, turning back to Tin. "But you have created a thing of great magic, fuelled by your own wonder, that responds to the stargold that lives in your blood, the lifeblood of Farallone itself. And it can be no accident that it takes the form of a spider, like the oldest of the Three Creatrixes of this land. Unfortunately, such a creation in the hands of the Brothers would mean certain disaster, for they would soon figure out how it works. The Brothers, for all their greed, are very, very clever men. If they were *ever* to discover that all the gold left on Farallone is hidden away in the blood of the Wild Folk, and to a lesser degree in the animals and a handful of human beings. Well…it is terrible to think of the carnage that would result."

"Are you asking me to destroy the Fiddleback?" Tin said. His voice came out broken and hoarse.

Thornton didn't reply for a moment. At last he said, "No, though at first I thought it best. Until I saw the spider and her egg sac. That little fiddleback spider has given this creation of yours her blessing and her trust. She has chosen it as her vehicle out of the City. She has given it all the stargold in her body. Old Mother Neeth was killed long ago, but still, this spider is very extraordinary. There are unseen things at work that we cannot fully understand. What I do know now is that you need to get out of the City, and fast. You need to go to the land of Olima and speak with the Wild Folk. They will not want to speak with you. They will probably try to kill you. They mistrust humans, and loathe City people. They are harsh in their hatred, but that hatred was born of real fear and loss. Still, you must make them listen to what you've told me, and even entrust your Fiddleback to their protection, if that is what they ask, far, far away from the Brothers."

"Will you come with us?" said Tin, soft. "If you're from there, and all? If you know the Greentwins too?" Immediately he regretted it, for Thornton turned abruptly away. Tin saw all the muscles in his neck tighten.

"I'm not leaving here until my work is done." The man's voice was harsh. "If I leave, I will not be able to come back, and the Mycelium will fall apart. If I leave, there will be no one to lead the resistance from within when the time comes. It is important that resistance comes from within the City as well as without, or what was broken will never be whole. I have made a promise."

"But why wouldn't you be able to come back again?" said Seb. "You must know the way."

"It wouldn't be my feet that couldn't get me back here, child," whispered Thornton, his voice soft again. "It would be my heart."

Tin, who never cried, wanted to. He didn't ask why Thornton had left and never gone back, for fear the older man might actually begin to weep. He only nodded, and acted as though he understood what this would mean: your heart belonging somewhere else.

"We are mapping the whole underside of this place," Thornton continued, steadying his voice, "making a web down here of every buried ghost of a creek, every ghost, really, of every creature or human buried under here long ago, who are nothing more than bones now. We are connecting each dot. And when we've mapped the whole underside of it and understood what it used to be, it'll be as easy as pulling one string in a web. The old creeks will flood the streets. The sand dunes will rise up. The City will be pulled apart by its own, buried wildness. It will be returned to that wildness. The people who live here will be freed from the yoke of the Brothers and their worship of stargold. We will create a new community, a new order. The Brothers do not worship the life force in the gold, but only their own power over it. Our mapping is just months away from completion. It's taken us eight years, because we must go so stealthily, so secretly, through the underground. When it is done I will call the Greentwins. It is they who will pull the string. It was they who told me how and where to begin, that day I met them in the Desert. *We will come*, they said, *when it is ready. When you have put back together the story of what the City once was. We will help it to live again. Wait for the Spider of Gold.*

Call for us then, and we will come."

"It was the Greentwins who told you?" whispered Mallow, a shiver running through his fur. "They never mentioned any spiders to me!"

"They told me once they are good at seeing glimpses of a bigger wholeness, little snatches of vision only," said Thornton. "They go around collecting these pieces. That's what they've done the last two hundred years. I learned all the stories I know from them. But their visions are never detailed, never specific. Perhaps they didn't know that sending you to Tin, in the City, had anything to do with the spider they described to me. Only that both pieces of knowledge were important."

"But – what is it that's going to happen?" asked Seb in a small voice. He had crept onto Tin's bed, and the boys were holding hands, pretending not to acknowledge the fear they felt, but comforted by their clasped palms. "Is – is there going to be a war? Will we be sent to fight? What happens if Farallone...dies?"

It was Mallow who replied. "Everything dies with her," he said, and a long shudder passed from his ears to his black tail.

Tin and Seb spent the remainder of the night resting in bed at Thornton's orders. The next morning – the boys had no way of knowing whether it was night or day, but Thornton did, by way of several hourglasses and a series of peepholes – Thornton and Tin repaired the Fiddleback's broken legs. Thornton tipped an imaginary hat solemnly to the small spider nestled against the bobbin. She'd made herself a tiny web tunnel, an ordinary white one. Anders brewed up a strong concoction of bitter herbs, which he told Seb and Tin would speed up the healing of their bruises and muscle aches. When they asked him where he got the herbs, seeing as he lived underground, he grinned and told them that all moles come up to the surface in the dead of night, and even the Brothers themselves could not stop the weeds from growing. That he knew the out of the way corners where they didn't dump their poisons. The boys choked down the dark cups of sludgy tea, but felt much revived.

Beatrix navigated the boat through the flooded old underground tram tunnels and culverted stream pipes towards the City edge, where Thornton would help them make their escape.

"Are we going over the ocean?" said Tin when Thornton told him where they were.

"Indeed," said Thornton. "You'll need to go south and then west, along the coast, to Olima, which juts out into the sea."

Seb had grown quieter the more Thornton spoke of

the boys' escape, and the nearer they came to the edge of the City. He sat apart from them on the bed, his nose close to a map of the underground that Thornton had let him study. Mallow dozed by the wood stove. Tin – caught up in his own dreams about the grass and the wind and the fir trees and the creeks that Thornton described to him as they worked on the Fiddleback – didn't notice his friend's strange silence.

"Will we have to go by boat?" asked Tin.

Thornton paused and looked at him with a glimmer in his eye. "My hope, Tin, is that you will be able to go by wing."

They reached the northern edge of the City in the darkest hour before dawn. Anders packed the boys a worn denim sack full of roasted roots, rice and several pairs of warm socks. Beatrix placed her hands on their cheeks, whispered words they didn't understand, and kissed their foreheads. Thornton led them to a packed dirt chamber just below the surface of the ground. Tin pulled the Fiddleback behind him along the damp, sandy earth. He thought he could hear the gentle swoosh of water close by. Mallow looked uneasy, and Seb stared down at his hands. Thornton lifted the lantern he carried to illuminate the walls. Suddenly they could see sliver after sliver of slender pale bones tucked into the dirt, and long orange bills.

The air around them moved, as if full of fog. Tin drew in his breath sharply. The fog took the form of a half-dozen huge white birds with long, ample bills. They unfurled right out of the bones themselves. Ghosts!

Thornton bowed his head low. The boys mimicked him.

"Greetings, White Pelicans," said Thornton. Then the ghosts of the white pelicans spoke at the same time, as one being. The sound resonated, wind in reeds, wind on waves. The words were unintelligible to Tin and Seb, but Mallow and Thornton listened closely. After several moments, as the boys stared wide-eyed at the ghostly birds, one of them winged off, right up through the soil.

"The pelican ghosts are generous of heart," Thornton said. "They do not trust people, but they do trust the Mycelium. They have sent a messenger to ask their living brethren from the Country to carry you boys, in the Fiddleback, down the coast. I've told them to drop you near a place I know in Olima, just beyond the border from a village called Alder." The name seemed full and heavy with meaning as he spoke it.

"I'm not going," blurted out Seb, trembling.

"What?" said Tin, turning to grasp his friend's arm. "Seb, what?"

"I can't come. I can't go out there. I don't belong out there. It's not my Fiddleback. And I don't have stargold in me, like you do." He was crying, avoiding Tin's gaze.

Thornton, silent, placed a hand on his shoulder. "I want to be a Mycelium," Seb continued in a trembling voice. "I'm good underground, with maps and things." He looked up at Thornton. The man smiled sadly, and nodded, seeming to understand the desperation in the boy's eyes as well as his words – that his heart was breaking, that it wasn't his journey at all, but Tin's.

Tin didn't say anything. He felt angry and betrayed and lost and ready to cry himself, but he kept his face impenetrable.

"Suit yourself," he said through clenched teeth. "Have a good life."

Seb's face fell into a deeper sadness, and he turned away. Mallow kicked Tin's leg then, and gave him a nip too. "Don't be a baby," hissed the leveret.

Tin balled his fists and ignored the hare, looking up instead as the rush of ghost-wings slipped back down through the soil, and the pelican ghost who had gone as a messenger returned.

"They're here," said Thornton. "We have to get you out before light, while you're just an odd shape hidden within a flock of pelicans, and not a Fiddleback and a boy and a hare dangling from the sky."

Suddenly, with a small sob, Tin turned and threw his arms around Seb. His friend's narrow chest quivered uncontrollably.

"You're my only brother," muttered Tin, choking back his own grief. "I expect to see the City overgrown with dandelions when I come back."

Thornton and Seb helped Tin push the Fiddleback through the narrow, sandy tunnel and out onto the beach, where fifteen living white pelicans floated like fallen pieces of moon. Tin gasped at the sight and Mallow leaned back onto his hind legs to snuff at the air, wondering if they were the sorts of bird who liked to eat rabbits. Satisfied that they smelled only of fish, he settled down again and groomed, nonchalant.

"Bless you, child," Thornton said, taking Tin's hand and cupping it a moment. "May you hide your Fiddleback well, and may we meet again." Thornton smiled very tenderly at the boy and opened the Fiddleback's triangular door. Tin didn't know what to say. There was so much in his mind and in his heart. He only nodded, and felt his throat tighten.

"I'll do my best," he whispered.

"There is nothing else to do," Thornton replied. But his eyes belied a flash of doubt, and of sorrow. "Take good care of him," he said to Mallow with a small bow. The hare inclined his head regally.

Tin looked back once at the edge of the tunnel for Seb

and waved. Then, with a deep breath, he climbed into the Fiddleback with Mallow in his arms, and was lifted with a sudden swoop into the winter sky by fifteen white pelicans. Their wings spanned two metres and their white feathers glowed in the moonlight.

Up and up the pelicans flew, and Tin clung dizzily to his Fiddleback as it glowed through the sky. At last he felt brave enough to look down. The City Wall was already far behind him. Below was the impossibly vast skin of a grey ocean. To his right stretched the Great Salvian Desert, silver in the starlight, and the soft, endless folds of the Salvian Mountains. In front of him the coastline was jagged and huge and fringed with green. The ocean crashed white against it. The sea air filled the Fiddleback and Tin breathed and breathed the smell until he was dizzy. It felt more like drinking than smelling. Suddenly the boy began to cry, first just a little bit and then in great, breathless sobs. The tears dripped down his chin. Mallow watched the tears and the boy with confusion at first – for hares never cry – and then with sympathy. He curled on the boy's lap and let the tears fall into his fur. Tin cried with sorrow for Seb, who was the only family he had ever known, and he cried for himself, for fear of what lay ahead, but mostly he cried because in all his life he had never imagined that the world could be so enormous and so beautiful.

Far away on the City's west-facing wall, a lone man stood by an old Star-Breaker with a spyglass to his eye, watching the extraordinary flight of fifteen white pelicans and the strange, spider-shaped contraption held between them. After a time, he put the spyglass away, satisfied, and descended back into the City.

9

COYOTE-FOLK

The following morning, Comfrey and Myrtle set off from the camp of the Basket-witches. The girl didn't look back, afraid that if she did she might lose her nerve entirely. She clutched the bit of madrone bark upon which Salix had drawn a map of Olima, peering at the lines scrawled there.

"Aren't I guide enough?" huffed Myrtle, bounding ahead through old fir trees and out into the open, where a grassy meadow gave way to cliffs and the ocean far below. "Isn't that why I'm here? Or do you not trust my hare ways?"

"Hush, Myrtle," said Comfrey, studying the map and not the path in front of her. "You yourself said a map might be useful when Salix drew it for me. After all, you haven't been *everywhere*. And certainly not among Grizzly-witches!"

"Watch it!" Myrtle cried. The path wound very near a steep cliffside ragged with coastal sagebrush and lupines. Far below, the ocean boomed. Comfrey started back with a gasp. "Honestly…" Myrtle groaned. "We're ages from the Grizzly-witches yet. Days and days and *days* of walking. I know the way at least as far as the top of the Vision Mountains. There we can get our bearings."

"All right," sighed Comfrey, tucking the madrone bark into her pocket. "So far my judgment hasn't served us very well, though yours has been little better…" She adjusted her pack and kept walking, trying not to feel afraid. The leveret sniffed and leaped ahead, nosing the path for succulent greens. Comfrey's bag was heavy with provisions the Basket-witches had carefully packed – a bundle of acorn cakes, several strips of dried meat, a small woven bag full of dried huckleberries, the otter-skin blanket, a fresh flask of water. Her shoulders ached already with the load.

For a time she kept her eyes on the path and on her boots, but doing so made her think of the nice shoemaker who'd been making her shoes since she was a girl, and that made her think of her mother's warm kitchen on a rainy morning, and *that* made her think of her mother's face and gentle hands and her smell of earth and lemon balm. Tears knotted her throat. Would she ever see her mother again?

Maxine would be desperate by now. Had she sent out a search party? Would she think to look beyond the boundary? Had such a thing ever happened before? Her father had gone beyond the boundaries of the Country, but not into Wild Folk land…

Myrtle hopped beside the girl, not taking much heed of her quiet. She was too relieved to be out of sight of the Fire Hawk to think about anything at present but the taste of the new grass along the side of the footpath, and the little sour leaves of sorrel. For a hare, it isn't possible to worry and to eat at the same time. A covey of quail cooed and rustled from inside a bush, and Myrtle thumped a friendly greeting.

"Myrtle," said Comfrey after another while, as the path passed through a thicket of young fir trees, their boughs tipped with bright new green from the winter rains. "What will happen if we fail? If we don't find the Elk or she won't help us, or we get eaten by Grizzly-witches first? Or any other number of other Wild Folk? And why *us?* How can a Country girl and a little hare possibly do something so big as all this?" Her voice shrilled at the end.

"To start with," the leveret replied in a haughty tone, "the Greentwins trusted me enough to send me to your window ledge in the talons of an owl. I may be little, but I am pretty fierce, on the whole. The Greentwins are wise, though it's hard to follow what they're on about half the time. As for the Fire Hawk, well, he made himself pretty obvious, dreadful sack of kindling and embers though he is. He dropped that feather right at your feet. He knew you wouldn't be able to resist. Who knows why he did it, but he did, and that's that. And as for the rest, you've clearly never been a hare. You humans are so good at worrying about every possible little detail that might or might not go wrong. For a hare, every day is a gamble! It makes things simpler. All we can do is go forward, and do our best, and enjoy the fine tastes of the leaves!" At this, Myrtle took another great mouthful of grass, and sighed happily.

Comfrey snorted, imagining herself down on hands and knees savouring the taste of leaves while such a task lay before her, but she couldn't help smiling at the leveret's good spirits. In a way, Myrtle was right. There *was* nothing to do but carry on. What was she going to do, run home at the first hint of a challenge? She, Comfrey, was being asked to bring the feather of a Fire Hawk to the Elk of Milk and Gold, a Creatrix of Farallone! Hadn't a part of her always longed for an adventure, to do something brave and important like her father had wanted to do? To meet the Wild Folk, face-to-face? Then the vision of burning destruction she'd glimpsed in the Fire Hawk's feather flashed before her eyes again. The bodies of Wild Folk bleeding across the ground. The hordes of metal-clad men, descending... She felt sick, and forced herself to put her mind to other things. It was too much to think about all at once. One foot in front of the other…

She looked out over the big blue skin of the ocean. She smelled the salt air. A flock of enormous white pelicans winged towards them along the cliff's edge. Their wingbeats were heavy and slow with prehistoric grace. As they flew nearer, Comfrey noticed that they carried something bulky and round and very odd-looking in their many feet.

"Myrtle, what is *that*?"

"Good grief!" exclaimed the hare, standing on her hind legs to look more closely. She sniffed the air, and her eyes grew wide.

The pelicans swooped abruptly higher, now almost level with the place where the girl and the leveret stood. Their wingbeats were laboured. The round thing they carried came into clear focus. It seemed to glow the colour of gold. It had strange, spindled legs, a glass door, and an open viewing hatch, out of which a boy with very pale hair peered, looking astonished. At his ankles, a small furred form with long ears peeked tentatively. Comfrey let out a shriek of surprise.

"Mallow!" cried Myrtle, keening.

At the sound of his name called out from far below in a voice he had known since birth, Mallow leaped up to the edge of the open hatch. Tin had to grab hold of him to keep the leveret from jumping out into the cold morning air. The white pelicans veered lower, towards the top of a squat fir tree.

"It's my sister Myrtle! Let me go, let me go!" said Mallow, squirming and kicking his strong legs into Tin's stomach.

Just as the white pelicans placed the Fiddleback in the top bows of the tree, thinking they were doing Tin and Mallow the honour of a comfortable perch, which any bird would prefer to the ground, Mallow took a flying leap out of the hatch, landing with a small groan some two metres below. Shaking himself, he sprang away down the grassy scrubbrush hill to a narrow dirt path.

Tin craned his head out of the Fiddleback's hatch and watched Mallow take flying bounds down the trail towards the other hare, who was also leaping with excitement. The white pelicans were already far away overhead, soaring out once more over the ocean. Even so, Tin raised a hand to wave his thanks, and the motion dislodged the Fiddleback from the tree. It hit the ground hard and rolled to a stop against a lupine bush.

Tin groaned, rubbing the side of his arm, and sat upright again. He leaned out of the door gingerly. On the path, Mallow and Myrtle were touching noses. For several minutes they stood still together, silent, whiskers moving. Mallow then groomed tenderly at the place along his sister's neck that had been burned by the Fire Hawk.

"How extraordinary…" Tin breathed. He felt a lump in his throat, a sweetness and a sadness together in his chest at the sight of the two siblings reunited. He thought of Seb, so far away now in the City with Thornton and the Mycelium, and the feeling got worse. They'd never been apart for more than an afternoon since Tin could remember. He clambered out through the little side door and sat down in the wet green grass of the hillside, trying to ignore the thought of his friend.

Instead, Tin looked around, and the beauty of the place overtook him. The sun had risen only an hour before, and was now turning the dew on the grass to a golden mist. The most extraordinary thing, he found, after several stunned minutes of staring, was the ground. At the break of dawn up in the sky with the pelicans, the world below had appeared to be a sea of rippled valleys and hills of green and darker green, and unbelievably lovely to Tin after twelve years of nothing but stone and cement. Now, the dewy grass soaked the seat of his trousers – a new pair from Thornton, baggy and patchwork. Under his hands the dirt was cold but somehow soft. It smelled sweet and musky and alive and so good that Tin's mouth watered. He lay down on his back and stared for several moments at the base of a lupine bush, thinking of plants and roots and how all along, his whole life, this place had been here, under a big sky and big winds, more beautiful than anything he could have dreamed. An unfamiliar calm stole across his mind; a stillness he had never known before.

He heard a scraping noise near his ear, the grind of little teeth, and then the face of a gopher popped up from a hole, harvesting grasses right by Tin's ear. The boy yelled in alarm, and rolled clumsily upright.

In his reverie of grass and slope and dirt and sky, Tin had momentarily forgotten all about Mallow, and the incredible appearance of his sister Myrtle. Nothing seemed impossible in a place like this. The two leverets were now a metre away on the path, staring at him. Standing between them was a girl, eyes light green against dark skin. He had never seen anyone like her before, and yet she looked oddly familiar. The expression on her face was one that Tin could only interpret as a kind of amused disdain.

"Never seen a gopher before?" she quipped, not knowing what else to say to this oddly dressed boy who seemed to have fallen from the sky.

"A gopher? Um, no, never," stuttered Tin, shrugging. "At least not for real."

Comfrey stared more closely at him, taking in his curls, which had been blown in every direction by the last few windy moments of the pelican flight, his odd, tattered canvas shoes with rubber soles, his sturdy canvas work coat, his paleness – there was almost no colour to his skin at all.

"Where did you come from, anyway?" she said.

"The moon, of course!" chimed Mallow, sarcastic, standing up for his young friend.

"I thought I missed you, but maybe I was wrong," Myrtle muttered, kicking her brother sideways.

"What?" Comfrey looked back and forth between the two leverets, then at the pale boy again. She'd been so caught up in all the excitement that only now did the strangeness of the situation truly hit her.

They *had* come down from the sky, in something that looked like a giant glowing spider. First the Fire Hawk, the vision in the feather, the quest for the Elk of Milk and Gold laid upon her, and now this! Really, it was all a bit much to absorb in a single morning.

"Are you from the stars? Or a ghost? Is that why you're so pale? And why've you got that big spider skeleton thing there?" she asked, trying to sound nonchalant.

Now Tin laughed. "Might as well have been the moon. But no. I'm from the Fifth Cloister of Grace and Progress." When Comfrey only continued to stare at him, her mouth partly open, he hastily continued. "In the City. It all sounds like a mouthful of nonsense, saying it here. Mallow's from, well, I don't know where he's from. He was dropped in the Cloister in the rain by an owl. My name's Tin."

The boy, trying to be polite, held out his hand, but Comfrey only glared back. Now she really felt ill. She swallowed hard and sat down on the hillside next to the boy, thinking of the City, and her father. Weren't City people evil? He smelled a bit strange, like mildew, but his smile and his outstretched hand were honest.

"Are you a…a Wild Folk?" the boy said into the silence.

At this Comfrey snorted. A giggle escaped her.

"Me? A Wild Folk? Myrtle, am I sprouting fur? Of course not, silly. I'm only a Country girl. You're not *really* from the City, are you? You can't be. *Nobody* is from the City. Not here."

"Well, I am," he repeated, studying her face. Now she looked frightened. "What's your name?" he added, trying to sound friendly.

Comfrey eyed him. She felt distant from herself; the edges of her world shivered and moved. Was he a spy? Perhaps they were trained to seem nice, to look eager and young.

"Comfrey," she replied in a strained voice. Myrtle sidled towards the girl and let her run her hands over her long ears. Comfrey looked down, startled at the leveret's sudden presence. *Was* it Myrtle? Or the other leveret? They looked so similar, though after a moment's study Comfrey saw that the other hare had a patch of white on his chest where Myrtle had none, and that she boasted one across her nose. "Hang on," the girl cried. "How come you've got Myrtle's brother with you, anyway? And what on *earth* were you doing up there in the sky?"

"It's Mallow, if you don't mind," interrupted the leveret before Tin could stammer out a reply. "Didn't Myrtle tell you she had a twin, and that we were both sent by the Greentwins?" Mallow glanced at his sister with big light eyes. Had she been so swept up in her new adventure she'd forgotten to mention him? Had she made a new friend so fast?

"Of course I did," said Myrtle, nosing at her brother's flank. "Only we're in just a bit over our ears at the moment. Understandably the girl may have forgotten."

"Do these terrifying burn-marks have anything to do with it?" Mallow asked sympathetically, eyeing his sister's singed fur. "We're not exactly in a good way ourselves."

"Well then," Myrtle retorted with mock good cheer. "We'll make a merry lot. We are travelling north to take the feather of the Fire Hawk to the Elk of Milk and Gold, right under the noses of the Grizzly-witches."

"The *what*?" sputtered Mallow. The white patch of fur on his chest quivered. "How did you manage all that so *quickly*, Myrtle?"

"It was mostly my doing," interjected Comfrey, feeling a little bit protective of the feather and her part in it all. "The Fire Hawk is dying. That's why he dropped a feather.

And I picked it up. That only happens at the end of the world, you know. Well, that's what the Basket-witches told me. They have reason to believe that the threat will come from the City, as it always has. From *your* people," she said, glaring at Tin, "I don't know when, or how. Only that what I saw in the feather meant the – the destruction of the Wild Folk... Maybe you are the beginning of all that, maybe you are their messenger, their spy!"

"How dare you—" began Mallow, but Tin had already jumped to his feet in anger.

"You are no better than we are," he cried, "assuming all City people are bad, just like I was taught that all Country people were diseased savages. Well, I know more about City greed than you ever could, and therefore hate it more than you ever could either. And I came here sent by the Mycelium to take my Fiddleback to the Wild Folk, away from the Brothers." He gestured back towards his eight-legged vehicle. "I know about the danger too. And I know about the Elk of Milk and Gold! Maybe even more than *you* do."

"I highly doubt it," snapped Comfrey. How dare he, and a City boy at that! What could he possibly know that she didn't already? Although, she reflected, she hardly knew anything about the Elk. This made her more angry than before. As for just who these Mycelium were, she didn't feel like asking, and revealing her ignorance on the subject. "And they're after *that* thing?" she continued, pointing at the Fiddleback. "You're bringing more City people behind you?" Her nostrils flared as her voice rose in anger. "How dare you come here! And how dare you help him!" She glared at Mallow. The hare leaped protectively onto Tin's lap. "You can't just come here with that contraption, whatever it is, and leave us all with the consequences!" Comfrey's cheeks were red with heat. She wasn't used to speaking to anyone so harshly. But this was all too strange and frightening.

The intensity of her anger silenced Tin completely for a moment. The thought of the Brothers invading the Country had been abstractly horrifying in the underground, with Thornton and Beatrix and Anders. Now he was here with this fierce Country girl berating him, glaring at him with sharp and intelligent eyes, and the sickening reality of what the Brothers were planning hit him. She looked so capable with her black messy braids heavy to her ribs, her dirty green wool dress and deerskin boots, and she was frowning at him, her thick dark brows furrowed.

There was a glow of strength about her that he'd never seen in a City person. All his life he'd been told that Country people were diseased and malformed, and here Comfrey was, rosy and dark with good health. And he couldn't shake the strange familiarity of her face. How could she possibly look familiar? Suddenly, he felt the full weight of the Brothers' plan. He felt the full gravity of the long story that Thornton had told them – Thornton, who was from this place. Why had he ever left the Country? But as the boy absently smelled a handful of grass and soil he felt that he knew the answer: you would only ever leave this place to protect it, even if it meant you might die trying to save it. Tin felt, in a small but growing way, like he might understand after all, just from breathing the salty air, just from landing in the boughs of a tree – a real, live fir tree! – and seeing a wild little gopher rustle up through the dirt. *Just for this*, Tin thought, *I might die too. Just for the feeling of aliveness in my lungs. I would die too, rather than let it fall into the hands of the City and become another wasteland.*

Comfrey, more irritated than ever that the boy hadn't replied to her at all but had instead gone vacant, staring at the trees, spat, "Didn't your mother teach you better?"

"I don't have a mother," Tin retorted, coming back to himself. "Or a father, for that matter. And this is not a *thing*. It's a creation. I helped ferry a very special spider out of the City in it. Not to mention…well, never mind. You probably wouldn't care anyway." With that he stalked back uphill and began unfurling the legs of the Fiddleback, brushing bits of grass and fir needles off the leather compartment, leaving Comfrey where she stood, scowling at him.

"Wouldn't care about what?" she ventured, curious despite herself.

Tin studied her. An ocean wind was whipping at her black hair, loosing more of it from the braids. He looked away and pulled the Fiddleback upright. The gold wheels glinted in the sun. Comfrey couldn't help but notice the odd beauty of the round seat-compartment suspended between those eight graceful legs. It really did look like a spider.

Tin crouched down to examine the engine and the golden silk, and to check on the little spider and her eggs.

"She's gone!"

"Who's gone?"

Comfrey hurried over to look, her curiosity overcoming both her fear and her pride.

"The fiddleback, the little spider! She wove all this golden thread for me in return for getting her and her children out of the City. I was her ticket. And she was mine." Tin wished he could have said a proper thank you, or goodbye, even if the spider wouldn't have understood. He wondered where she had scuttled off to so quickly, if she'd had somewhere very specific all along that she wanted to reach, perhaps to lay down her egg sac. He hoped she hadn't been pecked up by one of the raucous blue birds he now saw bobbing and cawing from a branch.

There was such a wistful, innocent look of wonder and

sadness mingled on the boy's face that Comfrey couldn't help but soften, just a little.

"You really *made* this whole thing?" she whispered, staring at Tin's skinny hands. "And…what kind of spider is it that makes golden thread? I've never heard of such a thing." She felt suddenly ashamed that she had behaved so haughtily towards Tin. He couldn't be all bad if a spider had been willing to spin silk for him.

"That's just it," said Tin. "I don't know. I don't think she was any ordinary spider. But that's only the beginning." He turned to Mallow, who was sniffing at the fiddleback's abandoned tunnel. "Come on, Mallow, let's show them," the boy whispered. "Stand back, you two!" he added, getting to his feet and waving for Comfrey and Myrtle to move.

"Stand back?" Comfrey said, raising an eyebrow.

"Boys!" huffed Myrtle, turning away to nose at a patch of wild radish with feigned indifference. But she kept one sharp eye on Tin as he climbed into the Fiddleback. When Mallow leaped up beside him, Myrtle watched with both eyes. When the vehicle flashed to life, every bit of it suddenly suffused with gold, the leveret bounded right into Comfrey's arms with surprise. For a long moment the two stood, transfixed, as the golden Fiddleback wheeled and turned, flashing sunlight, looking very alive indeed.

"How does it do that?" Comfrey asked when she could

find her voice. Tin could see that she was dazzled, and it made him feel glad and warm inside. Finally, something she didn't claim to understand! But…what should he tell her? He didn't really understand it himself, and this business of stargold inside his blood, and the Wild Folk, whose blood was all stargold, confused and frightened him. Then he remembered that Comfrey had said something about a feather, and the Elk of Milk and Gold. He looked at Myrtle, and at Mallow, and back at Comfrey, and suddenly the incredible serendipity of the situation tolled through him. It made his ears ring.

"It runs on stargold," he said at last. "The stuff the Brothers have been after for the last two hundred years, the stuff they tore out of Farallone for five hundred years in the time Before. I don't understand it, but it runs on *me*, and Mallow – and probably Myrtle, and…maybe you too. See, this man – the leader of the Mycelium in the City, the underground resistance – he told us a story. It was about the Elk of Milk and Gold and how at the time of the Collapse, in order to protect Farallone and the last of the stargold that the Brothers had been mining, she made the Wild Folk out of it. Their blood is all stargold! That's what he said. And that some of that stargold got into people and into animals too, just a little bit. I think maybe you and I should go to the Elk together. It seems like we are meant to. My Fiddleback—"

"Their blood," interrupted Comfrey, her face drawn and dark, "is stargold? The Wild Folk. Tell me, Tin, is it really? Stargold, the kind the Elk made the world from?"

"Yes," replied the boy. "Yes, the last stargold of Farallone. That's where the Elk hid all that was left, and if it is destroyed then all of Farallone will die."

"But that's exactly what I saw," Comfrey whispered. "In the feather, the Fire Hawk's feather. Wild Folk cut open by men in metal, and all across the ground this shining golden blood that seeped and seeped and the men were like demons leaping on it, scooping it up... And your Fiddleback has something to do with all this? It...detects stargold and comes to life? Isn't that very dangerous, in the wrong hands? What if they follow you, isn't it like bait?"

"Yes, but the Brothers have no idea where I am," Tin said. "They'll never think I came out here, and so far. Anyway that's the whole point, I'm trying to get the Fiddleback *away* from the Brothers and to the Wild Folk. To – to keep it safe, and hidden." His voice became strained. He hated the idea of giving the Fiddleback away, of never getting to ride in it or see it flash golden again, and the warmth that gold suffused him with.

"Was the vision I saw in the feather true, then?" said Comfrey. "Or false? How can we stop the Brothers from coming here? Don't you realize that your very presence might be the thing that makes the vision I saw come true?"

"Visions," interjected Myrtle, who had been trying to keep up with the twists and turns and emotions of human conversation, "are notoriously fickle. The Greentwins taught us so. They show possibilities, warnings, hopes and, only sometimes, truths. It doesn't much matter whether what you saw in the Fire Hawk's feather was true. It just matters that it's *possible*. And that's plenty bad enough!"

"Perhaps," added Mallow through a mouthful of young yarrow leaves, "we might chat about the end of the world and all that *while* we move? According to the laws and wisdom of harekind, standing about doing nothing is never a good idea unless you are eating, in which case you are decidedly *not* doing nothing."

Myrtle nipped her twin affectionately. "Glad we don't have to make a go of it alone, Mal," she whispered. He looked at her with affectionate golden eyes.

"That makes two of us," he replied.

"Good idea," Tin said with a rueful smile at Mallow. Comfrey scowled. The boy made himself busy spinning each golden wheel and checking the tightness of hinges and screws.

"New terrain," he muttered. "The thing's going to take a beating."

"Myrtle," said Comfrey quietly. "Can we really trust him?" She eyed Tin, and the bright wheels of the Fiddleback. Despite herself she felt a small tug to ask him what it had been like to live in the City as an orphan boy, working for the Brothers.

"Mallow's my twin," Myrtle said, ears back, not meeting Comfrey's eyes. "And the Greentwins – I don't think they would have sent my own brother to help someone untrustworthy." She paced around Comfrey's feet, worried. "Besides, we need all the help we can get, crossing through the land of the Wild Folk!"

"Fine," said Comfrey loudly, so Tin could hear her. "Let's go."

He grinned and, with a gallant bow, gestured for the girl to climb into the Fiddleback, followed by Myrtle and Mallow. Almost at once it surged to life, more golden than ever.

"Woah!" the boy exclaimed. "Looks like all four of us have a bit of stargold in our blood. It's going to be a wild ride!"

Comfrey flushed with pride, and smiled back, and Tin felt his stomach lurch at the sight of her open, lively grin. He slipped into the steering seat beside her and then they were off downhill through the firs and deep hills, wheels spinning. Comfrey let out a small shriek, first of fear, then of delight, as the small wind-stunted firs sped by them, the Fiddleback swaying and bouncing over rocks until it found the damp dirt of the path.

"Which way are we going?" said Tin once they'd

reached the pathway. Comfrey fumbled for the madrone-bark map the Basket-witches had drawn for her.

"Straight along this footpath until it turns inland at the alders," interjected Myrtle as Comfrey peered at the tattered bark. "Then we follow the creek until we reach a great meadow and some barns from Before. From there, we'll be close to the old road, the one that runs dead north."

"Guess you really *do* know the way," the girl said.

"Weren't you listening?" replied the leveret, "of course I do!" She flicked her ears smugly and settled against her brother's flank, enjoying the comforting warmth of his nearness, and the wordless peace of hares.

Up the eastern ridge, a Coyote-woman and her three sons watched the Fiddleback make its oddly graceful way along the path. They breathed the wafts of dust stirred up by the strange eight-legged contraption. They breathed the boy and girl smells, the leveret smells, the smells of metal and hinge and pedal and invention, and looked at one another, intrigued. With a pinch at her sons' long, black-tipped tails, the Coyote-woman led the way at a trot along the crest of the ridge, keeping her ears cocked for the skittering, whirring sound of the Fiddleback.

It took the children and the leverets until sundown to reach the meadow at the edge of the alder-lined creek. They stopped once for lunch where the path first turned inland, travelling under the deep alder-shade where the air smelled of sweet bark and water. Comfrey laughed at Tin's face when he took his first bite of acorn cake mixed with a handful of dried huckleberries. His eyes watered with the rich vibrancy of the flavours on his tongue. They didn't encounter any Wild Folk on the footpath, nor sense them watching from the trees and hills, save once when Comfrey glimpsed several very tall, very green women deep inside the alders bending over a fringe of new nettles. But the Fiddleback moved so quickly, and with such relative silence, that they were nothing but a blur behind her. They managed to startle up several flocks of quail, to whom the leverets apologized profusely out the front window, and after which Tin stared with open wonder. Their bronze and grey feathers! Their whirring cries!

The boy was intoxicated by the sights and smells of the wild land that whirred past the Fiddleback's window. The shapes of alder trees and their shadows; the muddy roughness of the footpath; the rich smells of forest humus and new grass and fir needles and moss. The largeness of the land unsettled him only a little, and its utter lack of discernible pattern – no walls or brick floors or beakers of mercury or terrible gleaming Wall in sight – made him feel light-headed, while his thoughts felt easy and free and glad.

They stopped in the meadow where their dirt footpath met a broader one to make camp for the night. Comfrey had grown easier around the boy. It had been such a peaceful, uneventful day, spent largely in silence staring out at the moving land. Perhaps it wouldn't be so hard, this task to find the Elk of Milk and Gold. Perhaps Olima wasn't at all like people had told her. Perhaps those were just stories. Perhaps they *could* succeed...

In the twilight, Comfrey set about looking for dry twigs and brush to create a small fire, eager to demonstrate her skill in such matters in front of Tin, who, as a City boy, would never have seen such a thing before. From a distance, the Fiddleback looked small and spindly and very strange in the middle of that meadow, like a great skeleton or a dream-creature, looming up out of the shadows.

"Comfrey!" came Myrtle's shrill cry. "Look up!"

The girl whirled, not knowing which direction the leveret meant for her to look. Standing right in front of her in the near-dark were four lean, very tall Coyote-folk, ears tall and perked. Three were young males with muscled, furred arms, who brandished little bone knives. The fourth was a female with a long scar across her face from one eye to the opposite jawbone. She grinned, showing sharp teeth, and Comfrey screamed. Behind her she heard another shout, this time from Tin.

"Quick, Comfrey, come quick!" he yelled.

She broke into a run. Now four more Coyote-folk surrounded the Fiddleback where it sat alone in the meadow not ten paces from where they'd laid down their packs.

"I don't know where they came from!" Tin cried.

"Astonishing sneakery!" moaned Mallow. "How did *we* miss them?" He jumped into Tin's arms.

"What do you want?" demanded Comfrey, striding towards the Coyote-folk who surrounded the Fiddleback. She gave them her very best glare. But they were fierce-eyed, and danced and leaped around the spider-legged vehicle on long, nimble legs, howling. When she tried to come nearer, one snapped his teeth at her and shot a furred hand out, almost catching her braid. She saw the jagged rim of those fangs in his human face, and leaped backwards just in time. "Go away!" she yelled, and threw a rock. They howled with laughter.

Tin scrambled to join her, tossing more rocks, but the four other Coyote-folk – the mother and her three neargrown sons – were all around them now too, yipping and shrieking their hunting cries.

Myrtle went still as death behind Comfrey's cloak, while Mallow hid himself in Tin's coat. Comfrey and Tin knocked into one another with panic at the sound and clasped hands without thinking. Then, quick as light, all eight Coyote-folk were upon the Fiddleback, each grabbing a long spindled leg. The Coyote-woman looked hard at Comfrey with star-bright eyes, and her tail brushed the girl's legs. Then she, her three sons, and her four brothers were off at a lope, the kidnapped Fiddleback lumbering and jerking along amidst them.

After a head-spinning instant of shock, Tin bolted after them, his skinny legs outstretched in a desperate gallop. Mallow, revived from his panic, leaped down to the ground and tore after the boy. Comfrey scrambled to gather up their backpacks and followed them with a cry of dismay. Myrtle bounded at her heels, her ears laid flat, her whole body streamlined in the night air. In the distance a chorus of long, high-pitched howls split the darkness.

THE HOLY FOOL'S INN

It didn't take long for Comfrey to catch up with Tin. She flew down the road, feeling the power in the gasp of her breath, the muscles in her legs, the trust she felt in her body as she sprinted through the dark, her braids thumping on her back.

The hares were now far ahead, just two creamy backsides down the dark road, sniffing at the ground and the laurel-scented air for the trail of the thieving Coyote-folk. For a good kilometre, their scent led straight down the centre of an overgrown old road from the time Before. The hares kept to it easily, pausing every so often to pant small misty breaths into the cold night air and wait for Tin and Comfrey to catch up. The Coyote-folk were quick, even with the clattering Fiddleback between them, and already the sound of their howling, the hiss of wheels, and the breaking of twigs and stirring of brush ahead of them, had grown faint.

The leverets' ears quivered with every other rustle and thump of sound as they ran. They followed the Coyote-folk's scent through a flat and scrubby meadow where cows had grazed in the time Before. Comfrey cursed as a remnant scrap of fence tore her green wool hem. At last she caught up with the hares, her lungs burning. They raced through a stand of willows, got wet to their knees in a creek, and emerged dripping and gasping at a crossroads in the middle of an abandoned ghost town from Before, with Tin close behind.

Comfrey stared in astonishment at the ruined houses that lined the road, now just skeletons of wood and stone that had collapsed inwards with the weight of time and blackberry brambles. She had never seen ruins like this in her life. All the towns of Before had been burned, she thought. One of the houses still stood here, and its elegant wooden walls amazed her. It was so tall, with a covered porch and balcony and windows made of glass that were bigger than she was, not just one row but two, the second high up beyond the height of the porch, as high as the trees. The dark grey paint peeled off the old building in great strips, giving it a mottled appearance. The porch leaned dangerously on the far side and half the balcony's railing was broken, held up by a just-leafing wisteria vine, but Comfrey still stared in amazement. A haphazard sign made of driftwood hung from a hook above the porch, with words painted red across it: *The Holy Fool's Inn*.

"Where are we?" she breathed. But Tin had hardly stopped to look at the old building – to him it was nothing unusual, only another half-decayed house like the many he had seen lining the City streets out of the Cloister windows. And the hares were busy sniffing the ground and night air.

"They're nowhere!" cried Myrtle.

"Coyotes have a habit of doing that," said Mallow. "They are consummate tricksters."

"What if they've figured out how to work the silk?" Tin said, running to the base of an oak tree and peering up. He heard a sudden, loud rustling and gasped. "They're up here! I can hear them!"

Mallow raised up onto his back legs and sniffed the air cautiously. It didn't smell like one of the Coyote-folk, but there certainly was something in the oak tree, and the leveret took a few more steps forward, listening.

A large, silvery being leaped from the branches and landed with the swish of a striped tail next to Tin. It was a Raccoon-woman in a dress all of scraps and bones, big and hunched and cackling with delight.

"Well well *well*," she crooned in a voice that rattled.

"Look at this fine specimen here, are you a human boy, are you indeed?" She reached out two strong, long-fingered hands and seized Tin's throat, pulling him very close. She had a woman's face, but grey-furred, with a black bandit stripe across her eyes and several long canine teeth that clicked and flashed as she spoke. Her breath smelled of fish and earth and rotten fruit, and Tin gagged, swallowing down a cry. She pressed her fingers a little tighter, scratching him with her nails, feeling along his throat and neck and down to his shoulders with busy, terrible hands, all the while talking. "I've always wondered what I would do if I could only get my hands on one of you," she muttered. "If I would dunk you in the stream and break you into pieces like a crayfish to eat juicy and raw, or if I would keep you as my pet on a string, and make you dance for me round my fire? Or maybe you'd be better seared on the fire and fed to my children, yes, perhaps that would be best, perhaps that would be fair, after all your kind did to ours long ago… And oh, I do wonder about all these strong *bones*… How nice they would look among my collection." She sniffed him with a strange, black-rimmed nose and flicked out her tongue to taste his skin. Tin screamed.

"Let him go, you nasty old creature!" Comfrey yelled, unable to bear the sight, or Tin's scream of fear. She picked up a willow stick, took a deep breath, and ran straight at the Raccoon-woman.

"Comfrey, don't!" cried Myrtle behind her. "You can't just *beat off* one of the Wild Folk! Don't you know what she might do then?"

"Listen, ma-madam," Tin was stammering, trying to think how he might escape. "Let's make a deal. You tell my friends whether you've seen a group of Coyote-folk go by with a big golden-wheeled spider, and I-I will come with you."

"No you won't, Tin!" Comfrey said, her willow stick raised, not sure what to do. The Raccoon-woman was very large and strong, and her hands flashed with sharpened claws. She turned towards Comfrey now, shrieking with rage and excitement.

"Do I smell *another* human child? Two at once! Indeed, indeed, I must have these lovely bones of yours, they will clatter and clink so beautifully in the wind, and what tales they will sing to my children!"

Suddenly the door of the dark grey inn opened with a loud creak. Golden light from within and the sound of music poured out across the covered porch and down the steps, illuminating them all.

"Delilah!" came a deep, rasping voice. A man with an unusually oblong forehead and no hair anywhere on his body stepped out into the pool of light on the porch. The Raccoon-woman looked up, her black eyes flashing.

"Can't you see I'm busy, you old Fool?" she hissed with disgust.

The man on the porch pulled three oranges from the pockets of his multicoloured, patchwork robes, juggled them once, then tossed them to Delilah. With a little distracted cluck of delight she let go of Tin and caught them in her long fingers.

"Let the children alone, and leave our doorstep at once," the man said. Although his voice was steady, Comfrey heard a hint of dread in it. "We Fools have only this place, and it belongs to no one but us. Unless you behave in a kind and gentle and tolerant manner, you may not come so near our Inn. These children are human and they are on *our* territory. Leave them to us."

"Very well, very well," Delilah muttered, looking irritated. "The boy tasted foul anyhow." She spat at Tin's feet, sliced an orange open with one long nail, and ambled into the darkness of the willow trees on the far side of the road, leaving the scent of citrus in her wake.

"Praise to all Hares!" wheezed Mallow, grooming at his fur to soothe himself.

"Who on earth are *you*?" said Myrtle to the man on the porch. "You are not one of the Wild Folk." She sniffed the air, appraising him.

"No, no," replied the man with a chuckle. "I'm Oro, and this is The Holy Fool's Inn." He spread his hands wide. "Come, come, get out of that darkness where Wild Folk lurk. Delilah is not all bad, but you must know that the

Wild Folk are not overfond of your kind." He was looking at them closely with his light eyes. "I assure you though that you are very welcome here, with us. It is *long* since we have seen another human being. What a delight it is! Do come up, children and leverets, do come up."

"We're in a desperate rush as it turns out," blurted Tin. "Would you mind just pointing the direction a pack of Coyote-folk and an odd eight-legged vehicle went, not more than twenty minutes ago? A vehicle like a spider?"

"Manners, manners," whispered Mallow, nervous at the sight of this strange outpost in Wild Folk land, trying to remember if the Greentwins had ever spoken of it. The Holy Fools, they did sound oddly familiar, but the Greentwins had told them so many tales, it was hard for a hare to keep them all straight. This man smelled human, but very strange, and humans in greater numbers and by firesides did, he knew, have a special fondness for roasted hare.

Oro cocked his oblong head, which made his forehead glint. "Is our Oddness already rubbing off?" the man said, bemused. "What a strange description. Makes me downright anxious with anticipation for the stories which lie ahead!"

"Well, have you seen them or what?" Tin persisted.

"Nothing of the sort, lad, I'm sorry to say. But night has fully descended, and as you have learned already, it's best not to be abroad in the dead of it, not as a human being, oh no. Much worse than Delilah, I can assure you, roam the darkness. If she had been a vengeful Mountain Lion-woman, your throat would have been slit before you could make a sound. A good rest and a meal, and you can be off again in the morning. And perhaps the laws of hospitality will oblige you to give us your story before carrying on. Stories make the world go round, eh? What a delight they are for us Fools. We take tales like other men and women take tea, or toddies. It's not often that Country Folk pass this way. Do come up, my friends. You look half-dead with weariness."

"But – my Fiddleback!" Tin said, his voice strangled.

"Hush, Tin," whispered Mallow. "The man is right. Nights in Olima are no place for hares or children to be abroad. And besides, the Coyotes *are* Wild Folk. Well, weren't we meant to bring the Fiddleback to the Wild Folk?"

"Yes," said Tin. "But – I wanted at least to have a word with them, to ask them about how it really works, with the stargold and all…" He trailed off. The truth was, he'd hoped that maybe the Wild Folk would let him keep it. That he wouldn't have to give it away to anybody after all.

Oro beckoned again, and Comfrey noticed with a sharp intake of breath that his hand had six fingers. She followed, mesmerized, the leverets at her heels. Tin groaned, thinking of his bright and beautiful creation being thrashed through the bushes by Coyote-folk. With a sigh, balling his fists tight in his pockets, he climbed the stairs after them.

Inside the high-ceilinged inn a fire flicked and lapped at a brick hearth. Woven tapestries in a hundred muted colours covered the walls, strung from corner to corner with red madrone berries and bells. Several dozen men and women milled about between the three front rooms, which were all open to one another by means of large, barn-sized doors so hidden behind shelves and side-tables and hanging tapestries they must never have been closed. In the far room was a long feast table. In the front, where they'd entered, furs and cushions were flung across the floor, and men and women and children, some younger than Tin and Comfrey, some as old as the village grandfathers, lounged. They played games with strange, leathery cards painted with crooked crowned figures; hit marbles painted like planets on a patch of wood; juggled winter lemons; strummed at fiddles and skin drums with their hands; read little books so old their leather covers drooped.

The third room, to the left of the entrance, was empty of people. A skunk slept curled up on a cushion beneath the room's far window, where a single candle guttered. The walls were lined with open cabinets full of strange and wonderful objects – a bronze orrery with planets that shone, a clay urn painted with dancing Egret-women, the vertebrae of seals dyed indigo blue, amber glass bottles with spidery labels.

"Yes, our Cabinet of Wonders, where all the stories go," said Oro with a sigh of pure delight. He leaned towards Tin and Comfrey, who were now both peeping through the door.

"Guests, guests!" a little boy cried just then, leaping up from a game of marbles. He pulled a small gold trumpet from the pocket of his loose robes and blew into it.

Mallow and Myrtle jumped into Tin and Comfrey's arms, respectively, at the startling sound of the trumpet. Tin looked more closely at the boy and saw that, like Oro, he was oddly formed – his lip was cleft down the middle, showing his teeth between, and one of his eyes looked towards his nose, not straight ahead. His feet were bare, and missing their big toes, making the boy prance in an oddly graceful way to keep his balance. Tin looked around, swallowing hard at all the commotion. He suddenly felt the fatigue of the day, which seemed endless – was it midnight, or later? Or only just after dark?

Everyone stared at the four of them. A kind-looking woman, who was reclining on deerskins on the floor, knitting a very large blanket on bone needles, chuckled. Her skin was mottled pale and dark, piebald between cream and chestnut, one of her eyes blue and the other brown, which made her gaze upon them, though friendly, feel dizzying.

Peering around, Comfrey and Tin both realized that everybody was slightly misshapen, oddly proportioned. Not Wild Folk, no, Comfrey thought – there were no hoofs or tails or fur in sight – just humans made a little different, and unlike any she had ever seen.

Oro caught them staring. "We all have our Oddnesses, you know. They are our gifts, our singular stories. Some carry them outside, that's all." He tapped his bald and oblong head. "Others, here." He tapped his chest. "Course, not everybody thinks that way, do they, Amber?" he added sadly, putting a hand on the shoulder of the piebald woman.

"Now, now, Oro. These children look half-dead with exhaustion," said Amber. She heaved herself to her feet, leaving her knitting on the floor. For a moment the striped pile of yarn seemed to rustle and stretch, just like a cat. Comfrey rubbed her eyes. "Looks like all they can manage about now is a meal and a hot bath, eh, lovey?" she said, patting Comfrey's head in a motherly way and tilting the girl's chin up to look into her eyes. Comfrey could barely hold the woman's gaze, looking at both the blue and the brown eyes at once.

"What are your names, children?" Amber said.

"I'm Comfrey. I'm from the village called Alder, just the other side of the boundary. This – this is my friend Tin. He's…" She turned to Tin, but he wasn't listening at all. He was too busy looking around. The people of The Holy Fool's Inn fit the description of the Country people he had heard time and again from the Brothers a bit better than Comfrey did, but there was so much warmth and strange beauty and kindness about them. He'd never seen so many easy, smiling faces, or heard so much laughter. Just being in their midst made him feel glad. Not for the first time that day, he marvelled at this land called Farallone, his own land, though he had been kept from it his whole life inside the City's Wall.

"Is the lad deaf?" Amber said after another moment. The little boy with the trumpet loped near and tugged at Tin's earlobe.

"Ow, watch it!" Tin exclaimed.

"Off in la-la land," said Amber, opening a cupboard in the main room to pull out fresh bedding, and shooing off the little trumpet boy with her free hand.

"He's from the City," said Comfrey.

The boy with the trumpet, joined by an older girl whose back was greatly humped, giggled and leaned in to sniff at Tin.

"The City, the City!" chortled the trumpet-playing boy.

"Is he indeed?" said Oro, peering more closely at Tin.

"Manners!" snapped Mallow. "It's not as if they are another breed of human there, he's just the same as anyone."

Oro chuckled. "Oh my dear little leveret, wouldn't we be the first to know? I am not judging him, only observing. We Holy Fools love difference more than we love just about anything. We, after all, are the greatest misfits of all. We fit nowhere. I'm merely fascinated, itching to hear your tale. Never have we met a City person before! What a delight, what a true delight!"

Warmth stole through Tin's chest at the man's kindness, and at Mallow's loyalty. It made his eyes prick. He looked away.

Amber turned to the boy with the trumpet and the humpbacked girl, filling their arms with the bed sheets. "Run along, you two, and make the beds and heat some water for washing," she said giving them both a gentle shove. Then, like a great matriarchal tide, she bustled Tin, Comfrey, the leverets and Oro to the hearth.

They ate supper sitting on threadbare pillows by the fire. Myrtle and Mallow were delighted when an old man with a drooping, trunk-like nose brought them a ceramic pot full to brimming with wild radish leaves from the garden.

Though the children were tired, they were fit to bursting with their story, with what had befallen them over the past days, and eager to see if these strange, kind

Fools might be able to help them or give them advice. Taking turns, Comfrey and Tin related the basics of what had come to pass since the night the Greentwins sent the leverets out across the land of Farallone. When Comfrey got to the Fire Hawk and his feather and the vision she had seen in it, her voice broke and she stopped, trying to catch her breath, not sure how much she should share. Myrtle, chewing radish leaves, leaped onto her lap and nipped at her sleeves, trying to comfort the girl.

"And you have this very feather with you now, my dove?" Amber asked softly, her merry face very still and very dark. "What a burden to carry for such a young creature as yourself."

"It is here, in my pack," Comfrey said. "I have been too afraid to unwrap it again. I don't want to see any more. It was too terrible, what it showed me."

"Dear girl," murmured Oro. "I have a knack for seeing. I can scry any old puddle. Quite a distracting habit sometimes. But perhaps I might have a look in this feather. A feather dropped from the wing of the Fire Hawk to herald the end of the world. Oh, earth, may it not be so."

"But everything is the same as ever it was!" said a girl with blind blue eyes. "Surely the world is not ending. I have smelled in the air that the plum trees will blossom early. Surely they would not blossom if the world was going to end any time soon."

"Ay, child," said Amber, but a cloud passed over her face. "Plums will blossom right until the end. Their business is to bloom." She sat silent a moment, full of stillness. "But we must remember, my loves," she continued, casting her two unmatched eyes all across the room, "that endings always carry new beginnings like seeds in their bellies. You just have to know how to look for them, and how to look after them, so that they can grow. That is our task, every single day."

"Here it is," said Comfrey, opening her rucksack. "I'll show you."

The Fools gathered near, nodding and murmuring and stroking one another's faces and hands to soothe their fear. Comfrey removed the sheaf of white, butter-soft deerskin from her bag and unrolled it very gingerly, as if it swaddled a child and not a feather. Tin leaned close. Earlier that day they had been so busy arguing that he hadn't stopped to ask just what this feather was, and what it had to do with the Elk of Milk and Gold, nor had he realized it had been in her backpack all along. Inside the buckskin was another wrapping, this time finely woven of usnea lichen. A smell of damp forest and smoke rose from the bundle, but the pale green lichen was unburned. Surely the feather wasn't *really* on fire, Tin thought. But then Comfrey lifted it from its final swaddling, holding the quill lightly between her finger and thumb, and he saw that he was wrong. It flickered just like an ember, its delicate edges licked by little flames. It was as long as Comfrey's forearm, and it lit the whole room with a dark and beautiful glow.

The boy with the trumpet let out a crow of awe and surprise, and Oro crooned.

"Oh my holy stars," he said, reaching out.

"I wouldn't do that if I were you!" said Myrtle, leaping forward to stop the man. "Look, don't touch. The Fire Hawk entrusted the feather to Comfrey alone. He's a very particular creature." She shuddered at the memory. "He might not take well to it being touched by anyone else. He might think it stolen, and come hunting us!"

"By all Haredom," muttered Mallow. "That's the last thing we need."

"Wise little leverets!" exclaimed Oro, snatching his hand away. "What was I thinking? You children are very fortunate to have these as your companions and not my sorry old self! What an extraordinary quartet you make. It is a blessing you have come to us. Now, let me look. I shall peer from a friendly distance, shall I?"

And he did, squinting and flaring his nostrils at once. The feather's light danced all over his bald head, making it glow. His face went very still as he looked. Then it darkened, losing all of its light. Horror spread through his eyes.

"Bedtime for the young ones," he said abruptly. "Off with you all, besides these two and their leverets, poor chits. You are too young for such things, and yet you carry them, and so you must know them."

A mewling outcry went up among the children, but Amber silenced it and herded a group of twelve or so out through the tall glass doors into the night-time, singing raspy lullabies that sounded like the calling hoots of owls.

"Is it that bad?" breathed Tin, studying Oro. Comfrey had hidden her face in her hands. The man was still staring into the feather. It sparked, throwing an ember onto the rug. No one dared touch it, so it burned a little black hole as it went out. Those who were left – another dozen adults of many ages and shapes – had gathered even nearer, holding each other. Comfrey wished that someone would hold her too. Myrtle quivered in her lap.

"It is," said Oro. "It is." He sat back and closed his eyes at last. "You may put away the feather, my girl," he said to Comfrey. "I cannot bear any more."

Her hand shook as she placed the feather back on its bed of lichen, trying not to look directly into its embered face. But she couldn't help it. Her eyes were drawn inexorably there. And in a flash she saw her mother at the round table in their kitchen, feeding soup to a strange, pale man.

"My mother!" she cried.

217

"Oh dear," said Oro. "Is that who I saw, then? A woman with fine dark eyes and a thousand dark, dark curls?"

"You saw her?" Comfrey half-sobbed, holding Myrtle very tight.

"Easy," wheezed the leveret. "I'm not used to being clutched except as a prelude to someone else's dinner." Comfrey loosed the hare and took hold of her black braids instead, twisting them.

"Briefly, but yes," said Oro. "I saw a gentle Country-woman with a strange, pale man at her table. A man with something amiss about him. Something cold and grasping and very, very clever. One of the City Brothers, in disguise."

Tin let out a moan, and Comfrey a strangled cry, but Oro stopped them with a hand.

"Better let me finish, my dears. That is not all I saw. I saw many more of them. I saw them as if I myself were a hawk flying out over all the Country. I saw them one by one entering all of the villages across the many gentle valleys and mountains of Farallone, disguised in Country clothes. I saw them beset and kill travelling merchants and traders to make their disguises."

"Are they after my Fiddleback? But how can they possibly know I am here, in the Country?"

"It is not clear, my boy, what they want," said Oro. "But whatever they are after, the worst of it all is that now they know. Now they know that the Country is not poisoned or diseased. That its waters are clean and its valleys bountiful, its people peaceful and unarmed. That it has healed itself while they were sealed away behind their Wall. That it is rich with all that must be lacking in that City. They will want to have it all, again. The Elk did not foresee this, she did not foresee the survival of the City at all. She was too tired and too heartbroken to understand the tenacity of poison and of greed."

At that moment, Amber came in. She took one look around the room and into the hollow, heavy eyes that met hers, and exclaimed, "My doves, it is far past midnight and time for sleep. Let's attend to these matters when we are not so weary. Only Fools would discuss the end of the world at the witching hour." And with one tidal sweep of her arms, she gathered both Comfrey and Tin to her warm, broad breast, squeezing them tight. "Visions clarify with sleep," she said. "We may be Fools, but there are gifts to be had here at The Holy Fool's Inn for those in need." Then, with her arms still about their shoulders, she herded Comfrey and Tin up a narrow flight of stairs. The leverets followed at her heels.

"But – my mother!" stammered Comfrey.

"And the Brothers! Does Oro know when the vision he saw took place? Has it already happened?"

"Sleep first, visions later!" said Amber, firm and motherly. "It can all wait until daybreak. Washroom's down that way." She pointed left at the top of the stairs down an equally narrow, white-panelled hall. "Third door on the right. And this is your room." She turned the glass knob of a door across the hall. "Afraid we've only one vacancy. Three are taken by ghosts. Harmless sorts, but they do make for a sleepless night. The fourth, that's Oro's. He stays in the inn proper each night; old watchdog he is. The rest of us, well, we prefer a more rustic style of sleep." She smiled and led them into the little room, lighting candles as she went, which illuminated a chamber with wrought-iron bed frames five hundred years old, quilts of soft floral patterns and stripes filled with wool, a wooden chest of drawers, and a chandelier of cut glass in the shape of flowers, lit with candles.

Amber moved to the window and opened the curtains, gesturing with a candle and spilling a little wax on the faded red carpet. "There – our tents," she said proudly. The shapes of a dozen or more snug, cone-shaped tents made of skins and tule scattered the edges of a grassy meadow ringed with apple trees. A few had fires lit inside. The children stared.

"Into bed with you, now. Fresh nightclothes are in the dresser there. I'll come and wake you for breakfast, and for your gifts. We can talk more about what you have seen, and what you must do, by the saner and kinder light of morning. Otherwise, none of us will ever sleep, and we will be quite hysterical by dawn." With a swift, violet-scented kiss on each cheek, she left them.

Comfrey and Tin took turns using the bathroom, cleaning their teeth with willow sticks and a jar of peppermint tooth-clay, bathing in the basin of a white tub with soap that smelled of orange blossoms. They climbed into bed without speaking, and though their hearts were dark with private fears, the soft linen nightclothes, the sun-dried sheets and heavy blankets, the scent of orange blossoms and mint and fresh night air, suffused them both with well-being. Myrtle and Mallow nestled together beneath the window, lay back their ears, and fell at once to sleep, exhausted by the day and so much bad news.

Tin glanced at Comfrey's shape in the dark, her hair loose and drying in a black-brown mass across her pillow, tangled and long. He'd never slept in the same room as a girl, and felt suddenly embarrassed for looking. He turned to the wall.

"Tin?" whispered Comfrey after a little while.

"Yes?" he replied, hesitant, hoping she was not going to ask him about the City, or the Brothers, or blame him for bringing the Fiddleback here. He felt sick. Amber was right. Sleep was a welcome balm. He could escape into his dreams for the night, and think about it all in the morning.

There was a silence. Outside a great-horned owl hooted gently, its voice like velvet.

"I'm glad you're here," the girl said in a shy voice. "I'm glad I don't have to do all this alone. My...mother, she'd be pleased to know I have a friend. Two friends," she added, looking down at the sleeping Myrtle, then back at Tin in the dark room. His own hair was a pale tangle amidst the covers, and Comfrey blushed, turning away just as Tin had done, for she'd never slept in the same room as a boy either.

"Me too," said Tin. He wanted to say more – about the way Farallone made him feel, how he didn't think he had ever really loved anything besides his friend Seb and his Fiddleback until he'd come here and felt the fullness and life force of this land and all of its creatures, its green plants and sun and hills and birdsong. But he was too tired and couldn't find the words, so he smiled into the darkness. "Me too," he said again, more softly.

Then they slept, so exhausted that they did not dream.

11

THE CABINET
OF WONDERS

Amber woke the children with a song about dawn and mothers and golden bells. Tin sat up with tears in his eyes, almost remembering his own mother's voice, though he had been only three months old when the Brothers took him into their Cloister. Comfrey woke teary-eyed too, thinking of Maxine. Amber touched each of their foreheads with rosemary oil. Both children kept their eyes closed for an extra minute just to listen to her voice – liquid, smoky amber, like her name – and to smell that rosemary smell, which pricked their noses and their lungs awake. She left a bundle of fresh clothing at the base of each bed and told them to come to the garden for breakfast. There was a long-sleeved, patchwork dress for Comfrey, made with sturdy red and yellow linen scraps, and a thick green wool vest. A beautifully knitted blue sweater with leather elbow patches sat at the base of Tin's bed, and stiff brown trousers. Myrtle and Mallow were gone, but Comfrey spied them through the window, grazing at the vegetable patch, their ears flicking back and forth with pleasure as they ate.

When the children came downstairs, they stopped in their tracks in the main room, bewildered and awed by the way the midwinter sun coming in through the windows of the inn glinted – off the glass panes, off the marbles left by the little trumpet boy beside the hearth, off hanging crystals, off tiny shards of mirror stuck to the walls, as if somebody had placed them just so, just where the morning sun hit. Amber found them thus, mouths agape, and herded them outside under the apple trees to a breakfast of fresh eggs and seedy dense toast covered in blackberry jam. Huge cups of a dark and bitter tea full of goat's milk steamed on the table. Their heat wafted up into the cold morning towards the branches of the apple trees, which were bare yet, with only the faintest hint of buds. A fire crackled in a pit in the earth, warming them, and the russet-coloured girl roasted apples in the embers. Nearby, the skin-tents where the Fools slept gleamed in the morning sun, and a man beat at a coloured rug with a stick, sending dust into the air.

"My mother," said Comfrey, staring at her breakfast,

but feeling suddenly unable to eat. "Tell me, is she in danger this very minute? Was the vision in the feather of now, or of what is to come?"

"The Brothers," Tin was saying at the same time, to Comfrey and to Amber and to the girl by the fire, to anyone who would listen. "Are they here, already? Do they know how to get to Wild Folk land? Will they find out…?" He paused, wondering at the danger of his own words, spoken aloud, wondering what these Fools knew. "That the last gold of Farallone runs through their veins?"

"By all the Fools, not if we can help it," replied Amber in a voice much fiercer than she had ever used before. "Now eat up, my chits. You must be hearty and strong to make it all the way to the end of Olima to bring that feather to the Elk of Milk and Gold. Your feet are already on the path most needed. Now you just know a bit more than you did before, and it'll speed your way."

"But what about my Fiddleback?" said Tin. "Why did the Coyote-folk take it? Do they know about the Brothers? Will they know how dangerous it would be for them to get their hands on it?"

Just then, a little skunk ambled up to the table and tugged at the boy's trouser-leg with her teeth. Tin almost yelped in surprise.

"Run along now to the Cabinet, Tin. Oro is waiting for you!" Amber said. "What you will see there, and what he will give you – these are all the answer and all the help we can provide."

In the Cabinet of Wonders, that room full of strange treasures that he had glimpsed last night when they arrived, Oro sat Tin down at a mirror-topped table and bade him look into it.

"What do you see, young Tin?" said Oro. The mirror reflected their leaning arms and the early morning sun that was coming through the window. It reflected Oro's pale, long head and Tin's tight curls still sticking out from sleep. A blue porcelain pot of tea left a ring of steam round itself on the table's mirrored surface. Tin looked a moment longer at himself, eyes a little puffy with sleep, then sighed, tired and confused.

"Nothing. Just us," he replied, trying to keep the frustration out of his voice. "I thought we were going to talk more about the Brothers, and the Fiddleback, and what we can do to stop them from coming any further!"

"Dear boy," Oro said with a sigh. "Sometimes talking isn't the best plan of action. What we are about to do will help you far more than anything I might conjecture. Now, let's have a cup of tea and look again. You will not truly see into a mirror like this one if your eyes are full of other things." Oro pulled the teapot close. It left a steamed streak on the glass. Then he turned to the bottom shelf behind them and balanced two chipped and un-matching teacups in one hand.

Tin saw that they left two circles on the wooden shelf, light and dustless, where they'd been standing beside the bronze orrery, the indigo glass bottles, a chess piece, a broom handle, a pincushion filled with marvellous shiny needles, and a battery chipped to the colour of silver. Oro poured a steaming spout of deep green tea into each cup. Tin drank, trying to clear his mind like Mallow had taught him on their first evening together, when they were hiding in the shadows of the Cloister's catacombs. That felt like another lifetime, now. He swallowed more tea.

Oro watched him. For a moment his eyes seemed to brighten, gold-flecked, like a cat's. Tin took a breath, and another sip. The taste of nettles and rosemary made his chest ease. The tea heated up his whole body. When he exhaled his breath steamed up the mirrored table too, just like the teapot.

"Well, now I can't see anything at all," he muttered, glancing up at Oro. The man only gave him a crooked smile. Then he gestured for Tin to look again.

Instead of foggy glass, Tin saw himself down in the catacombs of the Fifth Cloister of Grace and Progress. He gasped, and leaned closer. It was strange to see his own body from afar, there in that dark, stone-walled room where he had spent so many evenings working on his Fiddleback. He looked skinny and pale, his hair a light tangle in the darkness. It gave him a sad feeling in his belly to see himself from this distance. He looked so lonely and so solemn as he coaxed his creation together. And he was talking to himself! Had he talked to himself out loud the whole time he worked? How strange not to remember! There was a small half-smile on his face as he tinkered, his lips moving faintly all the while. Then he remembered – a story! He'd been telling a story aloud, one of the stories that were always running through his mind.

In the Alchemics Workshop the Brothers overseeing the boys' work forbade him from his "ceaseless infernal chattering". When he forgot himself once, he received three lashes across his tongue with a sharp metal cord that cut his cheek as well. He did not forget again. Instead, he told himself stories in his head as he heated the mercury by precise and careful degrees, as he stirred and stirred at a vat that might explode if ever the boys stopped stirring, and did his best not to breathe in the fumes. It calmed his mind to tell himself tales this way, it kept him from the panic or deadened exhaustion that many of the other boys suffered through the long and dangerous hours. What stories had he been telling aloud as he made his Fiddleback? As he watched himself, it almost looked like he was whispering a spell, but no matter how hard he tried he couldn't remember what he had said, only the feeling of intense focus and happiness that came over him whenever he was making something.

He peered so close his nose almost touched the mirror, craning to hear. It was then that he saw something extraordinary. He saw light extending from his own fingers and from his mouth, golden light that shimmered, coursing from his own body and into each part of the Fiddleback that he touched. The light unfurled from him like the tendrilled stalks of plants, and spread through the Fiddleback's wires and leather and engine. Without realizing he did so, Tin reached to touch his own gold-rimmed fingers in the mirror.

"Ah!" warned Oro, but it was too late. The vision had gone. "Well, well," the man murmured, resting his own hand on Tin's back. "Now I begin to understand…"

"You saw it too?" Tin breathed.

"Indeed, my lad, indeed. What a thing you made, and lost! With your hands and your words, you brought your Fiddleback to life. You have much creative power in you, dear boy. That is the golden light you saw. That is the true power of stargold. Oh it is quite splendid. It is a wondrous and rare gift!"

"Thornton, a man we met who is part of a group of rebels in the City – I never did get to tell you that part last night – he told me that the reason I could make the

Fiddleback the way I did was because I have a little stargold in my blood. Not like the Wild Folk do, only a very little bit. That lots of people have a little. Maybe – maybe you do too? But, what does it mean? The mirror only showed me something I already knew...just, more beautifully than I knew it." The boy sighed and looked at his hands, wishing that he could see that golden light now, that he could control it in some way.

"All that you say is true, my lad – of us, of Wild Folk, and of yourself," Oro replied. "Stargold is the life force of Farallone. Those who carry it in their blood have a duty to this land – that is how I understand these matters. But we are not finished. Look here." And as he pointed with his six-fingered hand, a woodrat scrambled up the leg of the table and trotted right to the centre beside the cooling teapot. He held a strange red object the length of a thumb in his jaws, and swayed his tail proudly. Tin started back.

"He has found your Oddness!" Oro exclaimed, gesturing towards the rat. Tin stared, confused. "He and his sisters and brothers build their stick nests in these walls. They gather treasures left over from the human world, from Before. And they listen to our stories. They always seem to know which small trifle belongs to which person, so to speak, or represents them in some way. In exchange, we give them bits of cheese and berries and apple twigs. It's a good deal, all in all."

"I don't understand," said Tin, staring still, feeling shaken by what he had seen in the glass mirror, and now by the woodrat who peered at him with very intelligent black eyes.

"You've just looked into the Mirror of Oddness, and seen the nature of your own," replied Oro. "Of course, you were born with it, your Oddness. That's what makes you you, and not me. But sometimes in life we have moments that show it to us very clearly, encapsulated, if you will. Source-points of our Oddness. It is also your strength, your gift."

The woodrat moved his whiskers and set the treasure down with his white-edged paws. It made a click against the glass. It was in fact longer than a thumb, but not by much, and about as wide. The red exterior was chipped. Inside it was layered and made of metal.

"What *is* my Oddness, then?" said Tin, peering nervously at the object on the glass before him.

Oro smiled. "Well, this thing here is called a penknife. Long ago every lad had one of these. As your Oddness, it carries the power of making and unmaking. Powerful and dangerous, both." He pushed the tool closer to Tin.

"I thought it was for the Cabinet," said Tin, not quite ready to pick up the compact little tool.

"It is. There are always two, like you and your shadow, you and your memory-you as you remember him." Oro reached for the reflection of the penknife next to Tin's hand, and with a sound like parting water, he picked up a second one out of the reflection of the real one. "For the Cabinet," he said to the woodrat, who took the little red object in his teeth and scampered it up a shelf on the wall, placing it beside a knight chess piece.

"I'll show you," Oro said, watching Tin turn the penknife over and over in his hands. He demonstrated to the boy how to use a fingernail to lift up the separate, nested tools: knife blade, tiny scissors, corkscrew, can opener, screwdriver, tweezers, wire cutters, pin. This last item was not like the rest. It was wooden, with a tiny thorn tip.

"Fiddleback spider venom in that," said Oro softly, and Tin felt a chill. "Don't prick yourself. It can only be used once, so use it wisely. As for the rest of these, they have two uses each: their literal use, like the knife for cutting, or the can opener for opening cans, or the screwdriver for unscrewing a screw, which I daresay you won't need, and then a metaphoric use too."

"Metaphoric?" said Tin, raising his eyebrows.

"Yes, yes. The can opener for opening those things which are sealed. The screwdriver for securing one thing to the next – hope to courage, for example. Or loosening them, detaching worry from joy, or what have you. Tweezers for removing something almost invisible that is hurting you." Oro smiled, as if it were all very obvious. Tin's mouth hung open.

"How—?"

"You'll figure it out, I assure you. It's all very intuitive. Remember, a penknife can carve a story too. At least, this penknife can. For that's what you do, my boy, isn't it? Tell stories with what you make?"

Tin couldn't think of what to say.

"My lad, keeping your eyebrows halfway up your head like that is going to give you a dreadful headache, and I could use your help out in the vegetable patch while Comfrey takes her turn. Enough of this intellectualizing, let's get our hands dirty!" With that, Oro rose abruptly, leaving a piece of cheese on the table for the woodrat.

Tin, dazed, followed without another word.

Oro took him straight to the beehives, to listen to their humming – *Good for the nerves after a round in the Cabinet*, he said – and then had the boy lend a hand turning a vegetable bed with a large rusty shovel to prepare it for the planting of winter greens. Tin glimpsed Comfrey through the apple trees, being led by Amber towards the Inn. Digging, turning, shaking the roots of weeds out of those shovel-loads of dirt, with Oro hollering for him to save the dandelion roots – *For heaven's sake, boy, they're precious medicine!* – Tin wondered what her Oddness would be, what little object the woodrat would bring forth from

233

the walls and place before her. Mallow, spotting Tin from amidst the patch of nasturtiums he was presently munching, bounded over and nipped at the boy's trousers, impatient to hear about the Cabinet of Wonders.

When Comfrey peered down into the mirrored table with Amber's mottled hand on her shoulder and the woodrat watching intently from the top of the shelf, she saw her own memory immediately, without any sips of the rosemary and nettle tea that Oro had given Tin. There in the mirrored glass was the Bobcat-girl in the scrubbrush hillside, looking back at Comfrey with green eyes, uttering her name: *Hello, Comfrey.*

But watching in the mirrored glass was much more vivid than remembering, and so Comfrey saw something she hadn't remembered, and also something that she could not have seen at all with human eyes. She watched herself lag behind her cousins, eyes roving, hands creasing at the fabric of her skirt. Then she bent over a little ditch along the side of the path where a seep of water made the nettles flourish late into the autumn. A red-striped garter snake flicked through the water and into the grass with one curving, shimmying motion. Instinctively she reached a finger to touch his scales, but he was already gone. Then her mother called and she stood quickly, realizing her family was far ahead.

That's when she saw the Bobcat-girl. From a distance, watching through the mirror, Comfrey could see the expression on her own face, an expression of utter shock and delight. Then, in the glass, the world wriggled and changed. Delicate threads became visible in the air around her. A long, thin one reached from her chest to the chest of the Bobcat-girl. Smaller threads reached from her fingers to the snake in the seep of water, from the snake back across the path to the place where he'd eaten a cricket only a few minutes before, from the cricket to all the blades of dry autumn grass. There were thin threads of connection between everything. The whole living world gleamed with them. All together, the threads seemed to be saying something to her, like the Bobcat-girl had; they seemed to form a word, or a series of words, that the girl could almost, for an instant, read. What did it say? She reached out to touch that word, to hold onto it, but it was gone.

"Your Oddness," said Amber after a moment's silence. Comfrey's hands and shins and chest and head tingled.

"My…Oddness?" said Comfrey, struggling to swallow.

Amber smiled, and explained to Comfrey what Oro had explained to Tin about Oddnesses, about Strengths. "Your Oddness is in seeing clearly, seeing the interconnections between all things," she said. "Seeing what others do not, what others have forgotten or are afraid to see. If you were one of us," Amber added, "wearing

235

your Oddness on your skin, you might look like this."

She placed her cream-and-chestnut-splotched hand where Comfrey's reflection floated, and the girl saw herself with eyes as big as a doe's and a strange lump in the centre of her forehead like a third eye, only closed and sealed by a great woven net of eyelashes. Comfrey raised a hand to that place on her face, moaning a little in horror. In the reflection her hands looked webbed because there were threads connecting each finger. Her real forehead remained smooth, her real fingers free. She gasped and closed her eyes.

A small clicking sound made her open them again, and she saw the woodrat pushing a pair of delicate gold-rimmed spectacles across the table with pale paws. Comfrey drew in her breath.

"Such eyes want to know about everything," Amber murmured, raising a thick brow at the radiant, embered feather that appeared in the mirror, held in the hand that Comfrey still had half-raised to her forehead.

"How…?" the girl stammered, lowering her hand at once to find no feather there at all. "Who *are* you people, anyway? And what is *that*?" She leaned towards the spectacles.

"Your gift, for our Cabinet. The encapsulation of your Oddness, procured from the stacks of the Wild Woodrat Library, where they have collected old gadgets and doodahs from that lost human world of Before."

Comfrey opened her mouth to say that this didn't explain anything at all, but then shut it again as Amber gathered up not one but two identical pairs of spectacles, pulling the second pair right out of the reflection, as if from the bottom of a pond. She handed the first set to Comfrey.

"Once, people used these if their eyesight was bad, or blurry, often when reading books. These are a little bit more special even than that, only to be donned when you absolutely need them. They don't make things bigger or smaller, they only help you see the threads between everything, and the language those threads speak, the words they make together. How one thing is bound to the next: the heartbeats of snakes to the life cycles of crickets, the downy seeds of a thistle to the nest of a goldfinch. These spectacles will help you to see the threads that bind things into one whole, and to read their meaning. But you can only wear them three times, three times ever, or your own dear eyes will go blind, as if you had stared too long into the sun."

"Oh, my," whispered Comfrey, touching the glass of the gold-rimmed spectacles very carefully. "How will I know? When to use them, I mean?"

"You just will. That's the trick. You just will. And that Myrtle, she may be of help, being a hare, and therefore in the centre of many threads of connection." Amber chuckled.

Late morning sun fell through the glass windows, and the skunk, who had been curled up asleep in that patch of warmth since she'd fetched Tin in to the Cabinet several hours ago, stretched at last and rose slowly on her four short legs. She wriggled the black and white plume of her tail. Comfrey lurched back automatically, not keen on the stink of a startled skunk.

"Ah, not to worry, not to worry. Our Rosie has no stink glands. That's why she's here. Can't manage out there in the wild world without them. Rather like us, I'd say. She's lacking the thing that would protect her against others. Confidence in numbers, you see? She's a marvellous wasper, as they say, eating the wasps from their ground nests so they don't disturb our bees. Wasps, to a skunk, are a great delicacy." Amber bent to give Rosie a pat on the head as she stood. Comfrey smiled despite herself, thinking of wasps as delicacies.

"Come along, dear girl. Let's show Comfrey about the humming of bees, and how in it you can hear the heartbeats of the flowers. We could listen to such a thing all day long, Rosie and I."

"Could we look into the mirror to see about my mother?" Comfrey ventured.

"Oh no, my lovely, no indeed. It is no scrying mirror but only a mirror of Oddness. We will go into the garden now and see what Oro thinks of all this. Then we will send you on your way with your new gifts in tow."

The skunk looked up at Comfrey with glinting black eyes and sniffed. Her nose was dark, with pink blotches. For a moment, Comfrey's hand grazed the spectacles where she'd placed them gingerly inside her dress pocket. She wondered, like a thirst in her chest, what the skunk would look like through them, what Amber would look like, the whole Inn, the sky outside... She wondered what the word was which she had almost understood when she'd looked into the mirrored table and seen it forming out of the threads strung between herself, the Bobcat-girl, the little snake, the autumn grass. She heard the Bobcat-girl's voice in her head, saying her name.

Amber sensed the girl's hand tightening on the spectacles and anticipated her thoughts. "Best to train your own eyes to all the details, big and little, first. You can see so much more than you think you can, with practice." Amber tapped the mirrored table, then headed for the door. She left a piece of cheese from her pocket on the top of the door frame, near an opening in the wall. The woodrat skittered out and gathered it up in his hungry paws.

They found Oro, Tin, and the humpbacked girl named Pieta sprawled in a patch of grass near the beehives, drinking cold cups of fresh-pressed apple cider. Their arms were all covered up to the elbows in dirt. Comfrey saw that Pieta had a smile that made her whole face sweet and bright as honey, a smile she was currently directing at Tin. Her patchwork robes were hitched up to her knees to reveal pale, shapely ankles and small bare feet entirely covered in mud.

"Turned the old tomato bed in record time with these two strapping young people!" exclaimed Oro, raising his mug of apple juice. "Comfrey, meet Pieta, Pieta, Comfrey."

The girl leaned forward, pushing her red hair from her eyes. "Tin's been telling me *all* about your adventures," she said, then sighed, holding her hands tight in her lap and glancing back at Tin with that sweet smile. The boy grinned back amiably, enjoying the attention.

Comfrey felt a very small twinge in her stomach, and raised an eyebrow at Tin, then replied to Pieta in a brisk tone, "I don't know what he's been telling you, but it certainly isn't like picking roses or digging vegetable beds for that matter. Seems like a nice spot here. I wouldn't want to leave it, if I were you. As it happens, things are really quite *bad* in the world at the moment."

"Yes, well," interjected Tin, "some people just have a roving spirit by nature, that's all."

"Oh, quite so, quite so. Maybe I have one of those…" murmured a wistful Pieta, nodding. Comfrey flushed, feeling angry at Tin, wanting to take back what she had said. Instead she turned to Oro, impatient to learn more about the fate of Farallone, and her mother.

"I would like to get a message to my mother," Comfrey said, casting a sidelong glare at Tin. "Is that possible from here? Can somebody be sent? Shouldn't the village people be warned about the Brothers? Maybe Tin could go—?"

"But we have to find my Fiddleback and get it from the Coyote-folk, to make sure it's safe!"

"The Fiddleback might after all be safer among Coyote-folk than among us," interjected Myrtle hastily. "If they're expecting it to be with a boy named Tin, they certainly won't think to look among Coyote-folk. Nor would any self-respecting Coyote let them near. And besides, Coyote-folk come and go from the First Bobcat's underworld. The Brothers would never know how to get there."

"Coyote-folk may be tricksters," added Mallow with a small hare-sigh, "but they are rarely traitors. No one is better at sneaking and hiding in plain sight."

"Safer? In the underworld?" Tin nearly shouted, thinking again of the sight of the Fiddleback jerking between the teeth of the Coyote-folk. "That doesn't sound very safe! And it didn't look like they were trying to be helpful to me! It's probably half-ruined by now!" But he could hear the childishness of his words even as they came out.

"Is that really all you can think about?" Comfrey snapped. "We have to get this feather to the Elk as fast as we can, if the Brothers are already here on Country soil. Myrtle, could you go to my mother, would you?"

"I have a feeling you will need me more to help you across the land of the Wild Folk," the leveret said, wrinkling up her furred nose with thought. "Mallow and I are the only reason you haven't been eaten or killed or kidnapped already. Wild Folk have seen us from the trees and fields and shadows, and let us be because we are wild hares, and wild hares don't travel with human children unless there is something unusual about those human children."

"But we abandoned my mother, and now we know trouble is heading for her and we have to warn her—"

"Now, now," soothed Oro. "One step at a time. I slept on what I saw in that fiery feather, I mused and mulled and worried it to pieces, and at last I found a clue. Praise earth! I found a clue, a hint, to ease your young minds. In that vision there were wild irises blooming purple by the roadsides where the Brothers walked. The wild irises have yet to bloom this year, though it has been warm, with early rains, so they are likely to open soon. In the next fortnight, I daresay. But this means, dear Comfrey, that your mother is safe for now. So you must hurry across the land of Olima to the Elk with your sacred feather. She is the only one who can protect the heart of Farallone. She will know what to do to protect us all, including your mother."

"May it be so, may it be so," murmured Amber in a voice like a prayer. "For if she does not, they will come for us too. We Strangelings have never been accepted by Country Folk, let alone City Brothers."

"Why not?" Tin asked, though even as he asked it he thought he knew the answer, and turned pink.

For a moment, both Amber and Oro were silent. Sorrow moved over their faces. The sound of children playing with a ball and sticks felt suddenly very loud, coming from beyond the tents and apple trees.

"Of course you've been wondering what our own story is, us Fools," said Oro. The words rang with a sad resonance through the silence. Tin and Comfrey looked from Oro's face to Amber's, then at each other, both feeling a chill at once.

"We are not too keen on regular human folk in general," said Amber, shredding a long golden grass blade between her fingernails. "That is, we are wary to trust them."

"What do you mean?" Tin said slowly, his stomach cold.

"We started out, well…" said Amber, looking at Comfrey, "like you, dear. Born in the villages of the Country."

"What?" It came out a gasp. Comfrey reached up and held the ends of her braids, as if this might steady her. "Why haven't I ever heard of you or of your inn?"

"Listen, child," said Oro in a steady voice. "You've never seen or heard of anyone like us in the villages, because we are all here."

"I don't understand, if you were born—"

"When a child is born Odd in the villages, you know, with a hump like Pieta's, or a head like Oro's, or skin like mine, they are taken away immediately by the midwife, to be exposed on a hill. Left out to die, in other words." Amber looked down as she spoke, and her voice was soft.

"*Exposed?*" said Tin, his skin crawling at the word though he wasn't sure what it meant. It sounded like being orphaned, like being left for the Brothers, only worse.

"Well, that's what everyone believes. That we die. The child is left out to be taken by wild animals, or by the Wild Folk, whichever get there first. The ultimate sort of Offering. Strangelings, we call ourselves. Poisoned Ones, we are called." Oro grimaced.

Comfrey let out a little gasp, thinking of her mother, wondering with horror if she'd had an Odd sibling before her that she'd never known about. What if Comfrey herself had been born with that lump of a third eye on her forehead?

"It's an ancient decree, from the time of the Collapse," said Amber, her voice stronger again. "During that time there was so much sickness and poison everywhere in the water and the air, and people were born strange from those poisons. Of course, a child shaped oddly, no matter the cause, is of no harm to anyone, but it was a dark time, a frightened time. It was believed that by leaving the Poisoned Ones out for the wild beasts or the Wild Folk to take, it would somehow protect the rest of the hamlet from a similar fate. Except that the midwives, they've always had a secret.

"The story goes that after the Collapse, at the beginning of the villages, a pair of twins was born conjoined at the hand and with green hair like buckeye leaves. But the midwife, when told by the leader of the hamlet to take the babies up and leave them for the wild animals, she couldn't leave them alone. She refused. She stayed up the hill under an oak tree all night, praying to the three Creatrixes. At dawn, a strange being emerged from the far edge of the oak forest. It was one of the Hill Folk. It looked like a very broad woman with a skirt of thick dirt and grass, with the big dark eyes of a vole. Her arms were twined with so many tiny rootlets they looked like they were covered in lace. She took the little twins in her arms and nursed them, not with milk, but with the sweet nectar that all hills have inside their veins.

"The next time another such child was among the villages, seventeen years had passed. The midwife of its village brought the baby up to the edge of Wild Folk terrain as she was told. She knew, from the stories passed between midwives, to call upon the Hill-woman. But the Hill-woman didn't come. Instead of her, the twins conjoined at the hand emerged from the shadows at dusk and took the baby in their three hands. They were only seventeen years old, but those twins had been nursed by a Hill-woman and so became part Wild Folk themselves. They knew all the languages of all the animals and plants and stones. For a while, they took up residence here in the inn, which was then very ramshackle. One by one, they took in little Strangelings. Eventually, after a few of them grew old enough to take over the running of this creaking inn, teenagers only, but that was old enough, and the twins had taught them about living, about tending bees and plants and birds, about playing, and never giving up on joy, the twins built a green cart. They charmed a small herd of Elk and set off to rove, to roam, to heal any and all who needed healing, to learn all the land of Farallone and its many stories, heedless of the boundaries and the walls that had been made. That was two hundred years ago. Now, they are called the Greentwins, and while they look like us Holy Fools, they are also Wild Folk, because they were nursed by one. They are mostly wild, and a little bit angel."

Myrtle and Mallow were sitting nose to nose, their ears and whiskers moving furiously, speaking together in their own hare-speech.

"Our Greentwins!" Myrtle exclaimed, turning back to the others. "They told us every tale except their own. All the spokes of the wheel except the middle."

"But I could smell something of them here all along," said Mallow. "They seem to be in the centre of so many different webs. Even the City's Mycelium. Remember what Thornton said, Tin? How he'd met them before he entered the City, how they said they'd come there when he called them, when the time was right?"

"Thornton?" said Comfrey. "Who is Thornton?" A sickening sadness had been swelling in her chest, how all along in her idyllic Alder village this terrible thing had been happening. She thought of her Offering bundle, and wondered if her mother knew about the babies left out just the same way. But now, the name of one of Tin's Mycelium friends, a man who had entered the City like her father had wanted to do, cut through her. She'd never heard him speak that name before, and it sounded terrifyingly, perilously close to her father's. Thorne, her mother called him. My Thorne. Papa, always Papa, to Comfrey. A dangerous kind of elation began to eclipse the girl's sorrow. Was it possible? Was it truly? A sob came out instead of any more words.

Myrtle leaped up into Comfrey's arms. Even in a short time she had learned that this, to a human person, was a comfort, like when she and Mallow groomed at each other's fur. Myrtle sniffed at Comfrey's chin, whiskers moving. She wondered not for the first time at the intensity of human emotions, how tangled they could become. It was like smelling the air before a thunderstorm. Tin, too, was confused by Comfrey's sudden outburst.

But then, they'd heard so many frightening revelations in the last day, he could understand if she was just overwhelmed.

"He's – he's the best man I've ever met," the boy said, surprising himself a little with the fervour in his voice. "He's the leader of the Mycelium, the underground rebels who are working to free the wildness that lives underneath the City still. But he came from the Country, years ago, he said. He came because he had terrible visions of the City destroying the Country that he couldn't ignore. He crossed the Great Salvian Desert and met the Greentwins there, who showed him the secret way in—" But Comfrey's heaving sobs stopped him. And he began to remember Thornton's own sorrow. The way every time he spoke of the Country, it looked like he was holding back tears. *It wouldn't be my feet that couldn't get me back here, child. It would be my heart.*

"What – what is it, Comfrey?" he asked, feeling his own throat tighten. An unexpected tenderness seared right through him. He wanted to comfort her, to hug her even, but didn't dare. He wasn't sure he'd even know how.

"The man you describe," Comfrey said between shuddering breaths, "the leader of the Mycelium, your Thornton. I think I know him as – as Thorne. It sounds too much like him to be a mistake! Could there be two men who left the Country for the City because of visions they had, with names so similar? It must be him, it must be my father!" And yet the words felt distant from her as they came out, only half-real. Could such a thing really be true?

Amber rushed to take the girl in her arms. She held Comfrey close and eight years of sorrow came pouring from her. Amber patted at her cheeks with a threadbare handkerchief, and crooned, and stroked her tangled hair. Tin watched and thought that it would take some practice to learn how to soothe a person like Amber could. In all his twelve years at the Cloister, nobody had ever taken a child up in their arms like that, to tell them they would be all right.

"My goodness," whispered Mallow to Myrtle. "I didn't know humans could create their own weather systems. It is quite extraordinary." He peered at Comfrey solemnly, twitching his nose.

"Well, wouldn't you feel just the same as a rain cloud opening, if someone came along and told you our own mother hare was alive and well, and waiting for us in the meadowgrass of our birth?" replied Myrtle. And for the first time in all her life, she felt the beginning of tears. But they did not come. Instead, she swallowed a few times and hastily ate a dandelion bud, to ease the strange discomfort in her chest.

"Your father..." breathed Tin, realizing now why Comfrey's face had looked so familiar to him the very first time he saw her. The unruly black braids, the pale green eyes and strong chin and otter-like grace. Only Comfrey was dark of skin too, which made her even more like an otter, dark from a life in the sun and dark from her mother, so that her pale green eyes were even more unnerving than Thornton's when they fixed you straight on. "Of course he is your father," Tin said to himself. "How did I not see it before?" There was such admiration in his voice that he blushed, embarrassed when he realized that Comfrey had heard him. But she smiled a wet smile at him, an upward tilt of her lips, and he felt in that moment that he'd never done such a good thing in all his life as bring Comfrey this news, and make her smile that way at him.

"Do you really think so, Tin? Tell me all about him, oh, do! I want to know everything, tell me everything he said. There is so much to piece together, so much to understand!" She reached into her pocket and clasped the golden spectacles tight, wishing that they could help her understand how all these threads connected. And her mother – she needed to tell her mother! Maxine, who had hoped for so long, against all hope.

"Sounds like a good conversation to have *while* we travel," interrupted Mallow, thumping his hind legs with impatience. "The sun grows high in the sky."

"There really isn't any time to lose," said Myrtle.

"I'm afraid the leverets are right," said Oro, rising to his feet, his face shiny with drying tears. "The Elk first, Alder village next, and we will keep our eyes and ears peeled for any word or wind of the Fiddleback or the Coyote-folk. Myrtle, Mallow, keep your ears to the bees. They will tell you what news we have to share."

Miss Limon, the master chef at The Holy Fool's Inn – a formidable-looking woman with only one thick leg like an alder trunk and very strong hands from all that exuberant dough-kneading – had prepared two delicious bundles of food for them. Sturdy oatcakes and smoked strips of salmon, hardy rolls and wedges of cheese, small apples, boiled eggs and little flatbreads made of seeds and honey. Amber packed their rucksacks full to the brim with the food bundles, and hitched on a flask full of piping hot tea for each of them, to be doubled as a water bottle. She tucked in extra flint, changes of socks, the clothing the children had arrived in – Comfrey's blue cape and green woollen dress, Tin's baggy trousers from Thornton, utterly mud-stained, now clean and pressed.

A parade of Fools followed Comfrey, Tin, Myrtle and Mallow down the wide old road that wound north from The Holy Fool's Inn for half a mile, singing and throwing calendula flowers into the air. They banged skin drums and played back-and-forth juggling games with lemons as they went. Gradually, the Fools peeled off back to their inn, kissing the children once on each cheek as they left, saying things like, *Be well and good luck, young Fools! Bless you, bless you.* Pieta turned scarlet when it was her turn to kiss Tin's cheek, and Comfrey hid a smile.

Amber and Oro came last, embracing the children and saying only, "Return, young Fools. Return to us."

The children stood up a little straighter, that they might be able to shoulder such a load, and strode on alone, the two leverets leaping and pausing to sniff and nibble at new shoots of grass along the way. None of them looked behind at the vanishing silhouettes of the trumpeting Fool's parade, for fear that they might, in looking back, lose their courage. For fear that they might not be able to continue forward, ever deeper into the land of the Wild Folk, towards the Elk of Milk and Gold.

12

THE BABA ITHÁ

They walked far that day, wending through the winter-orange branches of a willow valley before turning up a crooked footpath along the eastern flank of the Vision Mountains. It was a steep path through firs and sword ferns, little hazel shrubs and madrone saplings. Comfrey's pack felt very heavy. The feather and the thought of her mother weighed on her, but she had too many questions to ask Tin about her father to pay much attention to her aching shoulders or the dread that sat coiled in her belly. Once, as they climbed higher, she turned to look back. Far below, the willow valley looked like orange smoke, and she could see the faint ribbon of the road they'd followed from The Holy Fool's Inn. The willow valley became an estuary to the north, and then the thin needle of silver-blue water that was the Tamal Bay. Beyond it to the east were the steep golden hills, now tinged with the green of new grass that marked the edge of the Country.

Mallow and Myrtle took the opportunity, as the children stared wide-eyed at the view of the bay and the knuckled hills beyond it, to graze on the new soft leaves of the blackberry vines. They found the beauty in those tender, velveteen leaves infinitely superior to a view of blue bay and green hill, as lovely as it might be. After all, it couldn't be tasted, or touched, or munched between strong and leaf-biting teeth.

Comfrey sighed, pushing away the longing and concern that filled her at the sight of those Country hills, and continued to climb the footpath through the firs. *The Elk will know what to do. The Elk will help us all. The best thing I can do for my mother and for all of the Country is to carry this feather to the Elk,* she told herself. But it felt so heavy in her bag, and a voice in her head told her she would never make it, not a little Country girl; never could such a one survive an encounter with the Elk herself.

Tin lingered a moment longer, gazing out at the water. Seeing the undulating hills and valleys of Farallone from this vantage reminded him of gazing into the mirror in the Fool's Cabinet of Wonders and seeing himself there. It gave him new perspective, a fleeting sense of wholeness. He felt the cool weight of the penknife there in his pocket and wished that somehow he could use it to hold onto this beauty, so he could return to it again and again to understand it better. A wind came from the east across the bay, rushing up through the firs. Its scent was salty and resinous, cooling the sweat on his brow. Breathing in, Tin felt suddenly exuberant and fully, wildly, alive. He turned and ran after Comfrey, and the leverets bounded after him.

That night they made camp in a clearing at the top of the ridge. It was Tin's first night sleeping out under the stars, and so he hardly slept at all. He woke several times an hour to stare up from his bed of fir humus and wool blanket at that dizzy, speckled wheel of sky. The moon was close to full, and bright. There were so many stars they looked like the sun refracted on water. The lights along the City Wall had always dimmed the stars to a few. Tin had never seen even close to this many.

There was one constellation he found he liked especially, and kept looking for – the tiniest one of all, like a little leaf or a miniature soup-pan, made up of seven stars. He was bone weary, but those moving stars filled him up with a delight he had hardly ever known. He'd only ever watched stars from a window, not lain under them and felt as though they were a great tent, holding him, sweeping up all of his worries into their glinting hands. What was it like to be a tiny cluster of stars moving through the sky? Did they have any say in the matter, or was their spangled story wholly swept up in a greater one? And how was it that he had something of their matter in his own blood? How had the Elk made Farallone out of stargold? What star was it that had died, so long ago, and covered this land with its gold?

Eventually, towards first light, Tin fell into a deep sleep. He didn't wake until the sun was fully up, and only then because Mallow leaped onto his chest, sniffing the boy's nose and thumping at his ribs.

"Get up, you lazy rabbit!" exclaimed the leveret, making an old hare-joke about their softer, slower cousins. "Comfrey's already made a breakfast fire, and the tea's hot, and we'd better be on the hare-paths again before the dew is dry."

Mallow bounded off Tin's chest as the boy groaned and sat upright, rubbing his eyes and grimacing at the chill morning air and night-dew, which had made his wool blanket completely damp. He looked around at the small meadow where they'd slept: the twin nests Myrtle and Mallow had burrowed into the tall grass between the children's bedrolls; the way the fir trees, hung with lichen, moved their arms gently in the breeze. A blue jay landed in the top of one and began her raspy, scolding calls.

Tin heard the crackle of fire, and smelled it too, as the wind carried it towards him. He turned and for a moment saw Comfrey before she looked up from the small metal pot she was stirring, perched on stones in the fire. She had re-braided her hair, which had become full of fir bits and moss, pulled out of its confines in every direction from yesterday's climb. Her cheeks were flushed over the fire, her eyes bright. She crouched nimbly, feet wide and hips hanging between like a frog. She looked perfectly natural at a fireside, prodding embers, blowing at them, checking the pot. Tin felt envy at her competence and ease, an envy which masked his admiration.

"Nettle tea and acorn porridge!" she called, clanking a wooden spoon to the pot with a grin.

"How disgusting!" said Myrtle loudly from a patch of tender grass. "Mushy hot food. What could be worse? I'll never understand this concept."

Tin laughed, stretched, and joined Comfrey. He didn't say anything about the fire – how had she made it so quickly, and all alone? He didn't want her to think him an ignorant City boy, so he acted nonchalant, thanking her solemnly for the tea and porridge and apologizing that he had been asleep instead of helping her.

Comfrey had made the fire by friction alone, rising with excitement at first light to gather the sticks to do it with. She'd been hoping to show Tin something of her Country knowing, now that they were out here under the big sky and big firs, on their own. She could have just struck her flint, but she'd been trying to make herself feel competent that morning, strong enough and smart enough to make a journey such as this one, and was hoping to show Tin she could do clever things too, like him. Instead, he'd slept heavily, and of course she hadn't wanted him to figure out that she was showing off, so she made the tea and acorn porridge and pretended her own kind of nonchalance. In the tall grasses where they foraged, Myrtle and Mallow exchanged hare-laughter over the strange antics of humans, until they discovered a delicious patch of plantain, and lost interest once more.

When they broke camp and set out for the day, Myrtle and Mallow sniffed out what they deemed a "good path" with their swift-moving noses – a narrow, zigzagging deer-path that wove between robust green sword ferns and sudden stands of slim hazel trees just budding with tiny magenta flowers. Tin could hardly breathe for the wonder he felt at the size of these fir trees. They were wider than he was tall! Mushrooms grew everywhere through the duff at their feet. Comfrey gathered creamy white ones from a dead oak log for their dinner, showing Tin carefully how to identify them.

Small brown wrens sang sweet, elaborate songs in volumes that belied their size. Silver squirrels darted and scolded from the high fir branches, sometimes leaping to a nearby bay tree and making its limbs arch under their weight. Tin marvelled that they never fell.

"Do fir trees have Wild Folk?" Tin asked the leverets softly when they all paused by a small trickling creek to fill up their cups or, in the hares' case, dip their noses and tongues in for a sip.

"Course they do, like everything else," said Comfrey, matter of fact, sipping at her cup and taking a bite of one of the hard little apples Amber had packed for them. In truth, she didn't know a thing about the Wild Folk of fir trees, but she wanted Tin to think otherwise. She looked down at a puddle made by the creek, where a raft of ants was struggling, all clinging to tiny particles of hazel pollen to stay afloat. Something in Comfrey's chest hitched with tenderness, and she grabbed a flat leaf and scooped the ants out onto dry land. Tiny though they were, they seemed to shake themselves off like dogs, and pause to look up at her, antennae moving in a solemn thank-you bow. Comfrey gasped in wonder.

"Oh yes, they do indeed," Myrtle was saying to Tin as she groomed her face with two paws. Comfrey's exclamation interrupted her, and she looked up.

Tin had been watching Comfrey out of the corner of his eye. "If you go about saving every ant in a puddle along the way, we'll really never get there!"

Comfrey scowled at him. "If you were an ant, I wouldn't save *you*," she said.

"Ants are an honourable lot, you know," said Mallow. "Never a bad idea to do one a favour." He sniffed at the bark of a fir trunk, then tasted it thoughtfully as he turned back to Tin. "The creatures of the firwood are many, and shy. But they are all looked after by one Wild Folk called the Baba Ithá, the old lady of the firwood. There are others, her sisters, who look after the pinewoods, and the oakwoods too."

"She's not just a Wild Folk of the firs, you see," Myrtle elaborated, "but also the hazels, and the bays and maples, the squirrels and wrens and ants too. She tends to all of those who live in the fir forest. She is very secretive and very, very powerful. The Greentwins only ever met her once, and us, never!" She chewed experimentally at a fresh fir tip, then made a face.

"Good thing, too," said Mallow, going stiff and wide-eyed at the thought. "She has quite an appetite!"

"Fearsome, she is," added Myrtle. "Takes and gives life, just like the forest. Best not to cross her path, if one can help it. Come along now. All this talk is making me hungry, and the forage is rather bland in this endless shade!" She leaped onwards, but Comfrey could tell a shiver of fear had moved down the leveret's spine, and her bounding was an attempt to hide it.

A dead stick fell from the fir canopy far above, clattering down through the branches and landing nearby on the ground as a raven chortled and took off overhead. Tin started at the sound.

"How do you know it's all right we're in the fir forest, then?" he stammered. "I mean, what if this old lady of the firs doesn't like that we're passing through here? After all, Wild Folk hate humans!" The fir forest was darker than it had seemed a moment before, the birds quieter, the shapes of the trees more looming and more alive too, like they might pick up their roots and walk on giant feet.

"No, no," tutted Myrtle in a motherly voice. "This forest is so big, and we are only passing through a small part. We came this way dozens of times with the Greentwins, and never saw a trace of her. And Mallow and I, we would smell her way before we saw her, given she lives in a house of bones."

"Yes, and we'd hear her too, since the house walks on the giant legs of a spotted owl, and the Greentwins told us she's always humming a little song," added Mallow. "No, we're quite safe. Come on then, slowpokes!" And he was off, taking great leaps, as if to prove there was nothing to fear.

Comfrey and Tin exchanged a wide-eyed glance. Comfrey smiled, crooked, and shrugged, as if to say, *Well, what can we do here?* Tin gave her a *Yes, best carry on* smile, embarrassed to have appeared afraid, and they followed the leverets further and further down the trail through the firwood.

None of them knew that when the Baba Ithá's house walked, it walked with the utter silence of owls. Or that when she sang, she sang in the sounds of the forest – creaking tree limbs, winter wrens, woodpeckers.

Nor did they reckon that the Baba Ithá might come looking especially for them.

So as they sat eating their lunch in a damp clearing where bracken grew, they didn't hear a creaking hut made all of owl and vole bones come walking up behind them on feathered owl legs, the talons each as wide as the bases of fir trees. The hut came so quietly that not even the leverets could distinguish its approach from the sounds of the fir forest. It was Comfrey who first turned, her ears pricking, her neck hairs raising slightly, not with the animal knowing of hares, but with a kind of sixth sense, a human intuition.

"Ah, I see the girl has a furrier heart than the two of you leverets put together!" said the Baba Ithá as Comfrey's green eyes met her own black ones, small and long as a grey fox's.

Comfrey nearly choked on the bite of grainy bread and cheese in her mouth, and the leverets simultaneously leaped into the children's arms, trembling. Comfrey and

Tin struggled to their feet. Tin pulled his Oddness out of his back pocket and clutched it in his fist.

The Baba Ithá let out a big laugh that was equal parts fir-branch creaking and the screeching of owls. The sound made the whole bone house shake. Standing in the doorway, she herself was a very short woman, but wide as a fir trunk and as gnarled. Her hands holding her belly as she laughed were as ruckled and stumpy as burls of bark. Her hair was one long grey braid down her back, woven and strung with the vertebrae of salamanders. She was barefoot, and her feet were furred and long. Her ears were furred too, squirrel-small and silver. When she laughed she revealed a mouthful of teeth as sharp and numerous as a mole's. Her house of bones was round and flat-roofed, with a hollow leg-bone chimney that smoked and two windows like bright eyes. It cast a soft light of its own. A single spotted owl perched on the lip of the flat roof, eyes half-closed.

"Forgive us, Mother Ithá," gasped Myrtle in a tiny voice, trying to gather herself up regally in Comfrey's arms, but failing. She could hardly lift her long ears off her shoulders for terror. "We did not think—"

"No, indeed you did not," interrupted the Baba Ithá sharply. She hooted a low note and the owl legs of her hut lowered so that she could hop, toad-like, to the ground. "I always know when a new visitor sets foot into the woods that are mine to guard. The mycelia tell me, naturally."

Like Thornton, Tin thought, lowering his penknife and wrapping his arm around the quivering Mallow, whose claws were digging into his chest.

"It's very rude to brandish a weapon at a stranger, boy," snapped the Baba Ithá, taking a step closer. "Especially one of the Wild Folk. For that alone, I should feed you all to my hearth." Four sets of eyes widened in fear. "Well, how do you think my house walks, you foolish creatures, if he is not *fed?*" She pursed her wrinkled lips, narrowed her eyes. "You should be muttering prayers for a swift death, you two humans smelling of Country and of City, you who have trespassed your poisoned feet into my firwood, and left no Offering first."

"Baba Ithá," Comfrey said in the strongest voice she could muster, thinking fast. "It is not disrespect that kept us from leaving the Offering-bundle for you. I have left the Offering-bundle at the Alder village for my mother, and I know about the giving of gifts."

Watching her, Tin saw a flash of Thornton. It was the way her voice rang out with its own authority, how she stuck out her jaw as she spoke, how a little gleam of confidence danced in her eyes, behind the fear. Not for the first time he felt, mixed with his admiration, a pang of jealousy that she should have such a father.

Comfrey took a deep breath and continued. "It's only,

we are ignorant human-people, and we did not know you were here. Nor are hares in the habit of leaving Offerings. So you see," she finished, swallowing mid-word at the dry, frightened taste in her mouth, "it was an honest mistake."

"Yes, quite honest," chimed Tin. "Just say the word, and we will offer whatever you want." Mallow thumped the boy's chest in warning as he spoke, but it was already too late. The Baba Ithá was laughing again.

"Very prettily said, children, yes, fine words indeed. Offerings, yes, well, it's rather too late for all that now." She raised a woolly eyebrow, pulled a long elderwood pipe from the pocket in the front of her dress, scratched her nail to a rock to light it, and began to puff away at a rank-smelling mixture.

"What do you mean, too late?" ventured Tin.

"Well, for one, an Offering is only an Offering when it's not requested. What kind of gift is a gift that has been demanded?" The Baba Ithá took another long puff. "For two, dear boy, you've just offered me *anything* I desire, and I do love nothing more than a good game."

Mallow groaned into Tin's chest. The sun went behind a cloud and the light through the fir boughs shifted.

"But—" Comfrey stammered, a flush rising up her cheeks. "We don't have time for games!" Was it wise to mention the Fire Hawk's feather and the Elk of Milk and Gold to this terrifying woman?

"No time, you say? Well in that case…" said the Baba Ithá, scratching her chin in mock thoughtfulness. She had a few white whiskers there, like a goat. "It'll be hare stew to begin with, a great vat. Throw in some yerba buena leaves to season it, yes, how delectable! And then, well, I can't quite decide if I'd rather have two strong young children, bones and all, to feed to my hearth – you would keep the hut fed for a moon apiece! – or if I'd prefer to keep you, perhaps change you to two handsome robins, to speak with the worms for me. They can be such trying, slippery things to carry on a conversation with."

Panic flooded down the children's spines.

"Why?" Tin blurted, his fear suddenly replaced by anger. He thought of all the things they had yet to do, and all the people he wanted to see again – Seb, Thornton, Anders, Beatrix. "You're the Wild Folk of the fir forest! You watch over trees. But trees don't eat hares and children. They are gentle, and quiet. What gives you the right—?"

Comfrey grabbed his wrist and stepped on his foot to stop him from making things even worse.

"Forgive us, Baba Ithá," she gasped. "He is from the City, and doesn't understand the respect due your kind. We will play your game, please! Let us play it, let us at least try! We have time! There's always time for a game." She tried to smile, but her mouth quivered.

"Good sense, girl," barked the Baba Ithá. "I might have

lost my temper, and eaten you all right here, no soups or fires about it. As for your *question*." She spat the word out like a bad seed in Tin's direction. "Trees feed as much on the decay of the world, passed through the bodies of worms and mushrooms and beetles and tinier things, as they do on sunlight. They of course eat sun first of all, and also each breath you exhale, but their roots need the nourishment of the ancient bodies of the moles and salamanders, robins, owls and foxes that have become part of the dirt. It is a continuum, my boy, life to death to life again, and you, I'm afraid, are part of it. I sow just as many seeds, and caress just as many newborn squirrels, as I reap, and kill." She chuckled, coming near and pinching Tin's cheek, hard. Her breath smelled of forest humus and rotten roots. Tin tried not to lurch back, but he went pale at her touch. "So now, let's begin our game!" With that, she hooted out a final laugh, and gestured for them to follow her and the walking bone house up a hill, towards a clearing beyond the forest.

For a moment, the children couldn't move. They were stone, watching with timorous awe as the Baba Ithá and her creaking hut ambled up through the trees. Comfrey and Tin looked at each other.

"Should we try to run?" breathed Tin.

"Don't be an idiot!" hissed Mallow. "*Run?* The whole forest is her family. Just because you don't see any other

267

Wild Folk doesn't mean they aren't here, watching and waiting. At her command, they would surround us!"

Comfrey exhaled. "Come on then," she said to Tin and the leverets. Together they hurried up the hill after the Baba Ithá.

"There will be three tasks," the Baba Ithá said once they had all arrived. She climbed back up to her stoop and waved the spotted owl down to her broad shoulder. The owl mussed at her braid affectionately. She beamed like a child at the word "tasks", rubbing her hands together. "If you complete each of them in one day, I shall let you pass through the remainder of my woods, and with three blessings too. If you should fail, well, you know how that will go!"

"But...three whole days?" stammered Comfrey, thinking of the Brothers from the City and how far they might get in that time. Oro had seen that the Brothers would not infiltrate the villages themselves until the wild irises bloomed. Another couple of weeks then, at best. But how long would it take her and Tin to reach Tamal Point, where the Elk lived among the Grizzly-witches, and return again? Panic made her voice high. "We have to get all the way to the Grizzly-witches, and find the Elk of Milk and Gold, and – don't you know our whole existence might be destroyed by the Brothers who are coming from the City? Don't you know they might kill Farallone itself?" She couldn't help the whole truth from spilling out now. Tears were close to the surface. "Do you even care?"

"Dare you question my wisdom?" hissed the Baba Ithá. A terrible fury turned her face stony. "Dare you question how I care for the firwoods that I am guardian of? You forget that you are human, and these troubles were made by your kind. Why should *I* trust *you*? Why should the fate of Wild Folk rest in hands such as yours? Filthy, traitorous hands, your human hands. Hadn't I better see that they are worthy? Hadn't you better prove to me you are better off alive than in my oven? I'm not so foolish as to take your word for it." Her piercing tone silenced Comfrey completely. Myrtle had gone stiff in the girl's arms.

"Now, task number one," the Baba Ithá said in a lighter voice, seeing that she had made an impression. "See that pile of dirt halfway up the meadow hill, by that lichen-covered rock?"

Comfrey and Tin peered up the hill and nodded, mute, their shoulders touching for reassurance. Big clouds shaded and then revealed the sun, making the hill ripple and move. It was flushed orange with newly opened poppies. In the middle was a dark heap.

"That's only half dirt. The other half of it is the little black seeds of our darling poppy. By morning, I want to see two piles. One of poppy seed, one of soil, and not a grain amiss!"

"But that's impossible!" Tin protested. "How could anyone—?"

"Not my concern!" the Baba Ithá snapped, and with that, her whole round house of bones leaped once on its feathered owl legs and glided away above the fir-tops, all with no more sound than moving boughs make.

13.

POPPY SEEDS, PEARLS AND
GRANITE SHOES

For the first hour, Comfrey and Tin sat on the hill and tediously picked poppy seeds from handfuls of dirt. They tried not to curse when the seeds and dirt got stuck on their fingers. Myrtle and Mallow could do little to help, having no fingers, and so lay belly down in the grass, in the position of hares who have seen a hawk above and don't know where to run. *What a terrible mistake it was to come this way!* they whispered to each other in the language of hares. *How could we have been so foolish?* Their ears were flat down their backs with both remorse and terror, and they tried not to tremble.

A wind came and blew the two-centimetre-high pile of dirt all over the two-centimetre-high pile of poppy seeds the children had managed to make.

Tin jumped up in a rage, kicking at the hillside. "This is impossible!" he yelled, his face scarlet. The wind picked up his blond curls and threw them across his forehead. "How do we know she hasn't just set us an impossible task, to *make* us fail?"

"Wild Folk don't work like that," said Myrtle. "A game is a game, a bargain a bargain."

"Except Coyote-folk, of course," said Mallow. "All bets are off with them…"

"There must be a secret way," Comfrey said in her calmest tone, though she didn't feel calm at all. "A trick to all of this."

"Yes," ventured Mallow, "there's often a trick…"

"I've never tricked a poppy seed, only a bobcat," replied Myrtle. She inched nearer to sniff at the piles.

An ant ran across Comfrey's hand, and she shook it off. Another appeared. She remembered that little raft in the puddle, and how she'd scooped all those ants to dry land. She smiled despite everything, glad she'd done that one kind thing in the firwood before this, before taking Myrtle and Mallow right to the soup pot of the Baba Ithá.

When she looked at her hand once more, a whole trail of ants was marching across it. Mallow, behind her, sneezed and shook his nose, which was covered with ants making their way down to his paws, all heading right for the pile of poppy seeds and dirt.

"This is hopeless," Tin groaned. "Why don't we just make a run for it?" He looked over at Comfrey, who sat a few paces away and was now peering intently at the ground, grinning. "What are you so happy about?" he snapped. "Have you gone nuts? Have you lost it?" He went red again with exasperation. "Great, the adventures of Tin and Loony. Wonderful."

"Be quiet and come see this, Tin!" Comfrey whispered.

Myrtle and Mallow were pressed to her sides, watching too. Before their eyes the ants had begun to carry the poppy seeds, one by one, to a separate pile, leaving the dirt behind. They were so small and moved so delicately that they didn't disturb a single grain below their feet.

"You clearly made an impression on them, Comfrey!" exclaimed Myrtle, sniffing tenderly at the ribbon of black ants that now stretched past Tin, wide as a finger.

Tin's mouth hung open as he watched the dexterous way the ants each carried a poppy seed above their heads in ordered columns. "I'll never make fun of anyone for saving an ant again!" he said as he crouched next to Comfrey. "They've called all their ant friends to help return the favour you did them!"

Soon the whole pile was covered in ants. The children and the hares watched the ants work all through the long hours of the day, murmuring little words of praise and thanks until the moon set some time in the middle of the night. By then, the two mounds had each grown thirty centimetres tall. Huddled close, they all fell asleep in the grass with the wool blankets from their packs pulled up to their chins.

When the first rays of dawn touched them, the Baba Ithá's owl-legged house came stalking back up from the forest edge. Without a sound, it crouched low to the ground right beside them and the old lady hopped down on her broad, furred feet. She came towards the sleepers, clicking her sharp teeth together hungrily. When she saw the two immaculate piles, one of poppy seeds, the other of soil grains, her eyes flashed yellow and she hissed. She leaned close to the mounds, sniffing. Just then a wind picked up, blowing several pieces of dirt back onto the pile of seeds. The leverets both leaped up from their slumber at the sound of the Baba Ithá's low chuckle of pleasure. Their ears quivered.

A slow smile had spread across the old woman's lined face. It was not a comforting sight, the way her skin puckered and creased as the smile became a snarl. With a quick movement, she snatched both Myrtle and Mallow by the ears with one hand. The leverets, white-eyed, kicked out their hind legs furiously, trying to scratch at her arms and wrest themselves free.

"Mallow!" yelled Tin, startled awake by their cries.

Comfrey leaped up beside him and they both jumped

towards the old woman to snatch the leverets from her grasp. But she was nimble, darting back, laughing terribly, her breath a stench of death. Her smell so close was too much for the leverets to bear; it enveloped them, and they went limp.

"It was a handsome attempt," she growled, gesturing at the piles. "But I'm afraid the wind was not in your favour." She pinched the dirt-smudged poppy seeds between the gnarled fingers of her free hand and put them on her tongue. "Yes indeed, it looks like it's soup for me and worms for you!" She held up the trembling leverets, grinning and licking her lips.

"That's not fair!" cried Comfrey. Hadn't they all watched the ants sort the piles out with immaculate precision? "They were perfect when we went to sleep! How are we supposed to know you didn't sprinkle that dirt on the poppy seeds when we weren't looking?" She couldn't bear to see the leverets hanging from their ears that way, let alone the thought of becoming a robin for ever – or worse, being fed to the wood stove! – and of never seeing her mother or her father again. Her father, who was alive! Her stomach seized with fear, and she fought the urge to take Tin's hand.

"The piles were perfect!" Tin said, doing his best to glare. He didn't want to appear the coward but it was very hard to stare down such a woman as the Baba Ithá, whose eyes contained all the force of roots and bones. "The ants came from all around and helped us! Isn't it worth something, that because of Comfrey, a hundred thousand little ants came to our rescue?"

The Baba Ithá hissed again. The sound made the leverets start and kick their legs in a renewed attempt to escape. But the old woman's grasp was tight. Suspicious, she narrowed her eyes. "Ants, you say? Ants came to do this work for you?" She leaned closer to the children, studying their faces as if she was examining mushrooms after a rain, recording every mark. "Ants don't lie," she murmured to herself. Her ancient face softened ever so briefly, but then she looked down at the leverets squirming in her grasp and scoffed. "I won't stand for trickery!" she rumbled in a voice so low it sounded as if it was coming from deep within the earth itself.

Tin felt his legs going limp, and took Comfrey's hand to steady himself. She squeezed his hand tightly.

"From now on, you must complete the tasks without the help of your leveret friends!" the Baba Ithá growled. "I will keep them with me, in my house, in a cage. One wrong move and the soup pot is only a step away!" She let out a hoarse shriek, the sound of an owl on the hunt, and with it the smell of old bones.

Myrtle and Mallow keened with fear.

"Please, you're going to frighten them to death! Let

them go!" Comfrey started to beg but quickly realized the Baba Ithá wasn't the kind to respond to weakness, and changed her tone. "How can we be sure you won't just eat them right away?" she demanded. "How can we trust you?"

"*Trust me?* Don't try my goodwill, girl. Trust *me?* Do you know who it is that I am?" Her voice had gone deep and loud, like a storm through ancient trees. "Do you know, child, what I have seen? The question is not whether you should trust me, but why on earth *I* should trust *you*. Must I repeat myself? What have you human people done to earn *my* trust?"A note of such absolute sorrow came through the old woman's words that both Comfrey and Tin almost fell to their knees with the weight of it. There were ancient, slaughtered trees in her voice, cut down and dragged up by the root, so many of them that they were like a graveyard of splintered bones. There were spotted owl mothers whose eggs had fallen to the earth with cut tree limbs, and mole children whose tunnels had been filled with poisons.

Comfrey bowed her head in grief against these visions, and said, very softly, "I am sorry, Mother Ithá. We will trust you. We will do as you ask." She felt tears coming, and battled them down. "I am sorry, leverets," she whispered, and though Myrtle was trembling in the Baba Ithá's hand, she fixed the girl with a look of such trust that Comfrey began to cry after all. Then, with silent horror, the children watched as the old woman carried the leverets up into the darkness of her bone house. Comfrey's hand found Tin's and they clung to each other, the dread in the air between them so palpable that neither dared to speak. Tin fought the desire to run after the Baba Ithá, to wrench the leverets free, to attempt an escape. But he knew it was futile. The old woman *was* the forest. With her eye on them, there was nowhere to hide. Beside him, Comfrey wiped back tears and tried to put her fear somewhere small and far away. It would not serve her or the leverets. But then the Baba Ithá emerged from her bone house again, her ancient face unreadable, her great braid thumping against her back, and beckoned for the children to follow her. Fear leaped back out of the small, faraway place Comfrey had attempted to put it, and there was nothing to do but follow. The Baba Ithá led them up to the crest of the hill, where the land became tangled with coffeeberry and toyon, hazel and oak, and then fir again. The forest was very thick there, shaded and damp. A deep, fern-shaped moss surrounded the trunks and cushioned much of the ground. The Baba Ithá bent down and fished a small pearl, luminous as a moon, from the moss.

"Once, very long ago, I had a suitor," she said in a quiet voice. "A Seal-man who came to visit me at the edge of Tamal Bay. I was silly then, careless and young. I left only the owl to tend the firwood for hours at a time. I was in love, you see…" The Baba Ithá sighed, and Tin, astonished by the tough old woman's sudden softness, tried not to gape. "He gave me a long necklace I could wrap six times around my neck. It was made of three hundred tiny pearls from the wild oysters of Tamal Bay, which he had gathered one by one with teeth and tongue. I wore them for hundreds of years, long after the Seal-man was gone, until one day they caught on a fir branch, and the string broke, and three hundred pearls fell into the moss." She held the pearl up to the light. "If you'd like to see those leverets alive again, gather every last one for me by sunup tomorrow." Her voice was hard and full of the clicking of owl beaks. With that, she dropped the pearl back into the moss and left, a great whirl of bones.

The children crouched against the damp earth all day, elbows to the ground, sifting through soil and moss for pearls. They only exchanged the briefest of words. The thought of the leverets restrained in a cage of bones in the Baba Ithá's house made them both too sick to speak. Dread sat in their chests, on their shoulders, filling them each with tears they knew they didn't dare shed, not yet, not while there was still a little hope. But as the sun moved across the sky, and the light grew long and golden through the firs, their hope and their resolve thinned. They had only found nineteen pearls, several of them scattered much further across the dense forest floor than they had imagined. At last Comfrey could bear the dread in her chest no longer, and she ripped at the moss in frustration.

"What have we done, coming here?" she shouted, leaping to her feet and kicking at sticks, at the trunk of an old tree. Tears flooded down her face. "Oh, Tin, we've lost them! The poor leverets, we've lost them for good! That terrible old woman is probably building up the fire for the soup already! And us! We'll never get to the Elk of Milk and Gold in time. Everything will be lost." She collapsed against a fir tree and sank to the ground, her arms clenched tight to her body.

"Comfrey," Tin said, alarmed to see her so completely undone. "Comfrey, please, don't cry." If she gave in to despair now, there would be no hope for either of them. He put his hand on her shoulder, but he'd never tried to soothe a girl before and he wasn't sure if he should pat, or hold, or shake her. He tried to remember what Amber had done.

She wrenched away from his hand and refused to meet his eyes. Through her tears, she wanted to say venomous things about the City, and how he didn't even have a mother or a beloved Country to lose, how he couldn't possibly understand, but she managed to hold the words in and slow her breathing.

"Comfrey," he tried again, in a quieter tone. But still she kept her face turned away. He tucked his hand into his pocket, embarrassed. He was only trying to help. And maybe she was right anyway. The sun was going down. What hope had they, once night fell? Suddenly something bright flashed on the ground between them. "What are these?" Tin said, reaching down to pick up a delicate pair of spectacles.

Comfrey saw them and flushed. "Don't you dare touch those!" she snapped, grabbing her Oddness and holding it close.

Tin backed away, affronted. "What's so special about them?" he shot back. Comfrey didn't answer, but when he looked at her he saw that her face had brightened. The spectacles rested in her palm and she was gazing at them with a look of such amazement and relief that her eyes were again full of tears.

"They are my Oddness," she murmured, her voice wholly changed. There was a smile in it.

"Spectacles?" he whispered. He felt as though she had gifted him a great and secret trust, though he wasn't sure if Oddnesses were really secrets at all. "What can you see with them?"

"Of course! That's it!" She threw her arms around his neck in a quick, fierce embrace, which he was too startled to return.

"That's...what?" he asked, confused.

"I can only use them three times," Comfrey went on,

barely hearing him. "Any more, and I'll go blind. Though that's hardly important at the moment. What Amber told me is that they make the world light up with its true patterns. They bring out its smallest details and show them as they really are, each thing hitched to the next, all part of big and small designs, as if connected by spider strings." She held the spectacles up to her nose. The glass sparked with rainbow spots as the last of the sun went down beyond the ocean.

"Oh," Tin managed, eyes wide. It sounded extraordinary, and complicated, and she spoke almost feverishly, as if this was something she had seen before. The spectacles were delicate and beautiful, with rims of lustrous gold, and the glass contained a glow all of its own. They suited Comfrey, he thought – practical, yes, but striking, and a bit strange too. What story had she seen in the mirror that had brought them to her? "But – when you put them on," he reasoned aloud, suddenly worried, "won't you see a million of these patterns at once? I mean, we're in a forest! There must be a thousand things going on everywhere every instant. How do you know what pattern you're going to see? How will you sift out the pearls from all that?"

Comfrey frowned, thinking. "There must be a trick to it. A kind of focusing, or what would the use be?" She looked around for a moment, studying the lacework of the moss, the darkening fir needles, the flight of a flock of wood pigeons against the dusk. Her nose turned down ever so slightly as she pursed her lips in concentration. "Maybe, if I hold in my mind's eye the pattern of the pearls, and the fact that they were once a necklace, if I just repeat to myself again and again the image of a pearl necklace, it might reveal itself." She sighed. "Well, there's nothing to do but try. We haven't got another plan."

Their eyes met, desperately bright, and Tin nodded. Comfrey swallowed once, stood up, patted at her hair to gather herself, squeezed her eyes shut, and set the spectacles on her nose.

"Hold my hand for balance," she said to Tin, and he obeyed quickly. She opened her eyes. Night had fallen dark blue across the forest, but now, through the spectacles, it was stitched with light. The fir boughs were haloed and criss-crossed with the memories of robin feet and chickadee wings darting over and under them. Through the moss, Comfrey saw the paw prints of a mountain lion who had passed through the night before, and on top of that the path of a newt who'd waded through the moss to get to a creek. Inside the newt's trail she saw, for an instant, a dizzying map of the winter creeks of his ancestors. The more she looked, the more layers of spider silk-connection she saw around her, each strand holding the story and shape of a different forest creature. Those layers pulsed a little in their glowing and called up a yearning in her, the same one she had felt at the sight of the Fire Hawk's feather.

"Oh no," she groaned, dizzy. Tin had been right. She felt like she was swimming. She could hardly see through all of the glintings and pathways woven around her, dazzling and unbearably beautiful. She tried to take a step anyway, and reeled, falling to her hands and knees.

"What? What do you see?" Tin was crouched at her side, trying to steady her.

But Comfrey only shook her head, too dizzy to speak. She was unable to find him with her eyes. She kept looking up at the fir canopy as he said her name, until Tin, as gently as he could manage, so as not to scare her, put his hand to her chin and turned her face to him.

"A mountain lion, a pregnant one, she walked there…" Comfrey murmured, her voice trailing off.

"Comfrey, I'm here. Comfrey, remember what you said. Think about the pearls, think really hard. Think about a strand of them all belonging to each other," Tin whispered in encouragement, trying to keep the despair from his voice. In this state, they were worse off than before!

Comfrey leaned her chin into his hand, exhausted. "I can't," she moaned. "I can hardly move. It's like seeing when you've never seen before, too much all at once. I can't…"

"Nobody else can do it for you," said Tin, putting on his

firm, brave tone – the one he'd used when he and Seb were escaping the Cloister, when he was sure a dozen times they wouldn't make it, but had had to pretend otherwise. Taking a careful breath, he turned his face up to the treetops. Framed between the branches, he saw that tiny constellation of seven stars he'd watched two nights before. It gleamed delicately, that minute soup pot, that drifting leaf. Its small beauty made him sad, and also stronger. He didn't want the leverets to die. He didn't want to be fed to a wood stove. Worst of all, he didn't want this beautiful, wild land and its terrifying but beautiful Wild Folk to fall into the hands of the City. He wanted to look up and find that small constellation every night until he was a very old man. "Close your eyes, Comfrey," he heard himself saying in a soothing voice. "Hold one of the pearls in your pocket, and try to make your whole mind a pearl."

Comfrey reached out a flailing hand and Tin guided it awkwardly to her pocket.

"Okay," she said softly. "Okay. Just…Tin? Steady me, will you?"

He pressed his hand firmly against her shoulder, and she closed her eyes to focus. She imagined a string of pearls, each gathered in the teeth of a seal. She tried to picture the Baba Ithá in love, crooning to the hundreds of pearls strung around her neck. She felt the bead in her pocket and thought of each pearl, rocked by the ocean inside an oyster, the tides rocked by the moon. She kept her eyes closed tight until all of this was so alive in her imagination that she could taste salt in her mouth. Then she opened them, and gasped.

The moon had risen. A delicate strand of moonlight spiralled and zigzagged through the moss, glowing here and there with a pearl-sized light. Holding Tin's arm, Comfrey stood with slow, careful movements, then began to walk, keeping only the pearls in her mind. One by one, she gathered them up from along that string of light. Tin turned his jacket into a bowl, and she placed each one gingerly inside.

It took all night to find those three hundred pearls scattered far and near across the forest floor. More than once, the pull of other threads overwhelmed Comfrey's sight, and she had to sit among the bracken, her back to a tree and her eyes closed, until she could hold the story of the pearl necklace in her mind without faltering. Tin kept by her side. He counted the pearls aloud, describing each one, until she could see the moon-bright pathway between them once more.

By dawn, they were both so tired they could barely stand. Comfrey was bone-worn beyond any weariness she had ever known. When she at last took the spectacles off, a streak of dizzy pain split through her temples, and she had to cradle her head to keep from being sick. Tin held the coat full of pearls so tight his hands were numb.

With the first streak of sunrise, the Baba Ithá appeared. The children were huddled against a tree, trying to keep one another awake. Tin, seeing the old woman, carried the pearls to her at once and placed the heavy coat in her arms. The tiny beads sighed against one another, iridescent. The Baba Ithá bent over them and breathed in. Her eyes filled with tears, and though she hissed just as an owl does, she was pleased.

"Oh my lovelies," she said to the pearls. "It has been so long." She ran her gnarled fingers through them, crooning. Then she tipped them all into the pockets of her skirt. They made a sound like water as she poured.

"You better not have eaten the leverets," Tin said, seeing through a kind of daze that he and Comfrey had won another day for their friends He had no energy for pleasantries.

The Baba Ithá made a snapping noise, the threatening click of a beak. "Do you doubt me?"

"No, ma'am, no indeed." Tin bowed his head and avoided her eyes, regretting his words.

"They are alive. That is all you need know," the old woman snarled. "Is the girl ill?" She gestured towards Comfrey, who had not raised her head.

"Only tired," Comfrey managed in a hoarse voice.

Tin rushed back to her side, understanding without words that Comfrey did not want to tell the Baba Ithá about her spectacles, nor let on how weak they had made her. He lifted her up by the forearms, and she leaned heavily against him.

With a sharp grunt of assent, and no further questions, the Baba Ithá gestured them onwards, beyond the mossy part of the forest to a place where the trees grew further apart, and a wide trail passed through, opening into a sunny patch shaded on the far side by a madrone tree. To the left of the trail where it opened into sunlight was a small grassy knoll ringed with brush and an outcrop of granite.

"Those two tasks, they were child's play, horse fodder, compared to the final one," said the Baba Ithá, ruffling at her skirts and her braid as an owl does its feathers. "The whole ridge of the Vision Mountains is made of ancient granite, a hard and formidable stone. I want you to fashion two walking shoes – clogs, boots, whatever you fancy – from this stone. Granite walking shoes, for human feet, are a delicate and precise affair. Nearly impossible to make, I daresay. Now, hop to!" The old woman let out a deep, wheezing giggle at the pun she'd made. She pulled a yerba santa leaf from a patch growing in the shade, chewed it thoughtfully for a moment, and was gone, her skirts swinging, heavy with all the clicking pearls in her pockets.

"*Shoes?*" said Tin, incredulous. He slid to the ground with his back to the rock.

Comfrey was already leaning there. She groaned, then sank onto all fours. The world was still reeling round her, and her head split with pain. Each movement ripped through her in a tide of aching nausea. "I-I'm useless..." she managed in a small voice. "I can't move any more." She slumped onto her side and curled up on the ground.

"Comfrey!" Tin grabbed at her wrist to feel her pulse. He had seen the Cloister physician do such a thing before, when a boy had collapsed in the Alchemics Workshop from the effects of mercury fumes. Her heartbeat was quick and fluttering. He rummaged in their packs for water and tried to pour some between her lips, but it only dribbled out of the sides of her mouth again. Frantic, he wet part of his coat and laid the cool cloth over her forehead.

"Oh, Mallow, oh, Myrtle!" he whispered to himself. "What will I do without your help? You would know something to give her now, some bit of plant for her to chew." He looked around the knoll and the forest edge but the plants were all unfamiliar to him. He hadn't been paying attention before, when Myrtle ran off for a sprig of yerba buena, or Mallow came back chomping at hedgenettle.

Comfrey stirred a little under the damp cloth, and Tin

managed to coax a few drops of water into her mouth. He leaned back against the stone. This time, his despair was complete. Without the leverets or Comfrey, he was utterly at sea in this place. He was a City boy. The granite stones, the clearing full of grass, the forest edges; they made him feel small now, small and useless, without the words or the wits or the knowledge of anything that might orient him.

"Oh, Mallow," he whispered again. "If only you were here." He missed the leveret's plucky courage, his quick mind.

Well, Mr No Plan, we've managed the impossible before, he could imagine the leveret saying. This made him smile. Then, almost absently, he felt the warm weight of the penknife against his thigh. His own Oddness. It wasn't quite as mystical as Comfrey's spectacles, just a little folding tool. He took it out of his pocket to admire its metal lines, its neat little blade and strange unfolding parts. Each tool had a metaphoric use as well as a literal one, Oro had said. The screwdriver, for screwing hope to courage. Why hadn't he thought of that last night, with Comfrey? He shook his head. Oro had also said something about a penknife being able to carve a story too. What had he meant? Tin thought hard. Obviously, cutting stone with that tiny knife blade was not metaphoric – it was just impossible. The blade would break in a matter of seconds. But how could his Oddness, that granite rock, and his knack for stories ever produce a pair of shoes? It was preposterous.

He turned to face the rock where he leaned and thought for a moment. Comfrey was breathing more evenly but had her cape pulled up over her head now, to block out the light. She knew so much more about these matters than he did, but he couldn't bring himself to disturb her. She had pushed herself beyond the edge of her strength last night, braving her Oddness. He didn't want her to risk anything worse. It was his turn to be daring, to try something that seemed impossible.

"I can at least start by experimenting," he told himself, pulling out the knife. He cleared his throat and tried brandishing the blade, looking at the rock, imagining shoes. But the spark inside of him that always energized his creativity when he was making something was nowhere to be found. All he felt was silly, and afraid. What was he supposed to do now? A raven croaked conversationally in a nearby tree, and a jay cackled.

An Offering. First, you have to give it an Offering. Was that Mallow's voice inside his head, or Comfrey's?

Of course! He looked round, afraid that some creature would walk forward from the forest to berate or punish him. But only the raven remained, croaking now and then. An Offering, that was somewhere to start. Only he'd never left an Offering before. He'd watched Comfrey do it when they stopped to camp, placing a little bit of their dinner at the edge of the wood. But they were almost out of food, and besides, he didn't think a stone would be interested in a piece of stale bread. Perhaps a story would make a good Offering? Perhaps with a story he could coax a pair of shoes from granite? He clutched the penknife, and tried not to laugh at himself. He sighed and shook his head.

"Ridiculous," he murmured. "What a stupid idea, telling a stone a story to turn it into a shoe!" Still, talking to the rock was better than doing nothing. It was a start.

"Ahem. Ah, hello. I'm Tin and, well, I, along with my companions – two of whom are hares, and in very great danger – need your help." He stopped abruptly. *Offerings first. Don't just demand what you want. Offer*, the voice said again. This time it sounded rather like the Baba Ithá. He shuddered. "I have a story for you, old lord granite stone," he went on. "I'm not sure if you like stories, but I do, and since you've probably been here a million years or even more, I thought, you know, it might be nice to hear one…"

Tin wasn't used to telling a story to a rock, so he couldn't think of anything to say at first except to start with their own story – him and Mallow, and then how they'd met Comfrey and Myrtle, all the way up to the Baba Ithá herself. That took the better part of the morning, but the rock appeared no different than before – no hint of a change of shape, no small door opening, revealing shoes inside. So he kept going. He was getting hoarse by this time, but he had warmed up into that familiar storytelling trance. He had stopped worrying that he was wasting his time. He had decided that he'd rather die telling a story than weeping with despair. If he just kept talking, he could keep the fear away.

At one point, Comfrey murmured something, but her words were impossible to understand. She managed to reach a weak hand out from under her coat, and took hold of his ankle. Perhaps to anchor herself, perhaps to encourage him. He put his free hand over hers, and was glad she couldn't see his sudden blush. Her fingers were cold under his. Stammering, he launched headlong into a proper tale, a magical one, a story and not just a recounting of the days' events. *This* was his Offering, he thought as he began, but he told it as much to Comfrey as he did to the stone, though he didn't know how much she understood, being fevered and half-asleep. Even so, he told the story for her. Tomorrow, they might be kindling for the Baba Ithá's stove, or turned into robins, like she had threatened. Today he would weave the most wondrous tale he could imagine.

It was an elaborate story of three sisters who stole an apple from the apple tree of a king, and were swallowed into the ground where a dragon with three heads dwelled. Many young men tried to save them, but only one young man with a pair of granite shoes, which could sink deep down into the earth, could actually do it. In the story Tin told, the young man was a shoemaker of magical abilities, who could make a shoe out of anything – out of rain, or poppy flowers, or snake bones, or clouds. Granite was no big deal. The dragon was the bigger challenge, not the making of shoes.

"I came from the hot mouth of a dragon, you know," said a rough, deep voice as Tin was just getting to the part where the young man in his granite shoes finds the three sisters underground. Tin started so violently that he cut his finger on the knife's fine blade, which he'd been brandishing as he spoke. "Very hot down there," came the voice again. "Yes, oh yes it is, down in the centre of the earth. It's quite magma-tongued. Long time I spent there, being made. Just so, just so… Though I'm hardly a lady, no indeed." This was followed by a wry chuckle.

Tin looked frantically around for that lilting, stone-rasped voice. He looked more closely at the granite rock, then gasped. Sitting there was a man no bigger than Tin's two hands, dressed in neat trousers and a coat, all so precisely the colour and texture of the granite that the man looked at first like nothing more than an odd rocky extrusion.

"Oh!" Tin exhaled, amazed. "Are…are you a Wild Folk?"

The little granite man laughed. It was the sound of

stones grinding. "I suppose you could say so, after a fashion, though I have never before had cause to take this form. I haven't spoken so many words together in the last hundred million years, you know, but it seems that in this shape – well, my tongue flaps like a cricket's legs! I can't seem to stop it!"

Tin managed a shaky smile, his heart beating fast.

"That was the first story I've ever been told," continued the little man with some excitement, scrambling up to the top of the granite rock. "Very obliging of you! Perhaps you human folk do have some redeeming qualities after all."

"I-I can finish the story for you, if you like," offered Tin. He glanced up at the sun. It was low, the light long in the sky. So far the story of the dragon had taken him two hours to tell. He'd put his whole heart into it. He'd added details about the colours and shapes and small beauties of things he thought Comfrey would like, which he never normally did. Now, though, he regretted how long he had taken, worried about the waning light. There were perhaps three hours of it left in the day.

"In truth, my lad, I may positively expire from an overload of verbiage," said the little granite man. "No offence intended, of course, but one must get introduced to so many words slowly, so as not to have a stomach upset. So, no, thank you all the same, much as I enjoyed it. And anyhow conclusions have never much concerned me."

The little man peered at the penknife in Tin's hands. "What *is* that thing you hold; that thing you've been waving about all these hours as the words poured from your mouth like magma?"

"It's, well, a tool, for cutting and carving and undoing and also for making, um, metaphors. That is, in the real world, I mean…" Tin trailed off, clearing his throat, not sure how to explain.

"May I?" said the little man, reaching out a hand.

"It's very precious to me," said Tin. "Meaning no disrespect, sir, but how can I know you won't take it into your stone for ever?"

The little granite man climbed down to a place on the rock where he was eye level with the seated Tin. "It sounded to me, underneath your words, like you wanted a pair of those granite shoes, and rather badly." The man's eyes glinted, mica-black. "I'm a respectable fellow, young boy. A stone never lies. I only wish to give a gift in return for that story of yours which pulled this small human form right out of me, one I've never inhabited before. Very spry, these legs, these hands!" He gave an experimental jig, grinning. "Now, give me that. I understand a thing or two about making things. I think I may just be able to help."

Tin's eyes pricked with a relief and a joy so sweet he almost wept. Slowly, gingerly, he laid the penknife in the little man's hands. Open, the knife was half as tall as he, but the weight hardly fazed him. Being made of granite, he was very strong. He began to chip away at his own rock, singing merrily. Tin stared on, wide-eyed. The blade sparked and sang against the granite, but did not break. Bits of stone flew in every direction. Before Tin's eyes, the little man carved a granite clog with astonishing speed and precision.

"Voila!" he said at last. "Remarkable blade this, made of equal parts metal and human dream. Try it on!" He held up the shoe, which was as big as his whole body.

Tin gently lifted the shoe in his hands. It was elegant, tapered at the tip, and quite heavy. It fitted his foot perfectly, rooted him to the earth as heavy as a tree. "Extraordinary," he whispered. "Extraordinary!"

"Yes, well," said the little man with a toothy grin. "Now you must make the other. I'll show you."

As the sunset gathered above them, Tin and the little granite man bowed over the stone. Sparks flew from the hot cutting of that small knife blade. Comfrey stirred once, opening her eyes cautiously in the dusk light. But the sight of Tin glowing by some strange light from within the granite stone, and the little man who watched merrily over Tin's shoulder, were so strange, her head still so thick with pain, that she moaned and buried herself under her cape once more.

And thus, as starlight fell, Tin learned how to softly coax a shoe from a stone. He learned how to chip and carve tenderly, holding the thing he wanted to make in his mind light as a bird, letting his hand and the stone dance.

"Dance, dance!" the little granite man exclaimed again and again.

Tin cut his fingers several times on the blade. The blood got on the rock, and the little man stared at it, fascinated.

"You have fire in you too, I see. Magma." He touched the fallen drops like they were red gems from the heart of the earth, and smiled at Tin in a fatherly way that made the boy's heart ache.

When the Baba Ithá returned the next morning on the soft owl legs of her bone hut, she found Comfrey and Tin asleep side by side, curled against the granite rock, their coat and cape tucked round them along with their wool blankets. The ashy remains of a campfire made a ring beside them. Tin cradled two stone shoes in his arms, and a small granite man sat perched on top of the stone, looking down at them with more affection than the Baba Ithá had ever seen a rock muster.

With a long, solemn nod to the stone man, and a soft word to the bones of their cage, she released the leverets. They leaped out of the hut and made straight for Comfrey and Tin on shaking legs, and burrowed under their coats.

The children would never know it, but when the Baba Ithá saw them all tucked together, and the stone shoes complete, her face for a brief moment was suffused with the sweet brightness of poppies. She smiled, a warm grandmother's smile, a smile of relief and admiration. For like a fir tree, the Baba Ithá ate sunlight just as much as she ate the old, decayed lives that rested inside the soil. As guardian of the fir forest, she was as life-giving as she was dangerous. And in that moment, gazing down upon them, she was as gentle as the dawn.

14.

THREE GIFTS

When Comfrey and Tin woke from a deep and heavy slumber full of dreams of stone shoes and glowing spider threads, they found themselves no longer tucked against the granite rock with the small stone man looking on, but wrapped in blankets of bobcat skin by a hearty wood-stove fire. The smell of some sweet and smoky meat filled their nostrils, frying in an iron pan. Myrtle and Mallow stood over them, stiff-legged, watching the door with wary eyes.

"Mallow!" cried Tin.

"Myrtle!" cried Comfrey, at precisely the same moment.

The leverets permitted their ears to be stroked enthusiastically, and Myrtle even endured a kiss on the top of her head from Comfrey. But when pressed about the two long days and nights they had spent caged in this very house, the young hares refused to speak more than a few words.

"It is in the past now," said Myrtle. The solemnness in her voice was the only hint she betrayed of the numb panic she and her brother had endured for those two endless, black days.

"Hares do not dwell on what has passed," said Mallow.

"It is, after all, not unusual to have more than one run-in with death before breakfast, if you're a hare," added Myrtle. "This one was just a bit more prolonged than usual." She busied herself nibbling a bit of grass off Comfrey's cape, and the girl knew better than to press her.

"We won't lose you again," she whispered, stroking the leveret's long back.

The Baba Ithá came through the arched bone door then, pushing aside the deerskin that hung there. Her hands were full of wild onions and small quail's eggs.

"I hope we aren't part of the breakfast feast after all!" muttered Mallow, backing into Tin, his long legs quaking.

"What do you take me for, young leverets?" crooned the Baba Ithá in her most gentle, rasping tones. "I wouldn't *dream* of eating you! Not any longer, that is." She laughed then, sounding more like her old self. "Not today, anyway, no indeed. Thought I'd see you all off with a hearty breakfast, given that you've completed the three tasks to my satisfaction."

Comfrey looked at Tin, both of their faces still bleary and lined with that uncannily deep sleep. She thought of the pearls, how together they had gathered every last one. She thought of the terrible reeling pain in her head, how it had turned the whole world to spots of light and dark. How long had she lain useless, battling it? Had she really seen Tin lit by the glowing light of the granite stone, helped by a little stone man? Or were those visions only dreams? She had been so ill. The only thing she remembered with certainty was Tin's voice, weaving steadily at an elaborate and beautiful tale, which she recalled now only as flashes of silver and gold. She searched the boy's face. Smiling, he pointed silently to the stone shoes beside the wood stove, speckled black and gold with minerals and smooth as milk. Comfrey gasped with delight and for a long moment they beamed at one another.

"How did you do it, Tin?" she breathed at last.

Tin, still smiling, slipped the penknife out to show her. "My Oddness," he replied, and pride moved through him swift and bright as morning. "Would you like to hold it?" he added, suddenly shy. He looked older, Comfrey thought, his smile sweeter than she had remembered, and she hesitated before replying.

"A little help, please," the Baba Ithá interrupted sharply, hiding her amusement. "If you would kindly chop these and quit your grinning, young man, I'd be very

302

grateful." She handed Tin several wild onions, dirt still clinging to their roots, which he took hastily, trying not to go red. Comfrey almost giggled. "And not with that thing," the Baba Ithá added, gesturing at Tin's Oddness. She passed him a knife with an antler handle instead. "And you, my dear," turning to Comfrey, "be so good as to stir the venison sausages, would you?" She pointed to the meat sizzling on the wood stove, then set another pot full of quail's eggs and water next to it.

Soon the whole hut smelled of wild onions. The little eggs were perfectly boiled. Two heaping plates were placed in Tin and Comfrey's hands, to be eaten by the fire. The Baba Ithá ate nothing, only drank a cup of smoky black tea, same as she offered the children. It was creamy with milk. For the leverets she had strewn fresh-cut oatgrass and willow-tips across the floor. They refused to leave the children's laps, and had to be fed by hand.

The bone hut was little more than a round room with a wood stove, one big wooden table, and a pile of skins in the far corner where, the children presumed, the Baba Ithá slept. The ridged bone walls were hung with drying herbs, tied here and there and everywhere to the protruding scapula and spinal cords and vertebrae. Several barn swallows' nests clung in muddy piles to the ceiling. It felt more like a cave to Comfrey than a house, the way her own cob home had been a house, warm and bright and cosy.

Despite the rich and delicious flavours of the venison, the wild onions browned in deer fat, the delicate taste of quail's eggs, and the relief she felt – that the leverets were alive, and that she and Tin would not, after all, be fed to the wood stove or turned into robins – Comfrey couldn't really enjoy her breakfast. She felt uneasy still. She wanted to be out in the air, in the meadows and firwood and dirt roads, on their way. There was so far to go! And they still had no plan, no idea how they would ever be able to approach the Elk of Milk and Gold and survive.

"Well, I'm surprised you've yet to ask about your rewards. I had thought human people were rather greedier than the two of you!" the Baba Ithá exclaimed, pausing to lick venison oil from her fingers. "It is quite becoming of you."

"Our…rewards?" said Comfrey. She had forgotten all about that long-ago mention of blessings in exchange for the tasks.

"Yes, yes," said the Baba Ithá. She began to unwind the string of pearls from round her neck. "I always keep my word, like I said, as any tree would. You doubted me?" The old woman narrowed her eyes at Comfrey, who blushed and set her plate down with a clatter, not knowing what to say. Myrtle, despite her own fear, stood up on her hind legs in the girl's defence, raising her ears as tall as she could manage.

"Of course she did not doubt you, firwood mother," said the leveret in noble tones. "Only she is tired and had forgotten, as humans often do."

Tin hid a smile at the leveret's cheekiness.

"What are you grinning about, boy?" snapped the Baba Ithá. The pearls were coiled like a slim glinting snake around her hand, a dozen loops at least.

The smile faded from Tin's face and he too blushed, finding he had no ready retort, which made his cheeks colour further. Mallow, following the example of his sister, began to protest on the boy's behalf, but the Baba Ithá cut him off before the leveret could do more than grunt.

"Enough!" she barked. "I am thoroughly unused to the strange etiquette of humans, and those unfortunate leverets who must be in their company." The old woman's gentle breakfast countenance had changed to a fiercer shade. "I am used to being straightforward, and I am tiring quite quickly of the role of hostess. Listen – the poppy seeds, the pearls, the stone shoes, they are yours. The tasks are their own gifts."

"But the pearls," stammered Comfrey without thinking. "They were a gift to you, from the Seal-man, a lover's gift…" She trailed off at the spark in the Baba Ithá's small bright eyes, not certain if it was amusement or tenderness or rage. That story had touched Comfrey, and now her mother and father rose up in her mind. She wondered if

Maxine had a secret strand of agates or carnelians somewhere in a drawer, hidden away so as not to think of Thornton, but nevertheless treasured, so as not to forget him. Comfrey had only ever seen the spoon her father had carved from redwood – *The first gift he ever gave me*, Maxine had whispered to Comfrey when the girl was six, and she'd asked her mother why she always kissed its handle before she dipped it into the acorn porridge. The hint of a love story in the Baba Ithá's pearls made Comfrey sad, and she wondered if it was right to take a gift that had been a lover's token to someone else.

To the children's surprise, the Baba Ithá smiled a very gentle, very old smile. It made even Myrtle and Mallow relax.

"Now that is very thoughtful of you, child. Very sweet indeed. I might have missed them before, but now I am certain you will guard them as well as I. It is a very old love, by now, one hundred years gone. So it's as much your story as mine. And anyhow, you've yet to hear the great usefulness these three gifts will provide you," she said before pausing, dramatically, "in your journey to retrieve the Elk of Milk and Gold."

Tin and Comfrey exchanged an awestruck look, leaning in towards one another and the Baba Ithá, feeling their hearts lift.

"The oil from the poppy seeds has the power of sleep,"

continued the Baba Ithá. She reached into the deep sturdy pocket of her brown skirt and pulled out an ancient purple vial. "A little smear under the nose or on the temples, and voila, sleep! Swallow a spoonful and you will get a doubly deep heavy sleep. As for the pearls, they are the milk of the bay, you see. They have the milk of the tidal moon in their hearts. For the Elk of Milk and Gold, whose fur is the very same colour as pearls, whose violet eyes hold that same lustre, and who made the moonlight itself, they are the tastiest delicacy, like perfect berries, like tiny sweet candies. And you will need a very, very *precious* Offering in order to convince the Elk to trust you at all. I'd say it's lucky you stumbled upon me, wouldn't you?" The Baba Ithá chuckled and fed another log to the fire. It was engulfed at once in orange-blue flames.

Comfrey and Tin could only nod, swallowing, trying to keep their astonishment from bubbling out in a rush of nonsense, which they both wagered wouldn't impress the Baba Ithá very much at all.

"What about my granite shoes?" ventured Tin softly, breaking the happy silence. He felt a pride similar to that which he felt for the Fiddleback rising in him. "I mean… that is—" He trailed off, feeling foolish for presuming they might be his own.

"They are indeed a third gift," replied the Baba Ithá. Her voice was resonant now. "And without them you will never be able to get anywhere near the Grizzly-witches alive. On your normal human feet they'd be on your trail in a matter of moments. Let alone the Elk of Milk and Gold, for she can feel human footsteps through the ground in her strong golden hoofs, and she will be away the second she senses you near. For what cause has she to trust you, at first, any more than I did? But if you were each to be shod with one foot in stone, she would mistake you for the grumbling of granite underground. The whole tip of the peninsula, Tamal Point, where the Elk and her herd run, is granite, stem to stern."

For a long moment, the fire cracked and popped. A golden-crowned sparrow sang outside, followed by the chortle of crows and the more distant rush of creek, filling the silence inside the Baba Ithá's bone house.

"How did you know?" whispered Comfrey at last. "How could the tasks make just the gifts we would need?" The girl peered closely at the Baba Ithá, confounded by the old woman's mix of dark ferocity and this generosity, these perfect gifts.

The Baba Ithá only chuckled and sighed, spreading her warped hands in a shrug. "One should never know the answers to all of their questions," she said. "But suffice it to say, sometimes the gift is made by the task and the way that task is carried out. Perhaps I had nothing to do with it at all. Perhaps, in completing each task, you made what you needed, and I am only telling it back to you now. Perhaps if a different four – not Comfrey and Tin and Myrtle and Mallow – had sifted poppy seeds and gathered pearls and made shoes of stone, their uses would be entirely different. Isn't it said, that the medicine you seek is already within you? And didn't I say, someone had to make sure you were up for the job?" The Baba Ithá looked down her nose at them, as if over a pair of spectacles.

"You seem to know so much about the forest, the land, all of its ways," blurted Tin, thinking suddenly, wildly, of his Fiddleback and the Coyote-folk. He ignored the stomach-thump he received from Mallow. "Maybe you can tell us where my Fiddleback is! And if it is safe?"

"That's no proper thank you," growled the Baba Ithá. The whole hut seemed to darken, and Tin wanted to kick himself. Her neck, though hunched and heavy with hair, bristled. "Out of my house! I'm sick of the smell of you, human and soft. Too many questions! I do not like questions!"

The old woman stood and made to yank the bobcat skins out from under the children. They leaped to their feet and stumbled towards the door, grasping for their packs, which hung there on twin antler-hooks. The leverets darted between their legs, knocking ears and paws at the children's ankles, for the Baba Ithá's face suddenly looked very much like a hawk's, hooked and bright with hunger. Myrtle and Mallow jumped from the porch to the ground, despite the distance created by those raised spotted-owl legs. Tin and Comfrey followed as the Baba Ithá chased them to the door. The children's feet smarted with their hard landing.

"Don't forget these!" came the Baba Ithá's voice from the doorstep. The owl legs lowered so that the bone house was level with the ground, and the old woman placed the purple vial of poppy oil, the long strand of pearls and the granite clogs on top of a freshly dug molehill. Then, with a nod of her head that was brusque and sharp, the hut lifted up again, took two large owl-legged steps, and was gone through an opening in the firs.

Though the children couldn't see it, the Baba Ithá peered back once at them through the thick trunks with a look of sorrow, but did not look back again. Already her mind turned to other things. It turned to the slower, deeper whisperings of the firwood and all of its woven lives – mushroom, doe, newt, fir sapling, young fern.

In particular, her attention was caught by a peculiar new spider who had moved into a crevice in an old fir log, a small fiddleback who seemed to have walked a great distance carrying a heavy, golden sac of eggs on her back.

15.

THE GRIZZLY-WITCHES

Had the children and the leverets followed the main
old road, which they could have picked up again
down the far side of the Vision Mountains, it would have
taken them four days of steady walking to reach the tip
of Olima. But the leverets insisted that they continue on
deer paths and rabbit runs to stay out of sight. And so the
journey took seven days zigzagging through coyotebrush
and coffeeberry and cow parsnip; through scrubbrush and
forests of alder and maple along creeks; on old cow trails
across low grassy hills; down huckleberry and hazel-lined
trails on the eastern slopes of the peninsula near the bay;
and hugging that bay shore itself, with its soft lapping
water and little sandy coves.

The children and leverets came upon no Wild Folk at

all until the third day. Before that, they saw only brush rabbits (with whom the leverets exchanged haughty foot-thumpings and nose-sniffings); tiny chorus frogs; orange-bellied newts crossing the path for the creek; a bobcat walking down the path away from them at dusk (Comfrey gasped with delight, thinking for a moment it was the Bobcat-girl); too many deer peering up through tall grass at them to count; the early monarch butterflies; a hundred jays and ruby-crowned kinglets; juncos and spotted towhees calling from the bushes.

The Wild Folk they encountered on the third day were only the gentle Bombus Folk, small velveteen people not much larger than the little granite man, who flew around on bumblebee wings and tended to the ground-nesting bumblebee hives and the flowers they pollinated: bearberry and huckleberry flowers like white bells, the calypso orchids getting ready to bloom in the fir duff.

Comfrey and Tin were startled by the Bombus Folk's kindness. They'd assumed that every last Wild Folk would automatically hate them, but the Bombus Folk seemed to have little capacity for hate. Instead, they begged that the children each sing them a song. They loved nothing more than a song, given that the bumblebees themselves often had to hum and sing against the bell-shaped flowers in order to shake that hidden pollen free. Both Tin and Comfrey blushed in turn, fumbling to remember the words and embarrassed to be made to sing in front of one another. Tin sang the morning hymn from the Cloister because it was the only tune he knew, disliking it more than ever with its words of progress and conquest and cogs-in-wheels, while Comfrey sang the Offering Song in a sweet, surprisingly clear and deep voice, like lake water. The Bombus Folk were thrilled – *Like birds, like birds with such sweet voices!* they exclaimed over and over. They pressed pollen-bundles the size and shape of teacakes into the children's hands, following the four of them for some way across an open hillside, singing their own strange, humming songs.

Besides this encounter, the children and the leverets didn't cross paths with any other Wild Folk, nor any large mammals, such as the mountain lions which Tin kept asking Comfrey and the leverets about in tones of fascination that masked a streak of fear. Comfrey wasted no time telling Tin everything she knew about mountain lions – their hunting habits, their social habits, how to tell them apart from bobcats at a distance. (*It's terribly obvious*, she explained, *because mountain lions are so much bigger and have very long black-tipped tails, but as a City Folk, you never know what you might mistake for a mountain lion!*). She told him the story from Black Oak, the village over the hill from north of Alder, about the man named Ben Catseye, called thus because his left eye was blinded by a mountain lion when he came between her and her two spotted cubs. She told him how they'd probably already been seen by at least one mountain lion – and maybe even the one whose paw prints she'd spotted through the moonlight moss while wearing the spectacles.

A sort of traveller's rhythm emerged in those days of walking. At dawn, when the sky changed colour and began to lighten at the edges, Comfrey gathered sticks and lit the fire. Tin, a little bit shy, asked her to teach him on the second morning, and so for the next two they did it together – Comfrey demonstrating how to layer the sticks just so, and coax the hottest flame, Tin watching earnestly, and fumbling a bit with his first try, mostly because he was nervous to have Comfrey looking on with that little amused smile and the gleam in her eyes.

"It was my father's flint," she said on the fourth morning, allowing Tin to strike it on his own. He'd made the whole Fiddleback, and the granite shoes; lighting a fire was hardly a challenge in comparison, and yet it took a delicate, patient precision that surprised him. And to make a spark this way! It was nothing like the Cloister's coal burners, and it never ceased to make him laugh with delight. "He taught me when I was very small. Before he went away." There was an edge of bitterness in her voice, and she realized for the first time that part of her was angry at her father for choosing the City, and his visions, over her and her mother. Hearing about him from Tin, his life underground with the Mycelium pursuing his noble cause, had clarified the anger which had smouldered in her since she was small. It was selfish, she knew, but all the same she was angry with him for never once sending word to them, for never coming home. Tin understood something of that anger in her voice.

"He saw something like what you saw in the feather, Comfrey," he said, trying to make her feel better. "He did it to protect you; to protect us all." His voice swelled with admiration, and Comfrey felt her anger turn to guilt and sadness. After all, she had run off and left her mother alone now too, just as he had done.

"Well," she snapped. But she didn't finish her thought, because she was finding it hard not to cry, and turned back to the fire instead to blow it to life.

That night, as Comfrey lay on her bedroll in the cold February air, huddled close to the fire, what she had seen in the Fire Hawk's feather when she first picked it up came back to her very clearly, smouldering on her closed eyelids. Had her father too seen the Country on fire, and the Wild Folk bleeding gold across the earth? Had he too seen the hordes of armoured men descending upon their wounded bodies? She remembered Salix's words. How the Elk was the centre of the wheel of the basket of Comfrey's fate, the Elk whose milk made the stars, the Creatrix of Farallone itself. What would happen when she gave the Elk the Fire Hawk's feather? Comfrey sat up with a jolt. Her hands and feet felt cold with dread. She slept at last, but fitfully.

On the morning of the seventh day, they reached the beginning of Tamal Point. It was marked, the leverets explained, by an ancient cattle grid across the old road and the sudden narrowing of the land into a long-tipped peninsula, with ocean on one side and bay on the other. The sky darkened quickly as they passed over the grate, and a chill came in on the wind. Fat raindrops began to fall. Comfrey loosed her blue cape from its bundle at the bottom of her pack and flung it on. Tin did the same with his patchwork coat. The leverets shook themselves, making their own fur more water repellent.

"At least the rain will dampen our smell and sound from the Grizzly-witches," said Mallow, doing all he could to remain cheerful in the face of the task before them. "Quite a bit more difficult to smell specifics in the rain. It just brings up the smell of everything more vividly. But of course that also means it's hard to distinguish the scent trail of a Grizzly-witch from this morning, or three days past." Mallow lowered his nose and whiskers to the earth and sniffed intently at the grass and a few protruding granite stones.

"You mean, you can smell Grizzly-witches already, right here?" said Comfrey, feeling a little sick.

She and Tin had discussed a hundred different plans backwards and forwards about how they would get the Grizzly-witches to eat the poppy oil, but they didn't know very much about the Grizzly-witches to begin with, and Myrtle and Mallow could only provide a few scraps of description and story that they'd learned from the Greentwins. Now, with a cold, wet wind picking up from the ocean, and Tamal Point stretching before them, windswept and sparse, the Grizzly-witches seemed as big as the very slopes and knolls around them. By comparison, Comfrey and Tin felt woefully small and unprepared.

"Why yes," answered Mallow after a few more moments' sniffing. "Naturally. We have reached their territory, and that of the elk whom they tend. What concerns me most is that I fear the prints I smell are quite fresh, not an hour old. But it's impossible to be certain in the rain. Myrtle, what do you think?"

"Only an hour old?" exclaimed Tin. He fumbled at the buttons on his pack, his hands already growing stiff from the cold, reaching to pull out his granite clog.

"Oh yes, at most!" replied Myrtle after a long moment.

"Why didn't we assume they'd be out and roaming? Of course they are!" muttered Comfrey. "What did we think they did all day?" She looked at Myrtle.

317

"Don't look at *me*," retorted the leveret. "We could hardly follow the hundred strands of your outlandish plans! How could we have helped? All we ever told you, true now as it ever was, is that the Grizzly-witches always gather at dusk in the big ruined milk barn of the ancient ranch called Pierce, and share stew, and root tea, and the stories they found as they hunted and foraged throughout the day."

"Yes, but how far is that barn from here?" exclaimed Comfrey, wiping rain from her cheeks and chin with a cold hand.

"No idea," said Mallow cheerfully.

"So," interjected Tin, impatient. "We put the shoes on *now*, one each, and lock arms so it's like we're one creature. Then the Grizzly-witches will hear us as rumbling granite, slow like the earth, not people."

After a moment's consideration, the girl nodded agreement. She pulled the other stone shoe from her pack.

"This is it," she whispered, hooking her arm through Tin's, elbows locked. "You two lead the way!" She nodded to the leverets. "I can hardly believe we're doing this: walking headlong into the barn of the Grizzly-witches!"

"Not quite *headlong*, I hope!" exclaimed Mallow.

"I say we leave the vial on the doorstep, like a gift," offered Mallow as they began to move slowly through the windy rain. "For Grizzly-witches are part bear after all, and bears love gifts, especially sweet delicate ones. And that bottle is just the colour of a berry."

"But isn't that suspicious?" said Tin, wishing he had a hat. His curls were heavy, dripping water repeatedly into his eyes. "I mean, why wouldn't they be wary and wonder if it's poison? No, I like the idea of putting it in the stew, or the lanterns."

"But how will we get in, Tin, without them knowing?" said Comfrey, stopping to pull her cloak further over her head.

"No stopping now!" shouted Mallow. "This infernal rain is getting in my ears, and if you two dilly-dally for too long, the cold will set in. I say we use our instincts, stop thinking so much. Imagine being a bear. What would fool you?" The leverets bounded off deeper into the rainy scrubbrush prairie, weaving between the budding lupines, then doubling back to the children's heels.

Comfrey and Tin fell into a rhythm of stone-footed walking, trying to sync up their legs and feet so that their gaits were fluid and matching. Comfrey had put the granite clog on her left foot, and Tin on his right, so that their impact on the earth was balanced. They didn't speak more than a few words, following the leverets quietly and carefully, hoping the thud and swish of the stone shoes was enough to fool the Grizzly-witches, at least for the time being.

After half an hour's steady tromping through the thickening rain and wind, Tin exclaimed that he could taste salt from the ocean in that wind. Comfrey said, "Why do we need to make the Grizzly-witches fall asleep at all? With these shoes on, why can't we just sneak past and find the Elk, offer her these pearls, give her the feather, and be done with it?"

"Oh no," said Mallow. "It doesn't matter what shoes you're wearing. If any of the elk of Tamal Point are disturbed in any way, the Grizzly-witches know. Only the deepest of deep sleeps will keep them from coming straight to us. Their ears and hearts are so deeply attuned to the elk herd. They know each time something out of the usual order occurs."

"Besides," added Myrtle, "you're convincing only so long as you're just passing through, like migrating birds. Not stopping to talk to the Elk of Milk and Gold herself!"

"Shh," hissed Mallow suddenly, stopping stiff with ears raised and tail quivering. "Look."

On the crest of the next hill, so far away that at first she looked like just another rock, was a Grizzly-witch. Everything about her was grizzly-bear-like – her shaggy gold-silver body, the hump of her shoulders, her short tail. Only she had hands and feet in the place of paws, even though she walked on all fours. And her face was an older woman's, beginning just past the ears. It was furred but flat and delicate and human; no long muzzle, no dark wet nose. Her teeth, however, were still a bear's, plentiful and sharp. She was digging with long fingernails for wild parsnip roots, and hadn't noticed the children or the leverets. She hummed as she did so. The sound didn't carry to the children's ears, but it did to the leverets', who shivered. Comfrey and Tin looked at each other in alarm. In the rain, the Grizzly-witch's silhouette looked entirely bear, and a massive one at that.

"I don't think we can fool such a being," whispered Comfrey, her voice shaking slightly with fear and awe and cold.

"But at least the shoes seem to work," Myrtle whispered back, nudging Tin with her nose. The boy blushed with pride. "Without them, that Grizzly-witch would have been upon you already. They aren't fond of humans. And that's putting it mildly. As for hares, we're a dime a dozen, and clearly she's got an appetite for roots this afternoon."

"Mallow," hissed Tin suddenly, with a wild look in his eyes. "Can you outrun a Grizzly-witch?"

The leveret regarded the boy through the rain with a look that was equal parts horror and pride.

"Why – yes, I suppose. That is, if I got a little head start, I think so. I think I could," replied the leveret, puffing up his chest.

"Mallow, you're nuts!" said Myrtle. "Tin – no. Whatever you're thinking – no."

"But just listen to my plan," said the boy, holding up a hand. "There's no way we're going to slip some oil under her nose. She's probably digging those roots to bring back for the evening stew."

"Perhaps," sniffed Myrtle.

Indeed, even from such a distance, it was clear that the Grizzly-witch was placing roots into a basket, not right in her mouth.

"So, Mallow, if you go dashing past and tempt her out of sight, Comfrey and I can run over, pour some of the oil onto the rest of the roots in her basket, then hide. Then, once she's given up chasing you – because of course you're too fast for her! – we can follow her back, at a safe distance that is, and see if they eat the roots for dinner! Then, under the cover of night, we'll find the Elk of Milk and Gold, show her the feather, and ask for her help. Simple!"

Myrtle rolled her eyes and Comfrey swallowed hard, thinking of all the things that could go wrong with this plan. But Mallow's pride had been stirred up. He wanted to prove just how fast and darting and clever a leveret he could be. In fact, he was quivering with excitement at the thought. Myrtle sniffed at her twin.

"I can do it," said Mallow. "It's as good a plan as any, and this Grizzly-witch here is providing us the perfect chance."

He glanced at his sister. "Oh come on," he cajoled. "Two's better than one – much more confusing!"

Myrtle feigned disinterest, cleaning at her paws, which were muddy and damp. But even Comfrey was looking at her now in expectation. "All right, all right!" the hare said. "We *are* quick as a flash, you know…"

It was true. When the leverets burst at once from a lupine bush not ten metres from the oblivious Grizzly-witch, they moved so quickly and suddenly in the rain that they looked like lightning flashes, golden and fast. The Grizzly-witch dropped the roots from her fingers in surprise, left her basket, and lunged after the hares, for no bear can resist a hare when it's so close at hand. She skidded with her bulk in the mud, but was gone in an instant down the hill in pursuit.

Meanwhile, Tin and Comfrey crouched behind the same lupine bush, trying not to pant with fear at the nearness of that bear-woman and her rooty bear-musk smell. Clearly, the granite shoes worked. They'd been able to creep so close to the Grizzly-witch that they could see the rise and fall of her chest as she calmly dug and gathered, dug and gathered, murmuring loving words to each root. But the children were also very careful to keep low and out of sight, for it was better not to take any chances.

The moment the Grizzly-witch bounded out of sight, thrilled by the chasing of hares, but thoroughly confounded by their criss-crossing, zigzagging movements, Tin and Comfrey moved in as fast as they could to the place where the Grizzly-witch had been digging. Several thick, green wild parsnip stalks were scattered across the ground. Comfrey fumbled the cork out of the purple glass bottle and with a shaking hand dripped a few drops onto the roots lying there in the basket. The rain had lessened to a mist, but still she hoped the water wouldn't wash the oil away. Then, just in time, they shuffled back in the stone shoes behind a distant bush, to watch.

The Grizzly-witch had given up on the chase rather quickly. She was an older bear, and at their best bears aren't endurance runners. Her hands and feet were covered in mud. She shook her shaggy head. Tin and Comfrey stared. It was uncanny to see that furred human face in the body of a bear, and those fingered hands and feet with human toes padding the ground like paws. She was breathing heavily through her nose. When she reached her basket full of parsnip roots, she paused for a long moment, sniffing at the ground, at her basket, at the roots. Comfrey grabbed Tin's hand in alarm and they both held their breath.

But after all, the oil only smelled of poppies, and there were many clumps of them nearby, their seeds having dropped and grown for thousands of generations in that dirt. And the strange sharp smell of granite? Well, thought the Grizzly-witch, perhaps her nose was getting old too. She sighed and began to gather the fallen roots into her basket. Annoyed at the energy she'd wasted tearing after those silly young hares, she began her ambling way back home for the evening feast, muttering to herself. She looked back once over her shoulder, feeling something strange, some sense of eyes on her shoulders, but she saw only a kestrel, his tail tacking through the lessening rain as he flew past her and towards the pine trees where she too was headed.

When the Grizzly-witch was almost out of sight, Tin and Comfrey stood, letting out a sigh of relief. The leverets burst from a nearby lupine bush to join them, making Comfrey almost shriek with surprise. Tin clapped his hand over her mouth and stifled the noise.

"That was amazing!" the boy whispered. "Faster than anything I've ever seen!"

"Yeah, you should have seen her face!" chimed Comfrey. "She was so exhausted, she could hardly catch her breath!"

Mallow puffed his chest out for a second time, and Myrtle kicked him playfully. "No time to waste!" she said, grooming at her whiskers, trying to hide her own pride. "It won't matter how fast we were if the Grizzly-witch doesn't share those roots with all of her sisters! C'mon, we can hide outside the barn until dark."

They walked quietly along the wet trail created by the

Grizzly-witch, grateful for the lessening rain. They prayed that she wouldn't eat a root and fall fast asleep in the middle of a hillside before she reached the barn-den of her sisters.

But she didn't. She carried the roots all the way back to a wind-battered, peeling white barn beyond the row of pines where, half an hour earlier, the kestrel had settled to roost. Through a narrow barn door the children briefly glimpsed a flare of warm firelight and smelled a waft of delicious stew, simmering away.

They settled in to wait beyond the pines for an hour longer, until the sun was all the way down. As the first stars came out and the windows of the barn began to glow from the fire within, first the leverets, then Tin and Comfrey, crept up to a series of cracks and holes in the sides of the barn and peered inside. The wooden floors inside the Grizzly-witch's old hay barn were strewn with animal skins of all varieties – elk, bobcat, rabbit, fox. The gnarled roots of myriad plants hung from the rafters, drying. One whole wall was full of shelves and drawers, each labelled with the name of a different root medicine or berry jam.

When Comfrey and Tin looked more closely through the crack between the boards, they saw that each lantern was in fact the skull of an elk calf with a beeswax candle glowing from its eye sockets. In the middle of the room, a Grizzly-witch, with many silver streaks in her fur, stirred a pot. She did not rise up on her back legs to do this, just reached out with a furred hand, which presented such a strange union of human fingers and bear's body that the sight made Tin dizzy. The Grizzly-witch they'd followed back from the wild parsnip patch came forward with her roots and dropped them one by one into the stewpot.

Inside the barn, the boiling soup released the hint of bitter poppy oil into the air, and several of the Grizzly-witches – there were nineteen in all – sniffed suspiciously, then shrugged. Poppies did, after all, grow everywhere across the hills.

"Tell us about the bones you read today," said the Grizzly-witch who stirred the pot to one of her sisters, the one grooming at her fur with a delicate bird-bone comb. She lounged with several other Grizzly-witches, some of whom were grooming each other, but the one addressed combed only herself, and her eyes were milky. Comfrey almost gasped aloud when the bear seemed to look up and right at the place in the wall where she was crouched, peering.

"She's blind," said Mallow in the smallest voice he could muster.

"I smell hare," said the blind Grizzly-witch suddenly, not answering her sister's question. The leverets stiffened.

"Yes, Amurra, there's hare in the stew," came the reply. Myrtle moaned.

"No, living ones, young ones – leverets," replied Amurra, setting down her comb.

"Must be Sorr," said the Grizzly-witch at the pot. "She caught several this morning, the smell is on her hands still. Come, tell us what you read. The signs have been so unclear to us of late." There was a tone of impatience in her voice, and in the postures of the other Grizzly-witches – several of whom were passing round elk-skull bowls – as if they were used to Amurra's rambling ways.

Amurra sighed and shifted her weight, letting go of this conviction about leverets. "The reading, yes…" she said, trailing off again. "Perhaps I spoke of hares because I do not like to speak of what I read in the elk bones today." She paused once more and smoothed at her fingernails. The barn had grown very still. The Grizzly-witch at the stewpot held the steaming ladle in mid-air. The fire popped and sighed under the soup. Several Grizzly-witches laid down their grooming combs.

"It was the big fellow who died last winter, just beyond his first mating season. I left his bones up by the granite stones at Raven's Tor. They were clean and smooth under my hands for reading today. I honour his life and his fast hoofs and his strong heart." Amurra said these last words in the same tones Comfrey used when saying the Offering words, like a prayer.

"We honour his life and his fast hoofs and his strong

heart," repeated the Grizzly-witches in a great chorus of low voices, no longer impatient.

Comfrey and Tin, however, only grew more so as they listened, curious to hear this bone-reading, this fortune-telling – whatever it was. The sound of Amurra's voice sent chills down their spines and rumbled low as the soil and roots and stones. As she spoke, her milky eyes became as beautiful as the starlight.

"The curious thing, my sisters, is that no matter how I felt those bones, no matter how I sang to them, asking for their oracle, all that they shaped under my hands was the story of the Elk. Our Creatrix, the one we guard. This was strange to me. *The Elk the Elk the Elk,* the bones whispered and clattered. And yet it was not a soothing sound, not a hymn of peace and wholeness, as her mention usually is. It frightened me, my sisters. It sounded like a warning, a premonition. For a time, I could hear no more. I tasted ghosts on my tongue. I tasted blood and metal and death. *The Elk,* whispered the bones beneath my hands. *The Elk.*" Amurra's voice rang out now, as if she were reciting an ancient piece of poetry.

A low rumbling filled the room. Mallow took cover in Tin's coat, and Myrtle buried herself further into Comfrey's cape. It was the sound of a grizzly's growl, deep and resonant and terrifying. The walls themselves vibrated slightly.

"I'm afraid it gets worse, sisters," continued Amurra after a moment. "Imare, why don't you serve the soup, so our bellies may be full and quiet, better able to digest what is before us. It is hard to think calmly on an empty stomach."

Comfrey and Tin shared a look of anticipation mixed with disquiet – the soup would soon lull all the Grizzly-witches into a heavy sleep, yet they both wanted desperately to hear the rest of Amurra's bone-reading. Had she seen two human children in the bones? Did she suspect that someone might be coming for the Elk? Did she know more about the fate of Farallone, something that might help them all? Comfrey shuddered with fear and hope.

Imare, the Grizzly-witch by the pot of soup, ladled generous helpings into each of her sisters' bowls as they came, one by one, to the fire. When everyone had settled back into their places, Amurra took a delicate sip of her soup, grunted with contentment at its rich and bitter flavours, and continued. Around her, the other Grizzly-witches slurped hungrily.

"I was about to set the bones down for good and leave them, but something compelled me to cast them once more across the ground. This time they did not tell of the Elk. Oh no. They fell in a grid. They fell in the form of the City. Only the City had no Wall. Touching that pattern made pain sear through me. Then it was gone. I do not know, my sisters, what it means. But we must prepare ourselves, we must guard our Elk more carefully than ever before." Amurra sighed heavily and lifted her soup spoon a second time to her furred lips. There was no growling reply from her sisters, no outrage. Her ears pricked. "I know it is hard to hear of the City," she said, taking their silence for the stunned horror she too felt in her chest. "For what happened Before carries great grief."

But suddenly, Amurra found herself unbearably tired, heavy, yawning. Her head nodded onto her chest. Her soup bowl slid to the floor, spilling, and Amurra too fell asleep like the rest of her silent sisters.

THE ELK OF
MILK AND GOLD

Myrtle and Mallow emerged from their respective hiding places in the children's coats, ears moving with triumph, golden eyes bright with satisfaction.

"It worked, Mr No Plan!" exclaimed Mallow, nudging Tin's hand with his nose.

"It took two very fast, brave hares," replied the boy quietly, grinning.

"Well, come on then!" said Myrtle, flicking her ears against Comfrey's arm. The girl's eyes were still trained on the crack in the barn.

"But does she know we are here? Should we be doing this?" she said. "And what she saw, or read – does it mean the City will succeed?" She turned to Tin, her volume rising. "*Your people* will bleed every last Wild Folk for their stupid Star-Breakers, and turn Farallone to a Wasteland again!"

The boy's face changed when Comfrey said "your people" with such hatred in her tone, like she was spitting those words at him. They didn't feel like his people at all, but he had been a piece in the great machine of the Cloister for his whole life, without knowing there was any other way to live, and so somehow, he felt complicit. The thought made Tin feel sick.

"They're not my people," he retorted, angry and hurt. "I have no idea who my real people are. I'm an orphan, remember? I got left on the Cloister doorstep like the Stranglelings your Village people ditch on the hills." Now there was venom in Tin's voice too, and a red heat at his cheeks. Comfrey snorted and opened her mouth to reply.

"All right, all right, you two, time enough to argue later. Right now, we have to be quick!" interjected Mallow. "This is our *only* chance. The Grizzly-witches are asleep. By tomorrow, they will have noticed our tracks, we'll never be able to get close again! We have no idea how long this poppy oil will work, nor where the Elk is at all, so we'd better hurry up and get looking!"

With that, both Mallow and Myrtle bounded around the barn and off into the darkness, towards the pale hint of a trail that led through the grass. They sniffed furiously as they went. The rain had stopped for good, and the cover of cloud made the sky lighter, but it was still difficult to see.

"How are we going to get anywhere in the dark?" groaned Comfrey, choosing to ignore Tin and speaking instead to her feet as she tromped off, one foot heavy with that granite shoe. Avoiding one another's eyes, they followed the white flashing of the leveret's hind legs as Myrtle and Mallow bounded ahead, sniffing at every trail junction, pile of elk scat and patch of grass torn by elk teeth.

A cold wind picked up from the west off the ocean. Coyotebrush swayed in the foggy dark. A barn owl screamed, passing high overhead and the leverets froze. Now that they wore the granite shoes, the children didn't provide the same blanket of protection from hare-loving predators as usual. But the barn owl was out searching for its regular prey – the numerous slow-moving voles, or unsuspecting gophers. The leverets remained still for several minutes after the owl was gone. Then Myrtle, who'd hidden herself amidst a very big patch of iris leaves, began to smell at a torn patch of grass near her nose very intently.

"I think I smell her," breathed the leveret.

Mallow emerged from his hideaway in a lupine bush and joined the sniffing.

"How can you know?" asked Tin, amazed, watching those quick-moving noses.

"Should I use my spectacles?" asked Comfrey, ignoring Tin.

"No, no," said Myrtle, raising her head again from the grass. "We can smell her well enough. There are a hundred nuances to an elk-smell. We've been picking up scent-threads all along the way, Mallow and I, of dozens and dozens of elk. A large group of females. Several smaller groups of wandering bulls. They're separate again, now the courting season is over. The females travel around mostly together, in one big group, led by the oldest matriarch elk, because she knows all the trails, all the sweetest food spots and the safest calving grounds. She is the star at the centre of their constellation. And *she*, the old matriarch, is also the Elk of Milk and Gold, Creatrix of Farallone."

Tin and Comfrey both stared at the little leveret.

"You know all this stuff just from the *smell*?" whispered Tin, incredulous.

"Why of course we do!" interjected Mallow, not wanting Myrtle to get all the credit. "There are whole books, as you would call them, written in smell across the earth. This is how many of us four-leggeds talk to each other across time and space. Anyway, as Myrtle was saying, the Elk of Milk and Gold moves always at the centre of the female herd. She has a very different smell though. It's of stars, of gold and of milk. She seems to have been grazing here, not at the grass but at the *granite underneath*."

"But, how can you be sure it's really *her*?" pressed Comfrey, crouching to look at the torn grass and bits of stone in the dark.

"Look closely." Myrtle gestured her nose towards an imprint in the grass beside the iris patch. It was a hoof impression edged with glinting gold flakes. Its light was visible even in the darkness.

Comfrey touched the hoofprint reverently, her mouth falling open.

Tin crouched too, though he waited until Comfrey was finished to place his fingers against the indentation. When he lifted his fingers, there was gold dust at their tips. His heart skipped with excitement and he felt a strange shiver through his whole body, as if the tracery of stargold that lived in his blood was responding.

The four set off again, the leverets slowly following the scent trail that matched the smells of that gold-edged hoofprint. Comfrey took the Baba Ithá's strand of three hundred pearls from her damp pack and held them wound round her hand, in case they came upon the Elk unexpectedly. She wondered what would happen when the Elk saw them. The feather seemed to weigh very heavily upon her again, like there was a lump of iron in her pack. How could she, Comfrey, have anything to do with something so grand as a Creatrix of Farallone? But the voice of the Bobcat-girl rose up in her memory then, speaking her name, and a spark of new resolve kindled in her. She didn't understand why, but she'd known from that very moment that an unfathomable destiny awaited her. The basket of her own fate burned to ashes and all its spokes pointing towards this Elk.

The fog parted, revealing a waning gibbous moon. Below, the moonlight illuminated a female elk on the far hillside. She was pale as cream and her hoofs were golden. She rested in the tall green grass. As the leverets, and then the children in their heavy granite shoes, approached, she stood slowly – first her back legs, then her front. She was very, very old and her creamy fur clumped here and there with age. Her spine was an elegant but knobbed line. But once she had risen fully to her feet, her power and beauty cast their own light. Her eyes were the same purple as the wild irises when they bloom. The pale cream of her fur matched the moon. Slowly, with the grace of many ages, she turned her head and looked right into Comfrey's eyes.

Comfrey let out a little cry and sank right down to her knees in the grass. This was the Elk who had made the world out of Old Mother Neeth's spun stargold. This was the Elk of Milk and Gold. For a moment the Elk appeared vast, as vast as all of Olima, all of Farallone, all the sky and ocean crashing far below. Then she took a small step forward and was an ordinary size again. Tiny flakes of gold fell from her hoofs.

Tears filled Comfrey's eyes. The Elk took another step forward, her gaze fixed on Comfrey. The girl sucked in a ragged breath. She felt suddenly then that no matter what happened to her, no matter if in the next moment the Elk annihilated her with a single searing bolt of starlight, the experience would be worth it – to have been blessed by the gaze of those violet eyes. She felt unutterably and incandescently *whole*. Tears fell freely down her cheeks.

Tin, kneeling beside her in the grass, put his arm round her shoulders. He'd never seen anything so beautiful in all his life. He'd thought similarly of the stars, the open green, of fir trees and the ragged coastline falling away to ocean, of pelicans and alder trees. But the Elk of Milk and Gold seemed to hold all of these things in her eyes, her moon-pale fur, her glinting hoofs, as she took another step nearer. From where they crouched amidst the grass, Myrtle and Mallow regarded the Elk of Milk and Gold with similar expressions of deference and love. Around her they could see a light the human children could not, a thousand luminous strands hitching the Elk to the night sky.

Tin remembered then that they were still wearing the granite shoes, and he wondered if the Elk understood that they were human at all. It did seem extraordinary that she would walk so calmly towards them, if she knew what they really were. This thought made Tin's heart hurt. Why did being human mean all the wild ones automatically mistrusted them? Why couldn't they be like hares? How had they become so cut off from the rest of the creatures of the world that every new interaction was tainted by mistrust and fear?

The Elk was now standing very near, and Comfrey, as if in a dream, had risen shakily to her feet, hypnotized. The Elk lifted her head up higher. She snuffed the air with her broad, dark nose. Her violet eyes flashed and her whole body quivered as she took in their human scent fully. Then she lifted a sharp, golden hoof. Myrtle thumped the ground in warning. After all, it had taken only one stamp of the Elk's golden hoofs to send earthquakes shuddering through the fault line at the time of the Collapse. But none of them could move from where they stood, they were transfixed, and neither the leverets nor Tin could find the voice to speak.

It was Comfrey who moved at last, very slowly holding out the Baba Ithá's three hundred pearls. The Elk sniffed the air again as she caught sight of the moon-white strand. Her nostrils flared. Her eyes changed. Gingerly, she lowered her raised hoof and stepped nearer. Where her hoof touched down the grass shuddered and turned gold. The Elk walked right up to Comfrey's outstretched hand, then snuffed at the offered palm, then moved her furred lips against the strand of pearls.

"Oh!" exclaimed Comfrey, because it tickled and

because, this close, it was a little hard to breathe with the force of those violet eyes upon her. Tremors ran through her body. "These are for you," whispered the girl, unknotting one end of the string so she could slip the pearls off into her palm. They looked like pieces of moon. The Elk caught them in her lips and crunched. As she chewed, she regarded Comfrey and Tin, then Comfrey again, then the leverets. Each pearl seemed to bring a brighter lustre to her fur, and a new strength to her old body. She looked larger than she had before and when she stepped a little closer, Comfrey felt the ground beneath her quiver.

I know the one whose pearls these are. I did not think she would ever give a human girl her blessing. These words came into Comfrey's mind and she blinked, looking around. The Elk was watching her. It was hard to tell if the expression in her violet eyes was one of gentleness or terrible anger, or both. Comfrey bowed her head. *What do you want, human girl? I had not expected to see one of your kind again.*

Comfrey heard the centuries of sorrow in her voice, of regret, of weariness and of loss. She also understood, with a strange calm, that it mattered very much how she replied. The Elk of Milk and Gold was poised on the edge of flight and of violence. Her whole body shone. Comfrey didn't say anything. Instead she grappled with her backpack and pulled out the white buckskin bundle, unwrapping it with one hand. The smell of singed lichen filled the air. She shook the lichen free, and lifted the Fire Hawk's feather between her fingers, holding it up. It flared in the darkness. She heard Tin gasp behind her. For a moment the feather filled the night and its light gilded every fur on the Elk's body.

The Elk stood perfectly still, her violet eyes fixed on the feather. But all through the ground ran a shudder, and Comfrey understood, without knowing how, that the shudder was the Elk's. That she extended far beyond the physical form that stood in front of them now.

Lay it before me, came the voice into Comfrey's mind. *Lay it before me, daughter of the Country.* The Elk said these words with a tenderness that seemed to hold in it every mother's touch that Comfrey had ever known. The tears fell again down Comfrey's cheeks. She crouched to place the feather at the hoofs of the Elk of Milk and Gold.

"The Basket-witches sent me," Comfrey whispered. "I-I saw this feather fall from the wing of the Fire Hawk and picked it up without knowing what it meant, but only because I found it beautiful. Then the Basket-witches explained to me what it was, and some of them didn't want to send me. But the Fire Hawk burned my basket, and you had told them that the one who found the feather was the one who must bring it to you, and…" The girl trailed off, embarrassed by her own stammering. Her voice sounded so thin and young and quavering in the darkness, crouched at the glowing hoofs of the Elk of Milk and Gold. She lifted her head, trying not to look into the feather. The Elk had lowered her face to it, so that her nose almost touched its surface. Three tears fell, drop by drop, from her violet eyes, three tears that were liquid gold. They fell onto the embered feather. Its molten fibres swirled and hissed.

Oh my children, oh my leverets, oh my Farallone. The Elk's long, creamy nose was gilded with tears. The feather's light danced. Tenderly, tentatively, Comfrey reached up her free palm. She wanted desperately to lay it against the long neck. She wanted to lay her whole cheek against those creamy flanks, as she would against her mother's skirts.

Myrtle and Mallow, who had been silently transfixed by the Elk of Milk and Gold and all that was transpiring between her and Comfrey, both snapped to attention, making thin sounds of distress, as Comfrey raised her hand towards her fur.

"You can't touch her, you daft girl!" cried Myrtle.

But it was too late. She only turned back at the noise the leverets made after her hand had already fallen onto that milk-pale fur.

"Comfrey!" Mallow snapped, thumping the earth. The girl still hadn't taken her hand from the Elk's neck, but was kneeling, mesmerized, that velvet nose to hers, breathing the smell of grass.

"A Grizzly-witch is coming!" Mallow wailed. "How can she be so near already?" he cried to Myrtle, then bounded towards Comfrey. "There's hardly any use running, but for the sake of All Hares, *get your hands off that Elk!*" The little leveret was practically screaming, his whole body quivering. Tin lunged forward and took Comfrey by both shoulders, wrenching her away from the Elk's soft, mothering warmth.

Daughter of the Country, I will go with you to the Basket-witches. I will go with you to the Fire Hawk. It is time. My body is old and failing. It is time. And with these words ringing their deep bells in Comfrey's mind, the Elk took the embered feather between her teeth and ate it in three smouldering bites.

Comfrey, shaken from her reverie, gasped and looked around frantically through the darkness until, with relief, she found the leverets behind her.

"Didn't you hear what she said?" stammered Comfrey. "Weren't you listening? Didn't you see her…eat the feather?"

"Didn't you hear Mallow?" exclaimed Tin. "A Grizzly-witch is coming!"

"What she *said*?" Myrtle repeated, dazed. "But she was perfectly silent, my dear girl. You seemed to be doing all the talking."

Comfrey fixed them all with an astonished green gaze. "But – how—"

"I'm not so easily drugged to sleep as my sisters," came a deep voice from behind them. Comfrey shrieked and leaped, whirling to look over her shoulder, causing the leverets to scatter and Tin to stumble. The Elk of Milk and Gold only cocked her ears, calm. As Amurra approached, appearing slowly through the fog, the Elk's old, matriarchal eyes grew tender and sad at once.

"I am blind, after all," the Grizzly-witch continued, in that low voice with its rasping edges, the same voice the children had listened to while eavesdropping through the barn walls. "I see beyond what you see. I see what others don't. I sensed something amiss with that soup after my second sip, so my slumber was short. Clever, using oil of poppy. Clever little hares. I should eat you now, for bringing human children here, for daring to sneak under the noses of your own wild kind. You are traitors." The Grizzly-witch spat the last word, her voice full of hatred.

The leverets flattened their ears along their backs in fear, trembling so much that their whiskers were a blur. Amurra turned on Comfrey then, who was clasping Tin's arm and trying to breathe steadily. She had never been so near a being of such danger and power and wildness in her life, all muscle and shaggy coat and tooth. Even the Baba Ithá had been tamer, somehow. In the dark, Amurra looked almost entirely bear. The night air around her was electric.

"But you," she growled at Comfrey, leaning near so the girl could smell the root and meat and rankness of her breath. "You have laid your dirty, accursed human hands upon the Elk of Milk and Gold. You have *dared* to lay not just one finger but your whole palm upon her neck, like a blight, like a sickness. The shape of slaughter, your human hands. I will not let your kind kill another of the Three who made Farallone." Amurra paused, frothing at the mouth with her anger, her blind eyes roving.

Comfrey felt like she might faint with terror. Tin put his arm round her shoulders, trying to keep it steady, to quell his own shivering panic. Were these to be their last moments? Would Amurra bring them all back slung over her shoulders for tomorrow's dinner?

"It's only because of the Basket-witches and the Fire Hawk's feather that we're here at all," Tin found himself saying. "Comfrey doesn't have dirty hands or killing hands. Sh-she has the gentlest hands of anyone I've ever met! If you are going to punish anyone, punish me. It's my hands that are dangerous, trained by the Brothers." It came out in one gush, and a note too loud, ringing in the muffled, foggy night air like a set of shrill bells.

Comfrey looked at him, her heart in her mouth. Amurra's ears had pricked forward, despite their human shape.

"The Fire Hawk, you say?" she repeated more softly, settling back on her haunches in surprise.

"Yes, ma'am," said Comfrey hastily, her voice quivering. "The Fire Hawk dropped his feather – and I picked it up—" She turned, wondering why the Elk did not intervene and explain to Amurra what was going on. But the Elk only gazed back at her, impassive and ancient. For a moment, she looked as big as the night itself; her fur was tipped with stars, her eyes were pieces of moon. She watched with the stillness of the night and the earth, her nostrils smoking.

"Ah. Naturally, another trespass on your part caused all of this," hissed Amurra, but her derision hid the beginning of dread.

Comfrey shifted uncomfortably and the granite shoe still on her foot hit another rock. A look of slow realization crossed Amurra's fierce, furred face.

"Where did you get those granite shoes?" the Grizzly-witch snapped.

The children looked quickly at each other. How did she know, without sight?

"I-I made them, ma'am," stuttered Tin. "For the Baba Ithá, and then she gave them to us."

"The Baba Ithá," said Amurra in a broken voice. "Indeed…" Her face had become pensive, some of its venom gone. "Something is at work here," she murmured.

"And you're at the heart of it." She turned to the Elk as she said this, and the reverence in her voice startled the children. "The Fire Hawk calls you. The Baba Ithá of the firwood has given two human children a pair of granite shoes to fool us all. There are two leveret-hares at their side, leading the way. Perhaps this is what the bones spoke of, and I misread them, distracted by my own old angers…" She was talking to herself now, low and faint. Though her eyes were already milky with blindness, they clouded further, possessed by an old memory of the time when men on horseback shot and killed every last grizzly bear in all the land, so that they went extinct. The Grizzly-witches had no animal brethren left to tend and guard; they were the last and only beings resembling the old wild grizzlies of Farallone, and that knowledge was a sad and bitter weight upon their hearts.

"I should prefer to kill you now," she snarled, turning back to the children, her pale eyes flaring. "We could remain distant from the happenings of humankind. We could keep ourselves apart, as we have always done." For a moment her growling voice filled the whole night. But that softness passed over her milky eyes again, and she quietened to a grating murmur. "But I fear that time has passed. Now the Basket-witches and their Fire Hawk have reached their hands to us, and the Baba Ithá too. The Elk is very old. She is tired, and has grown weak. I dread what any journey will do to her." Amurra was quiet for a moment, moving her own gnarled hands against the dark ground. She turned to the Elk, who lowered her soft nose against the Grizzly-witch's shoulder.

Tears came to Amurra's eyes. At last she said in a low voice, "The Baba Ithá trusts you. The Elk trusts you. But we Grizzly-witches guard her because we know the true treachery of humankind better than any other creature. The Elk may go with you of her free will, but I will let the land be the judge of you. I will let the old ghosts of this place test you. The only way you will make it out of our land alive is by taking the ghost roads. The ones that pass through the Shadow Lands. Where the wraiths of the grizzly bears walk. Once you leave the grasslands of Tamal, you will be free to travel in the realms you know. But the ghosts of this place must prove to me that you are worthy to escort the Elk across Olima, or I will hunt you all myself and bring you back to my sisters for breakfast."

The Grizzly-witch didn't give them time to argue or ask a single question. She only made two quick, sharp patterns with her clawed fingers against the earth, and a terrible keening note deep in her throat. Suddenly, great silver wraiths surrounded them, lit with the waning moon. Amurra was nowhere to be seen. Only the Elk of Milk and Gold remained calm and did not baulk. Tin and Comfrey both let out muffled shrieks. Myrtle's eyes rolled white and she and Mallow threw themselves flat against the ground in fear. As far as they could see across the grassland in the moonlight, they were surrounded by a tide of massive, silver grizzly bear ghosts. One lunged at Comfrey, his face half ruined, blown open by the bullet that had killed him hundreds of years before. She froze, and her heart stopped entirely.

"Comfrey, move!" Tin yelled, pulling her down with him to the ground.

But the ghost bear's huge jaws and blunt teeth had already passed through both of them, bringing a seep of sickening, cold lethargy to their bodies. The children lay panting beside the leverets. Now all of their eyes were wide and white. The Elk stood very still, her head raised high, her eyes gleaming bright. The grizzly-ghosts seethed and swelled around her, but didn't touch her. Comfrey struggled for words, her hands pressed against her chest to warm the place that had gone so cold at the grizzly-ghost's touch.

"It's like his teeth cut me somewhere I can't see," she moaned, clutching at her heart. "Like all the hope has gone out of me." Her face was pale, and she struggled to sit up.

With great effort, Myrtle pulled herself off the ground and came to Comfrey's side.

"I don't think they can actually hurt us physically,

though," Tin said quietly, trying to rally his own courage. "They can only freeze us with fear."

"The boy's right," Myrtle said in a ragged voice so different from her usual cheerful tone that the children stared. Mallow was by his twin's side now, his haunches quivering but his eyes firm. "Physically, we can walk through this place without a hair harmed on our heads," Myrtle continued. "It's fear we're up against. Clever old Grizzly-witch, setting us against our own fear. Nothing paralyses like fear."

"Tin!" Comfrey exclaimed, a little colour coming back to her face. "Your Oddness! Will it help? Isn't there a knife? Can it cut through ghosts?"

But as she spoke three more grizzly-ghosts – an old mother and her half-grown cubs – came towards them at a lumbering gallop, full of moon and wind, their snarling jaws open. Tin, fumbling for the penknife, felt his hands go slack with panic. He could hardly use his fingers, let alone set one clear thought in front of another. The ghosts swept through them, and the sickness and dread they left behind made Comfrey wretch.

"We can't do this," Tin whispered. "Their hatred is too big. I can hardly move my fingers, let alone open my penknife and even try!" His hands were still shaking and he was leaning on the ground again.

Myrtle and Mallow had both leaped onto his lap, and

they cowered there. Comfrey had never seen the boy so afraid, and she instinctively took his hands in hers. Their warmth made the sickness in her chest ease. He looked up at her, his light eyes strange and bright in the moonlight. She saw them widen and fill with wonder, and something in her shivered softly. Why was he looking at her like that?

Then she felt the warm breath on her neck. The lap of velvet lips. The smell of sweet grass. She turned. The Elk of Milk and Gold was nosing the neck of her cape. A sense of well-being, golden as dawn, spread throughout the girl's body from where the Elk touched her. The creature's eyes were fixed on her, liquid and kind.

"Oh," breathed Comfrey. She fumbled in her pocket for the pearls, and held one out. The Elk didn't lap it up, but only pressed her nose against Comfrey's arm. The warmth and light that spread out from it made the girl able to think straight for a moment.

Climb onto my back, daughter of the Country. Climb onto my back, son of the City. Climb up, all of you, and I will carry you to safety.

Myrtle let out a small hare-cry of surprise. This time, the Elk had made her words audible to all of them. Tears pricked in Comfrey's eyes. She looked at Tin. One of her hands was still in his. The Elk butted her shoulder more urgently this time. Thick fog pulsed up from the ocean in new tendrils, seeping between the grizzly-ghosts, turning everything cold and indistinct. Several more ghosts were turning towards them again. An enormous male with scars all down his pale belly was rearing up on his hind legs, pawing at the air, readying to charge.

"Better be quick about it!" croaked Myrtle.

Comfrey turned towards the Elk, doing her best to stand up on wobbly legs. The Elk's eyes were very old and very calm. Comfrey felt tears falling down her cheeks.

"Up you go now. No time to waste! See how she is kneeling for you?"

It was true. The Elk of Milk and Gold had bent her forelegs so the children could hoist themselves up. Tin, who was bigger, climbed in front, and Comfrey settled behind him, taking hold of the back of his coat. The leverets jumped up onto their laps. And all at once the fear that had turned them cold and sick began to thaw. The Elk was a star all of her own orbit, shedding warmth into the sea of ghosts. The charging male bear pulled up short before the Elk and, like the others around him, moved aside to let her pass, his terrible, scarred face bowed to his chest, his ghost-claws drawn in.

"They are so sad," Comfrey whispered, looking out at all of them. "What a terrible world it must once have been." Her tears fell quietly, and she couldn't stop them. Tin, thinking of the City, of the Brothers, didn't have the heart to reply that the world he'd come from was worse still.

The Elk was moving faster now, at a gentle, dignified trot. Grizzly-ghosts clamoured at her heels, not with aggression and hatred this time, but something like love. In the dark, in the mist, their faces glowed.

"She honours them," Mallow whispered, for the Elk had slowed and was reaching her golden nose towards the outstretched muzzles of the ghosts.

"Why?" said Tin, feeling a strange tightness in his chest. He thought he might cry too.

"She is the Creatrix of the world, silly," whispered Myrtle. "She is their mistress, their sustainer, their Queen. Now they are nothing but sorrow and fear left to roam in the wind. She is easing their pain."

All night they moved through a tide of grizzly-ghosts. The Elk walked a snaking path in and out among a thousand silver wraiths. The children clung to each other and the Elk's neck, exhausted beyond hope. Despite the protection of the Elk's radiant back, every touch from a grizzly-ghost made their limbs weak. Myrtle had found a safe place tucked inside Comfrey's cloak, and Mallow had made himself very small under Tin's coat. The Elk had to walk very slowly, as if the ghosts really were a tide of salt water, and not air.

Just before dawn they reached the edge of Tamal Point. Comfrey and Tin were half-asleep, leaning into each other, trying not to fall off the Elk's back.

"Psst! Wake up!" came Myrtle's voice from inside Comfrey's cloak. Tin felt a nip on his thigh.

"Ow!" he grumbled. "What—?"

But Comfrey had seized his hand, and the Elk herself had come to a complete stop. The largest grizzly-ghost they'd yet encountered stood guard over the old cattle grid that marked the end of the Grizzly-witches' territory. And the Elk's warm light showed no sign of dissipating it. Strange, grating sounds came from him, as if he was speaking. The Elk watched the ghost with a level violet eye.

"What is he saying, Myrtle?" Comfrey hissed. "Can you understand?"

The little hare's ears were quivering as she listened, but in a thin voice she replied. "He calls the Elk Creatrix and Mother. He says it will be a betrayal if she leaves with you, with us. He calls you traitors and cheaters of life and says she can't abandon them all for us."

The grizzly-ghost bowed low before the Elk, beseeching.

I must, came the voice Comfrey had grown used to hearing in her head, like bells turned to embers, ringing. *I abandon no one. I am always here, I am everywhere. I am not leaving you, only changing, for a time. These ones will not betray us. Let me show you.* And the Elk turned her head to regard the children and the leverets with a single violet eye. *Daughter of the Country, Son of the City, Hares of the*

Greentwins, come down from my back and go into the arms of the grizzly-ghost.

"What?" sputtered Mallow.

"Holy Mother of Hares protect us!" wailed Myrtle.

"Has she changed her mind about us?" Tin said in alarm.

Only Comfrey did not sigh, or swear, or tremble. Very steadily, she slipped down off the Elk's back. She thought she understood what the Elk meant. Something had changed in Comfrey since she had held the pearls out to the Elk the night before; since she had ridden on her back through the tide of ghosts. Something had clarified in her, though she didn't know what it was that was clarified, or how. Only that she felt pure, a part of everything. And she could see that underneath the grizzly-ghost's hatred and sadness and rage was the desire to be loved once more as kin, as a part of something that could never be broken.

So Comfrey walked right up to the grizzly-ghost, and opened her arms. Terrible, aching cold splintered her. She thought her body would fall to pieces. But instead of shrinking into her fear, she took a deep breath and opened her eyes.

She could see nothing but a kind of silver mist. She was *inside* the grizzly-ghost. Her breathing hitched. Why couldn't she see anything, any way out? She could hear Tin's voice, calling her, but very faintly. How could that be? He was

355

only a few metres away! Cold lanced through her again, that deadening cold. She had meant to embrace the grizzly-ghost, to meet fear with love. But she could hardly breathe. She thought she would die from the cold, the hurt in her chest. All she could think to do was sing an old lullaby her mother had once sung to her. She hadn't thought of the song in a very long time. Now she sang it, breathless, and remembered her father singing it to her too, and realized that it was a love song.

"Sometimes I'm a fir tree
With the robins in my arms
And sometimes you're the robins
You're the soil and the sun

Just light us the fire
And brew us the tea
Come on my love
Come walking with me."

Comfrey felt a hand on her back. It was a warm human hand. The ears of a hare brushed her ankle. She reached for Tin's hand and hung on to it, hard. At the touch he began to sing too, stumbling, half-humming, trying to join his voice with Comfrey's, trying to remember his mother's face, and if she had ever sung to him. They heard a great, bear-like sigh. The cold mist around them eased, brightened. Then it was gone, and the grizzly-ghost with it. Comfrey, Tin and the leverets found themselves standing on the far side of the cattle grid in the light of the rising sun. A long curve of ocean coast stretched far below them to the west, white with foam and the first light.

Well done, young ones. With a song, and with your love, you have eased his soul as well as I might have done. The Elk's voice came through them all like warm light. *You have proven to the grizzly-ghosts, and to the Grizzly-witches, that humans have the capacity to heal others. It is not only Wild Folk who know how to tend. Now, climb on my back again, for time is short and I can move much more swiftly than you.*

17.

THE WILD FOLK

As the Elk walked, everywhere she stepped an unseen word unfurled through the ground, a little filament of starlight. Only the Elk herself knew the language of those threads, though if Comfrey had peered through her spectacles at the earth beneath their feet, she would have seen a golden web spreading through the soil. Still, even without using her Oddness the girl could feel it. Tin could too. It was like a sunrise underground. Invisible to the eye, but clear as daylight to the heart. It was the presence of life itself, suffusing the earth with each of the Elk's hoofbeats.

After a time, Comfrey gasped and tugged Tin's sleeve, pointing. Behind them a crowd of animals was gathering. Flocks of quail, their topknots bronze in the morning light, skittered along on quick feet. An extended family of grey foxes, their silvery faces shining as they trotted near, nipped their children to behave, black eyes fixed on the Elk. A clan of acorn woodpeckers with their flashing red heads darted from bush to bush, calling out their laughing calls. Myrtle made herself very small when she noticed the foxes, and several sharp-beaked hawks, swooping along on enormous wings. With every step the Elk took south across the land of Olima, more animals materialized from the brush, the tall grass, the firs and pines, the sky itself, and the underground too. Voles crowded at her hoofs, as did the blue-streaked fence lizards. Swallowtail butterflies flitted around the children's heads, their yellow wings suffused with sun. Hummingbirds with ruby throats buzzed back and forth and around in circles on blurred wings. Badgers with their great, sharp, shovelling claws, bobcats on quiet spotted paws, rattlesnakes with white diamonds on their backs, green-bellied chorus frogs, blind black moles, flocks of every kind of sparrow, enormous bumblebees, the quick, striped chipmunks and silver squirrels and soft-eared woodrats – they all gathered round the Elk and walked beside her, setting aside their own antagonisms for a time, so that rattlesnakes slithered beside mice, bobcats next to brushrabbits, without any violence. They all walked together in peace, and the air and earth were tangled with their songs and cries and barks.

Then it was Tin's turn to gasp, and shake Comfrey, and point. Where there had only been a crowd of animals before, there were now suddenly Wild Folk too. They seemed to have emerged out of nowhere, out of the shadows or the songs of birds. Raccoon-folk like Delilah, with bandit-masked faces and cloaks of bone; Owl-folk with very round eyes and great feathered arms; a being Comfrey felt sure was a Hill-woman, with a petticoat of roots and a body as rounded and green as a spring slope; Poppy-men who wore tall pointed green caps and left a wake of orange pollen behind them. Mallow moaned when he saw a family of Mountain Lion-folk in the crowd, and even Tin gasped. They moved with a muscular grace, their bodies entirely golden and long-limbed, their faces human, but with kohl-dark eyes and broad noses. They were both beautiful and terrifying. Comfrey watched them breathlessly, thinking of the Bobcat-girl. She scanned the crowd – surely the Bobcat-girl would be among them, somewhere?

It seemed that the presence of the Elk had sent forth a kind of clarion call across all of Olima. She wondered if the Basket-witches would hear it too, and come to meet them. Tin, with a similar thought, scanned the gathering throng of creatures and Wild Folk for the Coyote-folk. Surely they would come too, and at last he could ask about his Fiddleback.

The road had narrowed from the grasslands and open hills of Tamal Point to a winding trail that led up through pines at the foot of the Vision Mountains. To their right, thirty kilometres distant, Olima narrowed into the hook of the far western headlands, and the long fingers of an estuary gleamed. The Elk's pace slowed, and Comfrey scanned the path in front of them, wondering if the Bobcat-girl and her family might emerge from somewhere up ahead. She saw a glint of purple. She took in a breath. She looked more closely and the purple glint came closer into her view. It was a rich, dark, silken purple: the purple of a wild iris blooming like a crown by the side of the trail.

"Oh," Comfrey gasped. "Myrtle, look. An iris. The first iris." She felt a tremor move through her whole body, remembering what the Holy Fool, Oro, had said, and what he'd seen in the feather. It was early still for the iris to bloom! And it was warmer inland; what if the iris had been blooming all week in the land of the Country already? The Brothers – did this mean that the Brothers were already at the Alder village? But Myrtle didn't seem to hear her. Both of the leverets' ears were trained in the direction Tin was looking, off to the left, towards a grassy clearing amidst a handful of old and twisted pines.

An enormous Bobcat sat beneath the pines, watching them very keenly. Her coat was the russet of bracken, with tawny spots all over like stars. Her ears were tipped with lustrous black tassles of fur, her face striped and thickly whiskered, her eyes two pale green planets. Beside her bloomed half a dozen more purple irises. The Elk came to a stop. She lifted her head high and let out a little snort of recognition, moving through a low stand of brush into the clearing.

My old friend, came her bell-like voice.

Well now, the Bobcat said, her eyes very level and very sharp. Her voice, like the Elk's, seemed to move invisibly through the children, right down into their bones. Myrtle and Mallow simultaneously hid themselves inside Tin and Comfrey's clothing. The Bobcat turned and bowed her head low to the Elk, then raised it abruptly with a purr and circled her, teeth bared with excitement, short tail swaying, pawing at the Elk's ankles.

Comfrey couldn't breathe. Was this one of the Bobcat-folk? But it was so enormous, as big as the Elk herself. The Bobcat-girl Comfrey had seen was smaller than she was, and regular bobcats were not much larger than house cats.

"Is that...the First Bobcat?" Tin asked, hesitating, remembering the stories Thornton had told. Comfrey looked at him sharply.

"How would *you* know?" she hissed.

"It is," whispered Mallow. "From the beginning of the world, just like the Elk. The one from Thornton's tale. Don't you see how...*big*...she is?" He quivered in Tin's lap.

The Bobcat whirled back on Comfrey, snarling for real now. Like the Elk she seemed to glow. But when her green eyes met the girl's, they softened, flashing with recognition.

Impetuous kitten, this one is, the First Bobcat said, and purred between her sharp teeth. *But we've no time for disagreements or trifles now. I come with bad tidings. I see you are on the move, and so you must already know.* She raised her eyes to the Elk's and swished her bobbed tail to the left once. Two Coyote-men and one Coyote-woman emerged from the trees behind her, pulling the dusty, battered Fiddleback between them. Tin made to leap from the Elk's back and run towards his creation, but Mallow stopped him with a nip at the thigh so hard that it broke the skin.

"Don't *move*, you idiot!" the hare snapped. "For once, just watch, and listen, and wait. We are in far, far over our heads, hadn't you noticed?"

My old friend, came the Elk's voice, fluid through them where the First Bobcat's was ragged and startling. *What is this thing of metal that you bring before me? Is this your tiding?*

This is only the beginning, replied the Bobcat, nudging the Fiddleback with her black nose. *Or maybe, in truth, it is the end.*

Tin suppressed a moan and the terrible urge to throw himself between the Coyote-folk who dragged it and straighten his Fiddleback's bent legs, clean its muddy wheels and round seat compartment, test its levers and steering wheel.

The First Bobcat sighed, continuing. *The Brothers are after it. They are after us. This thing was made by the City boy who sits astride your back. The Coyote-folk, my old friends in chaos, my messengers from the underworld, took it from him when they discovered it and brought it down to me in order to protect Olima. It is a thing of power, a thing of danger and possibly death. It runs on stargold, on the stuff of creation. An accidental discovery on the boy's part, no doubt. When they showed it to me, it reminded me very much of Old Mother Neeth, the Spider who made us, who the Star-Priests killed. It smelled of both creation and destruction, like she did. But I could make no sense of it, for it is a human thing. I thought to bring it to the Greentwins, they who are both human and Wild Folk, they who all along have been studying the wholeness of Farallone, from the tip of Olima to the City's underground. But I and the Coyote-folk made it only as far as the Country village called Black Oak, and there met face-to-face with the Brothers who had arrived that morning, dressed in Country clothes. But under their clothes they hid our old enemy: the gun, the terrible black gunpowder. We caught one glimpse of them and their machines, and ran. We intended to run north to the land of the Grizzly-witches, to you, though I know we agreed of old that only the fall of the Fire Hawk's feather should bring you forth from your hiding, and I from my underworld. Yet you are here, carrying human children and strange hares… And behind me come the City's Brothers, while behind you walk the wild hordes of Farallone, all unarmed.*

With these words, the First Bobcat lowered her great, striped head all the way to the ground. Two silver tears fell from her eyes.

The Fire Hawk has indeed dropped a feather, replied the Elk, very calmly. Her violet eyes kindled with a low and gentle light. Behind her the rippling crowd of feathered, furred, clawed and winged beings made not a sound. *And it is these human children and their leveret friends who brought it to me, braving the old anger of all the Wild Folk of Olima, and succeeding. We go to the Basket-witches and to the Fire Hawk, where the Psalterium will be given over to be read. There is nothing else that can be done. It is the last hope, and the last of my power. You know this too, my old friend. You have known it from the beginning.*

I have, replied the First Bobcat, her head still bowed, her ears flattened back in grief. *Only I thought it would be many thousands of years away, millions maybe, when the sun itself went out. You cannot leave us so soon.*

"Leave us?" Comfrey stammered, putting her hands on the Elk's neck, no longer able to hold back her words, or her fear. "Where are you going?"

But even as she spoke, she heard a distant droning made not by bees or hummingbirds, but by something far larger.

At the same moment, an alarm cry went up among the many birds that had gathered round the Elk of Milk and Gold. It was a terrible, cacophonous, many-voiced cry – mournful, screeching, resonant and shrill. An osprey wheeling far overhead dived suddenly, whistling terrible warning notes. Quail-folk, with their indigo-dark headdresses and their wide hips, began to wail their own alarm, herding all the animals and Wild Folk around them into the bushes.

The noise grew louder, an engine's roar. Tin whirled, leaping off the Elk's back, and Mallow leaped with him. Voles, sparrows and lizards scattered into the tall grass. Downhill, behind the many-coated crowd of animals and Wild Folk that had gathered in the wake of the Elk, who left a gleaming trail of golden dust behind her, a machine on four wheels screeched towards them. It was one of the abandoned automobiles from Before that Tin and the other orphans in the Cloister had most often used for scrap metal in the Metals Studio. There'd never been enough fuel to run them efficiently, so they'd been left to rust. This one had most of its outer metal torn away so that its wires and joints showed, like a cadaver. The Brothers must have used some of the last of the City's stargold to get it here, Tin thought. At its wheel sat a broad, white-haired, pale-skinned Brother wearing the robes of the Cloister. Another sat beside him, slimmer, his face in shadow.

Tin's whole body flashed hot, then cold. It was Father Ralstein himself, and Brother Warren beside him. Dread unlike any he'd ever felt in his life almost paralysed him.

"*Now* we're in for it," whispered Mallow, and the hopelessness in his voice made Tin rally with a last surge of courage. He took several steps forward, brandishing his Oddness. The crowd of Wild Folk had gone very, very still. In their blood and bones they remembered the sounds of machines like the one racing towards them, and the terror of it numbed them. Even the Elk wouldn't move. She stood staring, the shine of her body dulled with sorrow. Comfrey clung to her neck, trying hard to breathe. Only the Coyote-folk were unafraid. The Coyote-woman rushed to Tin's side, snarling, the others close at her heels. Another six raced from the trees where they'd been hiding. For once, Mallow didn't quail at the sight of them. Something larger was at stake today.

"We need my Fiddleback," Tin said, turning to them. "We have to bait them, we have to distract them so the Wild Folk here can get away, and the Elk of Milk and Gold most of all. I will go to them. I'm what they're here for." He only fully understood the weight of his words as he spoke them. It was the truth, and it had been eating at him while the First Bobcat had told her story. He had to turn himself over to the Brothers, distract them from the gathering of Wild Folk here. They could not learn what it was the Elk had done with the last gold of Farallone. Let the Fiddleback distract them from this truth.

"No, Tin!" cried Comfrey, jumping down from the Elk's back too. "You can't! Not after all this, there must be another way!"

But one of the Coyote-men was already rolling the Fiddleback down from the clearing. Tin choked. It looked so small now, so dirty and battered, half-wild itself.

"There isn't, Comfrey," Tin said, his voice calm. "Don't you see, it might be my very presence here that brings about the fate you and Oro saw in the feather. We thought we were hiding the Fiddleback, and the secret of the Wild Folk, from the City, but all the while we were leading them right to the heart of it! I can't let that happen any more."

"You are braver than we thought, human boy," the Coyote-man said to him in a tone that half-mocked and half-praised, and ended in a growl. The battered Fiddleback was by his side.

Comfrey tried to take hold of Tin's shoulder, but he pulled away, unable to look at her, and began to stride down through the crowd of Wild Folk. The words of the Coyote-man gave him added strength. And it was as if his resolve and his courage released them all from their stupor. They scattered as he passed – birds and bobcats and rabbits and lizards and Mountain Lion-men and

Poppy-women and Raccoon-folk, all vanishing one by one back into the brush and the tall grass.

"Mallow!" shrieked Myrtle as her twin bounded off after the boy. But for once, her brother didn't look back. She trembled at Comfrey's feet, torn, unable to decide whether to run after him or stay where she was.

The old, gaping automobile skidded to a halt as Tin appeared through the wild lilac branches with Mallow at his heels and the Coyote-man beside him with the Fiddleback.

"Quick," Tin hissed to the Coyote-man. "Go! Don't let them see you! Don't you know they have guns?"

"Guns?" wheezed Mallow, remembering all at once their first harrowing escape in the Fiddleback, and the deafening shots fired into the air.

"Of course," said Tin. His hand shook as he took hold of the Fiddleback's door. But the Coyote-man wouldn't leave. He eyed Tin with a fierce, golden look, and grinned.

"Guns or no, it would be my dearest pleasure to bite these men, to spill their blood and eat their hearts out whole," he snarled. Tin swallowed, hard, and Mallow leaped into his arms, muttering, "Really, a hare can only take so much!"

"No," said Tin. "You don't understand. They will fire at you and kill you, and then your blood will spill gold and they will *know*. Please, run. I'll give myself over, and it will distract them, and they'll think it's enough, for now."

There were tears on the boy's face. What would they do to him when they caught him? Would they take him back to the City? Would they discover how the Fiddleback worked, and kill *him* for the gold in his blood, and Mallow, and then figure it out anyway and come back?

"Well, well, well, if it isn't the boy himself. Isn't this our lucky day! I thought we'd find you out here sooner or later. Looks like he's come round at last, Brother Warren," said the loud, terribly familiar voice of Father Ralstein as he stepped lightly out of the automobile. His robes were torn and dirty, his pale face smudged with earth and grease and blood, but he looked strong and flushed with the chase. Beside him, Brother Warren looked similarly dishevelled, and slightly paler, but he narrowed his eyes at Tin and smiled a grim, sneering little smile. Father Ralstein laughed and raised the barrel of his rifle so that it pointed right between Tin's eyes. "Now, Tin," he continued, his voice deepening to a snarl, "there will be no games today. Bring your creation to me and tell me the secret of its making, or I will simply kill you and leave you for these disgusting wolves to eat."

"They aren't wolves," Tin retorted in his strongest, loudest voice, clutching Mallow to him with one hand and the Fiddleback with the other. Why wouldn't the Coyoteman leave? "They're coyotes." He stalled, searching wildly for words, not quite able to move any closer.

Father Ralstein fired a shot right above Tin's head, and Mallow jumped from his arms. The Coyote-man yelped, lunging sideways, and the Elk of Milk and Gold, with Comfrey and Myrtle on her back and the First Bobcat at her side, came galloping down the hill through the brush towards them.

"No, no, no, *no*! Go back!" Tin yelled over his shoulder. "Take it, Father, take it, I will come willingly. I will tell you everything I know." He pushed the Fiddleback ahead of him, and Brother Warren slipped forward and snatched at it before Tin could murmur a word of apology to its spindly, golden body. But Father Ralstein had caught sight of the Elk as she, heeding the boy's warning, leaped to hide in the bushes, her hoofs flashing with stargold. Myrtle and Comfrey followed close at her heels, scrambling to hide in a wild lilac thicket and trying to creep into the deep scrub on their elbows and knees. Father Ralstein's eyes went pale with greed.

"There are *so* many riches in the Country that we did not know of," he hissed, swinging his gaze now to the leveret at Tin's feet. "So many perfectly healthy animals, such fertile land. Why, it's a sin this knowledge was kept from us so long by the greedy Country people. But not to worry, you'll tell us everything you learned, clever boy. You've made friends with the natives, haven't you? I will give you a great reward, and together we will punish them, won't we? And make up for lost time. Shall we start with dinner, Brother Warren?" With that, he whirled on Mallow, lowering the nose of his gun.

"No!" screamed a high, wailing little voice from the brush and the turn in the road where the Elk hid. Myrtle leaped from the wild lilac and flew downhill towards her brother. Father Ralstein lifted his gun at the sound and fired. Myrtle dropped, limp, to the ground.

Then everything was a blur. Comfrey struggled up out of the thick brush to follow after Myrtle and snatch the leveret in her arms, sobbing. Myrtle's blood was everywhere, streaked gold. Mallow let out a terrible keening cry that Tin thought would never end. Comfrey retreated back into the deep wild lilac branches to find the Elk and tend to Myrtle's wound.

Meanwhile, several Coyote-men attacked Father Ralstein and Brother Warren at the same moment with bared white teeth. More shots were fired. The air filled with the sound of a horrible, whining cry, and two of the Coyote-men fell dead. From the brush the First Bobcat let out a yowl, trying to call them off. She understood that none of them were any match for these men. Their blood was all stargold as it gushed out over Father Ralstein's feet. He staggered upright with a yell that became a shout of elation. Brother Warren sprang upon the coursing gold, taking it into his hands, up to his lips, tasting its metallic purity. Now both of their guns swung, aiming at the other Coyote-folk, at Mallow.

Tin stood, stunned. It was too late, everything was too late, he had failed; he had led the Brothers here, right to the heart of Olima and Farallone. With a scream of anguish and a final hope, Tin pulled the penknife from his back pocket. In the same moment a Mountain Lion-woman, who had been crouching in a nearby bush, lunged from her hiding place and took Father Ralstein by the neck with her long-clawed hands. But even her strength was no match for his gun. He fired, and she fell on top of him, her blood a river of gold that began to harden even as it touched the air. Brother Warren greedily shoved the Mountain Lion-woman aside in order to gather her golden blood into the pockets of his robes, but Tin was upon him then, screeching like a wildcat. He managed to scramble up the man's back, clinging to his robes. With a single, swift movement, Tin opened his penknife and shoved the poisoned pin tip into Brother Warren's neck.

The man dropped with little more than a gasp. Dazed, Tin clambered over him towards Father Ralstein, who was now stealthily making his way up the road to the place where the Elk and the First Bobcat hid with Comfrey and Myrtle, who was waning in the girl's arms. Mallow crouched at his twin's side, licking desperately at the place where the bullet had clipped her chest. Tin sprang at

Father Ralstein but didn't land with as firm a grasp as he had on Brother Warren, clinging instead to his waist. And Father Ralstein was much bigger and much stronger than Brother Warren. He whirled, dislodging Tin before the boy could open his knife blade.

"You little *savage*," he spat. "I will get answers from you, you little brat, though you will get no reward now. I have my ways, you know. You have not known pain, yet." And with a violent laugh he swung the butt of his rifle across Tin's brow with a crack. The boy crumpled to the ground. "And what is this strange little tool I see...?" crooned Father Ralstein, crouching over the boy's hand where he clutched the gleaming penknife.

But Comfrey's cry from the bushes made him turn away. "I'm coming for you, my pretties," hissed Father Ralstein up the hill. "You and that big fine elk you're hiding. I will bring the greatest load of stargold back to the City in two hundred years. And oh, how much *more* there is to be had where that came from... Extraordinary, that we never knew. Extraordinary... It was right under our noses all along, at the tip of our guns!" He chuckled to himself as he strode up the road towards the Elk of Milk and Gold. An entire family of rattlesnakes made a brave attempt to attack his ankles, but three blasts from his gun sent them sprawling in every direction.

Comfrey, laying Myrtle carefully to the earth against

the flank of the Elk of Milk and Gold, threw herself out of the thicket once more. She couldn't let Father Ralstein find the Elk, whose energy seemed to have waned almost to nothing as she watched the destruction of her own Creation around her, the ground slick with starry blood. Together in the deep brush she and the First Bobcat were trying to muster their last strength to open a crack in the world once more, to begin another earthquake, to release another plague. It had taken most of their generative abilities the first time, two hundred years before. Such disasters would strike Country and City equally, all the innocent and kind people across Farallone in addition to the Brothers and their supporters. Comfrey couldn't bear the thought. There must be something else they could do! It was only one of the Brothers against all of them. Surely he wasn't invincible. Rage spilled through her. Myrtle was badly wounded, Tin lay unconscious on the ground, the bodies of Coyote-folk and the Mountain Lion-woman sprawled next to him, sticky with gold.

She was unarmed save a small skinning-knife, but still she leaped at Father Ralstein, screaming her own impassioned war cry. A strong wind was gathering from the north. It bent the pine trees, making them creak and wail.

"You cannot have them, you cannot have any of them!" Comfrey screamed, running at him with her little knife out. "How dare you? Do you know that you upset the balance of the entire world, and that none of this will survive, not even for your own benefit, if you take the stargold from these creatures' bodies?"

"Is that so?" Father Ralstein drawled, amused at this young, dark girl who'd sprung before him, spitting with rage like a cat. With one strong sweep of his hand he knocked the blade from her grasp. She stood there panting, glaring at him and at the blade at his feet. He looked her up and down and began to smile. She was a healthy, sturdy thing, despite the dirt and the wild braids. Perhaps it would be better to bring her back alive with Tin. Perhaps…he turned to look over his shoulder at Tin. It would make it easier to get the boy to talk, with this girl as his hostage. Surely she knew all sorts of useful things about the riches of the Country. He smiled to himself. "I find that hard to believe, my dear. Coming from one who has never known the ease that stargold brings… Oh, you can't imagine, I assure you, the luxuries we would give to you if you were to help us, to show us the secrets of the Country. I'd wager there is no such thing as running water in this heathen place, let alone *hot* running water?"

A wind whirled around them sudden and sharp and full of ocean air. Comfrey's eyes widened.

"Yes, my daughter, you're intrigued, aren't you?" he crooned, edging closer, close enough to snatch her wrist. "Think of the jewels, the pretty dresses…"

But she wasn't looking at him at all. She was looking just over his shoulder, and a little smile had begun to spread across her face. The wind reached a pitch, then settled again.

On it came the countless grizzly-ghosts of Tamal Point.

Father Ralstein whirled, feeling a sudden cold dread seep through his entire body. A roar deafened him. Then the horde of grizzly-ghosts were upon him, laying their ghost-claws into his flesh, their ghost-teeth into his neck. They could not physically hurt him, but they filled him with such unhinged fear that he dropped his rifle with a scream as high and terrified as a child's. His eyes went wide and white as he tried to bat at the grizzly-ghosts with his hands, but at every touch cold panic spread deeper through his body. Snarling, the grizzly-ghosts thronged closer around him, and Father Ralstein turned and ran down the hill, stumbling as he tried to make his way towards his automobile.

The biggest grizzly-ghost of all, the one who had tested the children at the boundary of Tamal Point, paused before following him, bowing his head to Comfrey and to the Elk of Milk and Gold, who now stood above her on the road.

"Great One," he growled. "We heard the gunshots and knew. We made a wind and came to find our final revenge. We will follow him to the ends of the earth if we must."

And he was gone again, joining the other ghosts as they chased Father Ralstein, a silvery tide of claw and tooth and shaggy fur, right into his automobile. They did not slacken their pace as he sped away, but only surrounded him more closely, so that it looked as though a grey mass of fog was speeding down the road, round the corner, and gone.

The sudden silence rang through Comfrey's body. She stood, unmoving. No bird called or stirred. The wind had gone entirely still, and did not touch the grasses or the trees. It was as if everything held its breath, including Comfrey. Then she let it out with a great sob and ran to Tin where he lay, one arm sprawled across the cold body of the Mountain Lion-woman, clutching his penknife. The land exhaled with her, and a chaos of bird calls rose from the hills. Flocks sped off in five directions at once, like a net thrown over the hills. Mallow bounded to her side, his whole body shaking.

"Tin, wake up, Tin!" Comfrey shook her friend's shoulders and lay her ear against his chest. He was still breathing, though raggedly, and his heart sounded faint but regular. A line of blood seeped down his forehead, glimmering ever so slightly.

"We need the Greentwins!" Mallow wailed, throwing his ears back and his nose to the sky. "Myrtle is fading! I've chewed yarrow to staunch her wound, but she's lost so much blood. And now Tin!" The leveret put his paws on his friend's chest and nosed at his chin.

"Oh Mallow," Comfrey said, reaching out to touch his back, her chest tight with tears. Then she let out a swift breath. "What about the Elk? She is a Creatrix after all!"

But Mallow shook his head. "No, no, one can't ask such small favours from one such as her. Single lives are part of a much greater cycle to her." Still, he craned uphill to glimpse her golden silhouette.

"I'm going to try to move Tin into his Fiddleback, where he will be more comfortable, and maybe we can pull him—"

It was then that the First Bobcat began to yowl, a ragged, high, terrible cry unlike anything Comfrey or Mallow had ever heard. It dropped through them like a stone through water. Tin stirred. Comfrey clutched the boy's hand with gladness, but when she saw what it was the First Bobcat was crouched over, she leaped to her feet.

It was the Elk of Milk and Gold. She'd folded to her knees without a sound when the grizzly-ghosts were at last out of sight and the winds gone. Now she laid her head down on the earth and closed her eyes. Her breathing was slow and laboured. Only her hoofs shone gold. The rest of her looked like pure cream. Where she breathed, the purple irises bloomed right before their eyes, but it was as if something vital was leaking from her with each breath, back into the earth.

She is leaving. She is leaving us! cried the First Bobcat.

"But – she created the world!" Comfrey panted, running to kneel at the Elk's side. "She can't *die!*"

So long as the stargold of making remains, she will never die in essence, replied the Bobcat, her voice a mournful song. *But in form she will. She has been dying slowly since the Collapse. She will always be in Farallone and in the stars, but she will not always be the Elk of Milk and Gold. She will be there in the connections between all things. But if the Brothers prevail, and take all the last stargold of Farallone from the bodies of Wild Folk and use it in their Star-Breakers, then the Elk will be destroyed entirely and for ever, and all of Farallone will die.*

Comfrey swallowed hard, looking between the Elk, the First Bobcat, the unconscious Tin and the wounded Myrtle. She couldn't think of anything to say. Mallow looked back at her, his ears slumped.

"What a disaster!" the leveret said in a small voice. His eyes were desolate. "The Greentwins gave us such an important task, but what a dreadful mess we've made."

Despite everything, Comfrey cast him a crooked, desperate smile. "It's not your fault, Mallow," she said, trying not to weep. But the tears started anyway. "We've all done our best, every bit of the way… It's just, it must be just—"

But a shrill, searing cry filled the air above them then, cutting her off. And Comfrey knew without looking up who had made it. Her heart lifted, wildly. She turned her face to the sky. There was the Fire Hawk, wheeling and wheeling in the gathering dusk, his wings molten and bright, casting starry sparks.

Then she heard the sound of cartwheels and hoofs, and saw the Basket-witches coming round the corner through the pines. A great crowd of songbirds flew in their wake. Tears had left tracks through the dirt on their cheeks. Salix walked in front, her fennel-yellow dress torn from the speed at which they had travelled.

"Comfrey!" the Basket-witch exclaimed when she saw the girl. Comfrey thought she had never heard her own name articulated with such love and such relief. With a strangled cry, she ran right into Salix's wide, strong arms. "You are safe, my Comfrey, my sweet human child!" Salix murmured into the girl's hair. "You have done it, you have brought the Elk."

"But – we've failed, Salix!" Comfrey said into the Basket-witch's warm middle. "We were attacked, and now the Brothers know about the gold and – and – the Elk is dying!" Comfrey looked up, her face wet with tears.

"Oh no, my dear," said Rush, coming near to lay a kiss upon the girl's forehead. "You did not fail. If you had failed all the birds of Olima would not have come thronging towards us, crying out your name, and the boy's, praising your courage, begging that you be saved. The Elk would never have carried you upon her back, nor the Wild Folk come peacefully to walk by your side. It is true, our fight has only just begun, but you and the boy and the leverets have healed a very, very old wound. Now, come along, we will make camp higher up, where the trees are thick and we can be hidden, and see what we can do for the boy and the little hare."

The rest of that evening passed in a blur as the Basket-witches gently moved the battered Fiddleback, the weakened Elk, the wounded Myrtle and the half-conscious Tin to a clearing further up the mountain where the young pines grew very thick. They made up two beds in their red cart for Comfrey and Tin and insisted that the girl rest. Myrtle lay at her feet, her wounded side packed with yarrow and usnea and wrapped in a fresh cloth. Mallow huddled beside her, grooming her limp ears. Tin lay in a fitful sleep with a cool, lavender-soaked rag across his head. Comfrey had orders to coax a warm bone broth between his teeth every hour, and this she did dutifully and anxiously, talking to Tin in a low voice. The Basket-witches went back down again to bury the bodies of the dead Coyote-folk and the Mountain Lion-woman, and to clean their golden blood from the ground, burying it carefully in a deep hole beneath a wild lilac tree.

By the time they returned, Comfrey was already fast asleep. They went to the Elk of Milk and Gold then. She lay breathing very slowly in a fresh patch of purple irises. One by one, Salix, Rush and Sedge threaded yellow wood violets into her fur. Their hands shook and their tears fell freely onto the earth. Under their breath they sang old, old chants that only the willows, the rushes and the sedges knew.

The Fire Hawk joined them, perching neatly on a rock in the clearing. At his arrival, the Basket-witches turned away, understanding that what was to come was not for their eyes, and walked in mourning back to their carts.

Little speckled moths flitted in the air around the Fire Hawk, drawn to his light. The Elk opened one eye fully to look at him, and many words passed silently between them. The evening star glimmered, climbing the horizon. And as if it was that star alone which she had been waiting all day to see, the Elk of Milk and Gold gave a final great sigh and settled her old head more fully against the earth. A few violets fell into the grass from her neck. Her eyes, half closed, went still. A very faint shudder ran through the earth beneath her.

A gentle wind picked up from the east and more stars began to appear. After a time, the Fire Hawk opened his wings and drifted on the breeze, landing gingerly on the Elk's shoulders. He spread his flaming wings wide and lay them across the Elk's cold body, from forehead to tail.

As night darkened completely and the Milky Way began to gleam clearly above, the Elk of Milk and Gold burned in hot blue flames under the smouldering wings of the Fire Hawk. By morning, all that remained of her body was a pile of milk-white ash and a golden book with a thousand rippling pages.

18

THE PSALTERIUM

When Comfrey woke the next morning, from a heavy sleep, it took her a moment to remember where she was. Disoriented, she tried to sit up, but found she was tucked in under several heavy furs. The roof over her head was arched, made of long, woven willow sticks and covered with red cloth. A fire burned in a small stove. Then she saw the dark, kind face of Salix, her tall cone-shaped hair caught with thistles, the chickadee dancing about its crown. Tin stirred, yawning, and she felt a gentle, wet nose pressing into her hand.

"Myrtle!" she cried. "You're all right!" And with those words, all the events of the previous evening flooded through her again with a sickening clarity.

Myrtle lifted up her head and managed to quip, "Well

of course I'm all right! You didn't think I'd leave you to finish all this alone now, did you?" But her voice was a little breathless, and she didn't leap onto the girl's lap like she usually did, but stayed where she was, her head half lifted.

Salix smiled and thrust a cup of bitter-smelling root tea into Comfrey's hands.

"Where are we?" came a croaking voice from beside her.

"Oh, Tin!" Comfrey turned her head and smiled such a sweet, glad, relieved smile at the boy that he felt his heart lurch a little. He felt dizzy and sick, and his head throbbed.

"Where is the Elk? Is she all right? Did they take my Fiddleback? What—?"

"Hush, hush," soothed Salix, dabbing a fresh cloth to his head and handing the boy his own cup of bitter tea. "Your Fiddleback is safe. One of the Brothers is dead, and the other is far away. The grizzly-ghosts will have made sure of that. So the birds told us, and the First Bobcat. But still, ghosts cannot kill a man, and so he is alive, and being alive he is dangerous, because he saw the gold spill out of the veins of the Wild Folk. He will be back for it I'm sure. But I hope we will be ready for him next time. Oh my children, you came just in time. Just in time." Sadness shadowed her face. "The Elk gave us her Psalterium last night. In its golden pages are the last words of creation. Our only hope. So it was decreed long ago. I pray that we know how to read them."

"Her Psalterium?" said Comfrey. "But, does that mean the Elk is…the Elk is…no more?" She couldn't bring herself to say the word *dead*. She remembered what the First Bobcat had told her – that unless Farallone itself died, the Elk could not truly die, but only change form. Still, Comfrey had come to love the Elk of Milk and Gold, and tears gathered in her eyes.

A pot of acorn porridge on the wood stove began to bubble. Salix went to stir it, hiding her own tears, and just then Rush burst through the door, flushed and out of breath.

"They are coming, they are gathering already!" she panted. Then she caught sight of the children and the leverets, and came over gladly to kiss their cheeks.

"Who is coming?" Comfrey said with a start of fear.

"All the Wild Folk of every kind!" replied Rush, stroking her hair with a hand that smelled of wild roses. "To honour their Creatrix and to hear the reading of the Psalterium. Mole-folk must have spread the news lightning-fast through their mycelial networks and opened their tunnels for the safe and rapid travel of all."

"Perhaps we will see the Greentwins again at last…" breathed Myrtle.

"The Greentwins are not Wild Folk," said a sharp voice in the door. It was Sedge. "They will not be welcomed here. If they had not sent the leverets out to fetch these children, and the four of them hadn't come traipsing across Olima with their contraptions and their meddling human hands, we wouldn't be in this predicament at all! The Brothers would not have discovered us, the Elk would not have needed to come, and would not have died." Her voice was loud and thin and anguished, and Comfrey flushed with shame at her words. Tin, lying with his forehead covered in cloth, felt tears of frustration and exhaustion prick his eyes.

"Sister," said Rush, and her tone had none of its usual gentleness. Comfrey looked up sharply. The Basket-witch was flushed red with anger. "What a thing to say! Calm yourself. You are speaking from your own sorrow. I think we all owe the Greentwins an apology, and the people of the Country. These children have proven themselves brave, kind, generous and gentle to all Wild Folk. There was no way to stop the Brothers discovering what is in our blood. It was inevitable that they would invade again one day. They could not stay behind their City Wall for ever. The fact that their invasion and the coming of these children and leverets happened at the same time; well, this may be our greatest blessing of all. For without them we would not be standing here together. We would be hiding alone, in hate and in fear. Divided, we would never be able to resist the Brothers again. All together, we just might."

Sedge only sniffed with outrage, and whirled out again into the daylight. But Comfrey thought that she heard a single ragged sob escape the Basket-witch's lips, and she felt a surge of unbidden sympathy.

All day a crowd of Wild Folk gathered round the Elk's milky ashes and the luminous book at their centre. By the time the sun had begun to lower over the pines to the west, spilling amber light down through the meadow, the place was brimming with a tatterdemalion gathering of beings – furred and mottled and winged and clawed and strangely clad, with human faces or hands or feet. It was similar to the crowd that had followed the Elk from Tamal Point, only larger, more diverse, stranger and wilder and more solemn too. The Basket-witches built a fire there beside the Elk's ashes, so that all might gather and keep warm. Sedge held the Elk of Milk and Gold's glowing Psalterium to her chest, as if it might impart upon her very heart some of the Elk's ancient calm. She did not speak to her sisters, but sat apart in a daze of grief.

Salix and Rush insisted that the children rest inside the cart until the sun set, when they would begin the reading of the Psalterium. Tin and Myrtle were still very weak, and Comfrey cared for them both diligently as the sun wheeled overhead, remembering the patience and skill with which her mother attended to those in need back in the village, trying to keep at bay the heavy ache that filled her whenever she thought of Maxine. How many Brothers had invaded the Country? How many Brothers had already found Alder?

When the Basket-witches weren't looking she darted to the door to peek at the gathering crowd. She wondered if she would see the Bobcat-girl again. That October day felt like another lifetime. Mallow joined her, eagerly sniffing for the Greentwins on the breeze. But they could make out very little through the dense pines.

An hour before sunset there was a commotion at the far edge of the clearing. Comfrey could hear Sedge's voice pealing out high and sharp as glass. She sounded outraged, even a little afraid. A great chattering went up, as the voices of many Wild Folk clamoured all at once, some harsh, some gentle and excited.

"Mallow," hissed Tin, who was by then up and about, tinkering with his Fiddleback by the wood stove. "Can you hear what's going on?"

The leveret was already at the door, his ears straining. "I'm going to go have a look, it sounds important!"

"Should we come with you?" said Comfrey eagerly.

"The Basket-witches were very clear about us waiting until sunset," said Myrtle, still a little breathless. "I think they want you to make a grand entrance. Part of the ceremony, or some such…"

"Oh," sighed Comfrey. "But I'm desperate to see what's

going on! To know what's going to happen next! It's been an endless day of waiting…"

"Go on then, Mallow," urged Tin with a grin. "And come back quick and tell us!"

The leveret leaped off at a lean dash, his tail flashing in the golden light.

"Cheeky fellow," muttered Myrtle affectionately.

"You really think they want us to make a special entrance?" Comfrey said, turning back to Myrtle. She looked down at her green wool dress, remembering as if from a great distance that day in her bedroom in Alder when she had pulled it out of her trunk and put it on, thinking she and Myrtle were going for a quick jaunt to check the Offering-bundle, nothing more. The memory made her dizzy now. It seemed to belong to a different girl. She began to undo her braids, which as usual had become unruly and needed smoothing.

"That's what it sounded like to me," replied the leveret, hopping stiffly off the bed to warm herself by the fire.

"What are you doing?" Tin said, looking at Comfrey curiously. She was combing her hands through her hair with a strange, private expression on her face. She blushed and loosed her hair abruptly. It stood out around her face and shoulders in a black and wild cloud, falling in loose tendrils all the way to her waist.

"Combing my hair, silly!" she retorted hotly. "Since we

have to make a grand appearance and all, I want to look at least somewhat respectable. What? Have you never seen a girl comb her hair before?"

Now it was Tin's turn to blush and look away, down at his own torn clothing and ragged appearance. "We look like a pair of ragamuffin orphans!" he said with dismay. Comfrey giggled.

Just then Mallow came flying up the cart steps and skidded to a halt in the middle of the floor, his long ears swaying.

"In the name of All Hares!" exclaimed Myrtle. "What on earth is the matter?"

"Comfrey!" panted Mallow, only half-listening to his sister. "Tin! The Holy Fools are here, Amber and Oro and Pieta and all the others. They're here, the Mole-folk brought them, they've just emerged out of the ground. That's what all the commotion is about, and they're with – they're with—" The little leveret faltered, trying to catch his breath in his excitement and his amazement. He turned to Tin. "They're with two of the Mycelium," he breathed, shifting his eyes to Comfrey's face. "Our friends, and Comfrey's—"

"Thornton's here?" Tin cried, incredulous, leaping to his feet so fast the blood pounded in his head. Comfrey had gone very, very still where she sat on the floor, her hair wild around her face, her hands folded in her lap. She opened her lips to speak, then closed them again because they had started to tremble.

But before Mallow could reply, a man's voice boomed out through the clearing, and there was the sound of boots running through grass and pine duff right up the steps of the cart. The door latch jiggled. Comfrey sat transfixed, her chest heaving. Tin ran to open the door but it burst inwards before he reached it and Thornton came bounding through with one swift movement, looking more wolf than man in his wild desperation to find his daughter.

The strange spell that had held Comfrey so still, so transfixed, shattered all at once like thin glass. "Papa!" she cried, and flung herself upright straight into his arms. For a long time she didn't say anything more, and neither did he. Tears filled their eyes. "I knew it," she whispered into his shirt. "I knew you were alive."

"My sweet child, my Comfrey!" Thornton crooned hoarsely into the tangle of her loose hair, his cheeks wet. "Oh my stars, oh my gods, you are safe." For a long moment no one moved or made a sound, and Tin looked away, trying not to think about his own lost parents, and whether there was anyone in the world who would love him that way after all this time.

"Tin?" came a hesitant voice from behind Thornton's lanky form.

"Seb!" Tin cried, seeing his friend there for the first time.

Seb was paler, more wiry, and his dark eyes, always lustrous, were more striking than ever, perhaps in contrast to his light-deprived skin. They looked like two tunnels, emotive but dark as the underground. The boys hugged fiercely.

"I thought we'd never see each other again," Seb said, looking his friend in the face. "And – you found Comfrey! It's amazing, isn't it? Like it was all meant to be."

Tin went quiet, feeling suddenly protective of Comfrey and their difficult journey together. He realized with a jealous little start in his stomach that he didn't want to share her with her father or with Seb. *Comfrey isn't mine to share*, he told himself sternly, and managed to grin back at his friend. Myrtle limped over to smell at Seb and Thornton's ankles.

"Mallow!" cried Seb, upon seeing the leveret. "What happened?"

"Ah, no, that would be my twin. I'm Myrtle," said the leveret, miffed. "Just a little run in with a gun, you know," she said, trying to sound nonchalant.

"Oh! How terrible!" said Seb, blushing. For a moment he and Tin searched one another's eyes, feeling a draught of distance between them which they'd never felt before. They both had stories now that the other didn't know or understand, and that realization made them both grow suddenly shy.

"Seb, so much has happened, there's so much to tell

you," Tin stammered, wanting that distance to go away. "And – how did you both get here so fast? I thought Thornton said he would never leave, not until the work of the Mycelium was done. Did he call the Greentwins? What's happening in the City?"

There was a long silence as Seb tried to begin. But Thornton, releasing Comfrey from his embrace, cut in. "The Greentwins are missing," he said, sitting down heavily on one of the beds while Comfrey, her heart in her throat, rushed to bring him a cup of warm milk from the pan over the wood stove, adding a generous dash of brandy from the Basket-witches' cooking shelf. Then she sat down again beside her father and, feeling a little shy, took his hand in hers. Seb, seeing her fully for the first time, stared, his ears going pink.

"A week after you left us, my dear boy, you and your extraordinary Spider, I called them," Thornton continued. "But they did not come." His face went dark, its lines drawn.

Mallow and Myrtle let out twin keening cries.

"But – the Greentwins can't die! They can't be dead, surely!" said Mallow in a thin voice, his legs quivering.

"Worse, I fear," replied Thornton. "I think they've been captured. I think they're in the hands of the Brothers. I don't know how, but I sense it, for we could find no trace of them, no matter how many times I asked the Mole-folk to consult their own mycelial networks. By some terrible twist in the order of things, it seems they are being held in the City. But by the time I realized this, I had already witnessed and learned many more terrible things. I had seen the beginning of the Brothers' infiltration of the Country and could do nothing about it without giving myself away. It was so much worse than I had anticipated. And somehow they knew that you were here, Tin. Someone had seen that flight of white pelicans. The Mole-folk took me into their tunnels and told me all they knew about the Brothers, about the fate of the Country and the Greentwins and the Wild Folk. It broke my heart to pass beneath the village called Alder, but I vowed that once I had made sure the Fiddleback was safely hidden, I would return for my daughter and my wife at long last."

"But I'm not with Mother! How did you know we were here, together?"

"The Mole-folk, my child," said Thornton. "It was from them and their mycelial webs, which pass stories to and fro all across Olima, that we learned of your quest. That I learned of *you*, my sweet girl – you and the Fire Hawk's feather and the Elk of Milk and Gold. And that you were with Tin, of all wild and perfect fates! This was only yesterday evening. News came to us of the Brothers' attack at dusk. Of the Elk of Milk and Gold's arrival with human children on her back. We travelled all night and all day through the tunnels of the Mole-folk."

"Oh, Papa," whispered Comfrey, leaning her head against his arm, full of so many words and worries and hopes that she didn't know what to say.

"It is time," came Rush's voice from the doorway. She stood there in her pale skirts, glowing with the last light of day. "Come, my dears, it is time for the reading of the Psalterium. All are gathered, waiting for you." She nodded to the children and the leverets, and bowed her head to Thornton. Outside, they could hear a howling cheer beginning to rise through the trees. It was a sound unlike any Comfrey or Tin had ever heard; a thrumming chorus of barks and songs and wails and hoots that together created a startling and heartbreaking harmony.

Thornton kissed his daughter's hand and gave her a gentle nudge towards the crowd.

"It's for you they cheer," he murmured. "You four. Go on, they're waiting."

Comfrey and Tin looked at each other, their eyes wide, and both felt a little spark of pleasure at that shared look, for it held all the terror and wonder of their adventure together. Everything they had seen and spoken of and shared. Seb, watching them, felt an unexpected needle of envy, and tried without success to push it away.

"You're going to have to carry me," said Myrtle. "I'm still weak as a hareling!"

Comfrey smiled then, a wide smile suffused with a

happiness she thought she'd never felt so fully before. Here she was with her father, who had returned to her at last, and the three who had become her dearest friends in all the world, and although the threat to Farallone was no less than it had been the day before, she felt for the first time that all together they might, just might, be able to overcome it.

And so the children and the leverets descended the wagon steps, escorted by Rush, and made their way through the thick young pines into the clearing where the crowd of Wild Folk stood waiting. Thornton and Seb hung back, watching.

Tin thought he could feel the power of that crowd before it had even parted to let them through. As if the air itself was full of stargold, humming and gleaming. A Bombus-man was the first to catch sight of the children and leverets, and he let out a sweet-toned whoop of celebration. Then everyone was cheering all over again, and a dozen furred hands touched their arms and cheeks. Dizzy, Tin glimpsed faces like alder bark, the dark-rimmed eyes of foxes, wings like those of swallowtail butterflies, feet as long as fence lizards'. Amidst the cacophony, Comfrey heard a familiar, rasping voice holler out her name. Peering through the shifting mass of bright bodies, she caught the green eye of the Bobcat-girl, waving a furred, sharp-nailed hand in her direction. Her heart lifted and lurched, just as it had done the first time she'd seen her a lifetime ago. But then the yipping crowd surged around them again, pushing them towards the fire at the centre. Above them all, the Fire Hawk circled. Myrtle and Mallow sensed his sharp eyes above them, but puffed their chests out and ignored him. Now was no time to show fear! Tin saw Oro's great round head shining amidst the crowd, and Amber beside him, grinning and waving, with Pieta clinging starry-eyed to her hand.

In the centre by the fire, Sedge stood holding the Psalterium open in her arms, cradled there like a child. Her green headdress swayed in the sunset light. Salix herded the children and the leverets right to her side, near the heat of the fire. Up close, the Psalterium looked like no book they had ever seen. Its pages were as rippled and lined as spiderwebs. They glowed with a sourceless, creamy light. Comfrey held back a sob, thinking of the violet eyes of the Elk of Milk and Gold and the gentle warmth of her breath. Was this truly all that was left of her? How could that be?

"These children and their leveret friends," began Salix, pitching her voice to carry to the distant treetops. The crowd of Wild Folk and Holy Fools and animals quietened. "They have done a very extraordinary and a very brave thing. Something we all thought impossible after the Collapse." The chickadee in her hair sung a sweet, high note. "They have shown us the true kindness, courage and generosity of the human heart. They won the trust and love of the very Creatrix of Farallone herself, the Elk of

Milk and Gold, who carried them on her back across her land to reach us. They won the trust of all whom they encountered throughout Olima. They were sorely tested, but they proved themselves every step of the way, and taught us something of our own prejudices and our own fears. We are living through a dark and terrible time, a time of great sacrifices. The Elk of Milk and Gold has sacrificed her body to give us her last and greatest wisdom, her Psalterium. I know that some of you are angry at her passing. That you seek to blame these children. But something far larger is at work and at stake, and in her passing she has taught us about coming together. For here we all are, together. She offered herself, and all the knowing that her body holds, for the good of us all. Let us not forsake her." There was a great murmuring through the crowd, and a wind pushed through the tops of the trees, whispering. The sun's last rays caught their swaying tips, turning them molten. Salix turned to Sedge. There was a little warning in her eyes, for she knew that her sister still did not fully trust the children, and bore them no love. But Sedge's own eyes were lost in the pages of the Psalterium, already far away.

"The words of making and unmaking," she said in a drifting, high voice. Comfrey craned to peer over the Basket-witch's shoulder at the strange pages, and glimpsed marks like golden runes shifting there. "With these words we honour creation, with these words we seek to bring wholeness, to bring peace, to do no harm."

"*Wholeness, peace, no harm,*" came the reply of the murmuring crowd, a kind of prayer. Comfrey and Tin found themselves stammering along.

Sedge turned her face back to the golden pages of the Psalterium, and its light in the gathering dusk illuminated her sharp, long features, her woven green hair. "We have been studying these pages since daybreak. Their words are many, and strange. I who am mistress of patterns, with the help of each of your kind, still can read only a single page. Perhaps these are the only words the Elk wants us to read and understand. For these are clear as day, while the rest are a tangle of strangeness like the distant and unknowable bottom of the sea. Here is what I have read: *By the web, by the wheel, by the hand, by the dead. The spider weaves her veil where the world began. Go to where the world began, go to where the world will end, go the steepest way, after broken threads. By the Country, by the City, by the weaver, by the root. As above, so below, the spindle will show. When the Spider makes Gold the Land will behold the return of the Old.*"

Comfrey looked at Tin then, and Tin looked back at Comfrey, and the haunted expression in his wide, light eyes made her take his hand. In the girl's arms, Myrtle cocked an ear forward and gave an exasperated snort, breaking the luminous silence.

"I liked the Elk better when she wasn't a book!" the leveret said crossly. "Riddles make my head hurt!"

Sedge whirled, glaring at Myrtle, but it was as if the leveret's words had released some heaviness from the air. Rush began to laugh. Laughter moved suddenly through the crowd under the first star of evening. Comfrey grinned.

"I know what you mean," she whispered. "But I think she made it for humans, not hares. Humans like riddles. This one sounds like a kind of map…"

"You know how I feel about maps," sniffed Myrtle, but her tone was affectionate.

"I think," said Salix, resting a hand on each of the children's shoulders, "that your journey has only just begun. I think it's your hands that must do this weaving, and your wheels." She smiled at Tin. "Why else would the Fire Hawk have dropped his feather for you, and not us? Why else would the Elk have borne you across the land? Why else would this boy have created a machine that seems to have a soul – his Fiddleback? It seems clear to me that in these four is the salvation of all Farallone."

"The Psalterium speaks of Old Mother Neeth!" came a familiar, rasping voice from the back of the crowd. In the far shadow of the pinewood stood a house of bones with two owl legs. A broad old woman with a thick silver braid leaned from the doorway. Small furred ears poked out through her hair, and her feet were long and furred as well.

"It's the Baba Ithá!" Comfrey exclaimed to Tin, catching hold of his shoulder. The leverets instinctively bounded into the children's arms.

"I can smell the bones of that hut from here!" moaned Myrtle.

"Not again!" chimed Mallow.

"Surely not, Grandmother," chorused several Wild Folk at once, Salix and Rush among them. But Sedge only looked down at the Psalterium in her arms again, her eyes far away.

"Was she not killed a thousand years ago, with the coming of the Star-Priests of Albion?" rumbled Amurra, who had come up beside Sedge to examine the Psalterium.

"So the legends say," replied the Baba Ithá, leaping to the ground like a squirrel and making her way through the crowd. "That one of the invader's heroes killed her in her cave and set about building the City on top of it. They called her a monster, the terrible Arachnid. But did not the oldest stories call the place of her dwelling the beginning of the world? And did not the oldest stories say it was she, Old Mother Neeth, the Great Spider, who spun the gold of life down from the stars, and gave form to what was formless with her woven webs? Was it not from this that the Elk herself, and the First Bobcat too, were created? Was it not her threads that once held the life of Farallone together, as one?"

A low murmuring stole through the gathered Wild Folk.

"Am I the only one among you who still remembers? Are we old women a country apart?" the Baba Ithá bellowed, her face going dark. A cluster of Quail-people near her shrank away visibly, clutching one another's plump hands.

"No, you are not," murmured Rush gently. "All the old stories speak of Mother Neeth. The ancient Spider Creatrix whose webs hold the fates of all beings. Only it was so long ago that the Star-Priests killed her. If she is in fact still alive, why has she remained in hiding all this time? Where is she? And why has she allowed the destruction of the stargold of Farallone?"

"I thought the same as you," the Baba Ithá said, somewhat appeased, turning to the Basket-witch. "That is, until a little fiddleback spider entered my firwood the day I sent these children and twin leverets on their way across Farallone to the Elk of Milk and Gold. A fiddleback spider carrying a heavy egg sac on her back, who spun golden thread from her body, and had come a very far way, ferried by none other than the boy Tin who I had only just had the pleasure of meeting." Here her sharp teeth flashed with the memory of the three tasks she had set to the children, and the delight their terror had given her. "Ferried *from the City*. Well, then the stories began to come back to me about Old Mother Neeth, and I started to find it very strange that a City boy would meet with such an extraordinary spider, and create such an extraordinary vehicle in her likeness that ran as if by some invisible source of power. Something else, something older and more powerful, must be at work here, I told myself. However, I got quite distracted from these thoughts by word that reached me from the wood pigeons who roost in my most ancient trees. The Brothers had breached the Salvian Mountains… Only just now has the thought returned to me, that Old Mother Neeth is somewhere, somehow, still alive. And that the little fiddleback spider with her babies was sent by her."

"Well, what do you have to say?" Sedge demanded, turning to the First Bobcat. "Wouldn't you know if she were alive or dead?"

"Indeed, I would," said the sonorous, purring voice of the First Bobcat from behind Comfrey. She shivered at the sound and Myrtle, still in her arms, tried to make herself very small inside the girl's elbow. The ancient cat padded into the centre of the gathering and sniffed for a long while at the open pages of the Psalterium. Sedge did not flinch back, but her eyes, to Comfrey's satisfaction, did go rather wide. The First Bobcat was an arresting sight. The children were only as tall as her shoulder, and Sedge, though able to meet the First Bobcat's gaze at eye level, still looked insubstantial beside her.

"I remember Mother Neeth well," she purred. "You are

right. It was from her threads I was woven, as was the Elk of Milk and Gold, her threads spun down from the stars to the earth at the beginning of time. She sent us forth from her caverns to create the rest of Farallone, to give life as well as death to the plants, animals, stones, waters and winds. To watch over all of creation, while she spun her threads between the stars and the earth, the threads of stargold that spelled the fate of all things, that kept Farallone itself alive and whole. But neither the Elk nor I have felt her presence since the coming of the Star-Priests and their Star-Breakers. So I don't know how it can be she that the Psalterium speaks of. Though I could not say for certain she is dead, for one such as she would not be found in my Underworld."

"But how could she have been *killed*?" blurted Tin, the thought suddenly occurring to him. "Isn't she a – a god? An immortal?" His thoughts were wild with the memory of the little fiddleback spider and her bobbin of strong golden thread, of the Fiddleback's wheels and wires whirring all around him as he and Seb had careened through the Cloister's catacombs.

"Even stars die," replied the First Bobcat, her great, pale green eyes swinging to meet Tin's. Oddly, their colour and intensity reminded him of Comfrey's, and this made them a little bit easier to look into. "And did not the Elk die beneath the wings of the Fire Hawk? Though this fate

406

she chose for herself. It is true we do not have lifespans like yours, nor is it time and age that kill us. But we are not immune to violence. And all cycles must end."

"What we need to do," cut in the Baba Ithá, "is find that little fiddleback spider and ask her outright what the riddling Psalterium is trying to tell us, and if Old Mother Neeth is, in fact, still alive. After all, would not that spider from the City be the one to know? And if she is, then it seems clear to me that these children must go directly to her cave where the world began and consult her."

"But isn't that buried underneath the City? Can it even be found?" said Mallow, craning his head and ears out from the shelter of Tin's arms. "I've smelled the tunnels of that place, and I can tell you, finding an ancient Spider-woman in her cave would be no mean feat. Surely if she was there Thornton's Mycelium would already have discovered her?"

"First things first," interrupted the Baba Ithá with a scowl at the loquacious leveret. "We must find the little fiddleback. Who now, very likely, has a host of small spiderlings by her side. I can bring the children back to my forest with me in my bone house. It's only a morning's walk, in such a vehicle."

"Forgive me, witches and Wild Folk, all," Comfrey broke in, trying to make her voice very loud and certain. It faltered a little on the word *wild*, but she swallowed hard and kept going. She'd never addressed so many people before, let alone such powerful beings as these. "Before anything else, we have to go to Alder. My mother is in danger. I-I saw it in the Fire Hawk's feather." As she spoke, Tin slipped his hand into hers, and squeezed it. She stood up a little straighter, blushing. "I'm not going anywhere without warning her first. I think my father would agree."

At the sound of Comfrey's voice and the mention of Maxine, Thornton strode through the crowd with Seb close at his heels. He put his arm round his daughter's shoulders and kissed the top of her head.

"*Humans,*" spat Sedge. "You'd choose one woman over the fate of Farallone?"

"Easy, sister," said Salix, "things do not always have to be so black and white! This is the girl's mother. And after all, Comfrey has more than earned her way back home over the border. She is free to come and go from here now, like us. There is time."

"Is there?" Sedge hissed back. "Is there indeed? After the death of the Coyote-folk and the Mountain Lion-woman and the Elk herself? Now that the Brothers know our secret? And you say we have time?"

"For love, yes. Eight years ago I left my wife and my daughter in the name of the fate of Farallone," interrupted Thornton sharply. "I thought it was my duty to put the survival of this land over the survival of my own heart. But today I have been reunited with my child, and I can tell you that the heart that was half-dead within me is so full and so alive that it will not last another day without my child's mother to keep it whole. If she can ever forgive me. We will heal nothing without loving, without standing by the ones we love. I do not think we have to choose. I think that this is the only way we can ever truly succeed."

"These are fine words," Salix murmured with a little bow of her head.

"I will go look for the spider myself," interjected the Baba Ithá, "and then come directly to the edge of Olima, on the ridge above Alder, to tell you what it is I have discovered in my firwood, and to help you in any way I can. If I'm lucky, I'll have the fiddleback spider with me." Her voice was surprisingly generous now, warm as a hearth. "In two days' time, at midday, I will meet you there by the oak trees above the serpentine outcrop where Comfrey's people leave their Offerings." She addressed the children and the leverets with a solemn bow of her bone-twined white head.

"Let us guide you home through our tunnels," interjected a dark-furred Mole-man called Rute, patting at his vest with a large, clawed hand. "It will be much faster and safer. And your wheeled – contraption—" He faltered, eyeing the Fiddleback.

"My Fiddleback?" said Tin eagerly. "Will it be helpful

do you think?" His heart lifted. "It's very quick, you know, and quiet."

"Indeed I do believe it, just by looking at the thing!" replied Rute. "I think it will be very useful in our tunnels; we will positively *fly* through the twists and turns!" A gleam lit his black eyes.

"Twists and turns?" said Mallow, grimacing. "It's going to be a long journey…"

"You'll have to be *very* quick," interjected Sedge, still glaring at Comfrey. "Every hour matters. Every *minute*." Her voice cracked.

"We will be, Sedge," said Comfrey in a voice so gentle and so adult that at first Tin thought it was Rush who spoke. "I love Farallone as much as you. We all do." She glanced at Tin and Seb, at the leverets, at her father. "We won't fail you, I promise." She knew as she said these words that she could not truly promise such a thing when what they faced was so dark, so dire, and yet she meant them with all her heart. She reached out slowly and took Sedge's hand. The Basket-witch flinched, but did not pull away.

"Very well, Country girl," replied Sedge. "I will do my best to trust you." And for a single moment, a smile of warm admiration lit her face.

"What are we waiting for then?" interjected Myrtle, leaping impatiently around Comfrey's ankles. "For starters, I'd like to get this bumpy Fiddleback ride out of the way."

"You'd better get used to it," said Tin with a crooked smile. "I have a feeling there are going to be a lot of those in our future, especially if we are going all the way back to the City."

"Who knows," teased Salix, touching the leverets' foreheads gently with her forefinger, "it might be safer for you to travel back to the City carried in the arms of the North Wind, who is an old friend of the Wild Folk."

"Abominations!" cried Mallow. "Travel by owl was bad enough… But by wind alone? I won't do it, a hare can only take so much."

"Oh but I think we will in the end," said Myrtle, touching her nose to her twin's. "No hare that I've ever heard of has done any of what we have. We never could have imagined it, despite all the Greentwins' stories! One paw in front of the next and worry about it later. What else can we do till we've come to the end?"

"We can hope that it's no end at all, but a new beginning," whispered Comfrey, and the words sent their own wind through the gathered crowd, quiet though they had been. A breath of hope, luminous as stargold.

ACKNOWLEDGEMENTS

This book has been brewing in me since I was a girl, and so I have many people, landscapes and beings to thank for its creation and its birth. Thank you to all the authors whose books shaped me as a child – you makers of brave heroines, kind heroes, talking trees and wild magics whose words made me the writer, and woman, I am today. Thank you to my parents for always supporting me on this path, and to my mother for reading all my early drafts. Thank you to all the children and adults who subscribed to *The Leveret Letters* (the very first iteration of *The Wild Folk*) back in 2014, when it was a stories-by-mail project. Your support and excited letters in reply helped me to first birth the tales of Comfrey, Tin, Myrtle and Mallow. Thank you to my wise, wonderful and tireless agent Jessica Woollard for believing in this book, to my brilliant editor Anne Finnis for bringing it out into the world with such courage and vision, and to the whole team at Usborne for being so creative and full of heart in everything they do. Thank you to the plants, animals, stones, waters and winds of the Point Reyes Peninsula, the landscape that was the inspiration for Farallone and the place I gratefully and lovingly call home. And to Simon, for sharing in the old magic of story with me from the very first, and for reminding me how love sits at the centre of every true tale.

For more fantasy and adventure visit
usborne.com/fiction

First published in the UK in 2018 by Usborne Publishing Ltd., Usborne House,
83-85 Saffron Hill, London EC1N 8RT, England. www.usborne.com

Copyright © Sylvia V. Linsteadt 2018

The right of Sylvia V. Linsteadt to be identified as the author of this work has
been asserted by her in accordance with the Copyright, Designs and Patents Act,
1988.

Cover and inside illustrations by Sandra Dieckmann © Usborne Publishing, 2018

Map by Chris Jevons © Usborne Publishing, 2018

The name Usborne and the devices ♀ ⊕ are Trade Marks of
Usborne Publishing Ltd.

This is a work of fiction. The characters, incidents, and dialogues are products
of the author's imagination and are not to be construed as real. Any resemblance
to actual events or persons, living or dead, is entirely coincidental.

A CIP catalogue record for this book is available from the British Library.

ISBN 9781474934985   04452/4   JFMAM JASOND/18

Printed in the UK.

Look out *for* the
second magical adventure in

THE STARGOLD CHRONICLES

Coming in spring 2019

Find out more:

@Usborne

@WildTalewort

 @usborne_books

facebook.com/usbornepublishing

#TheWildFolk